IN GOOD FAITH

D1040939

IN GOOD FAITH

By

SCOTT PRATT

ISBN: 1480189871
ISBN 13: 9781480189874

This book, along with every book I've written and every book I'll write, is dedicated to my darling Kristy, to her unconquerable spirit and to her inspirational courage. I loved her before I was born and I'll love her after I'm long gone.

PART I

WEDNESDAY, AUG. 27

Eight men and four women. A dozen citizens, filing slowly past the defense and prosecution tables beneath the stern scrutiny of a white-haired judge. All wore the dazed look of people who've been forced to sit for days in a place they've never been, listen to the words of men and women they've never seen, and pass judgment on a fellow human being.

The gallery was sadly bereft of spectators. Misty Bell, a young female newspaper reporter with short chestnut hair and curious hazel eyes, sat dutifully holding her notebook in the front row to my left. Two seats to her right sat the victim's son, an overweight, sad-looking man in his sixties with sagging jowls and receding gray hair that curled around his ears like smoke from a smoldering cotton ball. Aside from those two and me—I was sitting in the center of the back row—the gallery was empty.

The defendant, a wiry man named Billy Dockery, stood next to his lawyer at the defense table as the jury filed past. Dockery was gangly and in his mid-thirties. His dark hair snaked past his shoulders, framing a flat face that had maintained a perpetual smirk throughout the two-day trial. He wore civilized clothing—a dark gray suit, white shirt, and a navy blue tie—but I knew he was anything but civilized. Beneath the veneer was a cruel and dangerous sociopath.

His lawyer was James T. Beaumont III, a longtime practitioner of criminal defense whom I'd known casually for many years. Beaumont was in his late fifties and was somewhat of a celebrity in northeast Tennessee. He favored fringed buckskin jackets and string ties and wore a beige cowboy hat outside the courtroom. A long, light-brown mustache and goatee, heavily specked with gray, covered his upper lip and chin. With his longish hair, clear blue eyes, and a deep drawl, he reminded me very much of Wild Bill Hickok—at least the way they portrayed him in the movies.

"Call your witness," sixty-year-old Judge Leonard Green said.

Beaumont nodded and stood. "The defense calls Billy Dockery."

Dockery got up, ambled to the witness stand, and took the oath, the smirk still on his face. I'd seen the proof in the case and knew Dockery should exercise his Fifth Amendment right to keep his mouth shut. He'd be a terrible witness. But I also knew that Dockery enjoyed the spotlight almost as much as he enjoyed thumbing his nose at the prosecution and torturing defenseless, elderly women.

After a few preliminary questions, Beaumont got to the point.

"Mr. Dockery, I'll ask you this question on the front end. Did you kill Cora Wilson in the early morning hours of November seventeenth?"

Dockery leaned closer to the microphone.

"No sir, I did not. I did not have anything to do with her death. I was not nowhere near her place that night. I ain't never hurt nobody and I ain't never going to."

The sound of his voice made me cringe. Five years earlier, Dockery had been charged with murdering another elderly woman during a break-in at her home. His mother hired me to represent him, and after a trial, the jury found him not guilty and set him free. The next day, Dockery walked into my office and drunkenly confessed to me that he'd murdered the woman. He offered me a five-thousand-dollar cash bonus, money he said he'd stolen during the break-in. I threw him out of the office, along with his filthy money, but since double jeopardy prevented them from trying him again and since the rules of professional responsibility forbade me from telling anyone, I couldn't do a thing about the confession. When I read in the newspaper that he was about to go on trial for killing another woman, I wanted to be there to see his face when they sent him to the penitentiary for the rest of his life.

"Did you know the victim?" Jim Beaumont said from the podium in front of the witness stand.

"Yessir. I done yard work for her sometimes and I painted her house last year."

"Ever have any problems with her?"

"No sir. Not nary a one. Me and her got along like two peas in a pod."

"Where were you that night, Mr. Dockery?"

"I was campin' on the Nolichuckey River more'n two miles from her house."

"In November?"

"Yessir. My mamma's got a cabin down there. It's got a fireplace and all. I go there a lot."

"Anyone with you?"

"No sir. I was all by my lonesome."

"Thank you, Mr. Dockery. Please answer the prosecutor's questions."

It was the shortest direct examination of a criminal defendant I'd ever seen, and it was smart. Up to that point, the prosecution had been able to establish only that Billy Dockery had done landscaping work for eighty-six-year-old Cora Wilson. They established that Dockery had camped along the Nolichuckey River about two miles from Ms. Wilson's home the night she was beaten and tortured to death, a fact the defense did not dispute. They established that a length of nylon rope found around Ms. Wilson's neck was the same kind of rope found in the back of Billy Dockery's truck. The prosecutor's expert witness could not go so far as to say the rope was an exact match, only that it was made of the same material, of the same weave and circumference, and manufactured by the same company. Unfortunately for the prosecution, the defense subpoenaed an executive from the company that made the rope, and he testified that more than fifty thousand feet of that very same rope had been sold within a twenty-five-mile radius of the courthouse in the past five years.

The prosecution's star witness in the case, a seventeen-year-old named Tommy Treadway, had initially confessed to breaking into the house with Dockery that night but refused to sign a statement. Treadway told the police that he left when Dockery began to torture Ms. Wilson. But Treadway was released on bond after he agreed to testify against Dockery and wound up driving his car off the side of a mountain in Carter County a month before the trial. His death was ruled an accident.

The state's only other witness—besides the routine information given by the cops and the medical examiner—was a degenerate drunkard named Timmons who said he'd overheard Billy Dockery say that Cora Wilson kept cash in her house and that he "might go get it some night." Beaumont had already destroyed the witness on cross-examination, forcing him to admit that his two primary activities as an adult had been drinking whiskey and stealing other people's identities so that he could afford to drink more whiskey.

Now the assistant district attorney had his shot at the defendant. It was usually a prosecutor's dream, but Assistant District Attorney Alexander Dunn had been aloof and distracted. His case was so weak he should have dismissed it and waited to see whether any more evidence could be developed, but his ego—or his boss— had apparently driven him to trial.

Dunn, in his early thirties, was wearing a tailor-fitted brown suit over a beige shirt. A kerchief rose from the pocket of his jacket, and expensive Italian loafers covered his feet. He stood before Dockery and straightened his silk tie.

"Isn't it true, Mr. Dockery, that you and another individual broke into the victim's home around 2:00 a.m. on the morning of November seventeenth?"

"No."

It was an inauspicious beginning, to say the least, and I sank deeper into my seat. Dunn had been ordered by the judge not to mention the dead witness, and the jury was sure to wonder why, if there was a co-defendant, he wasn't on trial at the same time or testifying for the state.

"And isn't it true, Mr. Dockery, that you beat and tortured the victim in an effort to force her to tell you where her cash was hidden?"

"No, it ain't true, and you ain't got no fingerprints, no blood, no hair, no witnesses, no nothin' to prove I was there."

"But you *did* tell Mr. Timmons that the victim kept cash in her home and that you intended to steal it, didn't you?"

"I never said no such thing. Timmons ain't nothing but a drunk and a liar. He was probably just looking for some reward money so he could buy whiskey."

"And you're a model citizen, aren't you, Mr. Dockery? I'll bet you don't even drink."

Dockery's eyes flashed with righteous indignation. He leaned forward and put his hands on the rail in front of him.

"Yeah, I may drink a little, but I'll tell you what I don't do. I don't parade around in a fancy suit and put people on trial for murder when I ain't got no proof."

"I object, Your Honor," Dunn said. "The witness is being argumentative."

"Sustained. Don't argue with him, Mr. Dockery," Judge Green said. "Just answer the questions."

"Isn't it true, Mr. Dockery," Alexander continued, "that you took thousands of dollars in cash from the victim's home the night you murdered her?"

"If I did, then where is it? Y'all tore my mamma's place, her cabin, our barn, and every vehicle we own apart looking for money and didn't find a thing. And you know why you didn't find nothing? Cause I didn't *do* nothing."

Alexander Dunn's cross-examination ended shortly thereafter. It was a monumental disaster. Jim Beaumont rested his case and Judge Green read the instructions to the jury.

The judge was long rumored in the legal community to be a closet homosexual, and he lorded over his courtroom like an English nobleman. Before I stopped practicing law, I'd appeared before Green hundreds of times, and although I hadn't laid eyes on him in a year, each grandiose gesture he made, each perfectly formed syllable he spoke, reminded me of his pomposity. During lulls in the trial, I found myself imagining him prancing around the room in a white periwig, pink tutu and tights, leaping through the air like a fabulously gay ballet dancer.

As soon as Green finished, the jury retired to deliberate. I thought I'd be in for a long wait, but in less than thirty minutes, I saw the bailiffs and clerks bustling around, a sure sign the jurors had made their decision. Five minutes later, they filed back into the courtroom. Green turned his palm upward and raised his right hand as though he were a symphony conductor coaxing a crescendo from the woodwinds. The foreman rose, an uncertain look on his weathered face.

"I understand you've reached a verdict," the judge said.

"We have, Your Honor."

"Pass it to the bailiff."

A uniformed deputy crossed the courtroom to the jury box, took the folded piece of paper from the foreman's hand, and delivered it to Judge Green. The judge dramatically unfolded the paper, looked at it with raised brows, refolded it, and handed it to the bailiff. The bailiff then walked the form back across the room to the foreman.

"Mr. Foreman," the judge said, "on the first count of the indictment, premeditated first-degree murder, how does the jury find?"

"We find the defendant not guilty."

"On the second count of the indictment, felony murder, how does the jury find?"

"We find the defendant not guilty."

"On the third count of the indictment, aggravated kidnapping, how does the jury find?"

"We find the defendant not guilty."

"On the fourth count of the indictment, aggravated burglary, how does the jury find?"

"We find the defendant not guilty."

"On the fifth count of the indictment, felony theft, how does the jury find?"

"We find the defendant not guilty."

I watched Dockery pat his lawyer on the back and walk out the door arm-in-arm with his mother.

He'd gotten away with it—again.

WEDNESDAY, AUG. 27

I fumed all the way home, muttering to myself about what an idiot Alexander Dunn had been. When I pulled into the driveway, the garage door was open. Caroline, my wife, must have forgotten to close it again. I parked my truck in the driveway and walked inside. As soon as I opened the door, I heard the sound of hard nails skidding across the wood floor. Rio, my German shepherd, came barreling around the counter, headed straight for me. I was carrying a bottle of water in my hand, and when he jumped up to greet me, his snout sent the bottle flying across the kitchen floor.

"Idiot!" I said as I walked toward the counter. "Why are you always so excited to see me? We're together all day every day."

The tone of my voice frightened him, and he lowered his head and slinked away. As I turned to reach for a paper towel so that I could wipe up the spilled water, I scraped my shin on the open door of the dishwasher. I reached down and slammed it closed.

"Where have you been?" Caroline said as she walked into the kitchen with her perpetual smile on her face. Caroline and I were high school sweethearts and had been married for more than twenty years. She owned and operated a dancing school where she taught jazz, tap, ballet, and acrobatics. She was leggy, athletic, and tanned, with thick auburn hair and soft brown eyes. We were still deeply in love, but at that moment, I wasn't in the mood for pleasantries.

"Caroline, why do you leave this dishwasher door open all the time?" I said as I knelt down and started wiping up the spilled water. "I just cracked my shin on it again. I've asked you at least a hundred times to close the dishwasher."

She stopped in her tracks and glared at me.

"Why don't you watch where you're stepping?" she said sarcastically. "Are you blind?"

"And why can't you close the garage door?" I said, still wiping up the spill. "Were you born in a barn? All you have to do is push a button and it closes itself."

"What difference does it make whether the garage door is closed?" she snarled.

"It keeps some of the heat out, and when we keep some of the heat out, the air conditioner doesn't have to work so hard. And when the air conditioner doesn't work so hard, it saves us money! But you don't ever think about that, do you? The money we have isn't going to last forever, especially if you keep leaving the garage door open."

"So you're saying I'm going to drive us into bankruptcy by leaving a garage door open? Sitting around the house for a year has driven you crazy, Joe."

I straightened up, wadded the paper towel, and tossed it into the wastebasket under the sink. I walked past her toward the bedroom. I grabbed a pair of shorts, some socks, a T-shirt from the dresser, and my running shoes from the closet and went back to the bathroom to change. Just as I finished tying my shoes, Caroline appeared.

"So do you want to tell me what's going on with you?" she said.

"Nothing's going on."

"You haven't been in the house five minutes and you've already terrified Rio, slammed the dishwasher, and given me hell for leaving a garage door open. Something's going on. Where have you been for the past two days?"

I looked up at her. The anger was gone from her face, and the tone of her voice told me she was genuinely concerned.

"I went to Jonesborough to watch Billy Dockery's trial," I said.

"I knew it," she said. "I've been reading about it in the newspaper. I knew you wouldn't be able to stay away. Is it still going on?"

"No. They acquitted him again. I don't think I've ever seen a prosecutor do a poorer job of trying a case."

"Come on out to the kitchen table," she said as she reached out and took my hand. "Let's talk."

I followed her out to the kitchen and sat down. She went to the refrigerator, pulled out two beers, and came back to the table.

"You're miserable," she said. "You're bored. I think you feel like you're wasting your life, and it's time to do something about it."

She popped the top on a can of Budweiser and handed it to me.

"I'm not miserable," I said. "I'm just a little upset. Seeing Dockery walk out the door today made me sick to my stomach."

"So why don't you do something about it?" she said.

"Do something? Like what?"

"Why don't you go back to work? I remember when we were young, you talked about going to work for the prosecutor's office. Why don't you give Lee Mooney a call and see if he can find a place for you?"

The suggestion took me by complete surprise. Even sitting there watching Alexander Dunn botch a trial, knowing I could do much better, going back to practicing law hadn't entered my mind. I'd quit a year earlier after spending more than a decade as a criminal defense lawyer. I made a lot of money, gained a lot of notoriety, and was good at what I did, but the profession eventually burned me out mentally, physically, and emotionally.

Friends and acquaintances had always asked me: "How can you go into court and represent someone you know is guilty?" My answer was always that my job was to make certain the government followed its own rules and to hold them to their burden of proof. It didn't have anything to do with guilt or innocence. I convinced myself for years that I was doing something honorable, that I was an important cog in the machine that called itself the criminal justice system. But over time, and especially after I realized I'd helped Billy Dockery escape punishment for murdering a defenseless elderly woman, I began to regard myself as something much less than honorable. A little over a year ago, after I'd helped a young woman walk away from a charge of murdering a preacher, the preacher's son tried to kill me in the parking lot outside the courthouse, and he nearly killed my wife in the process. That was enough.

I'd worked hard my entire life and had accumulated a fair amount of money, so I took a break, thinking I might eventually teach at a university. For the past year, I'd divided my time between watching my son play baseball for Vanderbilt University in Nashville and watching my daughter perform at football and basketball games as a member of the University of Tennessee's dance team. When I was home, I piddled around the house, worked out at the gym, ran miles and miles along the trail by the lake, and played with the dog. I enjoyed myself most of the time, but Caroline was right. I was bored, and I missed the excitement of playing such a high-stakes game.

"I don't know, Caroline," I said. "It got pretty bad there at the end. Do you really think I'm ready to go back?"

"If we were sitting here talking about going back into criminal defense, I'd say no. But I think you'd like prosecuting. You've always had a little bit of a hero complex. Putting bad guys behind bars might be right up your alley."

"You're ready to get me out of the house, aren't you?" I said. "You're tired of looking at me."

"How could I be tired of looking at you? You're gorgeous. You're big and strong, and you've got that dark hair and those beautiful green eyes. You're eye candy, baby."

"That kind of flattery will definitely get you laid."

"Seriously," she said, "I'm not tired of anything. I could live this simple little life we have now until they put me in the ground, but I know you, Joe, and you're just not happy. You have too much drive to be a professional piddler."

"So you think I should just call Mooney up and say, 'Hey, how about giving me a job?'"

"Why not? The worst he can say is no, but I think he'd be glad to have you."

I smiled at her. Caroline had a way of making me feel like I could conquer the world. She'd always had more confidence in me than I had in myself.

"Okay," I said. "If you really think it might be right for me, I'll give it a shot. I'll call Mooney first thing in the morning."

She stood and pursed her lips slightly. The next thing I knew she was pulling her shirt over her head. She slipped off her bra and turned toward the bedroom, dangling the bra from her fingertips as she looked at me over her shoulder.

"Now that's what I call eye candy," I said as I put down the beer and followed her. "Wait up. Let me help you take off the rest."

FRIDAY, AUG. 29

I felt the cool air conditioning on my face as I opened the door and stepped out of the oppressive September heat and humidity. It was a room the owner of the restaurant—a man named Tommy Hodges who fancied himself a local political insider—reserved for special customers, people he believed had power or privilege. It had its own entrance at the side of the one-story brick building. I was forty-one years old and had practiced law in the community for more than a decade, but I'd never set foot in the place.

The room was small and dimly lit, dominated by a single table, large and round with a scarred, blue Formica top. All four walls surrounding the table were decorated with autographed photos of state and local politicians. Lee Mooney, the elected attorney general of the First Judicial District, was examining a photograph of himself as I stepped through the door. Mooney was fifty years old, a lean, striking man with gray eyes, salt-and-pepper hair, and a handle bar moustache. I'd called him on Thursday morning and asked him whether he might consider hiring me, and he asked me to meet him at Tommy's place the next day. He turned his head when he heard the door open and grinned.

"Joe Dillard, in the flesh," he said, extending his hand. "It's been a long time."

At six feet five, Mooney was a couple inches taller than me. As his fingers wrapped around my hand, his white teeth flashed and his eyes locked onto mine. He held both my gaze and my hand a bit too long.

I was suspect of all politicians, but because I'd practiced criminal defense law for so long, I was especially suspect of the ego-filled megalomaniacs who typically sought the office of district attorney. A Texas A&M grad, Mooney had gone from ROTC cadet to officer training to the Judge Advocate General's office in the Marine Corps. He retired five years ago after the Marines passed on the opportunity to promote him to full colonel. His wealthy wife had persuaded him to move to northeast Tennessee, which was her childhood home, and he was immediately hired on as an assistant with the local DA's office. Before I stopped practicing law, I tried a half-dozen criminal cases against Mooney. I remembered him as a formidable adversary in the courtroom with an almost pathological fear of losing. I'd suspected him more than once of withholding evidence, but I wasn't ever able to prove it.

Mooney quit the DA's office two years ago when he smelled blood in the water. Word around the campfire was that his predecessor—a pathetic little man named Deacon Baker—had lost control of his own office and, Mooney must have sensed, the confidence of the voters. Mooney resigned and immediately announced he was running against his boss in the August election. When the last murder case I defended blew up in Deacon Baker's face just before the election, Mooney buried him.

"So what have you been up to for the past year?" Mooney said as we sat down.

"As little as possible."

"How's your wife? Is it Caroline?"

"Right. She's fine, thanks for asking."

"I've read about your son in the newspaper. He's some ballplayer."

"He's worked hard."

"Have you missed it? Practicing law I mean."

"Some," I said. There was a seductive element to defending people accused of committing crimes, especially when the stakes were at their highest. Having the fate of a man's life depend on the intensity of your commitment and the quality of your work was alluring.

Tommy Hodges, the slight and balding owner of the restaurant, showed up carrying two glasses of water and a pad.

"Don't I know you?" he said to me.

"I don't think so."

"Sure you do," Mooney said. "This is Joe Dillard, the best trial lawyer who ever set foot in a courtroom around here."

Hodges's eyes lit up.

"Oh yeah!" he said, pointing at me. "I remember you! That murder, the preacher, right? That was something. Big news."

"Yeah," I said, "big news."

"I ain't heard of you since. Where you been?"

"Sabbatical," I said.

"What?"

"Tommy," Mooney said, "how about a couple club sandwiches and a couple Cokes? Is that okay with you, Joe?"

"Sure."

He kept fiddling with a salt shaker with his right hand. After Hodges left, Mooney regarded me with a puzzled look.

"I always wondered why you were on the other side," he said as soon Hodges left the room. "I thought you would have made a great prosecutor."

"The reason isn't exactly noble. It came down to money. When I graduated from law school, I wanted to work for the DA's office. I even went for an interview. But the starting salary was less than twenty-five grand, and I already had a wife and two kids to support. I figured I could make double that practicing on my own, so I told myself I'd learn the law from the other side and then try to get on with the DA after I made some money."

"And before you knew it, your lifestyle grew into your income."

"Exactly."

"Why'd you quit?"

"A combination of things, I guess. It always bothered me that I knew my clients were lying to me, or at least most of them. And I was constantly at war with somebody—cops, prosecutors, judges, witnesses, guards at the jails, you name it. I got tired of it. But the bottom line, I think, was that I felt like I was doing something wrong."

"Wrong? How so?"

"Some of the people I helped walk out the door were guilty. They knew it, and so did I."

Mooney shifted in his chair a little and looked down at the salt shaker. "You defended Billy Dockery once, didn't you?" he said.

"He was the beginning of the end of my career as a criminal defense lawyer," I said.

"Alexander Dunn told me you were at his trial."

"I was curious."

"How'd Alexander do? It was his first big felony trial."

"The odds were against him."

There wasn't any point in telling him that Alexander was terrible and that he constantly referred to Cora Wilson as "the victim in this case" instead of by name. Even when he did mention her name, he referred to her twice as "Ms. Williams" instead of "Ms. Wilson."

"So what are you really looking for, Joe?"

"It's pretty simple. I want to do something that keeps me interested, and I want to do something that allows me to look in the mirror without throwing up."

Mooney sat back and smiled. "You looking to make amends?"

"Maybe. Something like that."

"You have to understand that Baker didn't leave me with much," he said, speaking of his predecessor. "He was so paranoid that he ran off every competent lawyer in the office. All that's left are a bunch of kids learning on the fly."

"Do you have anything open?" I said. I knew the budget in the DA's office was tight. State legislators tend to look at the criminal justice system as a necessary evil when it comes to funding.

"Not right now," Mooney said, "but I'll make room for you if you can wait a couple weeks. I was planning to fire Jack Moseley as soon as I could find someone to replace him."

"I don't want to cost anybody their job."

"Moseley's a drunk. Shows up late for work half the time, doesn't cover his cases, pinches the secretaries. Last month he disappeared for three days. We found him holed up at the Foxx Motel with a gallon of vodka and an empty sack of cocaine."

"I don't remember reading about that in the paper," I said.

Mooney winked. "Sometimes what the people don't know won't hurt them. I would've fired him months ago if I'd had another warm body. The job's yours if you want it."

"Exactly what would I be doing?"

"I've been thinking about that ever since you called. The best use for you would be to work the violent felonies, the worst ones. Murders, aggravated rapes, armed robberies. Dangerous offenders only."

I let out a low whistle. "Some job description."

"You really want to do something that makes you feel good? Here's your chance. You can make sure dangerous people wind up in jail where they belong. I'll keep your case load as light as I can so you can do it right."

"I guess it'll include death-penalty cases," I said. I'd spent a great deal of my legal career trying to ensure the state didn't kill people. If I took this job, I knew I'd soon be making some difficult choices.

"We haven't had a death-penalty case since Deacon left the office," Mooney said. "What's the point? The state's only executed one person in forty years, and there's nobody in Nashville complaining about it. I guess the legislature wants to have the death penalty in Tennessee but not have to worry about enforcing it."

"It'll change soon," I said. "People have a tendency to be bloodthirsty."

"Look at it this way. You'll be doing the same thing you did so well for all those years, practicing criminal law. The difference will be that you'll be working with the good guys, and you'll have the manpower and resources of the great state of Tennessee behind you. The pay is good, there's no overhead, and you get four weeks of vacation, state health and retirement benefits, the whole ball of wax."

I sat back and thought for a moment. The money didn't matter that much. Both of my kids had earned scholarships that paid a significant amount of their college expenses. Our house was paid for, and we had plenty of money stashed away. I'd already called both of the kids and discussed the possibility of going to work for the district attorney. Both were in favor, as was Caroline. All that was left was for me to take the plunge and see what happened.

"You make it sound like easy money," I said.

Mooney nodded his head. "There you go. Easy money. Piece of cake. Come by and see me Monday and we'll get the paperwork rolling. You start in sixteen days."

TWO WEEKS LATER
SUNDAY, SEPT. 14

Bjorn Beck glanced at the side-view mirror and watched briefly as the road stretched out behind him and seemed to melt into the distant mountains. He looked forward, and then back again. He thought about the constant comparison between what lay ahead and what lay behind. How poignant, he thought, this moment of pondering the future and the past. For Bjorn, ahead was his new life in the way of the Jehovah's Witnesses. Behind was the ignorance and intemperance of youth.

Bjorn's life was now filled with church activities. He was required to attend five meetings each week: the public talk on Sunday, the *WatchTower* study, the theocratic ministry school, the service meeting, and the book study. During these meetings, the doctrine of the Jehovah's Witnesses was being ingrained into his pliable mind. Already he'd learned that he was no longer required to salute the flag of any nation. He wasn't required to serve in the military or vote. His only allegiance was to Jehovah, the king of kings. He would no longer celebrate

Christmas or New Year's or the Fourth of July or Halloween. The only cause for special celebration would be the anniversary of Christ's death during Passover. Bjorn found the break from traditional Christianity—and traditional American life—liberating.

Bjorn, his wife Anna, and their two children, six-year-old Else and seven-month-old Elias, had spent the day at a church-sponsored convention at the Civic Center in Knoxville, Tennessee. Bjorn had been a convert for only eight months. He'd listened closely to the speakers, eager to absorb the words and ideas that would make him a better pioneer, a better servant of the church, and a better person.

He turned and stole a quick glance into the rear of the family's van. Else, blond and flawless with soft, round features, was sound asleep, her chin resting on her chest. Elias, another blue-eyed blond, was cooing contentedly in his car seat. Anna, whose hair had darkened to a sandy blond over the seven years since they'd been married, had slipped off to sleep in the passenger seat. Bjorn smiled and silently congratulated himself on his decision to move his family to Johnson City from Chicago a year ago. His children were safer, he had a better job, and he'd found Jehovah, or, more accurately, Jehovah had found him.

Two well-dressed, polite young men had knocked on Bjorn's front door on a cold, sunny day in January. Bjorn was impressed not only with their appearance, but also with their dedication. The young men were bundled up and traveling on bicycles, smiling and undaunted. They surprised him by asking whether Bjorn was satisfied with his relationship with God—he was not—and whether he might be open to alternative interpretations of the Bible—he was. They did not pressure him. He did not find them annoying. They left copies of two publications, *The WatchTower* and *Awake,* and asked Bjorn to read them. Then, if Bjorn didn't mind, they would return in a week and discuss the ideas in the publications with him and answer any questions he might have.

Bjorn had grown tired of the dogmatic approach of the Catholics, the religion of his youth and his parents— along with the scandals that hounded the church. He was tired of the aristocratic nature of the priesthood and the constant bickering over condoms and birth control, the role of women in the church, and whether homosexuality should be condemned. Bjorn considered those things insignificant and shallow. He longed for a deeper, more personal relationship with God.

Bjorn showed the publications to Anna, who shared his frustration with the church. The couple studied diligently. They learned of the Last Days, of the invisible return of Christ in 1914, of Armageddon, and of the Millennium, when Christ will rule over the Earth, the dead will be resurrected, mankind will attain perfection, and paradise will be restored. They learned that one hundred and forty-four thousand "true Christians" will rule the Great Crowd from heaven along with Jesus after Armageddon, until, ultimately, Jehovah, the all-powerful God, will rule again.

At last. A reasoned, intellectual approach to religion.

When the two young men returned as promised a week later, Bjorn and Anna had many questions. All of them were answered satisfactorily, and they accepted the young men's invitation to attend a public talk at the Kingdom Hall in Johnson City the following Sunday. A month later, both were baptized into the WatchTower faith.

Bjorn had become a pioneer, which meant he was required to spend a minimum of ninety hours each month proselytizing. It was his responsibility to turn nonbelievers into believers, or, in the parlance of the church, to turn goats into sheep. He was required to keep meticulous records of his activities so that the overseers and elders could keep tabs on his service. Bjorn didn't mind the accountability. In fact, he welcomed it. And he was naturally outgoing, so approaching complete strangers and inquiring about their relationship with God did not present a problem for him. Last month, he had exceeded his evangelical requirement by thirteen hours.

A roadside sign informed Bjorn that a rest stop was only a mile away. He'd been driving for only an hour, but the sun was going down and it was a beautiful September evening. The children could play for a little while, and he and Anna could stretch their legs. If God smiled upon him, he might even encounter a goat he could turn into a sheep.

As he eased the van off the interstate onto the rest area ramp, he touched Anna gently on the arm.

"Anna, I'm going to stop for a little while. Do you mind?"

His wife's eyes opened and she smiled.

"Where are we?"

"At a rest stop. We're not far from home, but I thought we might take a walk and let the children play for a little while."

"That's fine. I don't mind at all."

Bjorn maneuvered the van into a parking spot right in front of the restrooms. The rest stop was deserted. He saw Anna reach back and gently squeeze Else's knee.

"Else, honey, would you like to get out and play for a while?"

The child awoke slowly, rubbing the sleep from her eyes.

"I'm hungry," Else said in a tiny voice.

"Would you like a candy kiss?" Anna said. She reached for a bag of Hershey's Kisses in the console.

Bjorn parked the van, and husband and wife got out. Anna opened the sliding door and lifted Elias from his car seat. She handed the smiling child to Bjorn.

"He's wet," she said. "They probably have a changing table in the bathroom. If they don't, I can change him on one of the picnic tables."

"I'll do it," Bjorn said. "Take Else to the bathroom. I'll take care of him."

Bjorn pulled a diaper and a baby wipe from the diaper bag between the seats and walked slowly up the sidewalk. There were several picnic tables scattered on a lawn behind the bathrooms. Bjorn headed for the nearest table with Elias resting comfortably on his arm. Anna and Else strolled toward the women's restroom.

Bjorn enjoyed changing his son's diapers—even the smelly ones. It gave him an opportunity to provide comfort to the boy, to smile directly into his face and tell him he loved him.

Bjorn laid Elias on his back, smiled, and went into babyspeak as he gently and efficiently went about the task: "Are you Daddy's good boy? Yes you are. Daddy loves you. Can you say Daddy? Daaah-deee? You have to say Daddy before you say Mommy."

Elias grinned.

"Yes! That's my boy. You'll be saying it soon enough." Bjorn lifted the child into the air and kissed him on the cheek. "Let's go find Mommy."

As he started back down the hill toward the restroom, he noticed a green Chevy Cavalier had pulled into the parking spot beside his van. Goats, he thought. God has given me goats.

Bjorn saw them when he rounded the corner near the restroom to check on Else and Anna. He stopped short. Two of them, both males, were dressed in black from head to toe. Their hair was black, and they'd covered their faces in white pancake makeup. There was also a tall female, a redhead who was wearing a tight, pink miniskirt, a white blouse, black fishnet hose, and shoes with spiked heels. She was speaking to Anna, who was holding Else in her arms, while the others lingered a few steps away. On first glance, the redhead was attractive, with sharp features and full lips. Bjorn noticed a small tattoo on the side of her neck. It appeared to be a cross, but it was upside down.

"What a beautiful child," the girl said in a kind voice as Bjorn moved closer.

"Thank you," Anna said.

SCOTT PRATT

"I'd like to have a beautiful child like her some day. What's her name?"

Else buried her face in her mother's shoulder. Anna smiled. "She's shy. Her name is Else. Can you say hello to the nice lady, Else?"

Else turned to the girl and lifted a tiny hand.

"What's this?" the girl said.

"It's a Hershey's Kiss," Anna said. "She's offering you a kiss."

"Is everything all right?" Bjorn said as he cautiously approached. It was hard to tell with the makeup, but the two males appeared to be young, maybe twenty or so. One was tall and lanky, the other short and muscular. Both had small, silver rings in their pierced eyebrows, ears, and lips. The redhead was wearing a black spider web necklace, and the boys wore T-shirts that sported goat heads and pentagrams and advertised Satan. Bjorn immediately assumed that this meeting was destiny—he was being afforded a perfect opportunity to attempt to spread his new faith.

"It's a beautiful evening, isn't it?" Bjorn said.

"Yes," the redheaded girl said, "beautiful."

When she looked at Bjorn, he noticed something unusual. Her eyes. Heavy black eyeliner set off eyes that were different colors. One was a brilliant blue, the other green. Bjorn had never seen anything like it.

"May I ask you a question?" Bjorn said.

She looked at Bjorn suspiciously, but nodded slightly.

"Are you satisfied with your relationship with God?"

The girl stiffened. Bjorn heard one of the boys gasp.

"And how could that possibly be any of your business?" the girl snarled. She turned her head to the side and spat on the ground.

"I'm so sorry," Bjorn said. The smile on his face remained fixed. "I've offended you."

"You're offending me, all right," the girl said. "Who do you think you are?"

Bjorn stuck out his hand. He glanced toward the still-empty parking lot, silently wishing that someone else would come along. It remained empty with the exception of his van and the Cavalier.

"My name is Bjorn," he said. "And this is my wife—"

"I don't care what your name is." Bjorn was surprised, and a bit frightened, by the girl's anger. She ignored his outstretched hand, which he quickly retracted. Her eyes were locked onto him, and as he stood looking at her, he suddenly felt cold. He shifted Elias to his other shoulder.

"Please," Bjorn said. "The last thing I wanted to do was upset you. Perhaps we could go up to a table over there and sit and talk for a little while."

The girl seemed to relax a bit. She turned and smiled at her companions, then looked back at Bjorn.

"Talk?" she said. "You want to talk to me?"

"I'd love to," Bjorn said. "We'll just sit and talk. I'd love to share what I've learned about God's love with you."

She turned to the young man standing closest to her.

"God's love," she said. "He wants to share what he knows about God's love. That's nice."

She stood for a moment, seemingly pondering Bjorn's proposal. Finally, she said, "Okay, why not? Just let us use the restroom. Go on ahead. We'll be there in a minute."

The girl turned and walked into the building that housed the restrooms, followed by the males. Bjorn watched them go, then started back up the hill.

"Do you think this is a good idea?" Anna said. "They scare me."

"She seems filled with rage," Bjorn said. "Maybe I can help her."

"Bjorn, what about the children? What if something goes wrong? I mean, did you see what they were wearing? Those symbols on their clothes, goat heads and Satan? And all the black. They're hideous. And I could smell alcohol on the girl's breath. I think we should go."

Bjorn took his wife's hand. "This is a test, Anna. I'm sure of it. It's God's way of testing my faith." He gestured at the tree line a hundred feet away. "If you don't feel comfortable, take the children over there and I'll talk to them alone."

Bjorn took a seat at a picnic table beneath a maple tree. The sun was just slipping behind a mountain to the west, the shimmering orange light dancing through the poplar and oak leaves. What a magnificent sight, Bjorn thought, what a magnificent day. What a wonderful time to be alive and well in God's kingdom. It was a pity there weren't more people around to enjoy it.

Bjorn heard an engine come to life and looked back down toward the restrooms. He saw the green Cavalier back out of the spot near his van and pull away. Just then the two young goths who had been with the redhead came walking over the hill, heading in his direction. Puzzled, he stood and started toward them.

"Is your friend leaving?" he said.

The short, muscular goth raised his T-shirt and produced a pistol.

"Yeah, she's leaving," he said, "and you're coming with us."

SUNDAY, SEPT. 14

The voice eased its way through my subconscious and gently brought me out of sleep. I'd been napping on the couch, using the excuse that I'd be starting a new job tomorrow and needed to rest up. When my eyes opened, my wife's face was smiling down at me. She was offering me something—a telephone.

"It's Lee Mooney," Caroline said. "He says it's urgent."

Already, it had begun. The extreme importance of all matters legal, especially all matters criminal. I looked at my watch. Almost nine o'clock. I sat up and took the phone.

"Hey Lee," I said to the man who would become my boss in about twelve hours. I hadn't had a boss in nearly twenty years.

"Sorry about the Sunday call," Mooney said. "We've got a bad one. What would you think about starting a day early?"

"What do you mean?" I felt certain, even in my groggy state of mind, that the district attorney's office and the courthouses were closed on Sunday.

"It looks like we've got an entire family slaughtered out in the county," Mooney said. "They tell me there are a couple small children involved. I want to go out there and make sure everything's done right. Since it'll be your case, I thought you might want to come with me."

I processed the information slowly. My mind illuminated the high points—family ... slaughtered ... in the county ... small children. I rubbed my face and tried to focus.

"An entire family?"

"I don't have many details yet. Do you want me to stop by and pick you up or do you want to meet me out there?"

I didn't want to be entirely at his mercy, so I told him I'd meet him. He gave me the location, a place with which I was vaguely familiar. I could be there in less than an hour.

I hung up and splashed cold water on my face. I pulled on my jeans, a hooded sweatshirt, and an old pair of hiking boots. I pecked Caroline on the cheek and headed out the door. Rio started whining. He wanted to go. I dropped the tailgate on my pickup and he jumped in.

The place I was going was Marbleton Road, little more than a wide dirt path that intersected with Smalling Road near the mountains at the western edge of Washington County. The intersection was just north of Interstate 81 and just south of nowhere. You could stand at the intersection of Marbleton and Smalling Roads and unleash an arrow from a bow in any direction without fear of hitting anything human. The closest house was more than a half mile away.

I got there around ten. As I rounded a curve on Smalling Road, still a quarter mile away, I could see red and blue lights, plenty of them, flashing eerily off the trees surrounding the intersection. A young deputy stopped me about two hundred yards from Smalling Road and told me I was going to have to turn around. I showed him the brand new badge identifying me as an assistant district attorney that Lee Mooney had given me a few days earlier, and he waved me through. I spotted Mooney's SUV parked in a field to my left about a hundred yards south of the flashing lights, and I pulled over next to it and got out.

Rio's ears were pointed straight up, and his nostrils were flared. He was standing in the back of the truck, facing the intersection, and he was growling. The behavior was distinctly uncharacteristic. When I reached up to try to calm him, I noticed the hair on his back was at attention. I grabbed his harness and put him in the cab of the truck. I took a flashlight from the glove compartment, stuffed my hands inside the pocket on the front of my sweatshirt, and walked toward the lights. It suddenly seemed much colder than it was when I left home.

There were several unmarked cars and police cruisers, a crime-scene van, and three ambulances, all parked within a couple hundred feet of Marbleton Road. Just past the intersection was another van, this one from the local television station, Channel 12. A bright light illuminated a reporter sticking a microphone into the face of a man I recognized to be the sheriff of Washington County, a shameless publicity hound named Leon Bates. The flashing lights from the emergency vehicles made me dizzy. When I stepped up to the intersection at Marbleton, yet another young deputy accosted me where yellow police tape had been pulled across the road. I looked at him closely for few seconds as his complexion changed from light blue to light red to light blue to light red.

"Who are you?" he demanded. I knew nearly every cop in the county when I quit practicing law a year ago. I'd already run across two I'd never laid eyes on. The county commission wouldn't pay them a competitive wage, so a lot of them became disillusioned and moved on.

"Joe Dillard," I said, reaching for the identification and badge again. He looked at me warily.

"This is a crime scene," he said. "You can't go stomping around in here."

"Where's Lee Mooney? He told me to come."

The young officer turned and nodded toward the darkness. I could see beams from flashlights through the leaves on the low tree branches. They appeared to be about a hundred yards down the road. I also noticed brighter flashes of light. Someone was taking photographs.

"How bad is it?" I said.

"As bad as it gets. Walk through the trees to the left or the right. Don't walk on the road. They're making casts of foot and tire prints."

I made my way through the trees and looked up. The moon was creeping up behind a hill to the northeast, almost as though it was afraid of what it would see when it cleared the ridge. When I got to within twenty yards of the flashlights, I could hear muffled voices. I yelled out, "Lee Mooney!"

"Over here," a voice called in return.

"Can I walk on the road?"

"Stop where you are," Mooney said. "I'll come to you."

I saw the beam of a flashlight making its way toward me. I assumed it was Mooney. I waved my light at him. He stopped about thirty feet away and said, "Walk straight to me."

I nearly tripped in a small ditch and came up on the road. It was a little bit gritty and somewhat soft—a mixture of soil, sand, clay, and chat.

"Welcome to hell," Mooney said. He was wearing an overcoat and gloves, and he was shivering. When my flashlight hit his face, he looked as pale as the moon that was coming over the horizon.

"Do I want to go back there?" I knew perfectly well that I didn't.

"Depends on the strength of your stomach. Worst I've ever seen."

I'd seen dead bodies before, but it was long ago and far away. My experience defending murderers had sometimes required me to examine gruesome photographs, but I knew this would be different. I shrugged my shoulders.

"We've got four shot to pieces," he said. "Man, woman, and two children. They're all dead." His voice had a higher pitch than normal. In the cold darkness, it sounded almost as though it was being piped in over a transistor radio.

"What can I do?"

"Just come on back here with me and take a look around. Maybe you'll spot something we've missed."

Mooney told me to walk directly behind him. We rounded a slight bend, and I could see a man kneeling and gingerly picking up objects from the ground and placing them in an evidence bag. As I got closer I could see that he was picking up shell casings. A lot of shell casings. Another officer with "CSU" on the back of his jacket was pouring liquid plaster into a footprint on the ground. Others were searching the surrounding area with flashlights. A photographer was kneeling over something a few feet away. A light flashed.

I suddenly noticed two pairs of legs protruding from the ditch onto the road beneath the photographer. One pair of legs was longer than the other and covered with what appeared to be slacks. There were brown shoes on the feet. The shorter pair of legs was bare. The right foot was wearing a black pump. The left foot, like the legs, was bare. I noticed something else. The bottom half of the legs were bent at a grotesque angle.

I stopped cold.

Lying across the legs at right angles were the blood-soaked children, both facedown. The smaller child was on top of the longer pair of legs, the larger child on top of the shorter pair. I stared at them, momentarily unable to think.

"Somebody placed them like that after they were shot," Mooney was saying. "And there's something else— you see how the bottoms of the legs are bent? The killers ran over them when they left. Shot them point-blank and they fell straight back into the ditch. Shot the kids and placed them facedown on top of the parents. Then they ran right over their legs."

"Killers?" I said. "There was more than one?"

"At least two. Maybe more."

"How do you know?"

"There are footprints all over the place, but it'll take a while before we can sort it all out. The crime-scene guys tell me it looks like they came in one vehicle, a large one, van or truck maybe. They drove down the road a ways and turned around. There are footprints around the tire tracks where the vehicle stopped. They lined them up next to the ditch and executed them."

"How'd we find out about it?"

"Somebody heard gunshots and called it in. Young deputy, only been on the job four weeks, came out here and found them. He's sitting in a cruiser over there. I tried to talk to him, but he's too upset right now. He's just sitting there in a daze."

I could smell blood in the air. There was a lot of blood on the children, but I couldn't quite see the adults. The prurient in me urged me to move closer to the bodies, to take a look at their faces. I hesitated, and Mooney sensed what I was feeling.

"You don't want to look," he said. "The man and the woman were both shot at least six times. Both of them were shot in the right eye. So were the children. I wish I hadn't seen that little boy …."

His voice trailed off. I remembered that Mooney and his wife adopted an infant a few years ago. A little boy. Must be three or four years old now.

"Do we know who they are?" I asked quietly.

"We know who the man is. His name is Beck, Bjorn Beck. Thirty years old, Johnson City address. They left his wallet in his pocket. It had eight dollars in it."

"Nothing on the woman?"

"Not yet. I'm assuming she's his wife until somebody tells me otherwise. We've got TBI agents in Johnson City checking out the address right now. We should know something soon."

I began to rock back and forth and stamp my feet. Even though I couldn't see my breath, the cold felt as though it had penetrated the marrow in my bones.

"Cold, isn't it?" Mooney said. His voice was trembling slightly.

I didn't say anything, but I looked at him. When he looked back, I could see fear in his eyes.

"It wasn't this cold when I left the house," he said. "Seems like the temperature dropped twenty degrees when I got here."

"Yeah, I felt it too."

"You ever hear or read anything about evil?"

It was a strange question, one that I pondered briefly. Of course I'd heard of evil. Of course I'd read about evil.

"Ever read anything about Catholic priests performing exorcisms?" Mooney continued. "They say they experience a sensation of coldness, just like this."

"What are you trying to say?"

"What happened here was evil. The cold-blooded execution of an entire family. They didn't take his wallet, so it wasn't a robbery. All of them shot in the right eye. The way the children were placed. Running over their legs after they were dead."

I looked down at my boots for a moment. I'd noticed the drop in temperature. I'd noticed the reaction of my dog. I felt the presence of something I'd never felt before, but I didn't want to admit it or discuss it. All I wanted was to get out of there.

Mooney turned toward me again. His eyes were moist, his voice still shaky. "You have to promise me something," he said. "You have to promise me that when we find the … the *animals* that did this, you'll see to it that every one of them gets the electric chair. No screw ups. No deals. Whoever shot those two children needs to be removed from the gene pool."

The words hit me like scalding water. I'd spent a good portion of my legal career trying to keep the government from executing people, and now there I stood, in the dark, cold woods, listening to a man tell me I must promise to use my newly acquired power to make sure someone died. I looked at Mooney again. He was nearly in tears.

"I'll do what's right, Lee," I said, "as soon as I figure out what it is."

PART II

MONDAY, SEPT. 15

Tennessee Bureau of Investigation Special Agent Hank Fraley looked up from his desk to see a man walking through the front door.

A babysitter. Just what I need. I've got a loud-mouthed sheriff running around sticking his nose into everything, and now I have to deal with a lawyer.

Fraley had been awake all night, his head was splitting, and the acid in his stomach made him feel like he was being eaten from the inside out. He couldn't get the images of the dead family out of his mind. The eyes haunted him. All of them had been shot in the right eye. Thirty years of working homicide cases in Memphis and Nashville—places a lot more violent than this—had steeled Fraley, but nothing could have prepared him for the carnage he saw when he got to the murder scene. Those beautiful, innocent children. The girl was about the same age as Fraley's granddaughter, the boy just an infant. Who, or what, could do that to a baby?

And now he had to deal with Joe Dillard, the former defense attorney miraculously and suddenly turned prosecutor. Lee Mooney had invited Dillard to the crime scene, and now he was supposed to … what was he supposed to do, anyway? Mooney had called earlier and said he wanted Dillard involved in the investigation. His mission, Mooney said, would be to make sure Fraley didn't make any mistakes that would come back and cause them problems in the courtroom later.

"What kind of mistakes?" Fraley had asked.

"*Legal* mistakes," Mooney said. "*Constitutional* mistakes."

What a load of horse crap. Fraley was doing homicide work when Dillard was still sucking on a pacifier. He'd be as useless as teats on a bull. And besides, Fraley was looking for murderers, the kind of people who shoot babies at point-blank range. Screw *legal*. Screw *constitutional*.

The secretary buzzed. Fraley snuffed out his cigarette and told her to send Dillard in. He was a big guy, dark-haired, green-eyed and athletic-looking, at least twenty years younger than Fraley. He hadn't managed to put on the paunch yet, but his hair was just starting to go gray and the lines in his forehead and around his eyes were starting to run deep. He was wearing a charcoal suit, a nice one, and a blue shirt and tie. Movie star teeth.

Fraley had heard a lot about Dillard since being transferred up from Nashville to replace a bad cop named Phil Landers. There'd been a scandal about Landers soliciting false testimony from a jailhouse snitch who turned out to be Dillard's sister. Then Landers was accused of conducting an illegal search in a big murder case and subsequently lying about it on the witness stand. Dillard was the defense lawyer who finally took Landers down.

The bosses in Nashville sent Fraley in to clean up the mess. Said they needed a "stable" force in the office, which Fraley took to mean somebody old. They told him he could ride out his last few years with the TBI in the relative peace of northeast Tennessee. And now this, the worst murder he'd ever seen.

"What can I do for you?" Fraley said without shaking Dillard's hand. He didn't bother to stand. He wasn't about to make it easy.

"I'm not really sure," Dillard said pleasantly. "To tell you the truth, I don't really know why I'm here. All I know is that Lee Mooney said he called you and he sent me up here to help."

"I don't need any help, especially from a lawyer."

There was an awkward silence.

"How can I help?" Dillard said, standing in front of Fraley's desk, still smiling.

"Go back to your own office. Let me do my job."

"I'd love to," he said, "but my boss sent me up here. First day on the new job and all. Probably wouldn't be good if I disobeyed his order. So here I am."

"I didn't know a law degree qualified a person to be a homicide investigator."

A puzzled look came over Dillard's face. He stood looking at Fraley for a minute, then he smiled again and said, "Excuse me."

Fraley watched the man as he walked back out the front door. He thought he was rid of the lawyer, but about fifteen minutes later Fraley looked up from his desk again to see Dillard walk back through the front door and straight past the secretary. He was carrying a bag in

SCOTT PRATT

his left hand. He walked into Fraley's office, grinned, and stuck out his right hand.

"Hi, I'm Joe Dillard," he said. "I think maybe we got off to a bad start. I brought you some coffee and a couple sticky buns from Perkins."

Fraley looked at him deadpan, but decided grudgingly to at least shake his hand. "I know who you are," Fraley said.

"Mooney told me," Dillard said.

"Told you what?"

"That you can't resist sticky buns. I called him from the car, and he said I should bring you sticky buns." Dillard opened the bag. "How about it?"

Fraley wanted to tell him to stuff his sticky buns, but that isn't what came out of his mouth. What came out of his mouth was, "So you think you can bribe me with sweets?"

"Hope so. I don't have much money."

"You're a lawyer," Fraley said. "You've got more money than Sam Walton."

Dillard reached into the bag, pulled out a Styrofoam cup of coffee, and set it in front of Fraley. He pulled out a paper plate and a plastic fork, set those down, and then plopped a sticky bun on the plate.

"You want me to eat it for you too?" he said, licking the sticky stuff off his fingers. Fraley decided maybe he wasn't as bad as they'd made him out to be.

"Sit," Fraley said.

Dillard took his jacket off and sat down across from Fraley. He took the lid off a second cup of coffee.

"Long night?" Dillard said.

"The longest."

"Me too. I couldn't sleep."

"So enlighten me," Fraley said. "What do you think you're supposed to be doing here?"

"Extra set of eyes, maybe. Extra set of hands." Dillard licked some more of the sticky-bun goo from a thumb. "After you catch whoever did this, I'll be the one who handles the case in court, and I think Mooney wants me in from the beginning."

"He told me he was sending you up here to make sure I didn't make any mistakes."

"From what I've heard about you, you don't make mistakes."

"So you've been checking me out."

"And you haven't been doing the same?"

Fraley shrugged his shoulders.

"That's what I thought," Dillard said. "Listen, I'm not here to watch over you. I'm just here to help any way I can."

Fraley took a big bite of the sticky bun. Cinnamon, butter, sugar … so unhealthy, but so good. "So where do you want to start?" Fraley said.

"Maybe you should start by telling me what kind of evidence you've gathered so far."

"I got casts of footprints that are useless until I find the feet that match them. I got casts of tire prints that are useless until I find the tires that made them. I got nine-millimeter shell casings that are useless until I find the guns that spit them out. I got a bunch of slugs and I'll have more after the medical examiner finishes the autopsies. I got two Caucasian adults, a male and a female, shot six times each. Two little kids, one six years old and one ten months, shot three times each. All four of them shot in the right eye. After the adults were shot, someone tucked their arms against their sides and then placed the dead children at right angles across their knees in what appears to be the shape of a cross of some sort. The medical examiner called me a few minutes ago and said that after she cleaned up the father, she discovered that someone had carved a little message in the father's forehead."

"A message?"

"Yeah. It took her a little while to figure out what it was. I guess whoever carved it wasn't much of an artist."

"What did it say?"

"Ah Satan."

"Ah Satan? What do you think it means?"

"Who knows? The father also had an upside-down cross cut into the side of his neck. She decided to check on the others, and it turns out that all four of them have these little upside-down crosses carved into their necks. And take a look at these."

Fraley reached for some photographs and set them down on the desk in front of Dillard. The photos were of the bodies at the crime scene, taken from directly above.

"Does the positioning of the bodies mean anything to you?" Fraley asked.

The children had been placed across the adults' thighs. Dillard stared at the photos, then looked up at Fraley.

"Like you said, crosses," he said.

"Maybe upside down since they're across the legs instead of the shoulders. Do you know anything about upside-down crosses?"

"Some kind of satanic symbol maybe. I think they call them inverted crosses."

"Looks like devil worshippers."

"Either that or somebody wants you to think so. Have you identified all the victims?"

"They're local," Fraley said, "but they've only been here about a year. Bjorn Beck, thirty-one years old, address is 1401 Poplar Street. Clerk at a hotel over by the mall. His wife, Anna, thirty years old, worked at Starlight Marketing selling vacations over the phone. Else, six years old, just started kindergarten a few weeks ago. The little boy's name was Elias, ten months old. One of their neighbors said they went to a Jehovah's Witness convention in Knoxville yesterday. Haven't confirmed that yet. They were driving a Chevrolet van, maroon. We've got a nationwide alert out on the van."

"No witnesses?"

"Not that we know of. We canvassed within a mile of the scene. Nobody saw anything unusual. There's a guy who was checking out a building site about a quarter mile away who heard the shots and called it in, but he didn't go anywhere near it. As a matter of fact, he said he got cold chills when he heard the shots and headed in the other direction."

"What about family?"

"Both sets of parents are in Chicago, which is where Beck and his wife were from. Mr. Beck has—or had—a brother who's flying in from Panama City, Florida, this afternoon to make a positive ID on the bodies."

"I can't imagine having to do something like that."

The phone rang just as Fraley stuffed another bite of bun into his mouth.

"Fraley. Yeah? Already? Where? Ten minutes."

He looked at Dillard, trying to decide whether he wanted to tell him. He didn't seem like such a bad guy. Besides, maybe Fraley could get him to spring for lunch later. Fraley stood up.

"C'mon, boy scout," he said. "They found the van."

MONDAY, SEPT. 15

A patrol officer noticed the van about five blocks from the downtown area, where the Blue Plum music festival had been held over the weekend. I'd always thought it a strange name since plums, blue or otherwise, didn't grow anywhere near Johnson City. They cordoned off the streets and set up stages all over the blighted five-block area downtown, which had fallen victim to the convenience of mall shopping and the circular development of cities. There were a few junk shops, a couple bars where the college kids from East Tennessee State University hung out, a couple hobby shops, and a few lawyer's offices. If it hadn't been for a courthouse being located on Main Street, most of the buildings would have been boarded up.

Caroline and I had gone to the Blue Plum a few years earlier because both of us loved live music—it didn't really matter what kind—and the festival offered a little for everyone: bluegrass, country, rock, gospel, and blues. The city had billed it as a family event and it was supposed to benefit the merchants downtown, but they'd made the mistake of allowing the bars to give away beer and they let people drink on the streets. After a couple years it turned into a two-day drunkfest. People walked around in a daze, urinating in the alleys, and the more they drank, the more belligerent they became. There'd been several fights two years ago, and last year Caroline and I didn't even bother to attend. As I gazed at the van, I wondered whether our murderers shot a family of four and then went to Blue Plum to guzzle a few free beers.

There was nothing for me to do at the scene. Men and women with skills far superior to mine in the area of forensic-evidence gathering spent their time stooping and examining and picking and poking and photographing. I watched and stayed out of their way, hoping they'd find something that would help identify the killers.

I hung around until they hauled the van off to Knoxville on a flatbed truck, then I went back down to Jonesborough so that I could start getting set up in my new office, which was nothing fancier than a twelve-foot by twelve-foot sheetrock box. It was after three when I got there, and the place was nearly deserted. As I walked past the secretary, a forty-year-old, blue-eyed, redheaded bombshell named Rita Jones, she batted her eyes at me and handed me a stack of messages.

"You haven't even been here a day, and you've already got more messages than most of us get in a week," she said.

I'd known Rita for several years. She'd been a legal secretary for close to a dozen lawyers, had broken up more than one marriage, and had hit on me so many times that it got to be a sort of joke between us. My most vivid memory of her was at a Christmas party hosted by the bar association five or six years earlier. She wore red spiked heels, shiny red pants, a Santa hat, and a red knit halter top outlined in white fur that barely contained the bounty within. Sometime around nine, after everyone was good and soused, I was leaning against a wall talking to Bob Brown, a lawyer legendary for both his ability to ingest huge amounts of liquor and his insatiable sexual appetite. I was listening to one of Brown's stories when Rita and her bounty happened by. She stopped to say hello and Brown, without uttering a word, hooked his finger in the front of the halter and pulled it down, revealing her breasts. Rita didn't bat an eye. Nor did she attempt to cover herself. She looked directly at me, smiled coyly, and said, "All this, and brains too." I awkwardly excused myself and walked away, but I hadn't forgotten those breasts. They were magnificent.

"What's all this?" I said, looking at the stack of messages. "Nobody even knows I'm working here."

"All media. All about the murders," she said. She took the stack from my hand and began to go through it. "CNN, Fox, MSNBC, the big networks. The list goes on and on. Looks like you're going to be a celebrity."

She offered the stack to me again with a wry smile, but I refused to take it.

"Tell them no comment," I said. "If I have anything to say, I'll call a press conference and talk to all of them at the same time."

"I can't do that, cutie, much as I'd like to," she said. "You see, it isn't my *job* to tell them no comment. That'd be your job."

"Then just tell them I'm not here. I don't want my phone ringing every five minutes."

"You mean you want me to lie? Imagine that, a lawyer asking a secretary to lie."

"Don't act like you haven't done it before."

"But that was back when I was working for those awful private lawyers. Now I'm at the district attorney's office. Everybody here is honorable, honey. We're not supposed to lie. We're not supposed to do anything that would cast aspersions on the office."

"C'mon, Rita. You'll make an exception for me, won't you? I'm not used to being honorable. Maybe it'll grow on me."

"I'll tell you what. You make sure you wear some nice tight pants at least twice a week and I'll see what I can do."

"If I didn't know better, I'd swear you were sexually harassing me."

"And when can I expect you to do the same?"

"Sorry, Rita," I said, holding up my ring finger for her to see. "Still married. Still *happily* married."

"Well," she said with a wink, "we'll just have to see about that, won't we?"

I turned and walked back to my office with a strange tingling sensation in my stomach. I was flattered by the attention—it had been a long time since a woman had flirted with me so openly—but I knew Rita's reputation. She was a conqueror, a woman who chewed up men and spit them out like chewing gum. Besides, after twenty years of marriage, I was still madly in love with my wife.

The office was equipped with a desk, a computer, work station, and a couple chairs. The walls were antique white and bare. I'd left a box of personal items on the desk early in the morning, before I left to go to Fraley's office, and I started taking things out of the box and arranging them. I'd just set a photograph of my daughter doing an arabesque on the desk when the door opened and Alexander Dunn walked in. Dunn was a trust-funder, the beneficiary of a grandfather who struck it rich in the coal mines in southwest Virginia. He was vertically challenged, maybe five feet eight, and his brown hair was medium length, heavily moussed, and combed straight back from his wide forehead. He had thin, nearly indiscernible lips and pearly white teeth that didn't look natural. He was wearing a navy blue suit that was tailor-made, just like the suit he wore during Billy Dockery's trial. His Italian loafers were black instead of brown, but the white, silk kerchief was still rising out of the breast pocket. He strode straight up to my desk and stood there looking at me.

"The legend returns to the practice of law," he said. The tone was sarcastic, and he wasn't smiling.

I knew Alexander was a fairly recent hire in the DA's office. Prior to him becoming an assistant district attorney, he'd been an ambulance chaser and divorce attorney. He'd been with the DA's office for less than a year, and from what I'd read in the newspapers, he was trying mightily to make a name for himself by pressing for the maximum punishment on every case he handled. He wasn't having much success, though, and after watching him try Dockery's case, I knew why.

"Hello, Alexander," I said, looking back down at my box of goodies.

"Run out of money?"

"Beg your pardon?"

"Did you run out of money? Is that why you're working here?"

"Not exactly."

"Planning on running for office?"

"No."

"What then? Why are you here?"

"Thought it might be entertaining." I pulled another photograph out of the box, this one of my son Jack swinging a baseball bat.

"Entertaining?" Dunn said. "Well, just so you know, your pleasure is my pain. You're hurting my career."

"Really? How?"

"This new murder should be my case," he blurted. "I've been here longer than you." His tone had changed from sarcastic to whiny.

"Sorry. Just doing what the boss tells me to do."

"What makes you think you can just waltz in here and take over? People aren't happy about this, you know. People in the office. People in law enforcement. I've heard lots of bad things about you. Don't expect any help from anyone."

"Don't worry, Alexander. I wouldn't think of asking you for help."

"What's that supposed to mean?"

"It means I won't ask you for help. Now if you don't mind, I'm kind of busy here."

I looked up from the box and noticed that his lower lip had started quivering slightly, but he remained standing in front of my desk. He seemed to be having some kind of debate with himself about whether he should say what was on his mind. Finally, he spat it out.

"How's that sister of yours? Still a drug addict and a thief?"

It was true. Sarah had been a drug addict and a thief in the past, but she'd been clean for more than a year. She'd replaced her drug addiction with religious fervor, but given a choice between the two extremes, I'd take good old Southern Baptist fanaticism every time. I forced myself to smile at him, but I could feel my blood pressure steadily rising.

"I'm tired, Alexander," I said through clenched teeth. "It's been an extremely difficult first day on the job, and I think you should leave now."

"It's a shame," he said, "having an assistant district attorney whose sister is a career criminal. It doesn't look good for the office."

"Maybe you should take it up with the boss."

"Maybe I will." He sounded like a fifth grader.

"Let me help you with the door," I said, and I moved quickly around the desk toward him. I was a good five inches taller than him and at least forty pounds heavier. He started backing toward the door as though he was afraid I'd pull a gun and shoot him if he took his eyes off me. He opened his mouth to say something else, but I raised an index finger to my lips.

"Shhh. I'm not sure what might happen if you start talking again."

His eyes opened even wider. A trembling hand found the doorknob behind him. The door squeaked as it opened, and he turned and slithered out.

I stood there staring at the door for almost a full minute with the insult about Sarah ringing in my ears. I was consciously trying to slow my heart rate when I saw the doorknob turn. I couldn't believe it. The little fool was coming back, probably to get one last shot in. I made it to the door in two steps and jerked it open.

Rita, pulled off balance by the force of the opening door, stumbled into my arms.

"Rita!" I said, horrified. She backed up a step and smoothed her dress, the excess of her breasts escaping from her D-cup like wild horses from a corral. "I thought you were … I thought—"

"Don't you pay any attention to him," she said. "He's just jealous is all."

"You were listening?"

"I knew he'd do something like that. He's been upset ever since he found out you were coming to work here."

"He's a twerp."

"That he is, honey," Rita said. "But you still need to be careful how you handle him. Lee protects him."

"Why? Why is that incompetent little jerk even working here?"

"Because the boss's wife just happens to be Alexander's daddy's sister, and he's her favorite nephew. I'm sure I don't have to tell you that blood's thicker than water. Especially around here."

I knew exactly what she meant. Nepotism was alive and well in northeast Tennessee. The county clerk's office, the tax assessor's office, the county highway department, the sheriff's department, and the school system were all staffed by the sons, daughters, nieces, nephews, and cousins of county commissioners and their spouses. In the past, I'd always found the practice to be somewhat amusing—the hicks perpetuating their own myth—but this was different.

"So I'm stuck with him," I said, "no matter what he does."

"You step lightly around him," Rita said. "He's not very smart, but he's mean as a striped snake."

MONDAY, SEPT. 15

held my first press conference as an assistant district attorney late that afternoon on the courthouse steps. Lee Mooney asked me to bail him out, so I did, albeit reluctantly. I kept the details to a minimum and got out of there as quickly as I could.

I moved slowly the rest of the day, exhausted. After leaving the scene where the Beck family had been murdered shortly after eleven the night before, I'd taken the long way home and sneaked into the house so I wouldn't wake Caroline. I didn't want to describe to her what I'd seen, to try to put the horror into words. I went into the den and mindlessly watched television until after midnight, then lay on the couch and tried to sleep. I tossed and turned until an hour before dawn, the grotesque image of the broken legs glowing in my mind like an ember in the night wind.

I finally finished setting up my office a little after five. Besides Alexander, there were four other young lawyers in the office, and not one of them said a word to me all day. Before I left, I called Fraley to see if there was anything new to report. The only thing the canvas had provided was a witness at a house nearby who said she saw two people in black clothes and white makeup get out of the Beck's van sometime just after dark. I headed home.

We lived on ten acres on a bluff overlooking Boone Lake in a house built primarily of cedar, stone and glass. I loved the house and the property, and I loved the people and the dog I shared it with. The back was almost all glass and faced north toward the lake. The views, especially when the leaves turned in October and November, were spectacular. Rio greeted me with his usual enthusiasm, and once I calmed him down, I found Caroline in the bathroom, topless. She was standing in front of the mirror prodding her left breast near the nipple with her index finger. The sight made me more than a little anxious.

"It's bigger," she said, referring to a small lump just beneath the areola. "And it's hard. It's spreading out like a spider web."

"Have you called the doctor?" I said, keeping my distance. She was so sexy without the top that I knew I'd have trouble keeping my hands to myself, but it obviously wasn't the time.

"Not yet."

"Don't you think you should?"

"Probably, but I think it's just some kind of cyst. I'm too young to have breast cancer. And besides, there's no history of it in my family. I asked my mother about it. No history at all."

Caroline was so vital that it was difficult for me to even comprehend the notion that she might have cancer. She'd been dancing and teaching all her life: ballet, jazz, tap, and acrobatics, so she was in great shape. She'd noticed the lump, which had started out like a bee sting, almost three months earlier. I'd noticed it too, during moments when a lump in her breast was the last thing I wanted to think about. But it was there, and it was growing.

"Caroline, you need to go to the doctor," I said. "Wait, let me rephrase that. Caroline, you're going to the doctor. Tomorrow, or as soon as she can see you. If you won't call and set it up, I'll do it myself."

"I'll do it," she said, turning away from the mirror and toward me. "I'll call her tomorrow. I just dread it."

Still topless, she reached up to hug me. "Are you okay? The murders have been all over the news. It's terrible, Joe. Who could kill a child?"

"I'll let you know as soon as we find out."

"Do you have any idea?"

"None. The agents are working around the clock, but we just don't know yet. Maybe we'll get a break soon." She smelled inviting.

"They said the police found the van."

"Yeah. They're processing it now."

"Great way to start the new job, huh?"

"Just my luck."

I could feel the warmth of her skin through my shirt and I felt myself stirring. I pulled her closer.

"Sorry, big boy," she said, "Sarah's coming over."

"Sarah? Why?"

"She's leaving tomorrow, remember? I've got steak in the refrigerator."

"I forgot all about it."

My sister, the object of Alexander Dunn's earlier insult, was a year older than me. She was a black-haired, green-eyed, hard-bodied beauty who leaned toward extremism in all things and had spent most of her adult life addicted to alcohol and cocaine. We'd been close as children until one summer evening when she was nine years old. That night, my uncle Raymond, who was sixteen at the time, raped her while he was supposed to be looking after the two of us at my grandmother's house. My grandparents and mother had gone out shopping, and I'd drifted off to sleep while watching a baseball game on television. I heard Sarah's cries, the pain in her voice, and I went into my grandparents' bedroom and tried to stop him, but Raymond picked me up and threw me out of the room, nearly knocking me unconscious in the process. When it was over, he threatened to kill both of us if we ever told anyone.

Sarah and I went in different directions after that. I became an overachiever, subconsciously trying to prove to myself that I wasn't a coward, while she became a suspicious, defiant, self-destructive rebel. She'd been convicted of theft and drug possession half a dozen times and had spent a fair amount of time in jail. But last year, not long after our mother died, she and I had finally talked about the rape and its effect on our lives. Our relationship improved dramatically after that, and so did Sarah's life, or at least that's how it appeared. After she was released from jail a year ago, she'd moved into my mother's house, started going to Narcotics Anonymous meetings, and, to my knowledge, had been clean and sober ever since. She'd met a man at her N.A. meetings named Robert Godsey whom she said she loved. She was moving to Crossville, Tennessee, the next day to be near him.

Sarah told me her new boyfriend had been clean for five years, but I was concerned. Godsey had been a probation officer in Washington County for at least a decade, and I'd run across him several times in the past. My impression of him wasn't good, although I hadn't said a word about it to Sarah. I remembered Godsey as a belligerent bully, always filing violation warrants against his probationers for the tiniest of infractions. He was also a sanctimonious zealot, a man who apparently thought he knew all the answers to questions involving faith and eternity. I'd heard him harangue people in the courthouse hallways about getting right with the Lord more times than I cared to remember. One time a few years ago, I'd seen him back a young woman against the wall with his chest and shove her face with the heel of his hand. I started to confront him, but by the time I broke away from my client, he'd stormed out the door. Now he'd transferred to Crossville, and he was taking my sister with him.

Rio began to bark at the front door.

"She's early," Caroline said.

I walked through the house, quieted the dog, and opened the door. Sarah stepped inside, wearing black jeans and a pink, V-necked pullover top with short sleeves. I noticed she was wearing a silver fish on a chain around her neck. I'd never seen it before.

"Nice necklace," I said. Sarah's conversion to Christianity had been both recent and complete. Caroline and I had gone to her baptism back in mid-August. The ceremony was held on the bank of the Nolichuckey River behind the tiny Calvary Baptist Church near Telford where Robert Godsey was a part-time pastor. Godsey himself had immersed her in the brackish water.

"Thanks, Robert gave it to me."

"Come on in." I kissed her on the cheek. "Let's go sit out on the deck. I'll get you a glass of sweet tea."

A few minutes later, we were sitting on the deck beneath cirrus clouds that drifted high across the sky like giant kites. I looked beyond Sarah at the pale green lake below, the late afternoon sun glistening off the ripples like thousands of tiny pieces of hammered gold. An easy breeze was blowing, so pleasant that I thought of falling asleep.

"You okay?" she said. "You look tired."

"I'll be fine as long as we don't talk about the murders. I need to think about something else for awhile."

"No problem. The thought of it sickens me. Where's Caroline?" Her lips turned upward when she mentioned Caroline. She had a terrific smile, with deep dimples like miniature crescent moons.

"In the bathroom. She'll be out in a few. I think she's planning on grilling steak. You hungry?"

"Sounds great."

"All packed and ready to go?"

"I guess so."

"When do you start the new job?"

Robert Godsey's father owned an insurance agency in Crossville. Sarah was going to work for him as a receptionist.

"I start next week."

I took a deep breath and braced myself. I didn't want to get into an argument with her on her last day in town, but there was something I wanted to get off my chest.

"Can I ask you a question without you getting angry?" I said.

Her eyebrows arched.

"I'm serious. You know I love you and I only want the best for you."

"You're already hedging. What is it?"

"I guess I just want to ask you whether you're sure about this. Really sure. You've only known this guy for a couple months."

"His name is Robert, and I've known him for close to a year."

"But you've only been dating for a couple months."

"Three months, almost four," she said.

"Exactly. So why do you feel the need to pack up and move a hundred and fifty miles away? Are you sure you don't want to try the long-distance relationship thing for awhile and see how it goes? Get to know him a little better?"

"I'm leaving. The decision's been made."

"I know, but humor me for a minute. Does he make you thumpy?"

"Thumpy?"

"You know, pitty pat. Fluttery. Heart pounding inside the chest when he comes into the room, that kind of thing. Caroline still does that to me."

"I guess so."

"You see? That's what I mean. If he really made you thumpy, you'd know exactly what I'm talking about."

"I'm not a teenager. It isn't puppy love."

"So you love him. You're sure you love him."

"He's made me a better person. He led me to Jesus."

"I think you were a good person before, and I guess that's what's really bothering me. Tell me this. Would you be going to Crossville if you hadn't been baptized? Would Godsey accept you if you weren't a born-again Christian? Or was that part of the deal?"

Sarah's green eyes tightened. She'd always been quick-tempered, and I could see white lines begin to stretch toward her temples like tiny pieces of white thread, a sure sign I'd made her angry.

"How *dare* you say something like that to me," she said. "I think you're jealous. I think you hate the fact that I'm growing beyond you, that I'm leaving you behind in more ways than one."

"What's that supposed to mean?"

"You're a sinner, a nonbeliever. You have no faith. You think when you die you're just going to rot in the ground, that there's nothing beyond what you can see and touch and smell. I used to think the same thing, but I don't anymore. I think you envy me for it."

"You're wrong. I'm worried about you."

"Do you know what God did for you, Joe?" she said, the pitch of her voice rising. "Do you know He gave His only son for you? His only son? So you could be forgiven and have salvation? Think about that. Think about what a tremendous sacrifice that was."

"I don't want to debate the Christian religion with you, Sarah. I want you to think about what you're doing. I don't think this guy is right for you. I don't think this whole thing is right for you."

"I don't care what you think." She stood up from the table and picked up her purse.

"What are you doing?" I said. "Are you leaving? Can't we have a civilized discussion about this?"

I got up and followed her back through the house.

"Wait," I said. "C'mon Sarah, please don't leave. I'm sorry. I won't say another word about it. Stay and eat."

She kept walking.

"At least say goodbye to Caroline."

She stormed out the front door and down the sidewalk. About halfway to her car, she stopped and turned around.

"Tell Caroline I said goodbye," she said. "And tell her I'm sorry she's married to an atheist. You're going to hell, Joe. As sure as I'm standing here, you're going to hell."

THURSDAY, SEPT. 18

"How'd you get roped into this?" Sheriff Leon Bates said. He was sitting in my office in his khaki uniform with the brown epaulets.

"I volunteered for it, believe it or not," I said.

Two months earlier, before I went to work for the DA's office, Sheriff Bates and Judge Ivan Glass had gotten into a highly publicized snit. A public defender had filed a routine motion to suppress evidence in a drunk-driving case. During the hearing, a question arose about one of the sheriff's department's policies in giving breathalyzer tests. Rather than take a recess and send someone to get a policies and procedures manual, Judge Glass ordered a bailiff to contact the sheriff and tell him to come to court immediately to clear up the matter. The bailiff called the sheriff, and the sheriff replied that he was busy, that he was an elected official just like the judge, and that the judge didn't have the authority to order him to court. Glass told the bailiff to call the sheriff back and tell him he'd be held in contempt if he didn't show up in fifteen minutes. Sheriff Bates replied, "With all due respect, tell the court he can kiss my biscuits."

Enraged, Judge Glass drafted a petition and charged Bates with contempt of court, a misdemeanor offense but still a crime. In order for Glass to convict Bates, the district attorney's office had to prosecute the case in court. My second day on the job, Lee Mooney called me into his office and outlined the case for me. We both agreed that the judge had acted improperly, that there was no factual basis for the charge, and that the district attorney's office should recommend immediate dismissal.

"Would you mind handling it in court?" Mooney had said. "I don't want to get myself into the same situation as Bates."

"I'd be happy to," I said. "Judge Glass is one of my least favorite people on the planet."

Judge Ivan Glass and I had battled each other for more than a decade when I was practicing criminal defense. I'd successfully sued him when I was a rookie to make him stop jailing people who couldn't afford to pay their fines and court costs, and he'd returned the favor by making me and my clients miserable at every opportunity. A little over a year earlier, he'd attempted to send my sister to the penitentiary for six years. I managed to keep him from doing so, but the hard feelings still lingered.

The day of the hearing on Sheriff Bates's contempt charge had arrived, and Bates was in my office for some last-minute counseling. I'd talked to him several times over the past forty-eight hours and had come to genuinely like him. He was a tall, sturdy man in his mid-forties with light brown hair, brown eyes, a slightly crooked nose, and a mischievous grin. He was as country as they came, but he had a keen mind and a no-nonsense attitude when it came to law enforcement. Bates had been in office for less than two years, but his department had already made more drug arrests than his predecessor did during his entire term. He'd also begun to take on the local underground gambling industry, a move that was unprecedented in northeast Tennessee.

"I can't tell you how much I appreciate you doing this," Bates said. "I was afraid I was gonna have to go out and hire me some shark defense lawyer. Just like you used to be."

"No offense taken," I said, "and I'm glad to do it. It'll feel good to put Glass in his place for a change."

"He's gonna be one mad hombre, especially with all the folks I've got coming."

I'd asked Bates whether he could pack the courtroom. He was a popular sheriff, and since the judge was also a politician, I thought things might go a bit more smoothly if Glass had to face a courtroom full of constituents.

"How many are coming?" I said.

"I reckon they'll be quite a few."

"Almost time. Are you ready to go?"

"I'm nervous as a long-tailed cat in a room full of rocking chairs, but I reckon I'm ready."

"Just let me do all the talking."

I led Bates out the door and down the hall to the back steps. We walked in silence until I went through the side door into the courtroom.

"Wow," I said, "this'll shake him up."

The courtroom was packed with the good citizens of Washington County. Every seat was occupied, people were standing against both of the side walls, and there was a line outside the door. As soon as Bates walked in, everyone stood and a loud round of applause broke out. The door to the judge's chamber was closed, but I saw Glass peek out to see what all the commotion was about. His clerk had already taken her spot next to the bench, and the bailiffs were at their stations.

"Let's sit here," I said to the sheriff, pointing to the table traditionally used by the defense.

We sat down, as did everyone else in the courtroom. There was an eerie silence while everyone waited for the judge to appear. After several minutes, the door to his chambers opened, and Glass, wearing his ancient black robe that was frayed around the sleeves, hobbled carefully up the steps to his bench as the bailiff called court into session. I hadn't seen him for more than a year and was pleased to see that he looked awful. His face was colorless and gaunt, and the mane of white hair of which he'd always been so proud had lost its luster. Before, he'd carried himself as a smug adjudicator, one who believed himself to be morally and intellectually superior to others in every way. Now he just looked like a crotchety old man.

Glass sat down and surveyed the courtroom. When his gaze landed on me, he stared at me through his tinted glasses, a look of disgust on his face.

"I thought you went to work for the district attorney," he snarled.

"I did," I said without standing.

"Then what are you doing at the defense table?"

"Representing my clients."

"Is the sheriff your client?"

"My clients are the people of Tennessee," I said, feeling a bit silly at the pomposity of my own words, "and it looks like several of them have showed up today."

A murmur went up behind me, and Glass raised his gavel. "I don't know what all you people think you're doing here," he bellowed, "but if I hear a peep out of any of you, I'll have you removed from the courtroom immediately. I'm not going to allow myself to be intimidated by a mob."

"Stop acting like a jerk!" a voice called from the back of the courtroom. The remark was followed by a loud cheer and a round of applause.

"Order!" Glass yelled as the gavel banged. "Order or I'll clear this courtroom! Bailiffs! I'm ordering you to arrest the next person who opens his mouth!"

"Call the case," Glass barked at his clerk.

The clerk called the case of the State of Tennessee versus Leon Bates.

"Let the record show that Mr. Bates has been summoned here to answer to a charge of contempt filed by this court," Glass said. "The court is present, the clerk is present, the prosecutor and the defendant are both present. Mr. Bates, since you don't have an attorney, I assume you're representing yourself."

I stood and cleared my throat, more than a little nervous. I knew I was right, but taking on a man as powerful as a criminal court judge was always an uncomfortable experience.

"Mr. Bates doesn't need an attorney," I said.

"Oh really?" Glass sneered. "And why is that?"

"Because the district attorney's office refuses to prosecute him."

Glass's mouth dropped open and his complexion darkened immediately. He leaned forward on his elbows, his lips almost touching the microphone in front of him.

"Did I just hear you correctly, Mr. Dillard? Did I just hear you say that the district attorney is refusing to prosecute this case?"

"The charge has no basis in law or fact, Judge. You can't convict an elected official of contempt of court because he refused to appear when you called him on the telephone. You could have recessed the hearing and subpoenaed him, you could have sent someone over to the sheriff's department to get a copy of the manual, or you could have recessed court and held the hearing at a time that was convenient for Sheriff Bates. But you have neither the jurisdiction nor the authority to simply call an elected sheriff on the phone and demand that he appear in court, and you certainly don't have the authority to charge him with a crime when he doesn't."

The courtroom was absolutely still, the tension palpable. I was sure that Glass had never encountered a prosecutor who wouldn't do exactly as he ordered, and I had a pretty good idea how he would react. I braced for the threat and told myself to hold his stare and just keep breathing steadily.

"What I *can* do is hold *you* in contempt of court in the presence of the court and deal with it summarily," Glass said. His lips were barely moving, his tone full of anger and hatred. "I can fine you or send you off to jail, and I fully intend to if you don't do your job and prosecute this case."

"Go ahead, Judge," I said. "The first thing I'll do is file a complaint with the Court of the Judiciary and seek to have you suspended or removed from office. The second thing I'll do is sue you, and after that, I'll humiliate you in front of the Court of Appeals."

I held my breath, waiting for the explosion. Glass was infamous for his temper and for the pleasure he took in browbeating and bullying attorneys and defendants. I saw him draw in a deep breath, but then he sat back in his high-backed leather chair and began to contemplate the ceiling. Finally, he leaned forward and looked at the audience.

"Perhaps Mr. Dillard is right," he said. "Perhaps I acted hastily, even unreasonably. But I hope you good people will give me credit for recognizing my mistake and for dealing with it in a reasonable and appropriate manner. Mr. Dillard, after these fine people vacate the courtroom, I'd like to see you in my chambers. Sheriff Bates, the charge against you is dismissed with my apologies."

The courtroom erupted again in cheers and applause. As Glass made a hasty exit, dozens of people surged forward, clapping Bates on the shoulder and congratulating him on his victory. I was pleased for Bates, but I knew that the rift between Glass and me had just been raised to a new level. There was no way I was going back to his chambers. He hadn't ordered me to come to his chambers. He'd said, "I'd like to see you in my chambers." I took that as a request—and chose to ignore it. I wasn't in the mood to listen to any more of his threats. I just wanted to bask in the glow of kicking his belligerent butt in front of three hundred people. I slipped out the side door and took a seat in the jury room. I left the door open and waited until I saw Bates pass by.

"Hey Leon," I said as I caught up with him in the hallway, "congratulations."

Bates stopped and turned around, a wide grin spread across his face.

"Brother, I ain't *never* heard nobody talk to a judge like that," he said. "You got the *cojones* of a Brahma bull."

"Thanks," I said. "Let's just hope he never gets a chance to cut them off."

THURSDAY, SEPT. 18

When I got back from lunch that same day, there was a note stuck to my door from Lee Mooney asking me to come to the conference room as soon as possible. I walked in to find Mooney sitting at the table with a young man I didn't recognize. On top of the table was an evidence box.

"There's the man right now," Mooney said as he stood up. "We were just talking about you. I heard you handled yourself very well in front of Judge Glass this morning."

"I don't think I'll be invited to his retirement party," I said.

"He'll never retire," Mooney said. "The only way he comes off that bench is in a casket. But don't worry about it. You made plenty of other friends today, especially Sheriff Bates. He thinks you're a one-man dream team. Come on over here. I want to introduce you to someone."

The young man at the table stood up and offered his hand. He was a good-looking kid, late twenties, around six feet tall with short, straw-colored hair, blue eyes and a square jaw.

"This is Cody Masters," Mooney said. "Investigator Cody Masters from the Jonesborough Police Department." I vaguely recalled hearing or reading the name somewhere.

"Joe Dillard," I said, returning the smile.

"Have a seat," Mooney said. "We've got a little problem, and we think you're just the man to solve it. Cody has a case coming up for trial next month, and I want you to handle it. It's a sexual abuse case that got a lot of publicity a couple years ago. You might remember it. What did they call it in the papers, Cody?"

Masters blushed a little and dropped his head, obviously embarrassed.

"The Pizza Bordello case," he said.

"I remember that," I said. "The guy who owned Party Pizza in Jonesborough. What was his name?"

"William Trent," Mooney said.

"Wow, that case is still around?"

"Afraid so, and it's set for trial on October fourteenth. Can you do it?"

"You're not giving me much time to get ready," I said. "Who was handling it before?"

"Alexander," Mooney said. "But after the disaster with Billy Dockery, we can't afford to take another beating on a high-profile case. I want you to try to work out some kind of deal, but if you can't, you have to win at trial."

It sounded like an ultimatum.

"And if I lose?" I said.

"Let's not even think about that," Mooney said as he stood up. "Now, if you'll excuse me, I'll let you two boys get acquainted."

I looked at Masters and shook my head. "Maybe I should have stayed retired," I said. "Why don't you fill me in?"

For the next half hour, I listened while Cody Masters told me about William Trent, a thirty-five-year-old husband and father of two who opened a small pizza restaurant in Jonesborough a decade earlier. He was a member of the Chamber of Commerce, a Little League coach, and a deacon at the Presbyterian Church. He was also, from what Masters told me, one very sick individual.

Two years earlier, Masters was approached by two seventeen-year-old girls who told him that William Trent had been having sex with both of them for two years. Both were former employees of Trent's, and they told Masters a lurid tale. Trent, they said, hired only young girls who he believed would have sex with him. The girls were usually from broken homes, impoverished, weren't good students—the kind of kids most employers would shy away from. Trent let them know on the front end that certain things would be required of them if they worked at his restaurant, things that he termed "unconventional." The girls said Trent kept pornography running on a computer screen in the back office, hosted lingerie parties for the employees—he hired only young girls—in the restaurant after hours, kept a small refrigerator in the kitchen stocked with liquor, and occasionally provided cocaine, crystal meth, or marijuana. He also started them at ten dollars an hour, significantly more than the minimum wage. The girls said there was an unspoken allegiance among the employees—what happened at work stayed at work.

Trent immediately went about seducing them, and from what the girls told Masters, Trent's sexual appetite was insatiable. They had sex with him in the walk-in cooler, on the table in the kitchen where the pizza dough was rolled, in the bathrooms, on the counter and on the tables in the front after the restaurant closed, in his car in the parking lot out back. He wanted threesome sex, oral sex, anal sex, sex in bizarre positions—they even let him penetrate them with a catsup bottle a couple of times. And he insisted that the girls use birth control because he refused to wear a condom.

Masters told me that at least ten girls were involved over a three-year period, although some of the girls refused to cooperate with the police. The big problem with the case, Masters said, was that he was a rookie when he first met the girls, that the district attorneys were all away at their annual conference in Nashville, and that he had made several early mistakes that Trent's lawyer would undoubtedly bring up at trial.

"I probably should have waited until the DAs got back," Masters said, "but I wanted to get him off the streets. It made me so mad I threw the freaking book at him. I charged him with forty-two felonies. About half of them were aggravated rape and aggravated kidnapping. I tacked on statutory rape, aggravated sexual battery, sexual battery by an authority figure, you name it. He was looking at about twelve hundred years in prison. But his wife posted his bail and they hired Joe Snodgrass from Knoxville. He made me look like a fool at the preliminary hearing."

I knew Joe Snodgrass by reputation only. He ran one of the most successful criminal defense firms in the state.

He'd been the president of the National Association of Criminal Defense Lawyers and president of the Tennessee Trial Lawyers Association. He had a good reputation as a trial lawyer, and he'd written books on criminal procedure and pretrial litigation in criminal cases.

"What was the problem?" I said.

"I didn't read the statutes right. I'm not a lawyer. All the aggravated rape charges and all the aggravated kidnapping charges got thrown out after the preliminary. And Snodgrass made the girls look like trashy little sluts."

"What kind of evidence do you have?"

"Not typical rape evidence," he said. "We don't have any sperm or DNA, no bruises on any of the victims, no—"

"Wait just a second," I said, holding up my hand to stop him. "Do you have any physical evidence at all?"

"Not really," Masters said, shaking his head. "All we have are statements from some of the girls and a diary. Oh, and I got his payroll records so I could make sure the girls were working on the days when they say they had sex with him."

"How many girls?"

"I think only four are still willing to cooperate."

"Does Trent have any priors?"

"None."

"What about the computer at the restaurant? Did you have a forensics expert check it to see whether he was really going to porn sites?"

"I did, but it came up empty. After we got it back from the lab, I had one of the girls come down to the office and she said it wasn't the same computer. He must have gotten wind we were coming."

I sat back and thought for a few minutes. Lee was asking me to prosecute what boiled down to a multiple statutory rape case with no physical evidence and victims who were, at the very least, young girls of questionable character. The two I knew about had both said they'd engaged in consensual sex with their boss for a long period of time. The man accused of committing the crimes was a father, husband, reputable businessman, active in his church and community, and had never been in trouble before. And since he'd hired Joe Snodgrass, he was obviously well financed. I had only a few weeks to prepare, and in the meantime, I was supposed to be helping with the most intense murder investigation in the history of the district. What was it Lee had said when I met with him before I took the job? Easy money?

"I'm sorry, Mr. Dillard," Masters said. "I may have screwed this up beyond repair."

"Call me Joe," I said, "and don't worry about it. It would've been better if you'd waited until the DAs got back, and it would've been a lot better if you'd had the girls wear a wire on him, but it was a rookie mistake. No sense beating yourself up about it. What charges are left that we can prove?"

"After the preliminary hearing went so badly, Lee got involved for a week or so," Masters said. "One of the girls kept a diary, and Lee used it to convince the grand jury to indict Trent on ten counts of sexual abuse by an authority figure. We could have charged him with more than a hundred counts, but Lee didn't want to spend six months at trial proving all of them. He said if everything went well, Trent would wind up with thirty years."

"Did you say he used a diary to get the indictment?" I said.

"Yeah. Why?"

"Because we can't use it at trial."

"We can't? Why not?"

"It's hearsay and it doesn't fall under any of the exceptions to the hearsay rule."

"So what are we going to do? We don't have much of anything other than the girls' statements."

"I'll figure something out. In the meantime, I want you to go back and reinterview every single employee that worked there for the three years before he was arrested. If any of them will admit to having sex with him and if they'll come testify, we can prove a pattern of conduct. Once you get them lined up, I want to talk to all of them."

"Done," Masters said.

"When you did the preliminary hearing, did you get any sense of what the defense is going to be?"

"From the way the lawyer was questioning them, it looked like he was going to make them all out to be liars."

"So Trent is going to deny having any kind of sexual contact with any of his employees?"

"That's what he said when I arrested him."

"Did he give you a statement?"

"Nope. Lawyered up five minutes in. Acted like he didn't have a care in the world."

"Go ahead and get started on your interviews as soon as you can," I said. "Keep in mind that in order to convict him under the authority-figure statute, we have to prove three things. We have to prove there was sexual contact between him and the girls, we have to prove the girls were between the ages of thirteen and eighteen, and we have to prove that he had supervisory power over them by virtue of his occupation. The last two will be easy, but the first one will be the key."

"You know something?" Masters said. "Even if these girls aren't as pure as the driven snow, no grown man should be allowed to take advantage of them like that. They're just kids. They were only fifteen years old when he started having sex with them."

Masters slid the evidence box across the table to me.

"All the statements, the payroll records, and the diary are in here," he said. "You want to take a look?"

"Give the diary back to the girl," I said. "Have her bring it when she comes in to talk to me. I'll read it then. I'll take the rest of it home with me."

Masters shrugged his shoulders and took the diary out of the box. As I'd talked to him, an idea had formed in my mind, but the less he knew about it, the better.

"Guess I better get to work," Masters said as he rose, stretched, and started for the door.

"One more thing," I said. "Why did these girls decide to come forward after all this time?"

"They didn't come right out and say it, but I think it was jealousy more than anything else," Masters said. "Trent let both of them go and replaced them with a couple fifteen-year-olds. I guess he was tired of them."

"Women scorned, huh?"

"You got it. Hell hath no fury."

THURSDAY, SEPT. 25

Nearly two weeks had passed since the Becks were murdered, and despite the fact that Fraley and his fellow agents were working up to twenty hours a day, they hadn't been able to identify a suspect. Dozens of tips had come over the Crime Stoppers line, and we'd made a public request for help, but the killers were still on the loose, and we were no closer to catching them.

On Thursday morning, Caroline and I were sitting in a tiny, cramped office inside the Johnson City Breast Care Center. A faceless nurse had led us there quickly and silently upon our arrival. As I looked around, I could see it was an office where only one person worked, probably someone who input data into a computer. There were three chairs that looked as though they'd been placed hurriedly and haphazardly, one at the computer and two just inside the door. It was a lousy place to tell someone they had cancer, if that was what we were there for.

Caroline had already been through all the tests. Her primary care doctor had ordered a mammogram and a chest X-ray. I'd gone with her to both appointments, although she insisted she could handle it without me. She kept telling me I should be at work, but I insisted.

The mammogram showed a suspicious shadow. The doctor who read it wasn't able to make a diagnosis. She said from one angle, the mass looked like a benign cyst. From another angle, it looked like it could be something else. There was a 95 percent chance it was a cyst, she said, but just to be safe, she wanted a biopsy. Caroline had gone in four days later for the biopsy. We were there for the results.

Caroline sat down in one of the chairs. She was wearing a pair of jeans and a short-sleeved, red T-shirt. Plain attire, but she made the jeans look fantastic. She'd been quiet on the ride into town, and there was a distance in her eyes that told me she was frightened.

"Why couldn't they just call us?" she said. "Why do they make us come all the way up here?"

I didn't want to think about the obvious answer to the question.

"Maybe they want to show you the lab report," I said. "They're probably just covering their butts from a lawsuit in case something goes wrong later."

She gave me a look of uncertainty.

"Ninety-five percent," I said. "There's a 95 percent chance you're clean, plus the fact that you're young and you have no history of cancer in your family. You're going to be fine."

"What if it's bad?" she said.

"If it's bad, we deal with it. Think positive."

There was a soft knock on the door and it opened. Into the room stepped a black-haired, thirty-something male wearing a white shirt, brown tie, and khaki pants. There was a pager on his belt. I assumed he was a doctor.

Behind him was a chubby woman wearing a loud, print smock. I barely looked at her. There were now four of us in a room designed for one. I was beginning to feel a bit claustrophobic.

"Mrs. Dillard?" the man said.

Caroline nodded.

"And you are?" He looked at me.

"Her husband," I said.

"My name is Dr. Jameson," he said, ignoring the woman behind him.

I reached out and took Caroline's hand. Maybe it was the somber tone of his voice, but I knew this was going to be bad.

"As you know, we've conducted a biopsy on the mass in your left breast. I have the results here, and I'm afraid the news isn't what you want to hear. The tests are positive for cancer, Mrs. Dillard. Invasive ductal carcinoma. I'm sorry."

I heard the breath rush involuntarily out of Caroline's body. My own mind went temporarily blank, as though I'd been blasted with a thousand volts of electricity. I looked at her, she looked at me, and in that moment—that awful moment that I'll remember until the day I die—we were connected by something I would never have dreamed possible. It was fear. Pure, unadulterated fear. Neither of us could speak.

I could see that Caroline was fighting to hold back the tears, fighting to keep her composure in front of these strangers. Dr. Doom and his assistant were hovering awkwardly. Finally, I spoke.

"Could you give us a minute?"

"Certainly," the doctor said. He appeared relieved to have been given permission to leave the room. The two of them turned and walked out without another word.

I pushed the door closed and turned to Caroline. Tears were already streaming down both of her cheeks. I reached down and helped her out of the chair, wrapped my arms around her, and held the only woman I've ever loved. Her shoulders heaved, and she began to sob.

"Let it go," I whispered. "Let it go." I knew there was nothing I could say or do that would alleviate the shock and the terror of the diagnosis she'd just received, and as she stood there, leaning on me and sobbing, I tried to think of what I'd say when she was finished. After a few minutes, the storm began to subside, and I took a small step back. I took her face in my hands and looked into her eyes.

"You'll beat it," I said, wiping her tears away with my thumbs. It was all I could do to keep from breaking down and sobbing right along with her. "You'll beat it. Whatever it takes, whatever you have to do, you'll do it. I know you, Caroline. You're as strong as they come, and you've got a thousand reasons to stick around, not the least of which is standing right here in front of you. I'll help you. I'll do anything you need. The kids will help you. Lots of people will help. You won't go through this alone. I promise."

I don't know whether it was the look on my face, or some gesture I made, or some tone of desperation in my voice that reached her. It had to be something discernable to only a lifelong lover and friend because I didn't consciously do anything that would have caused her to do what she did next, something that took me completely by surprise.

She wiped a final tear from her cheek with the back of her hand and took a long, slow breath. Then she looked into my eyes, smiled, and said, "Don't worry, baby. I won't leave you. I'll never leave you. Why don't you tell the doctor to come back in?"

SUNDAY, SEPT. 28

Norman Brockwell was sixty-six years old.

An English teacher for nearly twenty years. Coach of the Washington County High School basketball team for eight years. And then the big break—appointed by the superintendent to serve as principal of Washington County High School. Twenty-one years in that position.

Twenty-one years.

Two grown children, both educators. An elder at the Simerly Creek Church of Christ. A Cub Scout troop leader. Past president of the Kiwanis Club.

And this is how it ends? Blindfolded and gagged in the middle of nowhere, wearing my underwear, tied to a tree like a dog?

They'd arrived at his house less than an hour ago. He had no idea what time it was; he didn't get a chance to put on his glasses and look at the clock. All he knew was he'd gone to bed at midnight while a storm raged outside his window. He'd been asleep in his twin bed upstairs, across the hall from Gladys, a retired mathematics teacher and his wife of forty years. Cheeky, his teacup poodle, hadn't made a sound until they came into the room. Cheeky had barked meekly, twice, before one of them beat her to death.

That's when he sat up, or at least tried to.

He'd seen a bright flash as something struck him above the left eye, felt himself being rolled roughly onto his stomach. Felt the warm blood oozing from the wound and creeping down the side of his face. Then the blindfold went over his eyes, the gag went into his mouth, and his hands were bound with tape. He wasn't sure how many there were, but it seemed like a small army. Hushed voices, both male and female. Short, sharp commands.

They'd pulled him up by his arms and walked him out the door, down the hall, and down the steps. They'd stuffed him into the trunk of what he guessed was a compact car of some sort, a compact car with a coughing engine and a faulty muffler. He'd ridden, tangled like a cord, in the trunk for maybe a half hour, the last minutes over extremely bumpy terrain.

Then they'd stopped. He heard the trunk lid open and was pulled out, once again by his arms. His joints shrieked as he was half-guided, half-dragged twenty steps or so. The ground beneath his bare feet was cold and wet, the air dead still. He smelled the clean smells of a mountain forest after a hard rain. They'd straightened him up and backed him against something hard. He knew now it was a tree.

A rope had been wrapped around him at least a dozen times, from waist to shoulders, the gag removed. He strained to see through the blindfold.

Yea though I walk through the valley of the shadow of death, I shall fear no evil. ... Gladys. What did they do to Gladys?

He listened. They were close to him now, in front of him. He could hear them breathing.

A female voice said: "Take off the blindfold and take the gag out."

Footsteps approached. Fingers reached behind his head. And then it was off. Moonlight filtered through the canopy above, casting long shadows among the trees. The car engine was still running, the lights were on. The gag was removed and he filled his lungs. The smell of exhaust reached his nostrils.

Jesus help me! Jesus, Mother Mary, and Joseph! What the …?

There were three of them, fanned out in front of him less than ten feet away, facing him. They were … what were they? Ghouls? Vampires? Two of them appeared to be wearing black clothing and had long, black hair. But their faces appeared to be bright white, even in the dim light. One of them, in the middle, was different. Was it a woman? Was this a nightmare? *Please, God, let this be a nightmare!*

"*Who are you?*" Norman Brockwell cried. "*Who are you?*"

The female at the center turned to her left.

"You picked him," she said to the lanky figure standing next to her. "Tell him who you are." The tallest of them stepped forward.

"Remember me, *Mr. Brockwell*?"

He could feel the boy's breath on his face, smell the acrid aroma of stale beer. He squinted, studying the figure before him, listening to the voice. He'd heard it before. Suddenly, he made the connection.

Boyer. Samuel Boyer. A freak. A rabble rouser. One of the worst he'd ever encountered. He'd disciplined him, suspended him, and eventually expelled him when he brought a gun to school. What else could he do? There were hundreds of other students in that school who were good people. They didn't deserve to be terrorized by the likes of—

"I brought a gun along," Boyer said. Norman Brockwell saw Boyer's lips curl into a half smile, half snarl. "How do you like it, *Mr. Brockwell*? How do you like feeling powerless? How do you like being humiliated?"

"Please, Samuel, I'm sorry," he said. "What can I do to make it up to you? What can I do to make this right?"

Boyer stepped back abruptly.

"Blow for blow, scorn for scorn, doom for doom," the girl said coldly. "Eye for eye, tooth for tooth. The vengeance of Satan is upon thee."

The principal watched helplessly as the two on the outside raised pistols, their shiny surfaces glimmering in the moonlight.

"No! Wait, please!"

"*Do it!*" the girl said, turning her back. "*Do it now!*"

Norman Brockwell's eyes glazed over and his chin dropped to his chest. "What did you do to my Gladys?" he asked softly.

And the night roared.

SUNDAY, SEPT. 28

By Sunday, our family and friends had all been told about Caroline's cancer and the rallying had begun. I thought the telephone call I made to our son Jack would be one of the most difficult things I'd ever done, but Jack didn't panic. He took the news quietly and said he was driving home immediately from Vanderbilt. I tried to talk him out of it—there was nothing he could do—but he insisted. He just wanted to see her, he said. He wanted to hug her.

I woke up a little after five in the morning and couldn't go back to sleep. Caroline was sleeping soundly, so I decided to wait until six thirty and then roust the kids. I wanted to take them to breakfast. I knew they'd rather sleep in, but we hadn't had a chance to be alone and talk about what was going on with Caroline.

We got settled into a booth at the Sitting Bull Cafe in Gray. Both were sleepy-eyed and wearing hoodies. Sitting there looking at them, I couldn't help thinking how lucky I was. Their appearances were opposite—Lilly was blond, green-eyed, and feminine while Jack was dark-haired, brown-eyed and rugged. They'd both grown into young adults I admired. They worked hard at the things they enjoyed, they treated other people with respect, they followed their conscience, and they loved to laugh. They'd had their share of problems and made their share of mistakes, but neither had managed to do anything dumb enough to have any lingering effects. I was grateful for them.

"I want to talk to you about your mom," I said.

"What is there to talk about?" Jack said. "It is what it is."

"She's looking at a long, hard road."

Both of them nodded without looking up from their menus.

"So how do you feel about it?" I said. "How are you doing?"

Lilly set the menu down and looked at me. "I'm scared," she said. "It's hard to think about her having cancer. It's hard to think about her dying."

"She's not going to die," Jack said.

"She could."

"But she won't. She's too tough. She'll probably outlive all of us."

"I've been doing some reading," I said. The truth was that I hadn't done nearly as much reading as I could have, or should have. The nurses had loaded us down with pamphlets and the Internet was full of information, but once I understood the basics, I didn't want to read any more. It wasn't as though I could gain any control by gaining knowledge. Like Jack said, it was what it was.

"There's been a lot of progress in the past twenty years," I said. "Her chances of surviving are excellent, but she's going to go through some rough times, and she's going to go through some changes."

"What do you mean?" Lilly said.

"Hormonal changes. Physical changes. She'll have to go through chemotherapy. It'll make her sick and she won't feel like doing much some days. She'll probably be cranky and irritable. It might even trigger early menopause. She'll lose her appetite. She'll lose all of her hair. She'll probably lose the breast."

"Better than the alternative," Jack said.

"Yeah, it is. But I don't want you guys feeling sorry for her, at least I don't want you *showing* her that you feel sorry for her. We have to treat her like we've always treated her. We have to keep her laughing. And I don't want either one of you using this as an excuse to feel sorry for yourselves. Your friends will be coming around asking, 'Are you okay? I'm so sorry about your mother.' Especially your melodramatic girlfriends, Lilly. Remember, you're not sick. She is. I don't want to see any Lilly pity parties going on. We're here to help any way we can. The more we help, the easier this will be on her. The best thing you guys can do for her is to keep on doing what you've always done. That makes her proud. That makes her happy."

I waited for one of them to say, "Okay, Dad, we're with you," or "Don't worry, Dad, we can handle this." Instead, Jack looked over at Lilly and said, "What'd you think of it?"

She looked back at him, puzzled. "Think of what?"

"Dad's speech."

She grinned. "I thought the reference to my melodramatic friends and the pity party was uncalled for, but other than that, it wasn't too bad."

"A little on the corny side," Jack said.

The waitress was approaching.

"If you two are finished making fun of me, it's time to order," I said.

We spent the rest of the meal talking about other things, primarily the Beck murder case, which was no closer to being solved despite the intense pressure being applied by the media and every opportunistic politician within a hundred miles. We got back to the house around seven thirty. Caroline was still asleep, and Jack and Lilly wasted no time heading back to their beds.

I took Rio and went for a run, washed my truck, read the newspaper, and puttered around the house until noon. I helped Caroline get lunch ready while Jack and Lilly rode into town to pick up a book Lilly needed for school. After lunch, we decided we'd drive up to Red Fork Falls in Unicoi County and do a little hiking. We were just pulling out of the driveway when my cell phone rang.

It was Lee Mooney, and the news wasn't good.

"I'm sorry," I said to Caroline. "I have to go."

Another gruesome trip, first to a modest, ranch-style home in a tidy neighborhood outside Jonesborough, then to a remote area near Buffalo Mountain. Two more dream-like walks through the scenes of unspeakable crimes.

The victims were Norman Brockwell and his wife, Gladys. Gladys had been beaten and stabbed to death in her bed at their home outside Jonesborough. Her daughter discovered the body after Norman and Gladys failed to show up for church. Norman had apparently been kidnapped and taken to Buffalo Mountain where he'd been tied to a tree and shot a dozen times. A couple hunters scouting deer signs for the upcoming bow season had discovered him about the same time his daughter was discovering his wife. Norman had been shot through the right eye. Gladys had been stabbed in the right eye. "Ah Satan" had been carved into Norman's forehead. Inverted crosses had been carved into both their necks. The Brockwells' dog, a tiny apricot teacup poodle, had been beaten to death, probably with the butt of a pistol.

I spent most of the afternoon in a haze of shock and disbelief. At seven, I met Lee Mooney in Jonesborough. He was waiting for me in a conference room just down the hall from my office. Sitting with him at the table were Jerry Blake, the special agent in charge of the TBI office in Johnson City, Hank Fraley, the agent who was running point on the Beck case, and Leon Bates, the sheriff.

All the murders had happened in the county, which fell under Bates's jurisdiction, but because both Bates and his lead investigators were relatively inexperienced in murder investigations, Mooney had assigned the case to the TBI. That hadn't stopped Bates from talking to the press about the case, but up to that point, he'd been excluded from the investigation.

"I want to form a task force," Lee Mooney said as soon as I sat down. "And I want you to head it up."

I looked at him, incredulous, then looked around the table at the others. The TBI agents were staring down at the table. Bates was looking at the ceiling.

"Me?" I said. "What do I know about heading up a task force, Lee?"

"You're a leader. People trust your judgment. And you know how to handle the press."

"And who would make up this task force?"

"Five or six guys from the TBI. A couple detectives from Johnson City. The sheriff and a few of his people. We might even be able to get one of the local FBI guys involved."

Jerry Blake was fiddling with a notepad.

"How long have you been a cop, Jerry?" I asked.

"Close to twenty-five years."

"Ever been on a task force?"

"A couple."

"What do you think about them? Be honest. Are they effective?"

Blake gave Mooney a sideways glance. "Not really."

"Why?"

"Turf wars, mostly. The different agencies don't trust each other, then they want to take credit for anything good that happens and they want to blame anything bad on somebody else. Lots of egos involved. You wind up with too many chiefs and not enough warriors. You have communication problems. Things that ought to get done don't get done. Information that ought to be shared doesn't get shared. It just doesn't work very well."

"That's what I thought," I said. "The only time I've ever seen a task force formed is when the police aren't making any progress in a case and they want the public to think they're doing something."

"But that's exactly where we are, Joe," Mooney said. "Word of these killings is already leaking out. By morning, everybody in northeast Tennessee is going to know about it and we're going to have a panic on our hands. We have to make people think we're doing *something*."

"Where are we now?" I said to Fraley. "What do you have that you didn't have before?"

Fraley looked around nervously, as though he was afraid to share information with Bates in the room. Blake's assertion about distrust between law enforcement agencies was already evident.

"We're still nowhere," he said quietly. "We've got more footprints that we'll compare with the Beck murder scene. My guess is that some of them will match up. We've got more tire tracks. We'll compare the shell casings and bullets to see if they match, and I'm betting they will. We've got two more bodies with crosses carved into them and wounds to their right eyes. They carved "ah Satan" into Norman Brockwell's forehead just like they did on Mr. Beck. We've got hair and fiber and a couple latent prints from the Becks' van, but we've run the latents through AFIS and haven't found a match. We've got hair and fiber from the Brockwells' home. We've got the rope they used to tie Mr. Brockwell to the tree. The medical examiner says Mrs. Brockwell was probably stabbed with an ice pick, but we don't have the weapon. She also says Mr. Brockwell had abrasions on his back, elbows, and knees. She thinks he rode out to the woods in the trunk of a car. We're checking to see if we can find any connection between the Brockwells and the Becks. Talking to family, friends, acquaintances, people they worked with, anybody we can think of. But as of right now, we don't have a single suspect."

"The first thing we should do is tell the media the cases aren't related," Mooney said. "That should at least keep people from panicking."

"Forget about the media," I said. "Somebody's going to leak it whether we tell them or not. And what do you mean by panic, Lee? Do you think people are going to riot in the streets? They'll put better locks on their doors and they'll buy guns and ammunition and guard dogs. They'll watch out for their neighbors. We don't need to start stonewalling, and I don't think we need a task force. We don't want to bring the feds and their egos anywhere near this, and as far as the local guys go, no offense to the sheriff, but the TBI agents are as good as it gets."

"So what do you suggest?" Lee said. "Status quo? Tell people we're doing all we can?"

"Give these guys some more time," I said, nodding toward Fraley and Blake. "Let them do their jobs. And how about we let the sheriff handle the media from now on? I'll brief him whenever he wants. He can do the press conferences, press releases, whatever. He has an outstanding reputation in the community and people trust him. What do you say, Sheriff? Will you keep the hounds at bay for me?"

"Whatever you need, Brother Dillard," Bates said.

I turned to Fraley again. He was in his early sixties, a little on the heavy side with receding gray hair, a pink complexion, and a bulbous nose. Despite our shaky start, I'd already developed a significant amount of respect for him. He was smart, tough, and hardworking.

"Surely you have some ideas," I said.

Fraley cleared his throat.

"A few," he said. I expected him to keep talking, but he sat there in silence.

Mooney stared at him. "Care to share them with the rest of the class?"

"Who kills a school principal?" Fraley said. "Think about it. Forced entry through the window at the side of the house, but there was nothing taken, so it wasn't a burglary that went wrong. Same M.O. as the Beck killing as far as the shooting goes. Shot to pieces. And if it wasn't just some random killing, then you have to ask yourself, who would want to kill a principal? And who would want to kill him and kill him and kill him?"

"Family member looking to speed up the inheritance?" Mooney said. "Disgruntled teacher? Or maybe it was the wife they were after."

"It wasn't the wife. They kidnapped Mr. Brockwell, took him for a long ride, tied him to a tree. They terrorized him. He was the target. They wanted him to suffer. His wife just happened to be in the way."

"So answer your own question," I said. "Who wants a high school principal to suffer?" I said.

Fraley shrugged his shoulders. "I'm thinking a kid. A kid with a grudge. Probably looking for revenge."

"But there were more than one," I said. "Maybe three or four. How do you explain that? And what about the Becks? Why would a kid, or a group of kids, want to kill the Becks?"

"I don't know yet," Fraley said. "But at least I know where I'm going to look."

FRIDAY, OCT. 3

"**M**r. Snodgrass is here," Rita Jones said over the office intercom.

"Thanks," I said. "Tell him to come on back."

William Trent, accused of having sex with his young female employees, was scheduled to go on trial in less than two weeks, and my case was in the toilet. Cody Masters, the young investigator who had originally brought the charges against Trent, had gone back out and interviewed more than two dozen of Trent's current and former employees. Nobody wanted to get involved in a trial that would undoubtedly be highly publicized and would cause as much embarrassment for the victims as it would for the defendant. Not one of them would cooperate with us.

Two of the girls who had originally given statements to Masters had recanted. Girls who had talked to him but refused to give statements were now telling him they had nothing to say. All that was left were the two girls who had originally made the complaint, Alice Dickson and Rosalie Harbin. Both were now nineteen years old. Alice, the girl who'd kept a very detailed diary, was shy and backward, and I was worried about how she'd do on the witness stand. Rosalie Harbin was a wild child who'd recently been arrested for forgery and theft. And the man who was about to walk through my door, William Trent's lawyer, knew I was in trouble. He'd called a week earlier to set up an appointment with me. I didn't have to ask what he wanted—he'd be looking to make a deal.

Snodgrass's appearance surprised me, to say the least. I was expecting a refined, smooth-talking pretty boy, but what oozed through the doorway was a gargantuan man who seemed to fill the entire room. Snodgrass was at least six feet seven and three hundred and fifty pounds. His face reminded me of a Chinese shar-pei, with rolls of fat across the forehead, sagging jowls, and a flat, wide nose. He looked to be around fifty, with a greasy shock of wavy black hair that fell to his collar. Small brown eyes that didn't seem to fit his face peered at me from behind thick glasses, and the white shirt he wore beneath a dark gray blazer looked like he'd been wearing it for a week.

"Have a seat," I said after I introduced myself and shook his moist, fleshy hand. His face was pink, small droplets of sweat had formed on his forehead, and I could hear him wheezing slightly. The effort of moving all that mass from the parking lot into the building and up the elevator to my office must have been almost more than his cardiovascular system could bear.

"Are you all right?" I said as he dabbed his forehead with a stained white kerchief.

"The cigarettes are going to kill me," he said in a deep, raspy voice, with just a hint of Southern accent.

"The wife's been nagging me to quit for years, but I don't pay any attention to her. I like to smoke. It's hot in here! Don't you people have any air conditioning?"

"Feels fine to me," I said.

I smiled at him, wondering how this blob of vulgarity had managed to build such a fine reputation and get himself elected to two of the highest state and national offices in the field of criminal defense.

"What brings you all the way up here this morning, Mr. Snodgrass?" I said.

He glared at me with his little eyes and kept dabbing his forehead with the handkerchief.

"You know good and well what brings me up here," he said. "We've got a trial scheduled in two weeks, and both of us know that you don't have a leg to stand on, legal or otherwise. So let's cut to the chase and dispose of the case this morning. It'll save the state some money and save you and your office some much-deserved embarrassment."

His tone was belligerent, his demeanor that of a wolverine rousted from sleep, and an air of superiority surrounded him like a fine mist. I kept the smile fixed to my face and leaned forward on my elbows.

"I'll bet you scare the pants off the young guys, don't you?" I said.

"You only have three witnesses on your list," he said. "Two of them are tramps and the other is Barney Fife. Do you have any idea what I'm going to do to them on the witness stand, Dillard? I'll filet them like halibut. You don't have a speck of physical evidence to corroborate anything they say. And my client had an impeccable reputation until your wonder boy with a badge ruined it. I'm thinking seriously of filing a civil suit against him and his department as soon as my client is acquitted."

"Your client is a perverted sociopath," I said. "I'm looking forward to meeting him."

"You can't be serious," Snodgrass said. "Surely you don't plan to continue with this charade. The jig is up, Dillard, the fat lady is singing, the show is over. I hear you're a good trial lawyer, and word is you've won a lot of cases, but you're not Houdini. There's no way you'll get out of the box I'm going to put you in if you insist on going through with this case."

I leaned back in the chair and laced my fingers behind my head. He was right about my case, but I had a plan to salvage it. And judging from the way he was conducting himself, I knew his ego would lead him down a path at trial that he'd later regret. But I wanted to be sure.

"Can I ask you a question, Mr. Snodgrass? Do you really think these girls made up a story just to ruin your client's reputation? I'm sure you've seen the statements from the other girls who are now refusing to testify. They corroborated everything Miss Dickson and Miss Harbin said."

"What I think doesn't matter," he snapped. "What matters is what you can prove beyond a reasonable doubt, and you can't prove that my client spit on the sidewalk, let alone convict him of all of these absurd sexual offenses."

"So he's going to deny having any sexual contact whatsoever with either of these girls."

"Of course he's going to deny it!" Small beads of spit flew from his lips as his voice grew louder. "And do you know why he's going to deny it? Because he didn't do it! Do you really think he'd have sex with either one of those nasty little skanks?"

I was sure the vulgarity and the tone were designed to see what kind of reaction he'd get from me. If I lost my composure and started battling with him or suddenly became self-righteously indignant, he'd be sure to bait me at trial. I kept my face relaxed and my voice pleasant. He didn't know it, but he'd just confirmed my strategy.

"You have your opinion, I have mine," I said. "Now I doubt if you came all the way up here just to argue with me and insult my witnesses. What is it you want?"

He shifted in the chair and rolled his head. When his chin dropped, it disappeared completely into the rolls of fat.

"I want to make you an offer you can't refuse," he said. "I want to give you an easy out, an opportunity to save face. I'm offering you a gift."

"I'm listening."

He took a deep breath and straightened his tie.

"In exchange for the dismissal of all the felony charges, my client is generously offering to plead guilty to one count of misdemeanor assault," he said dramatically. "He's also willing to pay a fifty-dollar fine plus the court costs on three conditions. One, he doesn't have to register as a sex offender. Two, you agree to unsupervised probation, and three, you agree that the charge will be expunged from his record after one year. Those are our terms. They're not negotiable."

I started laughing. I couldn't help it. The offer was ridiculous, but it was the way he delivered it that amused me. It made me think of a huge, animated purple blowfish, something you might see in *Finding Nemo*, pompously spouting his vastly superior intellectual theories to all the little shrimps around him.

"Sorry," I said, trying to stop laughing. His face was darkening, and even through all the layers of fat, I could see he was becoming angry. "I can't do that, Mr. Snodgrass. It's out of the question."

"Then rather than sitting there doing your impression of a hyena, perhaps you'd care to make some kind of reasonable counteroffer."

"I thought you said your terms were nonnegotiable."

"I might be willing to negotiate on the amount of the fine," he said.

I could see the conversation was pointless, so I decided to end it. Besides, he was beginning to get on my nerves. I leaned back and rubbed my face, as though I was giving his suggestion due consideration. Finally, I rested my chin on my fingertips and looked him directly in the eye.

"All right, Mr. Snodgrass. I'll make you a reasonable counteroffer. If your client will agree to undergo a simple procedure, I'll dismiss the charges. He can walk away clean."

"Procedure? What do you mean?"

"A medical procedure. I believe it's called castration. If he'll let a doctor remove his testicles so I can be assured he won't do this to any more young girls, I'll dismiss the case. Those are my terms, and they're nonnegotiable."

I noticed his hands tighten on the arms of the chair and his face went another shade darker. Slowly, he began to hoist himself to his feet.

"I'll be speaking to your superior about this matter," he said. "I'm sure he would want to be aware of your cavalier attitude, especially after I grind you into the dust. You might want to start looking for another job."

"Have a nice day, Mr. Snodgrass," I said without bothering to get up. "I'll see you in a couple weeks, provided you don't die of a heart attack in the meantime."

SUNDAY, OCT. 5

I knew I'd be spending most of Monday at the hospital with Caroline, so I called Tom Short and asked him if he'd meet me at my office in Jonesborough on Sunday afternoon. Tom was a forensic psychiatrist I'd known for years and whom I'd used as an expert witness in several cases I'd defended. He had an uncanny ability to diagnose personality disorders, but more importantly, he could analyze a set of facts or circumstances and make reliable predictions about future behavior. I wanted to show him the file and see what he had to say about the killers we were looking for.

He walked in wearing jeans and a red flannel shirt with the sleeves rolled up. He was just under six feet tall, with veiny blacksmith's forearms and a perpetual gleam in his astute pale blue eyes. He wore oval-shaped glasses and a two-day stubble. The worn stem of a tobacco pipe stuck out of his shirt pocket. The part in his thinning hair may have been a little farther from his ear than the last time I'd seen him, which was more than a year ago.

"You don't look any different," he said as he shook my hand.

"What were you expecting?"

"I don't know—maybe a jack-booted Nazi. I couldn't believe it when I read in the paper that you'd become a prosecutor, a minion of the government."

"I'm not a minion. I'm a civil servant, a proud representative of the people of Tennessee."

"Bull," he said. "You have too much compassion to do this job for long. My guess is you won't last a year."

"I appreciate your confidence," I said, motioning to a chair and anxious to get started. "Now, if you could find it in your heart to focus your laser beam on something other than me, I need your help."

I lifted a folder out of the file and spent the next half hour laying out everything we knew. The last items I showed him were the photographs from the crimes scenes and the autopsies. He leaned back and took his pipe out of his shirt pocket and stuck it between his teeth, unlit.

"They're young," he said. "And they're angry. Most likely male."

"You're sure of it?"

"Relatively. Crimes of this kind, where there are multiple killers, tend to involve younger people. There's something going on here besides anger though. Something a little beyond. I think you're dealing with a competition of some sort."

"Competition?"

"For attention, approval, that sort of thing. The number of wounds tells me they're trying to impress someone, maybe each other, with the amount of damage they're willing to inflict, the lengths they're willing to go. Maybe they're still establishing a pecking order of some sort. And the mutilation, the carvings and the broken legs at the first scene, the positioning of the bodies, they're taunting you, but at the same time, they're paying homage to someone, probably their leader."

"Do you think Satan is their leader?"

"I think the leader is flesh and bone."

"But do you think it's some kind of satanic cult?"

"Maybe, but more likely it's a group of fledgling sociopaths, obviously outcasts, rabidly angry, perhaps experimenting with how to best express their feelings to the world. Satan may be of some symbolic value to them, but I doubt they're dedicated in any meaningful way."

"How could anybody be dedicated in any meaningful way to Satan?"

Tom removed the pipe from his teeth and regarded me curiously.

"I don't remember religion as being one of your passions."

"Why is everyone suddenly so interested in my feelings about religion?" I said. I was thinking about the remarks Sarah had made to me just before she left.

"Is someone else interested?" Tom said.

"Never mind. Do you have any suggestions on how we catch them?"

"I assume you've checked out the goth bars."

"There's only one. The TBI agents have been there more than once. They came up empty."

"The only other way I could suggest, but I certainly wouldn't recommend it, would be to call them out. You could go public and insult them openly. Set yourself up as a target. They're obviously arrogant, so it wouldn't sit well with them. Of course, you'd be putting yourself, and probably your family, at extreme risk."

"No thanks," I said. "I'm not ready to die for the cause yet, and I'm not willing to put Caroline in any kind of danger."

He didn't say anything when I mentioned Caroline. He obviously hadn't heard about her illness, and I didn't feel like discussing it.

"Don't worry, you'll catch them," he said.

"What makes you so sure?"

"Like I said, they're arrogant. Arrogance breeds sloppiness. It's just a matter of time."

After Tom left, I walked back down to my truck, which was parked on the street beside the courthouse. As I approached, I noticed something had been tucked beneath the windshield wiper blade on the passenger side. It was a manila envelope, with nothing written on it. I got in the cab and opened it up.

Inside was a single sheet of paper. On it was a charcoal drawing. The drawing, which appeared to have been done by a professional artist, was in two frames, each taking up half the page. One half depicted two long-haired ghouls pointing pistols at a man tied to a tree. The man was elderly and naked except for his underwear, just like Norman Brockwell was when they found him. In the upper-left corner of the frame was a pair of fierce-looking eyes, one darkly shaded and the other lightly shaded, watching what was about to happen in the frame. The second frame was a drawing of a woman—maybe a girl—in a floppy straw hat. She was wearing a long dress and a shawl and was seated on a park bench beneath a tree, overlooking a river. Beyond her was an outdoor amphitheater, and behind her was a statue of a winged deer.

I immediately recognized the spot where the young woman was sitting because I'd been there hundreds of times. Caroline and I had spent many hours walking along the river at Winged Deer Park, talking about our hopes and dreams, about our children, our relationships, our problems. The spot depicted in the drawing was in the park. It was one of our favorite places.

My eyes fell to a written caption beneath the young woman on the bench. It said, "She knows. Come tomorrow."

MONDAY, OCT. 6

It had been twenty-two days since the Becks were murdered, a week since the Brockwells. The agents had interviewed nearly a hundred people and followed up dozens of false leads that had come in through hotlines set up by the TBI. The local newspaper editorialized that the police were incompetent. One editorial demanded a task force. Someone let it leak that the district attorney had already proposed a task force, but the idea had been vetoed by Joe Dillard, the prosecutor who was guiding the investigation and would handle the case when it went to trial. The paper pointed out that Dillard was also the newest member of the DA's office and that he had virtually no law enforcement experience. I didn't bother to confront anyone who'd been in the room during the discussion about a task force. It didn't matter.

On Monday morning, Caroline, Jack, Lilly, and I drove to the medical center in Johnson City. Caroline was scheduled for exploratory surgery, the first stage in her treatment. The surgeon was to open Caroline's breast, measure the tumor, and cut out a small section of skin above it and some of the surrounding tissue. He'd also remove what he called the sentinel lymph node.

He'd send sections of the tumor, the skin, the tissue, and the node to the lab. They already knew the tumor was malignant, but the lab would tell the doctor whether the samples from the node and the skin contained cancer cells. If not, he'd remove the tumor and a portion of the surrounding tissue and Caroline might be faced with only six or eight weeks of radiation therapy. That was the best case. If the tumor was large, however, or if there was cancer in the node or the skin, the treatment would be much different.

We sat in a waiting room in the surgery center until 10:00 a.m., nearly two hours after they wheeled Caroline away on a gurney. By that time, we'd been joined by Caroline's mother and two of her mother's friends whose names I didn't know, Sarah and her boyfriend—neither of whom spoke to me—a couple of Lilly's friends, and a man I'd never laid eyes on. It turned out he was from Caroline's mother's church. He put his hand on Caroline's forehead and prayed over her just before she was taken off to surgery. He asked the Lord to free her from this terrible disease. I didn't have much faith in his ability to rid Caroline of cancer, but I didn't object to him praying over her. I wouldn't have cared if a painted medicine man came in and danced circles around her. I was up for anything that might help.

Jack and I were walking back to the waiting room from a trip to the cafeteria when my cell phone rang. It was Fraley.

"You need to come out here," he said.

"What do you mean?"

"To the park. The girl in the picture. She's here. She wants to talk to you."

I'd called Fraley and taken the picture to him Sunday afternoon after I found it on my windshield. Both of us were skeptical, but he said he'd follow up.

"What?" I said. "Now?"

"As soon as you can."

"Caroline's in surgery. Can't it wait a few hours?"

"I guess it could, but we take a chance on her changing her mind or leaving."

"Where exactly is she?" I said.

"Near the pavilion. Right where you said she'd be. I'm holding the drawing in my hand and it looks exactly like what I'm seeing. It's weird."

I hung up the phone and looked at Jack. "I have to go," I said. He gave me a bewildered look. "We may have a witness in the murders. She wants to talk to me. Your mother will be in surgery for at least another hour, then she'll be in recovery for a while. As soon as the surgeon comes out, call me. I'll be back as soon as I can."

Winged Deer is a two-hundred-acre park located on the eastern outskirts of Johnson City. The western half of the park contains baseball and softball fields and a hiking trail that winds through a five-acre patch of dense forest. The eastern half skirts Boone Lake. Along the lake (which was the Watauga River until the Tennessee Valley Authority started building dams) are more walking trails, a boat ramp, a boardwalk, and a large, covered pavilion that people rent for outdoor gatherings and picnics. There are also a few benches scattered around beneath the oak and maple trees that dot the riverbank. I spotted Fraley's car in the lot and parked next to it. I found him pacing back and forth near the pavilion, nervously sucking on a cigarette.

"Sorry about this," Fraley said as soon as I walked up. "How's the wife?"

"Don't know yet. She's still in surgery, but thanks for asking."

"This one's strange," he said.

"How so?"

"You'll see." He nodded toward the water.

I started walking down the hill in the direction of the nod. My view of the bench was obscured by the tree at first, but then I saw her. It was as though the drawing I'd held in my hand the day before had come to life. I approached slowly. The dress she was wearing was cream colored and ankle length. Her feet were covered by sandals, her head by a finely woven straw hat that fluttered gently in the light breeze. A white crocheted shawl was draped over her shoulders. Her hands were folded in her lap, and she appeared to be looking out over the river, serenely contemplating the universe. I could see dark red hair curling softly down her back and shoulders all the way to her waist. As I approached, she turned toward me and lifted her chin. Beneath the brim of the hat was a young, smooth, face with high cheekbones and jawlines that melted into a slightly dimpled chin. Full lips were curved into a pleasant smile. Her nose was small and delicate. A flesh-colored patch, which was secured by a length of what appeared to be nylon, covered her right eye. Her left eye was the most brilliant, clear, cobalt blue I'd ever seen.

"I'm Joe Dillard," I said as I stood uncomfortably over her. The eye was beautiful, but at the same time, it was unnerving.

"Someone you love deeply is very ill," she said in an even tone. Her voice was calm and appealing, like that of a well-trained stage actress.

"What's your name?" I said.

"I see pain in your eyes. I sense regret. You've done things you'd like to forget."

"Who hasn't? I was told you have some information for me, Miss ... what did you say your name was?"

"You're skeptical of me."

"Comes with the territory. Do you mind if I sit down?"

She nodded, and I sat down at the other end of the bench. I looked out over the lake. It was placid, a vivid green. Some of the trees on the opposite bank were beginning to change to their fall colors of orange, yellow, and red. The sky was azure, the temperature warm.

"You did the drawing?"

She nodded again.

"You put it on my car?"

"You needed it. It was there."

"Why a drawing? Why not a phone call?"

"I thought the drawing was more likely to get your attention."

"Who are you? What's your name?"

There was an aura of calmness about her, a sense that she was perfectly at peace with herself and everything around her. She looked back out over the river.

"It's cancer," she said, "your wife."

Lucky guess. Coincidence. She knows someone who knows me and she's heard about it from them.

"No," I said. "My wife doesn't have cancer."

"You lie poorly. She's very strong, isn't she?"

"I don't have time for—"

"And so are you, but you draw much of your strength from her."

"I'm sorry, but you still haven't told me your name. You know, I could probably have you arrested just because of what was in the drawing. Would you like to continue this conversation at the police station?"

"You don't want to arrest me," she said.

"I don't want to sit here all morning and listen to you talk in circles either." I was becoming impatient. "Now what's your name?"

She looked back out over the river. "Alisha. Alisha Elizabeth Davis."

"Are you a psychic?"

"I see things that others can't see. I hear and feel things that others can't."

"I don't have a lot of time this morning, Alisha. If you know something about the murders, I'd appreciate it if you'd just tell me."

"They thirst for revenge, and they won't stop."

"Who are they?"

"One is Samuel, another Levi."

"Do they have last names?"

"Boyer. Barnett."

I reached into my back pocket for a notepad. I didn't have one, so I pulled a pen from my shirt pocket and started writing on the palm of my left hand.

"Samuel Boyer?"

She nodded.

"Levi Barnett?"

"You're saying Samuel Boyer and Levi Barnett did these killings? Do you know where they're from? Where can we find them?"

"They won't be hard to find."

"How do you know? And don't say you know things. Don't tell me it came to you in a vision."

"There's a third. One who commands. She believes she is the daughter of Satan."

"*How do you know*?"

My cell phone rang. I looked down at the caller ID. It was Jack.

"Excuse me," I said. "I need to take this. I'll be right back." I got up and walked twenty or thirty feet away from her, out of earshot.

"Tell me something good," I said when I answered.

"Surgeon just left," Jack said. His voice was hushed. "The tumor was stage three B, whatever that means. He said it was almost four centimeters long. There was cancer in the skin above the tumor and in the lymph node. He said the type of cancer she has is very aggressive. He already closed her back up. He said he left the tumor so they could see how it responds to chemotherapy."

"What did he say about the chemo?" It was the one part of the treatment Caroline had talked about the most. She was terrified of chemotherapy.

"Some other doctor is going to handle it, but he said most of the cases similar to Mom go through three months of chemo, then surgery to remove the breast and the rest of her lymph nodes, then three more months of chemo. After that she'll have to go through radiation for a couple months. He says she's looking at about a year before she's clear of it, and that's if everything goes well."

"Where are you?"

"I'm standing in the lobby."

"Where's your mom?"

"In recovery. The nurse told me we can go back in about a half hour."

"But she's okay?"

"Outside of the fact that she has cancer."

"How's Lilly?"

"Not good."

"I'll be there in fifteen minutes. Wait for me. I want to be in the recovery room when she wakes up."

I hung up the phone and walked back over to the girl.

She looked up at me, and I noticed a tear running down her left cheek.

"I'm sorry," she said.

I'd developed a keen intuition over more than a decade of practicing criminal defense law and listening to my own clients lie to me over and over again. Caroline jokingly referred to it as my "crapola detector." It wasn't innate; it was something that had developed through experience, but I'd learned to trust my ability to detect and sort through lies and to get to the heart of a matter very quickly. This girl gave me no indication that she was lying. Her voice was clear and steady, her manner calm and straightforward. The circumstances were certainly unusual, but I found myself believing her.

"Okay, Alisha," I said, "if you really want to help me, this is what has to happen. I'm going to go up and talk to that officer for a few minutes. Then he's going to come back down here and take a statement from you. He's going to write down everything you say. In the statement, you're going to tell him exactly what you know about the murders and the people you've mentioned. And more importantly, you're going to tell him *how* you know these things. We need details. We need something concrete if we're going to be able to get warrants and arrest these people. If what you say checks out, I'll probably need you to testify in front of a grand jury. You may even end up testifying at trial. Do you understand?"

A feeling came over me that reminded me of the way I felt the night I went to the Beck murder scene, but it was different somehow. I felt as though I was experiencing something unnatural, perhaps even supernatural, but the sickening sense of being in the presence of evil was absent. I wanted to talk to this girl, to question her, and I could sense that she wanted to tell me what she knew, but I couldn't stop thinking about Caroline lying in the recovery room, about to come out of the anesthesia-induced coma. Someone would have to break the bad news to her, and I wanted it to be me.

"I have to leave," I said, "but I'm going to go talk to the agent and he'll be back down here in just a minute. Just sit tight. Won't take but a second."

I jogged back up the hill to where Fraley was standing.

"Well?" he said.

"Write these names down." I opened my hand so he could see them.

"Who are they?"

"She says they're the killers."

"You're kidding me. You wrote them on your hand?"

"I didn't bring a notepad. Didn't know I'd need one."

"And I took you for a Boy Scout. At least you had a pen."

Fraley began copying the names down. "One of those names is familiar," he said.

"How so?"

"I put a list together of kids Norman Brockwell had serious problems with before he retired. One of them, Boyer, is on your hand. What's her name?" He nodded toward the river.

"Alisha Elizabeth Davis. Take a statement from her. Get everything you can. You know the drill. All we can do is check out what she says. And let's make sure we check her out at the same time. I have to get back to the hospital."

"Bad news?"

"You could say that. Go ahead, before she changes her mind. I'll call you in a couple hours."

I jogged back to my truck and pulled out of the lot. My cell phone rang less than a minute later. It was Fraley.

"She's gone," he said.

"What do you mean, gone?"

"I walked back down to the bench and she was gone. I don't think she could have

walked off without me seeing her, but she's not here. She disappeared."

MONDAY, OCT. 6

As soon as I got back to the hospital, I ran down Caroline's surgeon and talked to him for about ten minutes. One thing he said stuck in my mind: "The only way to deal with cancer is to kill it." From there, I headed straight back to the recovery room.

Caroline's eyes fluttered open when I rubbed my fingers across her forehead. She was lying on a gurney behind a flimsy curtain in a gray room that smelled of anesthetic and floor cleaner. A monitor loomed above her, its digital display reflecting her blood pressure, heart rate, and body temperature. A plastic tube carried anti-nausea medicine from a bag on a hook into a vein in her forearm. The skin on her face was dry and splotched with red, and when I leaned down to kiss her on the cheek, I noticed a bitter smell coming from her mouth.

"Hey, sugar," I said. "How do you feel?"

She looked up at me, and her eyes lit with a glint of recognition.

"My mouth tastes like a thousand skunks slept in it," she said.

"Smells like it too."

She covered her mouth with the back of her hand self-consciously.

"Just kidding, baby," I said. "Your breath smells fine."

"Liar. Would you get me some water?"

I poured some water from a pitcher that was sitting on a table near the bed into a plastic cup and helped her drink. Her lips were dry and scaly.

"I'm freezing," she whispered.

"Be right back," I said. I went and found a nurse, who directed me to a large cabinet just down the hall. I grabbed a couple thin blankets and went back to Caroline's cubicle. I laid the blankets over her and tucked the sides snugly beneath her.

"Is it that bad?" she said after I moved back to the head of the bed.

"What do you mean?"

"I can tell by the look on your face. And the kids aren't in here. If the news was good, they'd be here too."

"I just wanted to be alone with you for a minute," I said.

"So you could break the bad news to me?"

"It could be worse. I think you're going to make it."

She grimaced and adjusted herself on the gurney. "Was there cancer in the node?"

"Yeah, baby. I'm sorry."

"Skin?"

"Yeah."

I squeezed her hand gently.

"So I'm going to lose my breast?"

"I don't think you have much choice."

"What do I need a breast for, right? We're not going to have any more kids."

"They'll make you another one if you want them to. They do it all the time now."

"When do I have to start the chemotherapy?"

"A couple weeks. They want you to heal up from this for a little while first."

"Will you love me when I'm bald?"

Caroline wasn't particularly vain, but she loved her hair, and so did I. It was a reflection of her personality, beautiful but occasionally a bit on the unruly side. It was auburn and thick and curly and fell to the middle of her back. It turned a few shades lighter in the summer when she spent more time in the sun. Losing it was the side effect of chemotherapy that she dreaded the most.

"I'll shave my head if you want," I said. "We can be bald together."

Two hours later, after I'd rolled my wife out of the surgery center in a wheelchair, helped her into the car and taken her home, gotten her settled into bed, and made sure Lilly and Jack knew what to do in case something went wrong, I drove back up to the TBI headquarters in Johnson City. Fraley's office was buzzing. People were running in and out while Fraley alternately barked commands like a general and talked into the telephone. As I sat down across from him, he hung up the phone. He got up from behind the desk and walked over and closed the door.

"How's the wife?" he said as he returned to his seat.

"In bed. Resting."

"She okay?"

"Yeah, she's all right. What's going on here?"

"I can appreciate what you're going through," Fraley said. "I lost my first wife to breast cancer."

The comment shocked me. It was the first time Fraley had given me any indication that he had a life outside his job.

"I'm sorry," I said. "I'm truly sorry. What was her name?"

"Robin," he said, unconsciously smiling at the thought of her. He reached to his left and picked up a small, framed photograph. "Beautiful woman. It was thirty years ago. The treatment has come a long way since then, but at the time, there wasn't much they could do. It was too far along by the time it was diagnosed. Took her in a hurry. We'd only been married five years."

"Can I take a look?"

He handed me the photo. It was a studio portrait of a pretty young brunette, maybe twenty-five years old, sitting in front of a fireplace. She was holding an infant wrapped in a blanket, and beside her was a handsome young man, smiling the smile of a proud husband and father. I looked back up at Fraley and could see that the young man in the photo was him many years, many heartaches, and many miles ago.

"That's my daughter," he said. "She was three months old that day."

"Where is she now?"

"Nashville. Married to a banker. He's a good guy. She has a couple kids of her own."

"You raise her by yourself?"

"Yeah. Did the best I could. I don't think I messed her up too bad."

"Nice little family." I handed the photo back to him.

"She'll be okay," he said. "Your wife. She'll be okay."

"Thanks," I said. I briefly imagined Caroline lying in a casket covered in flowers, eyes closed, the serene look of the dead on her face. Fraley must have sensed what I was thinking.

"I'm sorry," he said. "I didn't mean to … I mean, I wasn't trying to make you think about—"

"Don't worry about it," I said. "I appreciate the concern."

"So I guess you're wondering what's going on here."

"You could say that."

"Reasonable suspects," Fraley said. "Boyer was thrown out of Brockwell's school the same year Brockwell retired. He has a long juvy record, mostly drug related, a couple assaults. His probation officer says he dyed his hair black recently, so he might be a goth. The other one, Barnett, is still a juvenile. He's only sixteen, but he's already spent a year in detention. He's got drug charges, a couple thefts, three assaults, one of them aggravated. The aggravated assault is what got him shipped off. Hit a kid with a baseball bat and broke his leg. He's only been out of detention three months. He's still on probation, and his probation officer said the last time she saw him, which was two weeks ago, he'd dyed his hair jet black. Looks promising."

"She said something about a third," I said. "I think she said 'one who commands.' Something about the daughter of Satan, so it must be a female."

"Did you get a name?"

"No."

Fraley raised his eyebrows.

"She was telling me all this stuff—it was weird. I think I was trying to figure out how she knew about the murders, then I got a phone call from my son and I had to leave. I thought she'd give the name to you. Sorry."

"Don't sweat it. If these two are the right ones, they'll lead us to the third. Are you sure you got the girl's name right?"

"Which girl?"

"The one in the park. Are you sure her name was Alisha Elizabeth Davis?"

"That's what she said."

"Alisha Elizabeth Davis was reported missing by her foster parents the day after the Brockwells were killed."

Fraley slid a piece of paper across the desk to me. At the top was a black-and-white photograph of the girl on the bench, eye patch and all. Alisha Elizabeth Davis, born April eleventh, 1989, one hundred and fifteen pounds, red hair, blue eyes, last seen on the morning of September twenty-eighth.

"I've got a couple guys talking to her foster parents now," Fraley said.

"This gets stranger by the minute."

"So what do you suggest we do next, counselor? Can we get arrest warrants or search warrants based solely on the word of a psychic, especially one who's listed as missing?"

"I guess we could put round-the-clock surveillance on them," I said, "wait and see where it leads us. But I'd hate to take a chance on someone else getting killed while we're waiting. I'd also hate to take a chance on somebody screwing up and them finding out we're onto them."

"Why don't we just pick them up?" Fraley said. "Simultaneously. We bring them back here, make sure they see each other, but keep them isolated. We play them off each other."

"And what if they refuse to talk to us? What if they say they don't want to come?"

"Is what you got from the psychic enough to detain them?"

"I don't know. It's a close call."

"But what if she turns out to be right?"

"We have to have probable cause to arrest them, but all we need is reasonable suspicion to detain them. I just don't know if the word of someone who claims to be psychic is enough, especially since she vanished. Not much legal precedent in that area. If we pick them up and somebody confesses, we risk losing everything on a motion to suppress later."

"No judge in his right mind would turn these people loose if they turn out to be the killers," Fraley said. "I don't care *what* the legalities are."

I sat back to think it through, trying to imagine the argument in front of a judge later on. We'd had six horrific murders within a three-week period and had enough similarities to reasonably believe the murders were connected. We'd received an unsolicited drawing from an anonymous source that very accurately depicted the second murder scene. We'd followed up on the drawing and located the witness, who said she knew who committed the murders but didn't say *how* she knew. She gave us her name and the names of the killers. One of the names she provided was at least indirectly connected to Norman Brockwell. We had another witness who said she saw two goths getting out of the Becks' van, and both of our suspects had recently dyed their hair black, at least indicating the possibility that they might be goths. Both of them had criminal records, including violence. The witness also told us the killers would strike again. We assessed the risk to the public and, in good faith, decided to act.

"The biggest problem I have is that there isn't a good-faith exception to the warrant requirement in Tennessee."

"Say again?" Fraley said. "In English?"

"You have to have probable cause to get a warrant, right?"

"Right."

"There have been federal cases and cases in other states where judges have ruled that the police lacked probable cause for an arrest, but because they acted in good faith, they upheld the legality of the arrest. It's called the good-faith exception. Tennessee doesn't recognize it."

"Maybe it's time they did," Fraley said.

"You're right," I said. "This may be the test case. You start getting your people together to coordinate the arrests and the searches and I'll go draft the warrants. See if you can get some lab people to come in early in case we need them. Which judge is the easiest when it comes to getting warrants signed?"

"Judge Rogers, especially after he's been home long enough to start drinking. He'll sign anything."

"Then Rogers it is. We'll pick both of them up, search their homes, cars, whatever. Let's put the screws to them."

MONDAY, OCT. 6

There were only thirteen Tennessee Bureau of Investigation agents assigned to the criminal field investigation unit in all of northeast Tennessee. Those thirteen agents covered twenty-one counties and eight judicial districts. Ten of them had been assigned temporarily to our murder cases, with Fraley at the point.

I was amazed at how quickly they'd been able to mobilize the agents, and once they were all up and running, it was impressive to see how much information they could gather and how quickly they could gather it. We'd identified two suspects at around 10:00 a.m. Fourteen hours later, computers had helped the agents gather information from the National Crime Information Center, local crime databases, local government databases, juvenile authorities, probation departments, and schools. I knew as soon as the suspects were arrested, most of the agents would head back out to execute the search warrants. They'd talk to parents, relatives, friends, acquaintances, employers—anyone who could provide them with information. It almost made me uneasy to see firsthand how quickly, and how deeply, the government could delve into an individual's life. What made me more uneasy was that all of this was occurring based on the word of a witness who might be crazy, lying, or just plain wrong.

It was almost eleven o'clock by the time I finished drafting the applications and affidavits required to secure the arrest and search warrants. I called Judge Rogers at home. He agreed to let me come over, and I found him sipping on a vodka martini in his den. The martini obviously wasn't the judge's first of the evening. It took me all of five minutes to convince him to sign the warrants. As soon as I left, I called Fraley.

Since I'd stayed in touch with Fraley by phone, I knew that as soon as I left his office that afternoon he'd ordered immediate, full-time surveillance on the homes—or at least the last known addresses—of our two suspects. None of the agents assigned to the surveillance had seen a thing until almost 10:00 p.m., when a banged-up green Chevrolet Cavalier rolled into the driveway at the address the computers provided for Samuel Boyer. The license plate was registered to Boyer. The agents reported that there were two passengers in the car. It parked in the driveway, the engine remained running and the lights stayed on, and what appeared to be a male got out and went into the house. The agents couldn't make a positive identification because the person was wearing heavy makeup. He was also wearing goth clothing. The male stayed inside the house for only a couple minutes and got back into the car. The agents followed the car to a cheap motel on the western outskirts of Johnson City, a place called The Lost Weekend. They were still there.

After the judge signed my warrants, Fraley told me to meet him in the parking lot of a Burger King a couple blocks from the motel. He flashed his headlights at me as I pulled into the lot and I pulled in beside him about fifteen minutes before midnight. I locked up my truck and sat down in the passenger seat of his Crown Victoria, warrants in hand.

"It's too early in the year to be this cold," I said as I closed the door and shivered involuntarily.

"I already talked to owner of the motel," Fraley said, ignoring the comment. "Boyer checked in under his own name. Doesn't seem to be trying to hide anything."

Fraley spit loudly into a Styrofoam cup. A pungent, wintergreen odor filled the car, and I noticed his bottom lip was sticking out as though he'd been punched in the mouth.

"That stuff'll rot your gums," I said.

"Been dipping off and on for forty years," he said. "They ain't rotten yet."

"Did the owner make a positive ID?"

"He couldn't tell from the photo I showed him. He says they always wear makeup."

"Always?"

"The guy says they've rented a room a couple times before in the past few months. Says they're weird, but they haven't done any damage."

"Do the dates coincide with the other murders?"

"Don't know. He said they pay cash and he doesn't keep records of cash transactions. It's not exactly the Ritz."

"Where's the owner now?" I was wondering whether he might be loyal enough to his cash-paying customers to alert them that the police were making inquiries. Fraley gave me a sideways glance.

"You really think I'm stupid enough to leave him alone?"

I shrugged my shoulders. "Sorry."

"One of my guys is in there keeping him company."

"Are there still three of them?"

"Small party. Nobody new has showed up."

"Any idea what's going on in the room?"

"They pulled the blinds and the curtains as soon as they went in. We haven't seen a thing."

"So what's the plan?"

"As soon as we get the go-ahead from the assistant district attorney—which would be you in this case—we'll take them down hard and fast. They're on the ground floor in a corner room, which makes things a little less complicated. Once we're in position, the agent in the office will call the room as a diversion. As soon as we hear the phone ring, Norcross will hit the door. He's our door-opening specialist. He's so good with a sledge hammer we call him Thor."

I'd been introduced to Norcross at the office earlier in the day. He was six and a half feet tall and looked like he'd been extracted from a slab of granite.

"Why didn't you call Johnson City?" I said. "They've got a SWAT team."

"I don't want to take a chance on someone leaking this to the press. The last thing we need is a bunch of reporters in the parking lot."

"Don't you at least have one of those battering rams? Or better yet, why don't you just get a key from the owner?"

"Because the door will probably be chained on the inside, genius. And trust me, Norcross and a sixteen-pound sledge is better than any battering ram ever devised."

He turned toward me and held out his hand.

"The warrants," he said.

"And what am I supposed to do? Wait in the car?"

"Go home to your wife," Fraley said.

"Are you serious? You want me to go home?"

"There's nothing you can do here. We've got the raid planned out, and the plans don't include you. Once we arrest them, we'll be interrogating them all night. I don't want you there."

"Why?"

"You can't participate in the interrogation because it could make you a witness, right?"

"Right, but—"

"And if you're a witness, you can't handle the case in court. It would be a conflict for you, right?"

"Yeah, but—"

"So you don't need to be there."

"I could observe. Maybe help advise you with the questioning."

"We don't need your help. We know what we're doing."

The tone of his voice was firm, the look on his face determined.

"Why don't you want me around?" I said. "Tell me the truth."

"How do you think this is going to go down? Do you think we're going to politely knock on the door and ask them to come along with us? Do you think we're going to take them back to the office, give them some cake and coffee, and ask them nicely whether they slaughtered six innocent people?"

"So what you're telling me is you're going to brutalize them."

"Brutalize might be a little strong, but we're not going to treat them like houseguests. And I don't want you second-guessing me. I don't want to be hearing about their constitutional rights while I'm trying to get information out of them."

"You need to be thinking about their constitutional rights or you could blow the whole—"

"Don't lecture me, Dillard. I was interrogating murder suspects while you were still in grammar school. I know what I'm doing, and the last thing I need is a lawyer looking over my shoulder while I'm doing it."

He spit into the cup again and stuck his hand out. Reluctantly, I handed him the warrants.

"We're on the same side, you know," I said.

"When this goes to court, I promise I won't try to tell you how to handle your case," he said. "But until it gets there, it's mine. We do it my way. Go home, counselor. Take care of your wife. Get some beauty sleep. You need it."

"Just let me ask you one question," I said. "Are you going to videotape the interrogations?"

"Let me ask *you* a question. Am I authorized to offer them anything?"

"You mean leniency? A break in sentencing in exchange for ratting out the others?" I thought about what Lee Mooney had said to me at the scene of the first murders. *You have to promise me that when we find the sick bastards that did this, you'll see to it that every one of them gets the electric chair. No screw ups. No deals.* "No," I said. "Don't offer them anything."

Fraley turned and looked out the window. He remained silent for a little while, then turned back toward me.

"Have a good night, counselor," he said. "I'll call you first thing in the morning."

TUESDAY, OCT. 7

"**E**verybody knows what to do, right?" Fraley said as he climbed from his vehicle, which was parked across a side street from The Lost Weekend motel. Seven men stood in silence. They were dressed in khaki fatigue pants and black jackets that said "POLICE" across the front and back. All were armed and wore bulletproof vests beneath the jackets.

"Any questions?"

Nobody said a word.

"Good. Remember, if we're right about these suspects, they've already killed six people. Shock and awe. I want all of them facedown on the ground in less than ten seconds. Keep a sharp eye out for weapons."

The men surrounding Fraley were locked in, their eyes wide in anticipation of the unknown danger behind the motel room door. Fraley thought about all the search warrants and felony arrest warrants he'd executed in the past and the inherent danger in breaking down a door without knowing what was on the other side. As the group of officers moved away from their cars and toward the motel, Fraley noticed his skin was tingling. It was a sensation he hadn't felt in a long time, and it reminded him of an irony he'd discovered years ago. It was in moments like this, when the prospect of sudden, violent death becomes real and immediate, that he truly appreciated being alive.

Fraley was in the back of the pack. Norcross led the way. The front was reserved for the young guys, guys with quicker reflexes, better cardiovascular systems, steadier hands. They jogged along the back of the shopping center, staying in the shadows, and across a side street that bordered the parking lot of the motel. Once they crossed the street, they turned toward the back side of the building. Norcross picked up the pace as they moved the length of the building to the shadows of the far-west wall and made their way back around to the front. Everyone squatted there while Fraley pulled out his cell phone and dialed the agent who was waiting in the lobby with the motel owner.

"One minute," Fraley whispered as he closed his phone and stuck it in his pocket.

Norcross led the way around the corner to the room. Four agents passed him silently. Three squatted beneath the window on the east side of the door, flashlights in one hand, guns in the other. The fourth took up a position next to a car in the parking lot about twenty feet away and trained his weapon on the door. Fraley, along with one other agent, stopped on the west side, less than five feet away. Still another remained behind and pointed his gun at the door. Everyone froze for maybe twenty seconds—it seemed like twenty years—waiting for the phone inside the room to ring. Fraley looked at his watch. With his right hand, he started counting down.

Five fingers ... four ... three ... two ... one ....

Nothing. No sound from inside the room. Fraley muttering, "Ring!" under his breath. Norcross looking back over his shoulder at Fraley, eyebrows raised as if to say, "What now?"

The telephone inside the room rang. Fraley saw the massive head of the sledge hammer looming above the door. The phone rang again, and then *Wham!* The door splintered as it exploded with the sound and force of a gunshot. Norcross tossed the sledge to the side. A man screamed. Lights flashed. A flurry of movement. Fraley's heart pounded inside his chest. Male voices: "*Police! Get on the ground! Get on the ground!*" A strange scent of incense hanging in the air. Flashes of candlelight. "*Give me your hands! Give me your hands! Now! If you move I'll blow your brains all over this floor!*" Bright light as someone flipped a switch.

And then only the sound of men breathing heavily.

"Are we clear?" Fraley said.

"Clear."

"Clear."

Three bodies lay facedown on the floor on the dirty shag carpet, hands cuffed tightly behind their backs. Two males and a female, all wearing black robes with hoods. Candles scattered around the room on the floor, on the nightstand by the bed, on the vanity near the bathroom. Black candles. A silver cup, a chalice, lay in the center of the floor, apparently overturned in the confusion. Fraley knelt beside it. Most of the liquid inside had spilled onto the floor, making a dark stain.

"Looks like blood," he said, resisting the urge to pick it up.

One of the agents was hoisting the girl onto her feet. She looked to be around twenty years old, redheaded, attractive at first glance, somehow familiar-looking. As she stood, the robe fell open in front. She was naked beneath it. Fraley glanced around the room as other agents pulled their prey up off the floor. The other two—the males—were wearing white, pancake makeup. They had black hair and rings in their eyebrows, noses, and ears. They were both naked beneath the robes, and blood ran down both their forearms. All of them seemed dazed.

"Get the cars," Fraley said. Three of the agents left immediately.

The girl began to mumble something unintelligible, quietly at first, then more loudly. Fraley couldn't understand a word she was saying.

"Shut your hole!" Fraley hissed as he moved toward her and jerked her cuffed hands upward behind her back. She winced and went silent.

"You're all under arrest," Fraley said through gritted teeth. "You have a right to keep your filthy mouths shut, you have a right to a scumbag lawyer. Anything you say can be used against you in court."

The agents arrived with the vehicles in less than a minute. Fraley shoved the girl toward the door.

"Get them out of here," Fraley said. He watched as the three were led out to the waiting vehicles. Once they were out of earshot, Fraley walked to the bathroom. He'd noticed three separate piles of clothing earlier: one pile—obviously the girl's—was on the vanity next to the sink. Another pile was near the wall next to the vanity, and a third was inside the bathroom on the floor near the toilet. There was a pair of shoes in each pile.

"Bag these up separately and bring them to the office," Fraley said to Norcross.

"Shouldn't they go to the lab?" Norcross said.

"They will. But first I have to make sure who they belong to. Watch and learn, my son."

TUESDAY, OCT. 7

As soon as Fraley walked into the office, he turned the thermostat to "Cool," set the temperature at sixty degrees, and made sure everyone knew to leave it there. The other agents brought the suspects in one at a time. Since there were only two interrogation rooms in the satellite TBI office, Fraley was forced to improvise. Boyer and Barnett were placed in the interrogation rooms. The redhead, the one they weren't expecting, was handcuffed to a chair in Fraley's office and left to stew. The door was left open and an agent was posted outside.

Fraley thought about what Dillard had told him. *One who commands.* A female. This might be her. The lack of makeup and goth persona certainly set her apart from the others, but she hadn't done anything or said anything to indicate she was a leader. After her initial attempt at speaking back at the hotel had been derailed by Fraley's hammerlock, she'd ridden from the motel to the TBI office in silence in the darkened backseat.

A search of the motel room and the clothing that had been strewn around produced nothing of value— a couple razor blades, the boys' wallets, a watch. They hadn't found even an ID card for the redhead. Fraley still had no idea who she was.

But the green Cavalier parked outside had yielded what Fraley hoped would literally be the smoking guns— two semi-automatic pistols, both nine millimeter. Drugs were also found in the car—a quarter ounce of marijuana, about a half gram of crystal meth, and a dozen pills, probably hydrocodone or oxycodone—were in the console. When Fraley opened the trunk and flashed his light inside, he saw what appeared to be a bloodstain near the spare tire well. If it was blood, it might be Norman Brockwell's. And then there were the shoes and clothes. Maybe the shoes would match footprints found at the scenes. Maybe the clothing would yield fibers. Maybe the tires would match the casts taken from the woods where Norman Brockwell was murdered.

The mobile forensic unit had been on standby at the office and was now going over the room and doing a preliminary on the car. Lab personnel were on standby in Knoxville. The forensics people would do what they could at the scene and then load the car onto a rollback and take it down to Knoxville along with the rest of the evidence. There was usually a significant waiting period for lab work, but this case had been moved to the front of the line. Fraley knew that by mid-morning, much of the lab analysis would be finished.

Fraley walked to his office and picked up a few files. The redhead stared at him but said nothing. Fraley did a double-take when he saw her eyes. One blue, one green. Piercing, as though they could see straight into his soul, and full of hatred. He made a quick trip to the bathroom and walked out to the snack room. He poured himself a cup of coffee and started slathering cheese whiz on a cracker. He looked up at the clock on the wall. It was 2:15 a.m. Fraley had been up for twenty-two hours, and it didn't look like he'd be going home anytime soon.

Fraley had asked Norcross and Taylor to Mirandize the suspects again. They were reading the suspects their constitutional rights and asking them to sign a form that acknowledged that their rights had been explained to them and that they understood. He'd already sent two other agents to Levi Barnett's home to bring back Levi's aunt, who was identified in his juvenile records as Barnett's legal guardian. Levi's father was in prison for dealing crystal meth, and his mother had deserted them a decade ago.

Fraley sipped his coffee and flipped through the files. When he came across the photos of the murdered children, the rage he felt when he thought about his granddaughter returned. He'd looked at the photos only once. They turned his stomach.

He thought briefly about how he would conduct the interrogations. The Reid technique was now standard operating procedure in law enforcement. Make the suspect as comfortable as possible. Make him think you're there to help him. Try to find some common ground and get him talking—it didn't matter what the conversation was about initially. The theory behind the Reid technique was that suspects would naturally feel guilt and want to unload their burden. The officer was there to facilitate the cleansing of the spirit. Get him talking, eventually turn the conversation toward the crime, and gently persuade him to confess.

Forget that.

If Fraley could have his way, he'd subject every one of them to torture. Maybe a little waterboarding would loosen their tongues. A few well-placed blows to the solar plexus or groin. Maybe even some electric-shock therapy. Then, once he had his confessions, he could proceed right to execution. No need for a trial and sentencing once they'd admitted it. Take them out back, shoot them in the head, load them in the back of a pickup truck, and haul them to the city dump. Get them out of the mix and be done with it.

When he came out of his fantasy-induced trance, Fraley noticed that guys were moving in and out of the snack room, trading good-natured insults and laughing. The mood in the office was lighter than it had been in weeks. The raid had gone off without a hitch. Arrests had been made. Evidence had been found and was being processed. The nightmare, it seemed, was over.

Norcross and Taylor came in and sat down, and the others filed out. Norcross had played defensive end at Memphis State before earning a law degree and joining the TBI ten years earlier. At thirty-five, he looked like he belonged on a poster for the Green Berets. His jaw was strong and square, his eyes hazel, and he kept his black hair cut to half an inch. Taylor was younger, a University of Tennessee accounting graduate who'd been an agent for six years. He was lanky and balding, with a nasally, high-pitched voice that quickly got on Fraley's nerves.

"What do you think?" Fraley said, looking at Norcross. He was too tired to listen to Taylor.

"The young kid and the girl are cold as ice," Norcross said. "And did you see that girl's eyes? Freaky."

"I take it they didn't offer to confess."

"The older guy, Boyer, is the softest one," Norcross said. "He's so scared he could barely sign the Miranda waiver."

"But he signed it?"

"Yeah. He was the only one who'd sign."

"Are they high?"

"Who knows."

"Nobody lawyered up?"

"Not yet."

"Did the girl say anything?"

"Not a word. Wouldn't sign the waiver, wouldn't tell me her name. Just stared at me. Made my skin crawl. I'd start with the soft dude."

"Have they brought the young kid's aunt in yet?"

"Yeah, but she's not happy. She keeps harping about his clothes. She says he's cold."

Fraley leaned back and stretched, thinking about the utter futility of what he was about to do. Since he couldn't offer any kind of deal, there was absolutely no reason for any of them to talk to him. What did they have to gain by confessing? Nothing. What did they stand to lose by confessing? Everything. He put his palms on the table and pushed himself up. Pain shot up his lower back from the beginnings of arthritis in his hips.

"Might as well get to it," he said as he moved to the sink and ran cold water over a dishrag. He glanced up at the clock. Nearly an hour had passed since the suspects had been placed in the interrogation rooms.

Fraley closed the door behind him as he walked into the room where Samuel Boyer was sitting. In one hand he held two plastic bags of clothing and the dishrag, in the other a manila folder. Boyer, still clad in the ridiculous looking robe, was sitting with his head down on the table shivering, his cuffed hands clasped in front of him. Fraley tossed the bags of clothing down in front of Boyer.

"Sorry it's so cold in here," Fraley said. "Something's wrong with the heat and we can't get anybody to fix it until morning. I brought you your clothes, but I wasn't sure which set was yours. You can put them on or you can sit there and freeze. Doesn't matter to me."

Boyer looked at the bags and reached for one. Slowly, he pulled on a pair of black jeans. Fraley unlocked Boyer's cuffs briefly so that he could put on a black sweatshirt. He pulled a pair of black boots out of the bag and looked at Fraley as if to ask whether he had permission to put them on.

"Go ahead," Fraley said. "For all I know you might be leaving in a little while."

Boyer pulled on a pair of socks and slid the boots over them.

"There. Feel better?" Fraley said.

Boyer didn't respond. Fraley sat back and watched as Boyer dropped his head back onto the table, into the same position he'd been in when Fraley entered the room. Fraley stood and walked to the door.

"Norcross!"

A moment later, the big man filled the doorway as Fraley sat back down.

"This young man's about to remove his clothes," Fraley said. "Once he does, I need you to put them back in this bag and tag them."

Fraley lifted the empty bag from which Boyer had removed the clothing and the boots. Boyer's head came back up off the table. He looked at Fraley curiously.

"Go on now," Fraley said. "Take everything back off and put your vampire robe back on. I'll let you keep it until we send you down to the jail."

Boyer hesitated, obviously confused.

"Take those clothes off now or I'll have my buddy Glenn here rip them off you!" Fraley yelled as he slammed a fist onto the table.

As Boyer began to remove his boots, Fraley allowed himself a smile. "I appreciate your help," he said to Boyer. "I thought those clothes and those boots were yours, but it might have been hard to prove until you put them on." He turned toward Norcross. "After genius here finishes taking off his clothes, take the other bag in there and do the same thing to the other genius. As soon as he puts the clothes on, make him take them off and turn the heat back up."

As soon as Norcross left the room and closed the door, Fraley tossed the dishrag onto Boyer's forehead.

"Wipe that white mud off your face," Fraley said. "I want to see who I'm talking to."

Boyer reached up with his cuffed hands and removed the rag from his face. He was a skinny kid, nothing but a sack of bones. He stared at Fraley for a second, then tossed the rag onto the table.

"The makeup's coming off," Fraley said. "If you don't do it, I will. If I do it, I promise you won't like it."

Boyer lowered his head back onto the table. Fraley waited thirty seconds. Boyer didn't move.

Fraley rose, picked up the rag with his right hand and grabbed a handful of black hair with his left. He jerked Boyer's head back and slammed it down, face-first. Boyer let out a groan. Fraley jerked Boyer's head up again and began rubbing the rag roughly across his forehead. The greasy makeup smeared, but very little of it came off. Blood began to run from Boyer's left nostril.

Fraley dropped the rag across Boyer's nose and moved back to his seat. "You shouldn't have resisted arrest back at the motel," Fraley said. "You wouldn't have gotten your nose broken."

Fraley opened the manila file and took out some photographs. Two were close-ups of the Beck children after they'd been cleaned up, with grotesque black holes where their right eyes had been shot out. One was a photo of Bjorn Beck with his eye shot out and the "ah satan" message carved into his forehead. Another was Anna Beck. All four photos clearly showed the inverted crosses carved into the necks of the victims.

"A little reminder of what you did," Fraley said as he slid the photos, one by one, across the table.

Boyer, holding the rag to his nose, glanced at the photos and then closed his eyes. Tears were running down his face, lightly streaking the makeup like lines on a road map.

"Look at them or I swear I'll staple your eyelids open," Fraley said.

Boyer opened his eyes and at least appeared to be looking at the photos. His eyes were dark, nearly black, surrounded by pink. Fraley leaned back and folded his arms across his chest.

"We found the guns in the glove compartment of your car," Fraley said calmly. "They're going to match the bullets we found at two murder scenes. Our evidence guys are going through your car with a fine-toothed comb, including the trunk. We think you gave Norman Brockwell a ride out to the woods in the trunk of your car. They're looking for little pieces of his skin, fingernails, saliva, hair, blood, anything they can find. And they'll find plenty, won't they? You know they will. You were too stupid or too high to clean it, weren't you?

"We're going to match the tread on your tires to the tracks we found out there in the woods where you tied Norman Brockwell to a tree and shot him. And those boots you just put on? My guess is they're going to match up to footprints we found at both crime scenes, you pathetic little piece of garbage."

Boyer's eyes had glazed over. He looked stunned. It was exactly what Fraley had been hoping for when he entered the room.

"And how do you think we found you in the first place? We've got a witness. Somebody already gave you up. Game's over for you, Sammy boy. You're going to get the death penalty. The *death penalty*. They're going to strap you into the electric chair and cook you like a Thanksgiving turkey. *If* we can keep you alive long enough. As soon as people around here find out we've arrested the gutless cowards that slaughtered a couple babies, they're going to want blood."

Fraley paused to let the words sink in.

"There's only one way out for you," he said, leaning forward. "Tell me what happened, tell me why it happened, tell me who was there besides you, and I'll tell the district attorney you cooperated. You know how it works. You've been in the system. The first one to the district attorney's office gets the deal."

Boyer's eyes rose to meet Fraley's. He didn't look like a cold-blooded killer. Sitting there with the streaks running through his makeup and his nose swollen and red, he looked like a scared, stupid clown.

Fraley picked up the photo of Bjorn Beck and pointed to the "ah satan" carved into his forehead.

"And just what is this supposed to mean?" Fraley said. "Was this supposed to scare us?"

"What k-k-kind of d-deal w-w-will you g-give me?" Boyer said. They were the first words Fraley had heard him speak.

"Depends on what you have to say." Fraley thought about what Dillard had said in the car. No deals. It didn't matter. It wasn't against the law for cops to lie to suspects during interrogation.

"Wh-where is sh-she?" Boyer said. His eyes moved slowly toward the door, as though he were trying to see through it.

"Who? The redhead? The question is *who* is she?"

"Sh-sh-sh-sh-she …."

"Take it easy," Fraley said. "She what?"

There was a sudden explosion as the fluorescent lights above Fraley shattered behind their plastic coverings. Fraley flinched and found himself on his knees beside the table, gun drawn, the room enveloped in darkness. Boyer let out a bloodcurdling scream.

"*Ahhhhhh! Ahhhhhh! It's her! It's her! She'll kill us! She'll kill us all!*"

The door flew open and Fraley could see the beams of flashlights in the hall.

"You okay in there?" Fraley recognized the voice. It was Norcross. Fraley rose from his crouch by the table and moved to the door. Boyer continued to scream.

"*It's Satan! She has the power of Satan!*"

"Shut up!" Fraley yelled at Boyer. He turned to Norcross. "What happened?"

"Not sure. Power surge or something. Whole building's dark."

"Stay with this guy."

The office was chaotic. Agents were running up and down the hallways, in and out of the front door, shouting commands and asking questions. Fraley moved out of the doorway and down the hall to his office. The agent who had been watching over the redhead was gone. The office was black. Fraley reached into his pocket for his Zippo cigarette lighter. He flipped open the top, flicked the wheel with his thumb, and stepped inside.

He could see her silhouette in the chair. As he moved closer, the lighter went out. He flipped the wheel again. Nothing. Again. It came to life briefly, just long enough for Fraley to see that she was smiling.

Fraley recognized her now. He'd seen her only briefly and she'd been wearing the big hat and the patch over her eye, but it had to be her.

The girl cuffed to the chair was the girl in the park.

TUESDAY, OCT. 7

I spent a sleepless night lying in bed next to Caroline. Her left breast was covered by a large, bloodstained bandage. Another dressing covered a stitched wound and a drain beneath her left arm. The medication she'd been given at the surgery center helped her sleep, but she moaned occasionally and mumbled almost continuously. At four in the morning, I tried to call the TBI office to see if I could find out how the interrogations were going, but a recording told me the number had been temporarily disconnected. I didn't want to call Fraley's cell phone. I knew he'd let me know when, or if, he needed me.

At 5:30 a.m., about forty minutes before sunrise, I gave up the idea of getting any sleep and got up to fix a pot of coffee. I let Rio out and wandered through the kitchen onto the back deck. The eastern sky was just beginning to streak with gray light. A soft breeze was blowing out of the southwest, sending the little blue and orange sailboat wind gauges that Caroline loved so much spinning slowly in circles. It was a time of day that I usually enjoyed, the calmness of the oncoming dawn. Typically, I used the time to contemplate the vastness of the sky, to appreciate the way the light played off the trees across the lake as the sun crept over the hill to the east, or to daydream about sitting in a luxury box at Yankee Stadium or Fenway Park some day, watching Jack play with the big boys.

But this morning I found myself in a dark mood. The murders weighed heavily on my mind, but even more disturbing were the thoughts of what was happening to Caroline. I knew Caroline would fight with every ounce of her strength and I sincerely believed she would survive, but I couldn't stop thinking that cancer would change her in some fundamental way. I imagined her without a breast, and I wondered if she would become somehow inhibited, whether she would lose her confidence or some of her zest for life. I wondered how such a drastic change in her appearance would affect our relationship, and selfishly hoped it wouldn't lessen the intimacy we'd always enjoyed. I thought about the scars she'd soon have, how a reconstructed breast would look, how I'd react to her losing her hair, what it would be like to make love to her.

At the hospital, I'd heard Sarah mention something about how fortunate we were that my new job provided insurance coverage that would pay for Caroline's treatment. From what I'd read, the treatment could cost a quarter of a million dollars, maybe more. I overheard Sarah tell Caroline's mother that God had intervened. It was God who had caused me to go to work for the district attorney's office. It was God who had saved us from financial calamity.

But as I stood on the deck, I didn't appreciate Sarah's reasoning or God's kindness. I would have much preferred He spare Caroline the pain and heartache she was experiencing by falling victim to such a terrible disease. How could the benevolent, loving God that Sarah described allow such a thing to happen to a person so kind, so gentle, so full of love?

Thoughts of God took me back to my grandmother's dining room table in the little house in Unicoi County where she and my grandfather lived with my uncle Raymond, who was then fourteen years old. It was a Sunday afternoon, two years before Raymond raped Sarah. My mother, Sarah, and I had made our weekly trip to my grandparents' house. Sarah and I would play while Ma fixed lunch in the kitchen. A little after noon, the door would open and Grandpa, Grandma, and Raymond, looking scrubbed and wearing their Sunday clothes, would arrive from church. I was six, old enough that I'd begun to wonder why we didn't go to church with them. For some reason, I thought that day would be a good day to ask.

As I sat at the table picking at a piece of fried chicken, I looked up at my mother.

"Ma, how come we don't go to church?" I said.

An expression of horror came over my mother's face and she dropped her fork. It clanged noisily off her plate and fell to the hardwood floor.

"Hush your mouth and eat," she said.

Everyone was quiet for a minute until my grandma spoke.

"Why don't you explain it to him, Elizabeth?" she said to my mother. There was a coldness in her voice I'd never heard. "Why don't you tell the boy why he doesn't go to church? I'd like to know myself."

At the time, I knew very little of my family history, but I knew my father had been killed in a war in a faraway place called Vietnam not long before I was born. Most mothers would probably have described a fallen soldier to their sons as a hero, but not my mother. His death was a "waste," she said. Politicians were to blame, politicians greedy to feed what she called the "war machine." My father didn't want to go to Vietnam. He didn't volunteer to go. He was drafted, forced to leave his home and his pregnant wife to fight a war in which neither he nor his country had any business. My mother was full of bitterness, contempt, and distrust for anyone or anything that might be able to exert power or control over her, including, as I was about to find out, God.

Confronted with my grandma's challenge, my mother turned to her with narrowed eyes.

"You know good and well why he doesn't go to church," she said. "He doesn't go because I don't want him to go. He doesn't go because he's my son, it's my choice, and I choose not to have his head filled with lies and false hope. He doesn't go because there is no God, and if you had the least bit of sense, you'd have realized it by now."

"How dare you!" my grandma yelled, rising from the table. "How dare you blaspheme the Lord in my home!"

I didn't know the definition of "blaspheme," but even at that early age, I was capable of discerning meaning from context. I'd never before heard Grandma raise her voice. She was trembling as she pointed her fork at my mother's face.

"Are you going to raise him to be a godless heathen?" she yelled. "How do you expect him to get through life without faith?"

"He'll get through the same way I do," my mother shot back. "He'll learn to rely on himself."

"Joseph!" Grandma said harshly to me. "Take your sister and go outside. Now! Raymond, you go with them."

I looked at my grandpa, who was sitting there with a bewildered look on his face. He rarely spoke, and it appeared that he had no intention of inserting himself into the battle I'd unintentionally started. I crawled down off the chair and walked outside to the front porch with Sarah and Raymond right behind me. As soon as we walked onto the porch, Raymond shoved me hard in the back and I went sprawling onto the front lawn.

"Moron," he hissed. "Why can't you keep your mouth shut? Now my dinner's gonna get cold."

I picked myself up off the ground and walked out to the barn. I could hear voices coming from inside the house, the voices of my mother and grandmother, shrill and forlorn as the argument raged. Eventually, the voices quieted. An hour later, my mother yelled from beside the car that it was time to go home. I descended the ladder from the hayloft, and as I climbed into the backseat, I could see Ma's face in the rearview mirror and I knew she'd been crying. The following Sunday, we stayed home for lunch. We went back occasionally on Sundays after that, but it was always well after Grandpa and Grandma had arrived home from church, and Grandma always prepared the meal. We never spoke of God again.

A couple years later, Raymond raped Sarah on that Friday night in my grandparents' bed. Less than a year after that, he drowned in the Nolichuckey River. Maybe his death was God's way of punishing him for what he did to Sarah, but I always wondered, if there was a God, why He would have allowed Raymond to rape a nine-year-old girl in the first place.

Around 7:00 a.m., just as the sun was beginning to show itself, the sky streaked with orange and lavender, my cell phone rang. I'd left it inside on the kitchen counter. I hurried inside to answer before it awoke Caroline, and as soon as I picked it up, I saw Fraley's now-familiar cell phone number on the caller ID.

"How'd it go?" I said.

"We need to meet," Fraley said. "I need another search warrant."

TUESDAY, OCT. 7

I told Fraley I'd meet him at a Waffle House near Boones Creek and went in to check on Caroline. She was so sore I had to help her to the bathroom and back to bed. Lilly was getting ready to drive back to Knoxville to school, and Jack was packing up for his trip back to Nashville. Once I got Caroline settled, I went upstairs to Lilly's room. She was already dressed, standing in front of the mirror by her dresser applying lipstick.

"Can you take another day off?" I said. "I have to go to work and I don't want to leave your mom here alone."

"Are you asking if I want to sleep in?" she said. "Are you asking if I'd mind not driving to Knoxville and going to class? Would I like to stay here and not have to eat in the cafeteria for another day? Sounds awful."

"Good. You're the designated nurse. Her pain medication is in the cupboard above the microwave. Two every four hours. I just gave her a couple, so she'll be due again around eleven."

Lilly grinned. "I guess this means I'll have to go down and get in bed with her."

I stopped by Jack's room to say goodbye. He'd spent the entire summer on the road playing baseball and had been in college for over a year, but it still broke my heart to see him go.

"Thanks for coming," I said as I hugged his neck. "It means a lot to both of us to have you around."

"Are you going to be able to handle all of this?" he said. "Can you juggle the work and everything?"

"Lilly's going to stay one more day, but after that, I'll be fine."

"All you have to do is call. I'll take a semester off if I have to."

"I love you," I said. "Have a safe trip."

The restaurant was less crowded than I expected, so Fraley and I were able to get a booth in the corner.

"I've seen corpses that look better than you," I said as soon as he sat down.

"You ain't exactly Miss America yourself." The waitress set a pot of coffee down in front of us, and we both ordered breakfast. Fraley, ever the picture of health, ordered four eggs over easy, sausage, bacon, hash browns with cheese, and four pieces of toast.

"So what's going on?" I said after the waitress left.

"The raid went fine. Took them down quick and got them out of there. We interrupted some kind of ritual or something. They were wearing robes with nothing on underneath, and the guys were bleeding from fresh razor cuts on their arms. There was a silver chalice with blood in it in the middle of the floor. I guess they were bleeding into the cup. They had candles all over the place. It looked like maybe they were getting ready to drink the blood or something."

"Vampires?"

"I'm not sure. Probably some kind of satanic ritual. I'll have to study up on it. We found two nine-millimeter pistols in the car, both stolen during a burglary back in July. All our lab people came in at five this morning down in Knoxville just to work this case. One of the ballistics guys has already matched several of the bullets we found at both scenes with the guns."

"That's fantastic," I said. "Looks like we've got our murderers."

"It gets better, and it gets worse. There were two pairs of boots and a pair of shoes in the motel room. The boot prints match up to prints at both scenes. They belong to the boys."

"Great. What about DNA?" I said. "Anything in the car?"

"They're running the tests," Fraley said. "It'll take a while longer, but I don't have much doubt they're going to find traces of Brockwell's DNA in the car. My main concern now is the girl."

Fraley filled me in on the details of the preceding night: the familiar-looking redhead who'd been arrested in the motel room; her cold, calculating demeanor; the interview with Boyer and the chaotic scene just as Fraley thought Boyer was about to break down and confess; Fraley's realization that the girl they had in custody looked just like the girl we'd talked to in the park.

"It took me a while to figure it out," Fraley said. "I went back to the juvenile records. You said the girl in the park's name was Alisha Elizabeth Davis. Like I told you before, Alisha Elizabeth Davis was reported missing by her foster parents a couple weeks ago. They said she woke up screaming the night the Brockwells were murdered, and she went missing the next day."

"Why was she in foster care in the first place?"

"Because her sister stabbed her."

"That's strange," I said. "Why did they take her out of the home instead of putting the sister in jail?"

"Because the sister's crazy," Fraley said. "The foster parents told the agents that the sister has some serious mental problems. She's already been in a mental institution, and for some reason the mother didn't want her to go back. So they put Alisha in foster care, I guess to keep her from getting hurt again. From what the foster parents said, Alisha's a great kid. They said she volunteers at the Salvation Army's homeless shelter and at the pediatric cancer ward at the hospital. She graduated near the top of her class in high school and is working her way through college now. She sells paintings and drawings and makes pottery in a little shop in back of their house and sells it at craft shows. They said she was happy there."

"So what does this have to do with the girl in custody?" I said.

"She's the sister," Fraley said. "The crazy sister. I went back into the records and took a closer look. Her name is Natasha Marie Davis. She's Alisha's identical twin."

I sat back and let it sink in for a minute. An identical twin. *The girl in the park has an identical twin? And she was trying to tell me that her twin sister is killing people?* I suddenly made a connection.

"You say the girl in the park was stabbed by her sister?" I said.

"That's right."

"She wore a patch over her eye. Was she stabbed in the eye?"

"In the eye."

"The patch was over the right eye, wasn't it?"

"You're catching on."

"Any idea what she used to stab her?"

"Ice pick."

"Tell me we have something that links Natasha to the murders."

"Not a thing. That's why I need the warrant. We're going to look for an ice pick, along with anything else we might run across."

"Where are you going to search?"

"Her mother's house. That's where she lives."

"I'm going with you."

"She has an inverted cross tattooed on her neck," Fraley said. "I saw it just before I left. And there's something else." He reached over and picked up a napkin and set it down on the table in front of him. He took a pen out of his pocket, scrawled something on it, and shoved it toward me. I looked down at the napkin. On it Fraley had written the same letters that had been carved into the foreheads of Bjorn Beck and Norman Brockwell – "ah satan."

"What about it?" I said.

"Write it out," Fraley said. "Backward."

TUESDAY, OCT. 7

our hours later, after I'd drafted yet another warrant application and gotten it signed by Judge Rogers, Fraley and I climbed the front porch steps of a small frame house in what was known as the Red Row section of Johnson City. It was an impoverished neighborhood in the southeast part of the city that bordered a massive "environmental center," what used to be called a land-fill and before that a dump. A small sign on the front door informed visitors that "A Christian Lives Here." Underneath the sentence, in ink, someone had printed, very neatly, "And a Witch."

I winced when I saw the woman who opened the door. She was tall and looked to be around sixty years old, although the information we had on her put her age at forty-seven. The skin on her face was sagging and had the faded yellow look of an old newspaper. Her unruly hair was a peculiar shade of red, and her eyes were covered by opaque glasses so thick that she appeared to be wearing goggles. She was wearing a full-length, flowered robe that made her body shapeless.

"Marie Davis?" I heard Fraley say.

"Yes."

Fraley produced an ID and introduced us. Four more agents stood at the bottom of the porch, waiting.

"We have a warrant to search your home," Fraley said, "and we need to speak to you about Natasha."

She sighed, muttered something under her breath, and moved away from the door.

Fraley motioned to the other agents to walk around the house, and he and I walked in. She led us to the kitchen table and motioned for us to sit down. As she walked to the counter and retrieved a pack of cigarettes and an ashtray, I looked around. The tiny den was a Christian shrine. An oversized King James Bible nearly covered the coffee table in front of the couch, and there were angels on every shelf, atop the television, and in every nook and cranny in the room. There were wooden angels, ceramic angels, plastic angels, brass angels, all different sizes. They gave the room the tacky look of a roadside flea market.

A large crucifix, at least three feet tall, dominated the paneled wall opposite the front door. On the wall to my left was a print of Da Vinci's *The Last Supper*. But it was the large print on the far wall that caught my attention. It depicted an eyeball atop a pyramid. The all-seeing eye of Providence.

"Is she dead?" Marie said as she sat down across from Fraley. The way she said it sounded almost hopeful. I watched her light a cigarette. Her teeth were the same color as her skin and as unruly as her hair.

"No ma'am," Fraley said. "She's fine. She's down at my office. We picked her up last night at a motel in Johnson City."

Marie stared off toward the living room for a long moment. She looked like she'd gone into coma without closing her eyes.

"Ms. Davis, are you all right?" Fraley said.

Smoke rose up in a spiral from the end of her cigarette. She had the slow mannerisms and defeated look of an addict. The house was dirty and poorly lighted. The carpet in the den was stained and matted. The linoleum floor beneath my feet was sticky, and a sour, musty odor hung in the air.

The sound of dogs barking and snarling suddenly came reverberating through the house from the backyard.

"Jesus!" Fraley said as he rose from the table, "Are they loose?"

"They're penned up," Marie said, "and I'd appreciate it if you wouldn't use the Lord's name in vain in my home."

Fraley stepped through the kitchen to a back door and opened it. The other two agents walked in, both looking a little pale. "Dobermans," I heard one of them mutter. "I hate Dobermans. My neighbor had one when I was a kid and it almost killed me."

"What can you tell us about Natasha?" Fraley said after he returned to his seat at the table.

Her expression turned hard and she looked away.

"I got nothing to say about Natasha," she said.

"Can you at least tell me why you won't talk to us about her?" Fraley said.

She blew out a lung full of smoke and turned back toward Fraley. The hand that held her cigarette had started to tremble.

"I reckon you'll find out soon enough," she said.

"What about your other daughter?" Fraley said. "What can you tell us about Alisha?"

"Can't say nothing about her either."

"Why not?" Fraley said. "Why won't you tell us anything about your daughters?"

"I'm gonna go in and sit in my chair," she said. "Y'all got no idea what you're getting into by coming here."

She got up from the table and began to walk stiffly to the den. When she reached the recliner, she sat down and picked up a remote control from the arm of the chair. She pointed it at the television and flipped it on. A televangelist wearing a bushy gray toupee was pointing back at her from his pulpit, warning her about the wages of sin.

"Ms. Davis," Fraley said, following her into the room. "This warrant says we can search your home, but you could make things easier on both of us. Do you know if there's an ice pick anywhere in the house?"

She responded by turning the volume up on the television.

"Fine," Fraley said. "We'll do it the hard way." He snatched the remote out of her hand and turned the television off. "Where's Natasha's room?" he said.

"Right down the hall," Marie said. "I don't go in there myself."

"Go check it out," Fraley said to me. "You guys go ahead and get started."

I walked through the den and into the dim hallway. About ten feet down the hall on the left was a door, painted black. I reached for the doorknob but hesitated, not wanting to go in the room alone. I could hear commotion coming from the kitchen as the agents began their search. I walked back to the edge of the den and waited for Fraley.

"What's wrong?" he said as he pushed past me into the hallway. "Scared of the dark?"

"I don't know," I said. "For some reason I like feel like I'm about to walk through the gates of hell, and I think I'd like some company."

Fraley turned the knob and opened the door. It was pitch black inside the room. Fraley started feeling along the wall for a light switch, found it, and flipped it on.

I stepped inside and looked around. The room wasn't much bigger than a prison cell, with a closet that ran the length of the wall to my right. At first glance, it looked like nothing special. I thought we'd find candles and pentagrams and inverted crosses. Instead, the room was just dirty, with clothing strewn all over the place.

A mirror over a small dresser caught my eye. I stepped toward it. Scrawled on the mirror in what looked like blood were the words "ah sataN." Beneath it was the phrase, "Hell is for children."

There was a stack of books on a table by the bed. Fraley picked up the book on the top, looked at the cover, then dropped it as though it burned him.

"What is it?" I said.

"*The Satanic Bible,*" he said. Fraley picked up another book and showed it to me, *Helter Skelter.* A third was *The Art of Black Magic.* "What kind of freak reads this stuff?"

"Did you see the print hanging in the den?" I said. "The one with the eye?"

"Yeah. What about it?"

"Do you know what that symbol is?"

"Enlighten me."

"It's on the back of paper currency. It represents the all-seeing eye of Providence. It may not mean anything, but all our victims were shot or stabbed in the eye. Do you see what I'm getting at?"

"We'll take it with us, along with the books and the mirror," Fraley said. "Let's finish up and get out of here. This place gives me the creeps."

Three hours later, Fraley and I stood inside a room in the TBI office that was used to monitor interrogations. Natasha had been moved from Fraley's office to the interrogation room while we searched her house. Sam Boyer had been taken to the county jail in Jonesborough while Levi Barnett was transported to the juvenile detention center in Johnson City. We could see Natasha on a video monitor, rocking slowly back and forth in her chair.

The agents had removed the mirror from Natasha's room, the print of the Eye of Providence from the den, and searched every inch of the house. We bagged the literature. We found some prescription drugs in a dresser upstairs in Marie's bedroom, but we didn't find an ice pick or any shoes that matched the smaller footprints found near the tree where Norman Brockwell was found. Outside the symbols, we had nothing concrete to tie Natasha to the murders. There was some circumstantial evidence—the fact that "ah satan" was Natasha spelled backward and the inverted cross tattoo on her neck—but I still had no way of proving Natasha was at either of the crime scenes.

"It looks like our only hope is if she confesses or if one of the others turns on her," I said to Fraley.

"She's not going to confess," Fraley said. "She wouldn't say a single word to me."

"Maybe you should take another crack at her," I said.

I sat down at the video monitor and watched while Fraley made another futile attempt to question Natasha. She refused to speak or acknowledge him in any way. She simply stared down at the table, unblinking, the hood of the robe pulled over her head. Fraley cajoled her and pleaded with her, then threatened her. Finally, he resorted to insults. He tried every tactic he knew, but he might as well have been talking to a flat rock. She didn't even look at him.

After nearly an hour of talking to himself, Fraley stood and walked out of the room. Natasha remained frozen.

"What are we going to do with her?" Fraley said, a look of defeat and disgust on his face.

"We don't have a choice," I said. "We don't have enough to hold her. We have to let her go."

TUESDAY, OCT. 14

There was an outrage in the community I'd never encountered. Word quickly got out that arrests had been made. By the time Fraley's agents took Sam Boyer to the county jail for booking, an angry mob had formed near the sally port. I watched the report on the news that night as they chanted "baby killer" at him and screamed insults. Some of them threw objects—the reporters said they were throwing baby rattles and teddy bears—as the agents took Boyer out of the van, covered him with their bodies to protect him, and shuffled him quickly into the jail.

Everywhere I went, I was accosted by people I didn't know. At the grocery store, at the post office, in the hallways at the courthouse, people would thank me for helping to finally arrest those who had been terrorizing the community. "Kill them all," they would whisper, "fry them." They thirsted for blood, for vicarious satisfaction, and I was the designated henchman.

I couldn't help wondering how Boyer felt, and whether the mob mentality might work to our advantage somehow. The other suspect, Levi Barnett, was transported to the juvenile detention center and was spared the mob scene. Natasha was released, though she was under twenty-four-hour surveillance, leaving Boyer the focal point of the hatred of an entire community.

We convened a special session of the county grand jury, and based on the evidence I presented, they indicted Boyer and Barnett for six counts of first-degree murder, five counts of especially aggravated kidnapping—one each for the Becks and Norman Brockwell—one count of felony theft for stealing the Becks' van, and one count of especially aggravated burglary for breaking into the Brockwells' home. I drafted the statutory notice that informed Boyer and his lawyers that the state was seeking the death penalty. I had plenty of evidence against the boys—Fraley and his companions had done an excellent job—but I was still uneasy about whether the arrest and search warrants would hold up once the defense lawyers found out about Alisha. I didn't offer to present her as a witness in front of the grand jury; I simply referred to her as a confidential informant. She was still nowhere to be found.

Since Levi Barnett was a juvenile, we couldn't seek the death penalty against him. Tennessee's death-penalty statute was indiscriminate when it came to matters of race, creed, or religion, but it drew the line at killing juveniles. In Tennessee, you had to be eighteen years old to vote, to buy cigarettes, and to get yourself killed by the state.

Boyer was arraigned via satellite three days after his arrest and interrogation. Judge Ivan Glass appeared on a television screen at the jail and informed Boyer of the charges against him and his rights. He also appointed

James T. Beaumont III to represent him, the same lawyer who had represented Billy Dockery a couple months earlier.

Levi Barnett was a little more complicated. Before we could get him into court to try him as an adult, we had to convince the juvenile court judge to transfer him to the jurisdiction of the adult criminal court. It wasn't much more than a formality, but the judge was vacationing in Italy and couldn't conduct the hearing for three weeks. We reached the judge by phone at his motel in Venice and asked permission to bring in a substitute judge, but true to form for a judge, he refused to give up his fifteen minutes of fame.

I spent the next week fending off the media, organizing as much evidence as I could, and preparing for the William Trent trial. Despite the fact that both Fraley and I told Lee Mooney we believed Natasha Davis was directly involved in the Beck and Brockwell murders, the extra TBI agents had been ordered to return to their respective assignments around the state. That left Fraley shorthanded, and after a week of men staring at the house on Red Row and seeing nothing, the surveillance on Natasha had been discontinued.

On Tuesday morning, the fourteenth of October, I got to the office at six and went back over my notes and strategy for the Trent trial. At eight, I looked up to see Lee Mooney standing in my doorway, sipping on a cup of tea.

"Are you ready for this?" Mooney said.

"As ready as I can be."

"Are you going to win?"

"Who knows? Depends on the jury, you know that."

"Why haven't you made a deal?"

"Because the only deal Snodgrass will accept is a slap on the wrist. No jail time, expungement, no supervised probation. I'm surprised he didn't ask for a public apology from the DA's office."

"This is important, Joe. Don't screw it up."

He turned and disappeared without saying another word, and I sat there wondering what would happen if my plan backfired and I lost the case. About fifteen minutes later, Cody Masters showed up, accompanied by our two star witnesses, Alice Dickson and Rosalie Harbin.

Alice Dickson was an attractive, introverted nineteen-year-old who'd grown up in a small trailer that perched precariously on a hillside in the Lamar community in the south end of Washington County. I'd visited the trailer and spoken to Alice's aunt while preparing for the trial. Alice had been born to a teenager named Tara Dickson back in the late eighties. Alice's mother was neither willing nor able to care for an infant, and when Alice was three months old, her mother wrapped her in a blanket, put her in a bushel basket, and left her on Jeanine Taylor's tiny front porch in the middle of the night. Jeanine was Tara's older sister. No one had seen or heard from Tara since. When I asked about Alice's father, Jeanine just shook her head. She had no idea who the father was.

Jeanine already had two small children of her own. Her husband worked at a factory in Johnson City earning just above the minimum wage, and Jeanine worked at a convenience store. They barely got by. When Alice was thirteen, Jeanine's husband, a hard drinker named Rocky Taylor, began to molest her. Alice immediately told Jeanine, who refused to believe her. But within a week, the molestation escalated to rape. When Rocky, in a drunken stupor, followed Alice into the bathroom late one Friday night, Jeanine caught him in the act. She gave him the choice of hitting the road or going to jail. Rocky chose the road, leaving Jeanine to raise three children alone.

The other girl, Rosalie Harbin, was nothing short of a hellion. Dark-haired, dark-eyed, flirty, she'd been raised by her Mexican mother and marijuana-dealing father about two miles from where Alice grew up. She'd been in trouble for various petty offenses—mostly thefts—since she was twelve. By the time she turned eighteen, she'd added forgery to her growing repertoire of illegal skills.

The girls met on the school bus, and though they were polar opposites, they'd been friends since they were six years old. It was Rosalie who'd heard from one of her other friends about the unusual circumstances at William Trent's pizza place, and it had been Rosalie who'd encouraged her friend Alice to go with her and apply for a job. Alice, who was desperately poor and barely over fifteen, had traded in her morals for the opportunity to make ten dollars an hour. Rosalie was the same age, but I got the impression that she would have done it for free.

"Now, remember what I told you," I said as we got up to leave for the courtroom. "Just tell your stories. When Snodgrass comes after you, stay calm. He's going to insult you, he's going to accuse you of being liars. Rosalie, he's going to bring up every theft and forgery charge that the judge will let him get away with. His entire strategy is to make both of you look like you're not credible witnesses, and that's exactly what I want him to do."

I turned to Alice. Her strawberry-blonde hair was shimmering, her blue eyes were clear. She'd worn a conservative, high-necked blue dress and looked like a young girl on her way to church. It was precisely the look I'd hoped for.

"Are you ready for this?" I said.

She nodded.

"Do you have it in your purse?"

"Yes."

"Don't mention it until I ask you about it. It won't be until after Snodgrass cross-examines you."

"Okay."

"Let's do it."

Four hours later, we'd picked a jury, broken for lunch, and were ready to start the trial. There were three newspaper reporters and two television crews in the gallery. The only other people in the courtroom were William Trent's wife and mother. Cody Masters was sitting at the prosecution table next to me while Trent and Joe Snodgrass sat at the defense table dressed in dark blue suits. Trent was a slight man, around five feet eight inches and skinny, with receding sandy-blonde hair and expressionless brown eyes. He was chewing his fingernails as I walked into the room.

The judge was Brooks Langley, a skin-headed, seventy-year-old retiree who was sitting in because both the regular criminal court judges had accepted campaign contributions from William Trent. I'd dealt with Judge Langley through a couple motion hearings and was impressed with both his knowledge of the legal issues and the way he ran his courtroom. I didn't think Snodgrass would be able to get away with much grandstanding.

The jury consisted of seven women and five men. All but one of the men had daughters, and all but two of the women were mothers. In picking the jury, I wanted to be sure I stacked it with as many women as possible. I intended to remind them what it was like to be fifteen.

During the initial questioning of the jurors, Snodgrass had strongly hinted that his client was falsely accused by two conniving former employees who became angry when they were fired for poor work performance and insolence. He intimated that the girls were planning to file a civil suit if Trent was convicted. It was the first time I'd heard that allegation.

The judge handed me the indictment, and I read it out loud to the jury. It charged William Trent with ten separate counts of sexual abuse by an authority figure. Mooney had framed the indictment so that I had to prove only five dates that the sexual abuse occurred. On all five of those dates, both Alice Dickson and Rosalie Harbin claimed that they had "threesome" sex with Trent. I was impressed with the way Mooney did it because it meant that each girl could corroborate what the other was saying on the witness stand.

As soon as I finished reading the indictment, Judge Langley asked me whether I wanted to make an opening statement.

"I'll defer to Mr. Snodgrass," I said.

Surprised, Snodgrass grunted and stood up. He'd cleaned up a little for the show. His hair wasn't greasy and his shirt wasn't wrinkled, but he still reminded me of Jabba the Hut. Snodgrass spent the next thirty minutes telling the jurors—in his uniquely bellicose way—what a wonderful human being his client was and that a terrible miscarriage of justice was being perpetrated on Mr. Trent by an unreasonable, even cruel, system. When he was finished, I walked over in front of the jury, spread my feet, clasped my hands behind my back, and looked them straight in the eye.

"This isn't going to take long," I said. "We don't have any physical evidence to present to you. I wish we did, but we don't. All we have is a story to tell you, and the story will make your skin crawl."

I turned slowly and pointed my finger at Trent.

"That man sitting right there, that perverted man, used his supervisory power and authority—power that he held by virtue of being an employer—to satisfy his own selfish sexual needs. He took advantage of his employees' youth and station in life, and he abused them over a long period of time in the most shameful of ways. When you've heard this story, and you've heard his pathetic denials and excuses for why he's being falsely accused, you'll come to the same conclusion that I have. He's guilty. He's guilty as sin."

I turned and walked over to the podium.

"Are you ready to proceed?" Judge Langley said.

"I am."

"Call your first witness."

"The state calls Alice Dickson."

Masters looked at me curiously from his seat at the prosecution table and mouthed the words: "What are you doing?"

My original plan had been to put Masters on the stand first to tell the jury how the investigation came about and then to follow him with Rosalie Harbin and then finish with Alice. It's the standard in trial work. You start slowly and then build to a climactic finish. But the more I thought about it, the more I became convinced that I'd call only one witness in this trial, and that witness was Alice Dickson. I knew Snodgrass would make Cody Masters look like an idiot on cross-examination. He'd referred to him as Barney Fife during his opening statement just like he did in my office a couple weeks earlier. I didn't want to give Snodgrass the opportunity to take the focus of the trial away from the real issue, which was whether his client was a pervert and had been sexually abusing underage girls for years.

I'd also decided not to put Rosalie Harbin on the witness stand. Rosalie oozed sexuality. She was also unpredictable and often flippant. I believed Rosalie would anger the women and make the men think she probably got what she asked for. She also had a habit of committing crimes of moral turpitude, things like theft and forgery, and it was entirely possible that the jury would dislike her so much that they'd acquit Trent on every count, no matter how convincing Alice might be.

So Alice was it. All or nothing. A multiple-count felony case with only one witness.

I'd never heard of anyone trying anything like it before.

TUESDAY, OCT. 14

Alice walked in with her eyes to the ground and slowly climbed onto the witness stand. Her hair was shoulder-length, her skin smooth and cream-colored. She looked frightened, and as I led her through the routine preliminary questions, her voice was trembling. But when we got down to it, she sat up straight and started talking directly to the jurors. I started at the beginning, questioning her about her life, how she'd been abandoned by her mother and had no idea who her father was, and how she'd grown up impoverished in a small, one-bathroom trailer occupied by five people. I asked her about the sexual abuse at the hands of her uncle, and she told the jury, in a moving moment, that she blamed herself for her aunt losing her husband. After twenty minutes or so, we got down to business.

"Do you know the defendant, William Trent?" I said.

"Yes."

"And would you point him out, please?"

She looked right at him and held out her hand. It wasn't shaking. "That's him, in the blue suit."

"Let the record show the witness has identified the defendant," Judge Langley said.

"Miss Dickson," I said, "would you tell the jury how you came to know Mr. Trent?"

"My girlfriend Rosalie and I went to his restaurant and applied for a job."

"How long ago was that?"

"Four years ago. I was fifteen."

"The indictment in this case alleges that William Trent used his supervisory power and authority over you to sexually abuse you. Did that happen?"

"Yes. Many times."

"Would you please tell the jury in your own words what happened?"

She began to speak, and for the next half hour she recounted the same tale that she'd told Cody Masters two years earlier. She described in explicit detail the mole on the head of William Trent's penis and the small tattoo of a pitchfork-wielding devil on the left cheek of his butt. She recalled the size of his penis as being "about the same as one of those Oscar Meyer wieners, maybe a little shorter. It wasn't very big."

She described the pornography, the lingerie parties, the liquor in the small refrigerator behind the counter. I didn't ask her about the drugs because she told me she never used any drugs. Rosalie was the one that liked the drugs.

Alice then went into Trent's sexual habits, his fetishes, his refusal to use a condom, and his insistence that the girls use birth control. She described his preference for having sex in places like the walk-in cooler. Snodgrass tried to object, saying that she couldn't testify to anything that wasn't alleged in the indictment, but after a short hearing outside the jury's presence, the judge ruled that the testimony could be used to prove a pattern of conduct and he let it in.

I ended the direct examination by asking her about the exact dates on which both she and Rosalie had sex with Trent and had her describe the events in detail. She was obviously embarrassed by what she'd done, but she also came across as contrite, apologizing repeatedly to the jury and saying, "I'm so ashamed."

When she was finished, I glanced at the jury. Three of the women were in tears, and a couple of the men looked like they wanted to jump over the railing and kill Trent. I could hear Snodgrass wheezing. He pushed himself up from the table and lumbered to the podium.

"That's quite a memory you have there, Miss Dickson," he said. She didn't respond. "Since you have such a fine memory, especially when it comes to your sex life, how about recalling for the jury your other sexual experiences."

Judge Langley looked at me, waiting for an objection, but I kept my mouth shut. The question was improper, but I already knew the answer, and I knew Snodgrass wouldn't like it.

"I haven't had any other sexual experiences," Alice said softly.

"I beg your pardon? Are you telling this jury that you've never had sex?"

"No, I'm not saying that," she said. "I've had sex with your client and my uncle raped me. That's all."

"Come on, Miss Dickson," Snodgrass said sarcastically. "Surely you don't expect this jury to believe that you would engage in what you've described as kinky, consensual sex with a man more than twice your age on a regular basis and not be sexually active otherwise. Are you saving yourself for marriage?"

Alice dropped her head and closed her eyes for a minute. I saw her shoulders rise as she took a deep breath. When she opened her eyes, a tear was running down her left cheek.

"I don't think I'll ever be married," she said. "No one would want me after what he did to me, after what I did with him. I feel ... I feel ... dirty."

She covered her face with her hands and began to sob quietly, and I felt a lump in my throat. After a half minute had passed, Judge Langley reached down and offered her a tissue.

Snodgrass had stepped in it. I looked over at the jurors and could tell that even the men were moved by the testimony. Alice was coming across as sincere, and I didn't think there was anything Snodgrass could do. He stood mute at the podium, waiting for Alice to regain her composure. When she stopped crying and looked at him, he went on the attack.

"I'm not even going to get into the specifics of these allegations with you because, frankly, I find them utterly preposterous," Snodgrass said. "So let's talk about the truth. The truth is that you don't have anything to prove that you ever had sex with my client besides you and your friend's word, do you, Miss Dickson?" he barked.

"I guess not," she said.

"The truth is that you don't have any of Mr. Trent's DNA to back up your claims, do you?"

"No. I don't."

"No pictures?"

"No."

"No video or audio tape?"

"No."

"No sex toys with Mr. Trent's fingerprints on them?

"No."

"No witnesses other than your friend Miss Harbin?"

"No."

"How many people would you estimate worked for Mr. Trent during the two years that you were there?"

"I don't know. People came and went some. Twelve, thirteen, maybe a few more," Alice said.

"And none of those people ever witnessed any of things you're claiming, did they?"

"Yes, they did. They just don't want to get involved."

"Don't want to get involved? They don't want to help put what you claim is a sex maniac who takes advantage of young girls behind bars? I find that hard to believe, Miss Dickson."

"I think they're ashamed. Like me."

"The truth is you didn't report this conduct until after Mr. Trent fired you, isn't that correct?"

"I needed the job. I needed the money."

"Are you saying that you couldn't have found a job where your employer didn't require you to have sex?"

"He paid us twice what anyone else would have paid. I couldn't have found a job making ten dollars an hour."

"So for two years, you allowed yourself to be sexually abused and you never told a soul. Did you tell your aunt?"

"I didn't tell anyone."

"You say you were raped by your uncle. Did you tell anyone about that?"

"I told my aunt. She kicked him out and divorced him."

"Did you tell her immediately?"

"Yes."

"Didn't wait two years?"

"No."

"So you tell your aunt immediately that your uncle raped you but then you allow yourself to be sexually abused for two years and don't say a word. Is what you want us to believe?"

"Objection," I said. "Asked and answered."

"Sustained," Judge Langley said. "Move along to something else, Mr. Snodgrass."

"Let's get back to the truth, Miss Dickson," Snodgrass said. "The truth is that you worked for two years for a man who paid you well and treated you with respect, isn't that right?"

"He paid me well," Alice said.

"The truth is that after you turned seventeen, you started using drugs with your friend Rosalie and your behavior became erratic, isn't that right?"

I stood again. "I object, Judge. There's absolutely no evidence that she ever used drugs. There's no foundation for the question."

"Sustained."

"The truth is that you started showing up late for work, when you bothered to show up at all, isn't it, Miss Dickson?"

"No, that isn't true."

"The truth is that Mr. Trent gave you several chances to conform your behavior, but he finally was forced to terminate your employment, isn't that right?"

"No. That isn't true."

"And the truth is that when Mr. Trent terminated you and Miss Harbin, the two of you concocted this story in order to exact revenge on Mr. Trent, isn't it? And if your little scheme works, you plan to file a civil suit against Mr. Trent, don't you?"

"I don't even know what that means," she said.

Snodgrass banged his fist down on the podium and bellowed at her. "The truth is that you're a liar! And so is your friend. Isn't that right?"

Alice looked down at her hands and shook her head slowly.

"Isn't that right, Miss Dickson?"

"No," she said quietly.

"That's all I have for this ... for this ... tart," Snodgrass said dramatically as he turned his back on the witness stand and plodded to the defense table.

I was anxious to get up and start the redirect. Snodgrass's attack had been passionate, and I didn't want to give the jurors much time to let it sink in. Finally, after a couple minutes, Judge Langley looked up from the notes he'd been taking.

"Redirect, Mr. Dillard?" he said.

"Absolutely," I said as I stood and walked back up to the podium. It was time to spring the trap.

"Miss Dickson," I said, "Mr. Snodgrass mentioned that you seem to have a very clear memory of the things that happened between you and Mr. Trent. Is there any particular reason why your memories are so vivid?"

"Yes," she said, "there's a good reason."

"And what is it?"

"I wrote it all down."

"Do you mean you kept a diary?"

"Yes," she said.

Snodgrass got to his feet as quickly as his mass would allow.

"Your Honor, I absolutely object to any mention of a diary. A diary is hearsay, it's an out-of-court statement, and it doesn't fall under any of the hearsay exceptions."

"Mr. Dillard?" the judge said.

"That would be true if I'd tried to use the diary during my direct examination," I said, "but Mr. Snodgrass opened the door to the diary when he saw fit to accuse Miss Dickson of concocting a story and called her a liar. The diary becomes admissible as a prior consistent statement, and I can use it to rehabilitate my witness."

"We had no notice of any diary!" Snodgrass yelled.

"That's because I wasn't planning to use it unless he attacked her credibility, and that's exactly what he did."

"He's withheld evidence from us, Judge! He has an obligation to allow us to inspect any evidence in his possession, and he knows it. This case should be dismissed, Mr. Dillard should be held in contempt, and the court should immediately file a complaint against him with the Board of Professional Responsibility."

"Judge," I said, "I knew of the diary's existence, but it wasn't in my possession because I knew it was inadmissible. I asked Miss Dickson to bring it along with her today in case Mr. Snodgrass challenged her credibility. She has a written record of everything that happened to her, and it will corroborate perfectly everything she said here today."

Judge Langley leaned forward and glared down at Snodgrass. "He's right, Mr. Snodgrass, and unless you've been hiding in a cave for the last several years, you should know it. The relevant parts of the diary are admissible. I'll take it back into chambers and determine which parts are relevant and which parts aren't. Court's in recess."

As soon as the jury filed out, Snodgrass and Trent disappeared into an anteroom. Because I'd practiced criminal defense for so long, I had a good idea of what the conversation would be like. Snodgrass was undoubtedly telling his client that his goose was about to be cooked, and that he'd better start living in the real world and accept some kind of deal. Otherwise, it was entirely possible that he'd spend much of the remainder of his life in jail.

Ten minutes after Judge Langley recessed court, a bailiff came up behind me and tapped me on the shoulder.

"Judge wants to see you and the defense lawyer in chambers," he said.

I walked back to the judge's office. Langley was sitting behind the desk with the diary open in front of him. He looked up as I walked in.

"Where's Mr. Snodgrass?" he said.

"Counseling with his client, I think."

"That was a dirty trick you pulled, Mr. Dillard," he said.

"I know."

He smiled and looked back down at the diary. I heard the door open, and Snodgrass walked in. The wheezing was a little louder than it had been earlier.

"You can't let this in, Judge," he said. "It's a reversible error. It'll wind up right back in your lap."

"Spare me the melodramatics, Mr. Snodgrass," the judge said. "Listen to this."

Judge Langley picked the diary up off the table and began to read.

"I got my first paycheck today. Bill made me do oral sex on him in the bathroom before he would give it to me. He shot his stuff all over my face. He is really sick. I wish I could quit but we need the money so bad so I just try to imagine that I am floating on a cloud until it is over. I made over four hundred dollars. I gave half of it to Jeanine to help with food and rent and I am saving the rest. I need to get a car as soon as I can so Jeanine will not have to pick me up every day. I should have enough by the time I am old enough to get my license."

He set the diary back down on the table and looked at Snodgrass.

"Are you sure you want to continue this?" he said. "If the jury convicts him, and I have no doubt they will, he'll be looking at a minimum of thirty years. Even if they don't convict on the counts involving the second girl, I'll max him out. That child was the same age as my granddaughter when he got a hold of her. This is one of the most disgusting things I've ever seen."

Snodgrass seemed to deflate. His giant head turned slowly toward me.

"If you'd told me about the diary in the first place, we could have made a deal and finished this," he growled. "How much time do you think he deserves for dipping his wick in a willing teenager?"

"Ten years if he serves it flat," I said. "Fifteen if he wants to take his chances with the parole board."

He turned and started shuffling slowly toward the door, his huge, rounded shoulders slumping forward, the soles of his shoes making a swooshing sound as he dragged them across the carpet. When he got to the door, he turned and glared at me again.

"I'll sell it to him," he said, "but don't you think for one second that I'm going to forget what you did to me today. Somewhere down the road, I'll find a way to even the score."

WEDNESDAY, OCT. 29

The transfer hearing in juvenile court for Levi Barnett was straightforward and uneventful. Fraley and a couple TBI lab experts took the witness stand and laid out the evidence we had against him—his shoes perfectly matched footprints left at both crime scenes and his fingerprints were on both of the guns found in Boyer's glove compartment as well as on the steering wheel of the Becks' van. Fraley had sent the prints from the van to AFIS early on, but Barnett's prints hadn't made it into the system. The judge, after a short speech, surrendered jurisdiction to the adult court. Barnett, swarthy, stocky, acne-scarred and dressed in a pair of jail-issued orange coveralls, sat stoically through the hearing. He didn't utter a sound, not even to his court-appointed lawyer.

The following Wednesday, Boyer and Barnett were scheduled for their first public appearance in criminal court. Barnett was to be arraigned again, this time as an adult, the judge would appoint him a lawyer, and a trial date would be set.

As I drove toward Jonesborough early Wednesday morning, I passed a convenience store about a quarter mile from the courthouse. In the parking lot less than thirty feet from the road, someone had constructed a gallows. Hanging from the two nooses were dummies with bright white faces, black wigs, and black clothing. I knew both Boyer and Barnett would pass the spot on their way to the courthouse from the jail, and I took some small pleasure in thinking about their reaction.

The scene on Main Street outside the courthouse was chaotic. I counted eight news vans and trucks already parked in the street. As I passed by the front of the courthouse, I saw at least fifty people milling around on the steps and the sidewalk. Court didn't convene for at least an hour. I'd done defense work in Washington County for more than a decade, and I'd never seen anything even remotely similar. I circled the courthouse looking for a parking spot. There were none. I turned back onto Main Street and looked in both directions. The street was packed with cars. I finally found a spot nearly a quarter mile west of the courthouse and pulled in.

I walked south one block, headed east, and managed to make it unnoticed to the back door of the county assessor's office on the ground floor. From there, I took the steps up to my office. Fraley was already there, leaning back in a chair with his legs crossed and his feet up on my desk. We talked for a while, mostly about Caroline, until it was almost time to go down to the courtroom.

"Ready to meet the soldiers of Satan?" Fraley said.

"You don't really believe that garbage, do you?"

"What do you believe, counselor? Are you a religious man?"

"None of your business."

"So you're not a religious man."

"I didn't say that."

"You didn't have to. If you were religious, you'd have said so."

I scowled at Fraley. I liked him and I'd grown to respect him, but we weren't so close that I felt comfortable talking personal religious philosophy with him.

"It's all right," Fraley said. "I'd rather have an atheist prosecuting this case. I think it would be easy to lose your focus if you were worried about what God wanted you to do."

"I'm not an atheist," I said.

"Don't tell me you're one of those gutless agnostics," Fraley said. "One of those sissies who doesn't believe in God but doesn't have the gumption to say so."

I looked up at the clock. Almost nine.

"Let's get this over with," I said.

I stuck my head into Lee Mooney's office on the way out.

"Aren't you coming?" I said.

"No," Mooney said, not bothering to look up from the newspaper he was reading, "it's your show."

The biggest case in the history of the district was unfolding, and Mooney had become like a ghost in the office, appearing and disappearing seemingly at will. He was keeping his distance from me, the case, and the media. I wondered whether he was showing political restraint or whether he was just plain scared.

Fraley and I took the back steps down to the second floor and walked down a private hallway into the courtroom. The place reminded me of the day Bates packed the courtroom. Every seat in the gallery was occupied, and people were standing against the walls. Television cameras and reporters were crammed into the jury box like frat boys in a phone booth.

There were two lawyers at the defense table, Jim Beaumont and Herb Dunbar. Dunbar, who was about to be appointed to represent Levi Barnett, was a bellicose, belligerent bully with a belly that stuck out a full foot in front of him. His clothes were always too small, and his face was the shape and size of a serving platter. He wore his strawberry-blonde hair in an afro, and his complexion was the color of zinfandel wine. He'd been known to step on opposing lawyers' feet during bench conferences, to belabor minutiae to the point of filibuster, and to drive judges and other lawyers nearly insane with his constant bickering. I once heard him exclaim that he believed his job as a defense attorney was to "create a mountain out of every molehill and force the state to come and fight on my mountain," and from everything I'd seen and heard, he stubbornly clung to his creed.

The door to Glass's office opened, and the bailiff hailed court into session. Glass took his seat and snarled at the bailiffs. "Bring in the defendants!"

Boyer and Barnett walked in ringed by sheriff's deputies, and the courtroom went dead still. It was the first time I'd seen Boyer in person, and the first thing I noticed was how young and frail he looked. He was walking with his head slumped forward, eyes on the ground in front of him. He was around six feet tall, slight, and pale with straight black hair that fell to his shoulders. The hair had been dyed; the roots were light brown. His face was angular, his upper lip paper thin. As he walked past me to the podium in the short-sleeved jail jumpsuit, I could see pink scars the length of both his forearms.

Barnett was at least six inches shorter than Boyer, with a thick neck and long arms that, like Boyer's, were covered with pink scars. He leaned forward when he walked, his arms hanging loosely like a gorilla. Unlike Boyer, however, Barnett wasn't looking at the floor. He glared defiantly around the courtroom as he plodded to the front. Judge Glass stared down from the bench as the attorneys scurried forward to the podium to stand next to their clients.

"State versus Samuel Boyer and Levi Barnett," the judge said. "Case Number 40,665. Let me see the indictments."

A clerk handed the thick document to the judge and he glanced over it.

"You're both charged with six counts of first-degree murder by premeditation. In the alternative, the state has charged you with six counts of first-degree felony murder. You're also charged with five counts of kidnapping, one count of robbery, and one count of especially aggravated burglary. Is this a death-penalty case, Mr. Dillard?"

I nodded in his direction. "It is, Judge. The state is seeking the death penalty against Mr. Boyer. Mr. Barnett is a juvenile." I never dreamed I'd hear myself utter those words.

"Filed your notice?"

"We have."

"Fine. I've appointed Mr. Beaumont to represent Mr. Boyer and Mr. Dunbar to represent Mr. Barnett. Since Mr. Boyer's already been arraigned, I'll ask Mr. Dunbar. Do you waive the formal reading of the indictment?"

Herb Dunbar cleared his throat. "We do, Your Honor."

"How does your client plead?"

"Not guilty, but we'd like—"

Suddenly, Barnett turned his back on the judge and began to chant something, quietly at first. I couldn't understand him, but then Boyer slowly turned and joined him. Boyer looked tentative, as though he was unsure about what he was doing. But he quickly settled into it, and the words became loud and clear. It was the same phrase that had been carved into Bjorn Beck's forehead.

"Ah Satan, ah Satan, ah Satan, ah Satan, ah Satan, ah Satan …."

Both of them appeared to be staring at the same spot in the back of the courtroom. The looks on their faces were emotionless, their voices monotone.

"Ah Satan, ah Satan, ah Satan, ah Satan, ah Satan, ah Satan …."

"What the …? What are they saying?" Judge Glass was sputtering. "Stop that! Stop now or I'll have you removed from the courtroom!"

Beaumont backed quickly away from his client, but Dunbar stupidly reached up and tried to put his hand over Barnett's mouth. I saw Barnett smile as he bit down hard on one of Dunbar's stubby fingers. Dunbar howled and jerked his hand away.

"He bit me!" Dunbar cried. "He bit me!"

"Get them out of here!" Judge Glass was standing, retreating toward the steps that led down away from the bench. I could see fear in his eyes, and I didn't blame him. There was something about the tone of their voices, the robotic manner in which they spoke, the continuous use of the word "Satan." No one said a word. Nobody moved. It was as if no one was breathing.

Several bailiffs converged on Boyer and Barnett, grabbed them by the arms, and began to drag them out of the courtroom. As they did so, both boys continued to chant, and they continued to look at the same spot in the courtroom. I followed their eyes and almost gasped. Standing in the back against the wall was a tall, red-headed young woman in a black leather jacket.

Natasha.

The chanting faded steadily as the bailiffs and the defendants went down the hallway outside the courtroom. Beaumont and Dunbar had moved to the defense table. Dunbar was wrapping a handkerchief around his finger; Barnett had bitten him so hard he was bleeding. I heard him mutter something to Beaumont about a tetanus shot, but Beaumont looked too stunned to respond.

There were at least a hundred people in the courtroom, and it was so quiet I could hear the ancient clock on the wall above me ticking. It took Judge Glass a couple minutes to regain his composure. Finally, he looked down at Beaumont and Dunbar and said, "I've been on this bench for forty years and I've never seen anything so disrespectful. The young people in this nation are going to hell in a handbasket, I tell you. Hell in a handbasket."

"Judge, we can do the scheduling without them," I said.

"I know that!" he snapped. "Don't you think I know that, Mr. Dillard? Do you think you're the only person in this room who knows what's what?"

"I didn't mean any disrespect. Just trying to move things along."

The judge looked out over the crowd. "You folks came to see the show," he said. "I guess you got your money's worth." He turned to his clerk. "Give me a trial date. Six months."

As the clerk looked through her calendar, I glanced over my shoulder. Natasha was still there, and she was staring at me. I didn't hold the gaze, but over the next several minutes—as Judge Glass set the trial date, motion deadlines, expert deadlines, and plea deadlines—I periodically looked back at her. Each time, she was looking directly at me, seemingly sneering. I felt she was trying to intimidate me, and by the time we were finished and the courtroom began to clear, I was angry. I stood motionless at the table as first the judge, then the lawyers and the crowd, moved out. The reporters and cameramen were packing up their gear. I continued to look in her direction. She didn't move.

"What are you doing?" Fraley said from over my shoulder.

"Natasha's here." He followed my stare.

"Unbelievable," he said.

"She's been staring at me since they made their scene."

"What are you going to do?"

"I don't know," I said, "but do me a favor. Shoot her if she tries to kill me."

I started to walk toward her as the last of the crowd moved through the double doors. As I pushed through the low swinging door that separated the lawyers from the spectators, she remained perfectly still, like she was glued to the wall, her eyes boring into me. When I was five feet away, I stopped.

"I know what you did," I said to her. "We'll be coming for you soon."

Her face tightened and she moved off the wall. Her eyes were mesmerizing; I couldn't break her stare for a full thirty seconds. She started speaking, but I couldn't understand a word. It sounded like gibberish, but the words were being delivered with purpose, the volume steadily growing. She took a couple steps in my direction. I felt a droplet of spit hit my cheek as she continued. The veins in her neck and forehead began to swell.

A strong hand closed around my bicep and pulled me in the opposite direction. I turned and realized it was Fraley. Behind him was a television camera sitting on the shoulder of a man, pointed directly at me. When I looked back, Natasha was gone.

"What did you say to her?" Fraley said as soon as I gathered my briefcase and we got out of sight of the reporters.

"I think I was trying to tell her I'm not afraid of her," I said.

"I hate to tell you this," Fraley said, "but it looks to me like *she's* the one who's not afraid."

WEDNESDAY, OCT. 29

I made the news on the local CBS affiliate—at six o'clock that night and again at eleven, the next morning at six, and one more time at noon. What made it worse was that they used the story as a teaser to lead into all their newscasts. By noon the next day, nearly every citizen in northeast Tennessee and southwest Virginia had heard Natasha's vitriolic response to my threat. Luckily, the cameraman hadn't gotten there in time to record what I said to her. Caroline taped one of the newscasts, and we sat that night watching it over and over, trying to figure out what Natasha was saying. She spoke in what seemed to be a strange, guttural language, something I'd never heard.

The phone rang around seven. The caller ID was blocked, but I picked it up anyway. An unfamiliar woman's voice on the other end asked to speak to Mr. Dillard.

"Who's calling?" I said.

"I don't want to tell you my name," she said in a heavy Southern accent, "but I work with your sister at Godsey's Insurance Agency. You need to go see her."

"Beg your pardon? Did you say I need to go see her?"

"Yes. Right away. Tonight if possible. And it would be best if you didn't tell her you were coming."

"Why? What's wrong?"

"Please, Mr. Dillard. Please go to Sarah. She needs you."

"Crossville's over two hours away," I said. "I don't think I'd be inclined to jump in the car and go down there on the basis of an anonymous phone call."

There was a pause at the other end. I heard her draw in a deep breath.

"She's been injured," she said.

"Injured? Is she all right? Has she been in an accident?"

"No, I … I … you have to promise me you won't tell her it was someone from work who called you. She'll know it was me."

"What's going on?" I said. "If she's hurt, I want to know what happened."

"It was Robert," she whispered. "He beat her up."

Her words stung me like a swarm of bees. I knew he was wrong for her. I knew he was a hothead. I was afraid something like this might happen, but I hadn't had the guts to come out and say it to Sarah.

"Where is she?" I said, trying to remain calm.

"She's at home. I just left there. It's bad, especially her beautiful face."

"Did she go to the hospital? Did she call the police?"

"She won't do either one. She begged me not to call the police."

"Do you know what happened?"

"I've known Robert since he was a little boy, Mr. Dillard. I've been working for his daddy, and his granddaddy before that, for thirty-five years. Robert's a bad seed. He'll do it again."

"No he won't," I said. "I can promise you that."

I talked to her for a couple more minutes and then thanked her for calling.

"Mr. Dillard?" she said before she hung up. "I just want to tell you that Sarah is so proud of you. She brags on you all the time."

I hung up the phone and tried to control my anger. *Think. Think. What should you do?*

Caroline, who'd had her second chemotherapy treatment a few days before and was just starting to recover from the effects, wandered into the kitchen.

"Who was that?" she said.

"A friend of Sarah's down in Crossville. She says Sarah's boyfriend beat her up. She says I need to come down there tonight. Apparently it's bad."

"I've seen that look on your face before," Caroline said. "What are you thinking about doing?"

"I was just asking myself that same question."

"Why don't you call the Crossville police?"

"Because they'll go pick him up and take him to jail for twelve hours. They'll charge him with a misdemeanor and let him out in the morning. He'll go to court and swear he'll never do it again and they'll slap him on the wrist and send him home."

"Don't you think he should go to jail?" she said.

"I think he should suffer. I think he should feel the same pain he inflicted on Sarah. And I intend to make sure it happens."

Caroline walked over and took my face in her hands. "I won't try to stop you," she said. "If you want to know the truth, I feel the same way you do. But you're not going alone."

"I don't want you to go, baby," I said. "You're sick, and besides, I don't want you to see what I'm going to do to him. I don't want you to see me that way."

"You need to take someone," she said. "I want somebody looking out for you."

"I'll call Fraley."

Just before eleven, Fraley and I rolled off the I-40 exit into Crossville. Before I left home, I looked in my Rolodex for the telephone number of the man who had been Robert Godsey's boss at the local probation department. I reached him at home, and yes, Godsey had left a forwarding address. It would just take him a minute to get on the office database on his computer. Yes, he'd be glad to give it to me. Was I going down to visit, or was I working on a case?

Fraley had been home watching television. He was up for a road trip, he said, and after I told him why I was going, he became even more enthusiastic. I picked him up at his house, which was just a couple blocks from the hospital in Johnson City.

The ride down had been largely silent as the debate raged within me about whether I was doing the right thing. I finally decided I didn't care whether it was right. It was what I was going to do. As we turned onto Live Oak Road about a half mile from Sarah's apartment, Fraley spoke up.

"It was self-defense, Your Honor," he said. "Mr. Dillard went to confront Mr. Godsey about assaulting his sister, and Mr. Godsey attacked him. Mr. Dillard merely defended himself. I swear it on a stack of Bibles."

I turned and looked at him. He had a smile on his face.

"I appreciate this," I said. "I'll make it up to you sometime."

The house Sarah rented sat atop a small knoll about fifty yards off Live Oak Road. As I pulled into the driveway, I saw her car, the used red Mustang she bought with some of the money Ma left her. The house was on a good-sized lot, maybe three quarters of an acre, surrounded by a fifteen-foot-high hemlock hedge.

"No way the neighbors would have heard anything with that hedge," Fraley said.

"Sometimes there's such a thing as too much privacy," I said.

"You want me to come in with you?" Fraley said.

"Yeah. I want someone besides me to see her."

We walked down a brick path and up a set of concrete steps, and I knocked on Sarah's door. A brisk wind was blowing; it cut through the light nylon jacket I was wearing and I felt myself shiver. I heard footsteps beyond the door, then a rubbing sound as she leaned up against the peephole inside. There was a long silence.

"Sarah," I said, knocking again. "Open the door."

"What are you doing here, Joe?" she said from the other side.

"Somebody called me. Are you all right?"

"Who's that with you?"

"A friend. He's a police officer."

"I don't want any police around."

"He's not here to arrest anyone. He just rode along to keep me company."

"Go away, Joe. I don't want to talk to you right now," she said.

"I'm not leaving, Sarah. If you don't open the door, I'll kick it in."

We stood there for a couple more minutes when finally I heard the dead bolt slide and the doorknob turn. The door opened slightly, and I pushed my way in. Sarah had already turned and started through the house. She walked into the kitchen and stood at the sink looking out the window with her back to me, wearing a white ter-rycloth bathrobe with her shiny black hair hanging over the collar. I followed, stopping at a tiled counter. Fraley stayed a few steps back in the den.

"What happened?" I said softly.

"It was stupid," she said. "We got into an argument. I don't even remember what it was about. We both said some things we shouldn't have said, and then ...."

I noticed there was a buzzing sound to her words, a form of pronunciation I'd never heard from her, as though she wasn't opening her mouth all the way.

"Turn around," I said.

Her head fell forward and her shoulders slumped.

"What are you going to do, Joe?"

"Turn around. Please."

She turned slowly, her chin on her chest.

"Look at me," I said.

When she lifted her chin, it was all I could do to keep from grabbing Fraley's gun and heading straight to Robert Godsey's house. Her left eye was swollen completely shut, and an angry purple bruise was spreading out like the wake from a raindrop on a pond. Both of her lips were swollen; her bottom lip had been split wide open. It looked like a puffy pink grub worm that had been chopped in half. As I moved toward her, I could see bruises on her throat. She'd obviously been choked.

"Come here," I said and opened my arms. She leaned against my chest and I held her close.

"It was my fault," she said, her voice breaking. "It was my fault. You know how I get sometimes. I just don't know when to shut up."

I waited for her to calm down and took a step back. I reached out and lightly touched her cheek.

"I'm so sorry this happened," I said. Rage was slowly building in me, constricting arteries, causing me to tremble slightly and my field of vision to narrow. I could feel my heart beating inside my chest. "Are you all right? Don't you think you should go get checked out by a doctor?"

She must have sensed my anger because she looked directly into my eyes and said, "Don't hurt him, Joe. It isn't worth it. I'll be fine."

I put my hands on her shoulders. "I'm going to go talk to him. I can't just let this go."

"Promise you won't hurt him. He has problems. He didn't mean to do it."

"I'll be back in a little while. In the meantime, put some things in a suitcase. You're coming home with me."

"No. I don't want—"

I squeezed her shoulders tightly.

"No discussion, Sarah. He *beat* you, and I don't care what you said, you didn't deserve it. I'm going to go talk to him, and then I'm going to come back here and pick you up. You need to think this through for a few days, and you don't need him around while you're doing it."

She let out a sigh and nodded her head. I leaned over and kissed her gently on the cheek. "Get ready to go. I'll be back."

"One second," Fraley said, reaching into his pocket and pulling out a digital camera. He handed the camera to me. "Take some pictures of her," he said. "You never know when it might come in handy."

I'd seen Godsey use his size and his belligerent demeanor to intimidate his probationers several times. I guess he thought he could do the same to me because he opened the door immediately when I knocked. He was shirtless, barrel-chested, and hairy. I could see the hair on his shoulders backlit by a lamp in the den behind him as he loomed in the doorway.

"What do *you* want?" he said as he opened the storm door and glared at me.

I clocked him without saying a word. I had a picture of Sarah, battered and bruised, in my mind, and I hit him in the nose so hard that blood shot out like a red geyser. He staggered back into the house, his eyes wide with surprise, and I bull-rushed him. I got my shoulder into his chest, grabbed the backs of his thighs with both hands, lifted his feet off the ground, and drove him into the floor with a loud thud just inside the doorway. I heard at least one rib crack, and he let out a pathetic groan as the air rushed out of his lungs. I could hear myself talking, yelling, cursing, but I wasn't conscious of what I was saying. As soon as I got him on the ground, I pinned his hips with my knees and got my left forearm under his chin and against his jawbone. I turned his head and pinned it sideways against the floor and started hammering him with my right fist and elbow. I hit him in the temple, in the side of the face. My forearm slipped once and he turned his head toward me, so I hit him square in the mouth. I hit him until he went limp.

Something in my brain told me to stop, but I couldn't. I just kept on hitting him, over and over. My knuckles were smashing into the hard bones in his face and skull, but I couldn't feel a thing. Suddenly, I was lifted off his body and dragged backwards, my butt skidding along the hardwood floor. A voice was saying, "Enough! Enough!" Strong hands lifted me to my feet and pulled me through the doorway into the night air.

A familiar voice said, "Come out of it, Dillard …."

I stood there gasping for breath, temporarily unable to recognize the face in front of me. It slowly came into focus, like a ship emerging from a thick fog, and I realized it was Fraley. I turned and looked inside the house. Godsey was lying on his back, his legs spread. I walked back in and stood over him. He was breathing, but he wasn't moving, his eyes staring up at the ceiling.

"I didn't know you were going to go ballistic on me," Fraley said. "Were you trying to kill him?"

"Can you hear me?" I said loudly to Godsey. He blinked. Both of his eyes were swelling, and his nose was smashed sideways onto his cheek. He was bleeding from the mouth, nose, and a cut above his left eye. I shoved his shoulder with my foot and he groaned.

"Don't ever come near her again," I said. "Don't call, don't write, nothing. She's gone. She's out of your life. Do you understand?"

"Let's go," Fraley said.

"Do you understand me?"

"He understands," Fraley said as he pulled me out the door and toward the truck. "I promise you he understands."

Later, as we drove east on I-40 toward home, I heard Sarah stir in the passenger seat. I was driving her Mustang while Fraley followed in my truck. She hadn't said a word since I loaded her suitcase in the trunk and we started home. I turned to look at her, and in the dim light from the dashboard, I could see the ugly purple lump where her left eye should have been.

"Joe?" she said in a soft voice. "Did you hurt him?"

"Not too bad."

"Seriously, what did you do to him? Tell me."

"The truth?"

"Please."

"I don't know, maybe a broken nose, a couple fractured ribs, maybe a fractured jaw or something, maybe a concussion. He'll probably live."

She was silent for a couple minutes. I saw her chest rise and fall as she let out a long, slow breath.

"Thank you," she said, and she leaned her head back and went to sleep.

THURSDAY, OCT. 30

Sheriff Leon Bates shivered as he sat alone inside the Dodge Dakota he used for surveillance. Nothing glamorous about this part of the job. Bates was parked inside a barn less than a hundred yards from his informant's house. The temperature outside had dipped to near freezing, and even though Bates was out of the wind, he was colder than a witch's teat in a brass bra. He looked down at his watch. The target was supposed to show up at 10:00 p.m. Almost time.

Above him, Bates knew there was a large room filled with gaming tables, video slot and poker machines, even a roulette wheel. Bates had busted the man who owned the property less than a week ago. After a few hours of interrogation and a threat to call in the feds, the man had revealed something that Bates had suspected for several months but hadn't been able to prove. Now was the time.

Five minutes later, Bates saw headlights coming over the ridge to the east. The car slowed as it reached the driveway, turned in, and crawled slowly along over the rutted clay.

"That's it," Bates whispered, "come to Papa."

SCOTT PRATT

The lens of an infrared digital camera was positioned in a hole in the barn wall and trained on the front of the house. Yet another tiny lens was in the ceiling above the kitchen table inside the house. The informant inside was wired for sound. All Bates's brand-new high-tech toys had been purchased with money his department had seized from drug dealers over the past year and a half. Bates got out of the vehicle and turned on the camera. Once he was sure it was working properly, he reached back into the Dakota, flipped the switch on the recorder, donned the headphones, and moved to a spot where he could peek through the slats and watch.

The car parked in front of the house, and a man got out. Bates shook his head slowly as the man walked up the front steps and knocked on the door.

"Son of a gun," he whispered. "My boy wasn't lying."

"What's going on, playah?" Bates heard his informant say through the earphones. The equipment was working perfectly. "C'mon in out of the cold."

Bates heard muffled breathing and the sound of footsteps as the two men walked through the house. When the footsteps stopped, Bates heard the target's voice.

"Put your hands on the table and spread your legs," the target said.

Bates immediately recognized the voice. He wasn't worried about the target frisking his informant. The listening device was wireless and undetectable.

"Where's your wife?" the target said.

"Went to a movie with her sister," the informant said. "She won't be back for a while. Have a seat there—take a load off. How 'bout a beer?"

"No time. I just need to make my pickup and go."

"So you're just gonna take the money and run, huh? You got no manners at all."

Bates squirmed in his seat. "C'mon, Lacy," he whispered to himself. "Get him to say something about his boss."

"This is business," the target said. "It's not a social call."

"Well, business ain't what it used to be with that sheriff running around arresting folks. Y'all's monthly payment is starting to cut a little deep."

"You just make the payment and keep your mouth shut. Let me worry about the sheriff."

Bates heard a beer can pop. "How much are y'all taking in on this little venture of yours?" the informant said.

"None of your business."

"Yeah, well, I reckon it's a pretty good lick or you wouldn't be taking the risk. What's your boss's cut?"

"When did you get so nosy?"

"Just like to know where my hard-earned money's going. Besides, it looks to me like you're the one doing all the work."

"You make your money by stacking the odds and skimming the juice," the target said. "There's nothing hard about it."

"So what's his cut?"

"More than it should be. Give me my money. I need to get going."

The earphones went silent again except for the sound of footsteps and the informant's muffled breathing. Bates heard what he thought might be a drawer opening, then more footsteps.

"There it is," the informant said. "Two grand. Cash."

His equipment was so good that Bates heard the sound of a heavy envelope landing on a table. A chair leg scraped, and Bates assumed the target was picking up his extortion money.

"It's all there," the informant said. "You don't have to count it."

"It better be," the target said. "I'll see you next month. In the meantime, why don't you move someplace closer to town? I hate driving all the way out here."

"I'm not moving my operation. For two grand a month, you can afford the gas."

Bates listened to the footsteps again, then watched as the target walked back out to his car. The target was easily identifiable, as was the number on his license plate. The camera above the table would leave no doubt. Bates allowed himself a smile.

"Gotcha," he said out loud. "You're mine now."

FRIDAY, OCT. 31

Halloween morning broke dreary and cold, with the wind whipping out of the southwest. A front was moving in, and as I drove to the office, I watched the burnt-orange and blood-red leaves cling stubbornly to the branches that served as their lifelines. About two miles from Jonesborough, I noticed something strange to my left. A leafless, dead oak stood naked against the charcoal sky. Perched in its branches were at least two dozen carrion birds, vultures, each the size of a large turkey. As I passed beneath the tree, they all took flight at the same time, their huge wings spreading out like giant arms. For the rest of the trip into town, I had the unshakable sensation that they were following me, circling above, flying messengers of death.

I arrived in Jonesborough early and parked in the lot behind the courthouse. I looked up as soon as I got out of the truck and was relieved that the vultures were nowhere in sight. I walked around the courthouse and across Main Street to a small coffee shop.

I'd just started reading the newspaper when I noticed a man walk through the door. He was wearing a long, blue denim coat and a floppy black felt hat and carrying a walking stick with an ornamental carving of a lion's head at the top. His gray hair cascaded out from beneath the hat to his shoulder blades, and his bushy beard, also gray, nearly covered his face. As soon as he stepped through the door, he looked directly at me. I nodded and looked back down at the paper. He shuffled past me to the counter. A couple minutes later, he was standing over me with a steaming cup of coffee in his left hand.

"Mind if I sit, neighbor?" he said.

There was only one other person in the shop at the time. He could have sat at any of a dozen tables.

"Suit yourself," I said, and he lowered himself awkwardly into the chair across from me. His nose was crooked and crisscrossed with pink veins. His eyes were small, close-set, and almost black. I folded the newspaper, smiled, and offered my hand.

"Joe Dillard," I said. His hand was half the size of mine, his fingers rough and calloused.

"I know who you are," he said in a deep, throaty drawl. He didn't return the smile. "I saw you on the television."

"Pretty embarrassing," I said.

He poured some cream into his coffee and began to stir slowly.

"The young lady could be dangerous," he said.

"Yeah? What makes you say that?"

"Unusual language she was speaking, don't you think?"

"Was it a language? I thought it was just gibberish."

He took a sip of coffee. As he set the cup down, he lifted his eyes. They were so dark I couldn't discern iris from pupil, like two dime-sized, bottomless holes.

"It was a language, and that's why I'm here, neighbor," he said. "To warn you."

"Warn me?"

He leaned forward, his lips tightening over his jagged teeth, and lowered his voice.

"The language she was speaking is called Enochian. Some say it's a language made up by hoaxsters, that it has no real value or power. Others say it's an ancient language passed down through the pagans, a secret language spoken only by those who worship the lord of darkness."

"And you know this language?"

He closed his eyes for a moment. "When I was a younger man."

"So which were you, a hoaxster or a devil worshipper?"

He flinched a little, as though the directness of the question stung him.

"There was a time when I was lost," he said, "but no more. Do you want to know what she said?"

"Not unless she was confessing to a crime."

"She was reciting an Enochian passage that I'm sure she found in *The Satanic Bible*. It's the only place she could have found those exact words."

It made sense since we'd found a copy of *The Satanic Bible* in Natasha's bedroom. I sat there stirring my coffee, waiting for him to continue, trying to act as though I wasn't alarmed.

"She put a curse on you," he said. "A satanic curse. One that could bring terrible wrath and violence down upon you."

Wrath and violence, psychic witnesses, inverted crosses and bullet holes in the eye. I was beginning to think I might be dreaming all of this. If I was, I wanted to wake up. I kept smiling, choosing my words carefully.

"Even if what you're saying is true, she doesn't have any power over me," I said. "I don't believe in Satan, and I don't believe in curses."

He shook his head and sighed. "To each his own, but if I were you, I'd take great care until the conflict between you and the girl is resolved."

"Oh, it'll be resolved," I said. "You can bet on that."

"It would be a mistake to underestimate her."

I took one last sip of my coffee and stood up.

"You know what?" I said. "I have to go. Thanks for the warning."

I walked toward the door. Just as I opened it, I heard him say, "Excuse me, Mr. Dillard?"

I stopped and turned back to face him.

"If the curse is real, there's only one way to break it."

"What's that?"

"One of you has to die."

FRIDAY, OCT. 31

J im Beaumont's motion to suppress all the evidence we'd gathered against Sam Boyer and Levi Barnett arrived by courier from his office less than an hour after I sat down at my desk. Hugh Dunbar, Levi Barnett's attorney, had joined the motion, but I knew the work was done by Beaumont. It alleged a variety of violations under the Fourth Amendment to the United States Constitution and asked the judge to exclude any and all evidence found as a result of the warrants I'd obtained the night we made the arrests. I'd been expecting the motion, but as I sat leafing through it at my desk, a feeling of uneasiness came over me. Beaumont, who I knew to be a fine lawyer, got right to the heart of it. The primary question would be: Did the warrant applications, which were largely based on the testimony of Alisha Davis, an informant, set out enough facts to show that the informant had a reliable basis of knowledge? Beaumont argued very persuasively that it did not. If a judge agreed with him—and we were going in front of Judge Glass—we'd lose everything.

As I sat at my desk, rereading the motion for the third time, the telephone rang.

"Have you read my motion?" It was the distinctive baritone of Jim Beaumont. I was immediately suspicious because I'd watched Beaumont practice criminal defense for years and had talked to him many times. I knew he didn't trust prosecutors, and I knew he wasn't the type to call and chat.

"Looking at it now," I said.

"You're on some thin ice, counselor," Beaumont said. "Arrest warrants based on a drawing from an anonymous informant? That's a first for me, and I've been doing this a long time."

"She turned out to be right," I said. "That should help her credibility. Besides, there's a lot more to it than the drawing."

"I took the liberty of calling the judge's secretary," he said. "The hearing's set for November tenth."

"In a hurry, are we?"

"I hate to do this to you, Joe," he said, chuckling under his breath. "I've always liked you, but when the judge throws out your evidence and these boys walk out the door, they're gonna run you out of town on a rail."

"Did you call to gloat?"

"A little bit, but the main purpose of the call is to tell you that my client wants to meet with you."

"Boyer? You're kidding me. What could he possibly have to offer?"

"It seems he's been sitting in that jail cell over there in protective custody, all by his lonesome, without the influence of others, with nothing to do but stare at the walls and think. Hypothetically speaking, he *might* just be starting to feel like he's getting a bad rap since he's the only one looking at the death penalty. And because he's become offended by the injustice of the situation, he *might* just be able to provide you with some valuable testimony regarding someone else's involvement in these crimes."

"Natasha Davis?"

"Let's just say it might be a person of the female persuasion, and this person might be directly responsible for all six killings."

"You're not trying to tell me that Boyer didn't kill anyone."

"He's willing to admit his involvement, but the killings were committed while he was under this third party's influence."

I thought about Alisha's comment, *one who commands.*

"And what would you expect in return for this information?" I said.

"We'd certainly expect some consideration."

"How much?"

"I'm thinking something along the lines of second-degree murder, run everything concurrent, twenty-five years at Range One."

"He'd be eligible for parole in eight years," I said. "Eight years for six murders? You're out of your mind."

"You know as well as I do that the parole board won't let him out. He'll serve at least twenty, and who knows? Maybe with a little luck one of his fellow inmates will kill him for you."

"Glad to hear you haven't lost your compassion."

"I don't have any compassion for him. I've seen the evidence you have. Looks to me like he helped kill six innocent people. But we all have a job to do, right?"

"I can't do a thing without talking to the boss," I said.

"Figured as much. How do you like being on a leash, anyway? Under the thumb of a politician."

"It has its ups and downs, but it beats running interference for scumbags every day."

"Ah, you cut me to the quick. Just one more thing before I let you go. Even if your boss gives you the okay, I'm not going to let you talk to him until after the motion hearing. You never know what a judge will do."

"You don't really think Judge Glass is going to let them walk away from this, do you? Especially after the little show your boys put on in the courtroom."

"Like I said, you never know. He might seize the opportunity to get a little payback for what you and Bates did to him. I'll see you on the tenth."

I buzzed Lee Mooney's administrative assistant a few minutes later, and she told me to come on back. When I walked through Mooney's door, I was surprised to find Alexander Dunn seated in a chair in front of Mooney's desk.

"Sorry," I said. "I thought you were alone."

"No problem," Mooney said, motioning to a chair next to Dunn. "Alexander and I were just discussing a few of his cases."

"I need to talk to you," I said.

"Personal or professional?"

"Professional."

"Go ahead. You don't mind if Alexander sits in, do you? He might learn something."

I *did* mind. I didn't trust Alexander, and I didn't feel comfortable discussing anything about my case in front of him. But I remembered what Rita told me—that he was Lee's nephew and that Lee protected him—so I didn't think asking him to leave would be particularly wise. I sat down in the chair.

"I just got off the phone with Jim Beaumont. Sam Boyer wants to deal."

Mooney was wearing a dark blue jacket with a miniature American flag pinned to the lapel. He reached up and began to finger his handlebar mustache.

"What does he have to offer?" Mooney said.

"He says there was a third person involved, and he's willing to give her up. I think it's the girl I've told you about. Natasha Davis."

"Is she the girl that was in the room with them the night they were arrested? The one you had to let go?"

"Yeah, that's her."

"The same girl that was on television barking at you like a dog?"

"Yeah."

"That was priceless," Dunn chimed in. "You should have seen the look on your face when you turned around toward the camera. You were white as a sheet, looked like you were about to pee your pants."

"So anyway, I think she ordered the murders," I said. "Maybe even participated. We have some circumstantial evidence that leads us in that direction. And now Boyer wants to tell us what happened."

"What kind of circumstantial evidence?" Mooney said.

"The first witness we talked to turned out to be Natasha's identical twin sister. She's the one who put us onto them in the first place. Then Natasha turns up in the motel room when we go to arrest Boyer and Barnett. But the most compelling thing is the carvings in two of the victims' foreheads."

Mooney had seen both Bjorn Beck and Norman Brockwell up close, and he was certainly aware of the carvings. But the only involvement he'd had in the case was to visit the crime scenes and assign the investigation to the TBI. I'd tried to discuss a couple things with him early on, but he put me off both times, telling me to "handle it any way you see fit." He'd barely mentioned the case since the night I argued against forming a task force. He hadn't looked at the file and was blissfully unaware of most of the facts and the evidence. All he knew about the case was what I'd told him, and if anyone else asked him about it, he simply referred them to me.

There was a legal pad sitting just to his right, and I stood up and slid it over in front of him. I told him to write down "ah satan." He did so, and said it out loud.

"That's what was carved into Bjorn Beck's and Norman Brockwell's foreheads," I said. "It's the same thing the boys were chanting in court, and they were looking at Natasha Davis while they were chanting. Now write it backwards."

I glanced over at Dunn, who had slid forward in his chair so that he could see what Mooney was doing. His hair was combed straight back and plastered to his head, and he smelled of cologne and cigar smoke. Mooney finished writing and looked up at me.

"Natasha," he said.

"I know she was involved. I just can't prove it yet."

"You can't convict her solely on the uncorroborated testimony of a codefendant," he said.

"I know, but we don't need much. The fact that she was with them when they were arrested and the carvings in the foreheads may be enough. Besides, if Boyer opens up, I'm betting we'll find more."

"And Boyer wants a break in exchange for information that will convict her?"

"Exactly."

"How much of a break?"

"Beaumont asked for twenty-five years at Range One. I didn't agree to it, but I was thinking somewhere along the lines of twenty-five years day-for-day might not be out of the question. But it's up to you, Lee. I remember standing at the scene where the Becks were killed and you said no deals."

He leaned forward and folded his hands on his desk in front of him. He looked at Alexander for a long minute, then turned to me.

"I hired you because I trust your judgment," he said. "I want you to handle this case your way. If you think making a deal with Boyer will help you get another murderer off the street, and if making a deal is the only way, then do what you have to do. I'm going to leave it all up to you."

I stood up. "Thank you, Lee," I said, "I appreciate your confidence. I trust everything that was said in this room will stay in this room." I glanced sideways at Alexander, who immediately turned and looked at the wall.

"Absolutely," Mooney said.

I walked out of his office and back down the hall knowing that I'd just been set up. I'd seen it before with other prosecutors and their assistants. Lee's decision to let me have free rein on the case had nothing to do with him having confidence in me. It had everything to do with accountability. He'd turned the case over to his trusted assistant, an experienced trial lawyer who he believed was perfectly capable of handling anything that came his way, and he'd instructed him to handle the case "your way." He even had a witness.

If something went wrong, he was off the hook.

I, on the other hand, would be left twisting in the wind like an outlaw at the end of the hangman's noose.

SATURDAY, NOV. 1

Saturday evening reminded me why I enjoyed being away from the cruelty and ugliness that made up the criminal justice system. Lilly had come home for the weekend and Jack called just to check in around six o'clock. Caroline felt well enough to cook steaks on the grill. After the three of us ate supper and cleaned up, I grabbed a couple beers and sat on the back deck and watched the stars twinkle in the vast black sky. Around eight, Caroline, Lilly, and I curled up on the couch and watched *Monty Python and the Holy Grail*. It was so good to hear Caroline laugh, and Lilly even provided a bit of vaudeville when she tripped over Rio and tossed a bag of popcorn all over the den.

Just as I was starting to think the world wasn't such a bad place after all, the phone rang. It was Sarah.

"I just wanted you to know that I'm going back to Crossville tomorrow," she said. "Robert and I are going to give it another try."

I was dumbfounded. Sarah had always been unpredictable and headstrong, but I couldn't imagine she would put herself back into an abusive situation.

"Are you crazy?" I said. "Are you ill? Are you back on the sauce?"

"Don't start on me, Joe. I'm a grown-up. I can handle it."

"He blacked your eye and split your lip, Sarah!"

"Don't yell at me!"

I knew from years of experience that shouting wouldn't work. The more I shouted, the more she'd shout, and the chances of reasoning with her would steadily melt away. I tried to think of a way to convince her that she was making a terrible mistake, but in the back of my mind, I knew it was futile.

"Sarah, please. It hasn't been a week. You haven't even *healed* yet."

"We talked on the phone for a long time yesterday," she said. "He's sorry, Joe. He's really sorry. He broke down and cried like a baby."

"I can't believe I'm hearing this. Why don't you at least give it a month or so? Let yourself try to get past this."

"I don't want to give it a month. I want to go back and try to make it work. We're going to go to counseling."

"Counseling? What kind of counseling? A karate class?"

"Stop being so cynical," she said. "He's really a good man."

"No, he isn't. Good men do *not* beat on women. *Period*."

"He just has some problems. Surely you, of all people, can sympathize with that."

"No, I can't sympathize with it. He's a bully. He takes his rage out on people who can't defend themselves."

"The pot calling the kettle black," she said.

Here we go. The classic warped Sarah logic. She's worse than a judge.

"What do you mean? I did what I did because he deserved it. And he's *bigger* than I am."

"He said you didn't give him a chance."

"And what about you? Did he give you a chance?"

"He's willing to give me another chance, in spite of what you did."

"So now you're blaming me? This is absolutely unbelievable."

"I didn't ask you to come down there. I could have handled it just fine myself."

"What were you going to do, Sarah? Bleed on him?"

"I'm not going to argue with you anymore," she said. "I just called because I felt like I owed you the courtesy of telling you I'm moving back."

"Sarah, he's going to do it again. When he does, don't call me."

I hung up on her, frustrated and angry. Caroline, who'd heard the shouting, walked up behind me and started rubbing my neck.

"She's going back," I said quietly.

"I know," Caroline said. "I heard."

"What's wrong with her? I just don't understand how she could do something so foolish."

"She still hasn't gotten over the rape. She thinks she deserves abuse. If she's not doing it herself, she finds someone to do it for her."

"Something bad's going to happen," I said.

I turned to her and she kissed me on the cheek. "And if it does, you'll be right there for her, just like you've always been. C'mon, let's get some sleep."

SUNDAY, NOV. 2

I opened my eyes Sunday morning to streaks of silver light shining in from behind the blinds in our bedroom. I threw my legs over the side of the bed, reached up, and pulled back the blinds. Massive gray clouds that looked like buffalo humps were receding to the west, replaced by a blue sky brightened by the sun in the east. As I sat there looking out the window, I suddenly felt like something wasn't quite right, but then I realized what it was. Rio greeted me every morning as soon as my feet hit the floor. He'd lay his snout across my thighs, look up at me with those expressive brown eyes, and wait for me to scratch his ears. He'd spent the night at the veterinarian's after being neutered the day before. I hated to do it to him, but as he grew older, he was becoming more aggressive. We kept him in the house most of the time, but anyone who came to the door was greeted by a snarling, 90-pound missile just itching to launch itself. He calmed quickly and had never bitten anyone, but I'd also received a couple complaints from people who happened to walk or jog by the house when he was outside. He apparently guarded the edge of the property with the same zeal that he guarded the house. I hoped the neutering would calm him down.

I stood and looked at Caroline, who was sleeping peacefully. She'd lost all her hair—even her eyebrows were gone—but I'd already grown used to it. As the sunlight illuminated her face, I thought to myself again how beautiful she was. I'd tried to tell her, but she scoffed at the compliments, referring to herself as "onion head."

She'd done amazingly well. By scheduling her chemotherapy treatments on Friday, she was able to endure the sickness she experienced immediately afterward on the weekends and get back to her beloved dancing classes on Monday. She wore a wig to the dancing school that almost, but not quite, matched the color of her hair. I'd suggested that she didn't need to wear the wig, but she said she was afraid her baldness would frighten the younger students, and I knew she was right. When she was around the house, she usually wore a knitted cap of some kind. She complained of pain in her bones, slept late most days, and had to take a nap in the afternoons, but she'd managed to keep her sense of humor and a positive outlook.

I put on my robe and walked into the kitchen, clenching and unclenching my right hand. The knuckles were still swollen and discolored from my trip to see Robert Godsey. I thought about Sarah and shook my head.

I made a pot of coffee and wandered outside to get the newspaper. A slight breeze was blowing out of the southwest, and I could hear the gentle rustle of the brittle leaves that remained on the trees in the woods across the street. I retrieved the newspaper, walked back down the driveway into the house, poured myself a cup of coffee, and sat down at the kitchen table to read.

The headline, above the fold on the front page, said:

Prosecutor Seeks Deal; Shocking New Details in Multiple Murders

The story was written by Misty Bell. As I read, I felt anger rising in my throat:

> The Johnson City Banner has learned that recently hired Assistant District Attorney Joe Dillard is seeking to make a deal with one of the suspects in six recent murders. Sources close to the investigation confirmed yesterday that Dillard is willing to offer Samuel Boyer, 19, a twenty-five-year sentence in exchange for information that will lead to the arrest and conviction of an unidentified third party that law enforcement officials believe was involved the murders.
>
> And in a shocking, previously unreported discovery, the Banner has learned that the phrase "ah satan" was carved into the foreheads of two of the victims....

I threw the paper down on the table in disgust. Jim Beaumont, Lee Mooney, Alexander Dunn, and I were the only people who knew of Beaumont's offer and my discussion with Lee Mooney. Beaumont had no incentive to leak it to the newspaper, nor did Mooney. I knew I hadn't done it, so that left only Dunn.

I wondered whether Natasha Davis had seen the story, and if so, what her reaction would be. Would she run? Try to get to Boyer? Clean up any mess that might still be lingering?

"I'm going to strangle him," I said out loud. "I'm going to crush his windpipe with my bare hands."

A blond head peeked around the corner near the refrigerator. It was Lilly, who'd been coming home from school every weekend since Caroline's diagnosis. The director of the dance team had graciously agreed to let her take some time off, and although I'd tried to talk her out of it at first, I was glad to have her around. She stepped around the corner wearing an oversized, bright-orange University of Tennessee T-shirt that hung almost to her knees, her long hair rumpled from sleep.

"Who are you going to strangle?" she said.

"Sorry honey, I didn't know you were there."

"Is everything all right?"

"Yeah, everything's fine. Let me fix you some breakfast. Are you up for a run this morning? It's beautiful outside."

"Are we racing?" I saw the competitive glint in her eyes. She'd been running seriously for several years, since she turned thirteen, and she'd been dancing her entire life. She was in great shape, but this was the first time she'd ever asked me to race.

"Do you want to race?" I said.

"Depends."

"On?"

"On how mad you'll get when I beat you."

"Care to put your money where your mouth is?" I said.

"How much?"

"Five bucks."

"Deal. How far are we racing?" Lilly said.

"Up to you."

"Three miles. How much of a head start do I get?"

"Who said anything about a head start?"

"C'mon, you're a man, Dad. And a jock. You've been running your whole life."

"I'll give you one minute."

"Five."

"Three."

"Okay. Three."

"We run to the oak on the bluff and back. That's three miles, right?"

"Right."

Thirty minutes later, Lilly and I were standing on a ten-foot-wide trail that ran along the northern bank of Boone Lake. The trail was developed for recreation by the Tennessee Valley Authority and wound for five miles through a wooded area on property owned by the TVA. It was only a couple hundred yards from our house, so we'd both run the trail a thousand times.

As we stood there stretching, she reminded me so much of her mother—beautiful, strong, and intelligent. I wondered briefly where she'd be in five years, ten years. I hoped she didn't stray too far.

It was perfect on the trail. No one was around, the breeze was still blowing, and the temperature was climbing along with the sun. I put my finger on the stop watch on my wrist.

"Ready?" I said.

"I apologize in advance for the embarrassment I'm going to cause you," Lilly said.

"Five ... four ... three ... two ... one ... Go!"

Lilly took off, and I pushed the button on the watch. I stretched some more and bounced around, watching her disappear around the first bend as I waited for three minutes to elapse. Two minutes into my wait, I heard what sounded like an animal growling followed by a piercing scream. It was a woman's voice, not that far away, coming from the direction Lilly ran. I listened intently.

Lilly? Was that Lilly?

The woman screamed again, and I heard another sound. A bear? A dog? Coyote? I took off down the trail as fast as my legs would carry me. I heard it again, but this time the voice was screaming for me: "Dad! Help me! Dad!"

I rounded the first bend and headed up a small rise, my lungs already burning. As I topped the rise, I caught a glimpse of her. She was on the ground, about a hundred yards in front of me, just to the right of the trail. She was screaming and crying and poking at something with a stick.

"Lilly!" I yelled. "I'm coming! Hang on!"

"It's trying to kill me!" she screamed.

As I closed in on her, I saw the dog. It was a Doberman. And then I saw the blood on Lilly's face. Her jacket was ripped and her exposed shoulder was bloody. She was swinging a small tree limb in her right hand, desperately trying to keep the dog at bay. I kept running and started looking for a weapon.

"Hey!" I yelled. "Here! Here! Come get me!" The protective, parental instinct had taken over. I wasn't thinking about anything but getting the dog away from my daughter. Even without a weapon, I headed straight for it with absolutely no idea what I'd do when I got there.

Kick it, I told myself, punch it, pick it up and smash it against a tree if you have to.

The dog moved toward Lilly. Thirty yards. She swung the stick she was holding, and the Doberman yelped and backed off a little. About fifteen yards short of Lilly, I spotted a thick branch beneath a white oak. I grabbed it up, still running. Then I was between Lilly and the dog. Lilly was crawling backwards crying. The dog lowered its head and snarled; its canines looked like white spears.

The dog lunged and I brought the tree limb down hard on the top of its head. The oak limb was a perfect club, between three and four feet long and hard as steel. My hands buzzed from the shock as the blow drove the dog's snout into the dirt beside the trail, stunning it. It snarled again and tried to get up, but then staggered forward and collapsed. I looked at the dog for a brief second, and then I turned and looked at my daughter, who was cowering near a bush. She was covered in blood. I turned back and raised the limb. Brought it down hard. Again. And again. The dog's head became a bloody mass of hair and brain matter. I dropped the club and rushed to Lilly.

"It must have come from under that bush," she was saying, pointing to a nearby laurel. "I didn't even see it until it knocked me down."

Terrible thoughts were racing through my head. *The dog is rabid. Lilly's been infected. She could die.*

"We need to get you to a hospital," I said as I quickly tried to examine bite marks. Her forehead was streaked with red. "Did it bite you on the head?"

She nodded. I parted her hair and could see a gash in her scalp.

"Where else?"

She pointed to her shoulder, about three inches from her neck. There were at least two puncture wounds near her collar bone and more on her forearm.

"You did good, fighting him off," I said. "You did good, honey. You're going to be fine now."

I picked her up off the trail and put her arm around my neck.

"Can you walk?"

She nodded.

"Let's get out of here."

SUNDAY, NOV. 2

T he lights were bright, the floors clean, and the smell antiseptic as the doctor in the white coat looked at us sympathetically. His nametag dubbed him Ajeet Kalam. He looked to be in his late thirties, very slightly built, with a roundish face, small teeth, and suspicious dark eyes. His accent told me he was born in India.

I was standing next to a gurney on which my daughter was lying. She'd been sedated, but she was awake. We'd been in the emergency room for three hours, and the Indian doctor was about to tell me something I didn't want to hear.

"It's good that you brought the dog with you," he said.

"It wasn't much fun going back there and dragging him out," I said.

"It was a female, actually." I hadn't bothered to look, and I really didn't care. "How did you kill her?"

"I bashed her head in with a tree limb."

"A violent way to die," he said wistfully.

"I didn't exactly have the time or the means to do it more humanely."

"Rabid dogs are a terrible problem where I come from. They kill tens of thousands of people every year. Especially in the poorer provinces."

Another time, under different circumstances, I might have been sympathetic to the public health problems in India, but at that moment, I couldn't have cared less.

"Do you have the test results?"

He nodded his head.

"And?"

"The dog wasn't rabid," he said. "Lucky for you."

There was a collective sigh of relief as Caroline, Lilly, and I realized that Lilly wouldn't have to undergo the painful treatment for rabies.

"So what's the plan?" I said.

"You look familiar to me," the doctor said. "Have we met?"

"I don't think so."

"I can't put my finger on it. It seems I've seen you recently. Perhaps on television?"

I shook my head, but he looked at me more closely. I could see he was about to put it together.

"Can we get back to my daughter?" I said.

"The crazy woman!" he said triumphantly. He pointed at me. "The crazy woman! You are the lawyer who the crazy woman yelled at on the television!"

"Please," I said.

"Do you know what she was saying? It sounded like a bunch of babble."

"I think she was trying to put a curse on me," I said, immediately wishing I could grab the words out of the air before they reached his ears.

His voice lowered and his eyes widened. He spoke slowly.

"Ah, a curse. Very dangerous. Very scary for you, no?"

"No. Not scary. Now if you don't mind—"

"Right." He looked as though he'd just awakened from a dream to find a young girl lying on a gurney. "How did you come across the animal?"

"We were jogging," I said. "We were going to race. She went out first, and I heard her scream …."

He looked down at Lilly, then back at me.

"Perhaps it is the curse," he said. "Perhaps you should be more vigilant."

"Is there anything else you should be doing?" I snapped. The look on my face must have told him not to mention the curse again because he quickly got back to the matter at hand.

"I'll give her an injection that will help fight infection," he said. "And I'll prescribe some pain medication. The stitches will dissolve, but you need to take her to her doctor in ten days or so just to make sure everything is healing properly."

"Can we take her home now?"

"You can. The test is very reliable, but I want you to keep a close eye on her for a few weeks. If there is any sign of headache, fever, irritability, restlessness, or anxiety, you must bring her to the emergency room immediately."

I patted Lilly on the hand and reached down and kissed her on the forehead.

"You're gonna be fine," I said, as much for me as for her. "You're gonna be fine."

"If you will excuse us, the nurse and I will go ahead and give her the injection. You can come back in about ten minutes."

I winked at Lilly, took Caroline's hand, and walked out of the room, down the hall, and through the automatic doors that led into the sunshine.

"What's this about a curse?" Caroline said after we stood in silence for several minutes. "I thought you didn't know what she was saying."

"It's nothing. Really. Don't worry about it."

"Whatever happened to being open and honest?" she said. "I thought you weren't going to hide things from me anymore."

In years past, I'd made a habit of keeping things from Caroline, things I didn't think she needed or wanted to know. But last year, shortly after my mother's death, I'd finally opened up to her. I told her about Sarah being raped when we were children and about my shame in being unable to defend her, about my terrifying experiences in the military, about the mayhem I witnessed every day at work, about the frustration I felt at being raised without a father. The conversation seemed to lift a psychological burden I'd been carrying for years, and I'd promised to tell her everything in the future.

"I'm not hiding anything," I said. "I just thought you had enough on your mind. Besides, I'm not taking it seriously."

"Who told you she put a curse on you?"

"It was just some old guy who came into the coffee shop the other day."

"So tell me about it."

"I'll tell you on the way home. Let's go get Lilly."

A nurse brought me a wheelchair, and I rolled Lilly out to the car. During the drive home, I told Caroline and

Lilly about the old man who came into the coffee shop Friday morning. I left out the part about one of us having to die, and I didn't say anything about the Dobermans outside Natasha's house the day Fraley and I searched her room.

"Did he tell you his name?" Caroline said.

"I didn't want to know his name."

"Do you think he was some kind of Satanist?"

"I got the impression that he used to be. I guess he's seen the light."

"Doesn't it scare you?"

"No. It doesn't scare me. And it shouldn't scare you either. Don't even think about it."

As we pulled into the driveway, it was strange not to be greeted by an overly excited German shepherd. Rio had been gone for only two days, but already I missed him. Since Jack had moved out, Rio had become my closest male companion.

I parked Caroline's car in the garage and helped Lilly out of the backseat and upstairs to her room. Caroline walked back to our bedroom. Just as we got to the top of the stairs, I heard Caroline yelling my name. The urgency in her voice told me that whatever had alarmed her was serious. I told Lilly to go on to bed and that I'd check on her in a few minutes.

I took the steps two at a time and walked quickly through the house. Caroline was just coming through the bedroom door. All the color had drained from her face. Her left hand was covering her mouth, and with her right she was pointing toward the bedroom.

"What is it?" I said.

"The bathroom."

I walked through the bedroom and into the bathroom. I saw it as soon as I stepped through the door. On the mirror above Caroline's vanity, scrawled in what appeared to be red lipstick, was "AH SATAN."

There was only one explanation.

Natasha had been in my house.

SUNDAY, NOV. 2

I called Fraley, who came over immediately. While I was waiting for him, I searched every nook and cranny of the house. Outside the message in the bathroom, there was no sign of Natasha. Fraley dusted the vanity and the mirror for prints but found nothing, took a few photographs, and then the two of us searched the house again. When we were finished, we stood in the driveway beneath the bright sun.

"What do you think?" Fraley said.

"I don't know. At least the dog will be back tomorrow. No way she gets in the house if Rio's here."

"She's just trying to scare you."

"Yeah? Well, she's doing a pretty good job of it. I don't know why I got back into this business. I should have listened to Caroline and gotten a nice, safe teaching job somewhere."

"And miss all this fun?" Fraley said. "Relax. We get through the hearing, you go see Boyer and make your deal, and then we'll get her psychotic butt off the streets for good."

"What am I supposed to do in the meantime? Sit up every night with a shotgun?"

"You've got some options. Your daughter's going back to school, right? You and your wife can move in with her mother until things calm down, or maybe you could ask the sheriff to put some guys out here until we can get her picked up."

"I'm not going to my mother-in-law's," I said. "I'll call Bates."

I called the sheriff, who had become my biggest admirer since the court hearing with Judge Glass. He agreed to post two deputies, in two cruisers, at my house until Natasha was arrested. I was still concerned, but at least I breathed a little easier.

First thing Monday morning, I waited for Alexander Dunn in the parking lot in back of the courthouse. It was chilly, the sky fast moving and slate gray. He got out of his black, 700 series BMW wearing a navy blue suit covered by a tan, calf-length trench coat. His hair was slicked back as always. His gloved right hand held an expensive black leather briefcase.

"You've got diarrhea of the mouth," I said as soon as he shut the door. "Do you have any idea how much damage you've caused? How could you be so stupid?"

"I don't know what you're talking about," Dunn said as he pushed past me and started toward the courthouse.

"I'm talking about running your mouth to the media. I'm talking about interfering with a murder investigation. I'm talking about obstruction of justice."

He stopped and turned, a smug look on his face.

"Are you referring to the story in the paper yesterday morning about your proposed deal with a murderer?"

"What do you get in exchange for doing something like that? Brownie points? Will she make you look good somewhere down the road? Do a feature on you? Will she turn her back if you make a mistake? Tell me, Alexander, what's the trade?"

"You obviously said something to someone you shouldn't have," Dunn said.

"I didn't say a word to anybody. The only people who knew what was going on were you, Lee, Jim Beaumont, and me."

"Then Beaumont said something to someone, or he leaked it himself."

"It wasn't Beaumont."

"How can you be sure?"

"Because Beaumont's a decent human being, which is a lot more than I can say for you."

"You're a crazy man." Dunn turned and started walking away.

"You still haven't answered my question," I said, catching up to him and leaning against him with my shoulder. "What's the price for betrayal? Did she give you thirty pieces of silver? I swear if you weren't Lee's nephew, I'd kick your butt all over this parking lot."

"Speaking of kicking butt, Lee got a call from the Crossville district attorney's office late Friday," Dunn said as he continued to walk. "Have you been to Crossville recently by any chance?"

He caught me totally off guard. After a long silence, I said, "What I do outside the office is none of your business."

"It seems that one of the probation officers down there—I believe he's dating your sister—got beaten up pretty badly. He had to be hospitalized overnight."

"Is that a fact?" I said stupidly, unable to think of anything else.

"Yeah, it's a fact. You know what else is a fact? He told them you did it. He doesn't want to press charges for some reason, but why would he tell them something like that?"

"I guess he doesn't like me."

"Imagine that. Lee isn't very happy about it. And who can blame him? A member of his office, an assistant district attorney, going into another district and committing a crime? It's embarrassing. It's downright *shameful*, is what it is."

We reached the door to go upstairs to the office, and I broke away from him and headed for the front of the courthouse. He was having entirely too much fun at my expense, and I didn't want to listen to any more of it.

"He also said you had someone else with you," Alexander called as I walked away. "My guess is it was your buddy Fraley."

I ignored him and walked up the sidewalk to the corner and turned left toward the front steps. As I walked through the front door of the courthouse, I saw Sarge Hurley, the seventy-something security officer who'd saved my life a year and a half earlier. I'd stopped by to talk to Sarge a couple times since I started working for the district attorney's office. He hadn't changed a bit. Still tall and lean with thinning silver hair, liver spots, and hands as big as country hams. Still had the youthful sparkle in his eye. Still carried his can of pepper spray, and he was still a living, breathing oracle of courthouse gossip. He started smiling as soon as he saw me.

"Well, I'll be danged, if it ain't Mike Tyson," he said. "Or since your first name's Joe, maybe I should call you Joe Louis."

I was horrified. How could he possibly know? Had Alexander Dunn broadcast news of my trip to Crossville over some private law enforcement network I didn't know about?

"What are you talking about?" He was frisking a skinny teenager.

"I hear you got a right hand like a jackhammer and you're mean as a badger."

"Who told you that?"

"Little birdie in a tree. No, that's a lie. It was a fat birdie, ain't no way he could sit in a tree. You didn't think you could do something like that and the news not get out, did you?"

Fat birdie. Fraley. It had to be Fraley.

"I have absolutely no clue what you're talking about, Sarge."

He released the teenager and walked over and put his arm around my shoulders as I headed for the steps.

"Son, I'm proud of you," he said. "Any man that would beat on a woman deserves exactly what you gave him. I wish I coulda been there to help you, though the way I hear it, you didn't need help."

"Do me a favor, will you? Don't spread it around."

He let out a rich laugh. "Too late for that, counselor. Word's already spread like jelly on a biscuit."

On the way up the stairs I dialed Fraley's number.

"Thanks a lot," I said when he answered.

"For what?"

"How many people have you told about what happened the other night?"

There was a long silence. "Just a couple."

"Great. In case you didn't know it, what I did was against the law. It's called battery."

"What you did was *karma*," he said. "What goes around comes around. Eye for an eye, all that. It was justice. And you did it with such *conviction*. If I hadn't seen it with my own eyes, I would've never believed it."

"You need to tone it down. Mooney already knows about it. He'll probably fire me as soon as I walk in the door."

"I didn't mean to cause you any—"

"Not your fault," I said. "Somebody from the Crossville DA's office called him."

"Are they going to prosecute you?"

"I don't think so. Just let it die down, okay? No more stories."

Rita Jones was at her post in the reception area, smacking a piece of gum and wearing a turquoise sweater that clung to her like cellophane wrap.

"Mr. Mooney would like you to come to his office," she said. I noticed Alexander Dunn standing by the coffee pot, acting as though he wasn't paying attention.

I walked straight back to Lee's office. His assistant waved me through without saying a word. I found him sitting at his desk, framed by the American and

Tennessee flags, reading the newspaper. It seemed that every time I went into his office, he was reading the newspaper. Did he do anything else?

"Close the door and have a seat," he said without looking up. His tone was firm and businesslike, unfriendly.

I set my briefcase on the floor and took a seat across from him. He folded his paper, removed his reading glasses, and sat there pinching the bridge of his nose between his thumb and forefinger.

"Alexander was just in here," he said. "He says you accused him of leaking information to the newspaper."

I breathed a sigh of relief. "Didn't waste any time, did he?"

"He said you threatened him."

"That's an exaggeration."

"I knew there would be some resentment when I hired you, but I thought you were confident enough to look over it."

"There's a difference between resentment and sabotage," I said. "That article could have a tremendous effect on my case."

He held up his hand. "I know. I know it could affect your case. Do you have any proof that Alexander leaked it?"

"No, but there were only four people who knew what was going on. Me, you, Beaumont, and Alexander. Beaumont had no reason to leak information to the press, I didn't do it, and I don't think you did. That leaves Alexander."

"There are dozens of ways it could have gotten out. One of the guards at the jail might have overheard Boyer and Beaumont talking. One of Beaumont's partners, one of his secretaries, a paralegal, anybody. He might have discussed it with Dunbar. Someone in our office might have overheard you talking on the phone. There's just no way to be sure it was Alexander. Now I want the two of you to cease fire, and I want you to make an effort to control your temper."

As I sat there listening to him, I began to remember a few of the other reasons—besides money—that I never quite made it down to apply at the district attorney's office. Inter-office politics. Nepotism. Lectures from the boss. It all seemed so silly, so ridiculous.

"I don't think I have much of a temper," I said.

"Really?" His brows raised and he began fingering his moustache. The habit was starting to annoy me.

"It takes a lot to set me off, Lee."

"So what set you off last Wednesday?"

"I beg your pardon?"

"You know exactly what I'm talking about. I got a call from the district attorney in Crossville."

"Yeah, Alexander mentioned something about that."

"You want to tell me about it?"

I looked down at my hands, suddenly ashamed. I felt like a schoolboy in a principal's office.

"There's this guy, Robert Godsey, used to be a probation officer here. He and my sister started dating. It got pretty serious, and then Godsey decided to transfer down to Crossville where he grew up. So my sister follows him down there. And then Wednesday night I get a phone call and this woman tells me that Godsey has beaten my sister up. So I go down there. And when I saw her, I don't know, Lee, I just snapped. Her eye was swollen shut and her lip was split and she had marks on her throat where he'd choked her. I went over to his house. I tried to convince myself to just talk to him, maybe scare him a little, but when I saw him standing in the door, all I could think about was Sarah and how she looked, and I guess I sort of went off on him."

"Sort of? You broke his nose and a couple ribs."

I nodded my head. There wasn't much I could say.

"The DA didn't mention anything about him beating up your sister," Mooney said. "I guess that's why he's not going to pursue it in court."

"I'm sorry, Lee. I didn't mean to cause you any problems."

"He said someone else was with you. Who was it?"

"Just a friend. I'd rather not say. I called him and asked him to go. He was doing me a favor."

He leaned forward on his elbows and rested his chin on his fists. "I like to keep a low profile, Joe. I like for my employees to do the same. This isn't defense work where you have to get yourself in the newspaper and on television to be noticed. The cases come to us whether we get publicity or not. You've handled yourself pretty well up to this point, but lately I see you making some questionable decisions. That little show in the courtroom the other day with Natasha, while amusing to some, was embarrassing to me. You had no business approaching her in the courtroom. And now you've gone to another district and assaulted a man, and I get a telephone call from an outraged district attorney who wants to know what kind of people I'm hiring. This job is hard enough without having to deal with that kind of nonsense."

"You're right," I said. "I apologize."

"I knew Godsey when he was here, and I thought he was a jerk. And I know Alexander's a snit, but my wife loves him and I'm stuck with him. Now I don't want to give you an ultimatum, Joe, but I don't want to see any more of this kind of behavior. Do I make myself clear?"

I was so embarrassed I couldn't look at him. I nodded again.

"Good. Leave the door open on your way out."

TUESDAY, NOV. 4

Caroline started her chemotherapy treatments on the seventeenth of October. In the week leading up to the first treatment, she seemed distant and resigned. The night before she was scheduled to go to the cancer center, she bought a bottle of wine and drank it in less than an hour. While I didn't think it was the healthiest thing she could do, it was at least good to hear her laugh for a little while. Unfortunately, the laughter soon gave way to tears of fear and frustration. She fell asleep on the couch with her head in my lap. I sat there stroking her hair and wondering what the next few months would bring until I finally drifted off to sleep sometime early in the morning.

I drove her to the cancer center early that Friday, just under two weeks after her first surgery. The stitches from her breast and underarm had been removed only the day before, but the cancer was aggressive and quickly advancing, the doctors said. They didn't want to waste time getting started.

As we walked into the room where the chemotherapy was to be administered, I looked around and was immediately struck by the atmosphere. The place was set up like a beauty salon. Five reclining chairs were aligned in a space no more than thirty feet long and ten feet wide, all facing a television perched on a shelf high on the wall. The floor was shiny white linoleum, the walls gray. Frosted plastic sheets in the drop ceiling concealed banks of fluorescent lights. To the right was a long counter, behind which sat three nurses in colorful smocks. One of the nurses, a gray-haired woman with a gentle face, took Caroline into the hallway and directed her to a set of scales. After recording her weight, the nurse led Caroline to a room where another nurse stuck a needle in her arm and withdrew blood. They would use the blood sample for a variety of things, she said, but of primary importance were Caroline's white and red blood cell counts.

An hour later, after she'd been returned to the beauty parlor and her blood had been analyzed, another nurse wheeled an IV tower up behind Caroline. The surgeon who had removed part of the tumor and the sentinel lymph node had installed a port just beneath the skin next to her collarbone. Into the port the nurse stuck an oversized, hook-shaped needle, and I saw Caroline cringe. A plastic bag containing clear fluid was suspended from the tower. A tube ran from the end of the bag and was hooked into another tube that was attached to the hook-shaped needle. For the first thirty minutes, the medicine that flowed through the tube into Caroline's port was to prevent the nausea that the chemicals were sure to cause. Once the bag was empty, the nurse switched to a drug called Adriomycin, a cytotoxin designed to kill fast-multiplying cells. The doctor had explained that cancer cells multiply quickly, as do many other cells in the body. Adriomycin would kill the cancer cells, he said, but in the process, it would also kill other fast-multiplying cells, including those that grow hair and fight infection. After the Adriomycin finished dripping into Caroline's vein, the nurse switched to another drug, Cyclophosphamide, that was supposed to attach itself to the cancer cells' DNA to keep them from reproducing.

I sat by Caroline's side for three hours that first morning. We talked, played cards, watched television. As I tried to distract her, I watched the nurses go about their duties in a starkly efficient manner. All the chairs were filled, and I'd discovered there were private rooms off the hall. Those too were full. Ninety percent of the patients were women, all in varying stages of treatment. Most wore caps—some nylon, some knitted, one crocheted—to hide their baldness. There were dark circles under their eyes, and their faces were sullen and gaunt. I was shocked by how many there were. One would finish the treatment and leave, and another would immediately take her place. The business of cancer was booming.

After an hour, I noticed a distinct change in the smell of Caroline's breath. It was a mixture of metal and almonds, different than the one caused by the anesthesia a few weeks earlier. It reminded me of the smell of cyanide. The irony was undeniable; in order to save her, they had to poison her.

We drove home in the afternoon and waited for her to turn purple, to faint, to vomit. Nothing happened. She felt fine Friday night and most of Saturday, and we began to tell each other that maybe she was one of those special people we'd heard of. Maybe she would remain immune to the side effects of the powerful drugs.

Saturday evening, she began to complain of fatigue. Her bones ached, she said. She slept fitfully, tossing and turning and moaning. On Sunday morning, she got out of bed, and I fixed her a hard-boiled egg. She ate it slowly, almost cautiously, as though she knew what was about to happen. Fifteen minutes later, she was vomiting in the bathroom. I knelt beside her as her body lurched and heaved. I put a cold compress on her forehead, wiped the dribble from her chin and cheeks, the sweat from her temples, the tears from her eyes.

She stayed in bed for the next thirty-six hours, barely able to lift her head. All I could do was help her back and forth to the bathroom and make sure she took in water. I'd never felt so helpless.

Almost three weeks later, I was awakened by an unfamiliar sound at four thirty in the morning. I lifted my head from the pillow and looked around. Caroline was sitting up on the other side of the bed. I could see only shadows in the darkness, but it looked like she'd pulled a sheet over her head. I reached over and touched her back.

"Are you all right?" I said.

Her response was a stifled sob.

"What's wrong?" I said. "What hurts? What can I do?"

She continued to cry in the darkness, so I pulled my feet up under me and slid over to sit beside her on the bed. I put my arm around her and pulled her toward me. As I did so, I reached up with my right hand to stroke her hair, but she'd pulled the sheet tightly across her scalp. I touched her cheek and could feel the wetness of tears.

"What is it, baby? What's wrong?" I said.

Slowly, she lifted the sheet, and as I ran my fingers beneath it, I realized what was going on. She dropped her head onto my shoulder and continued to sob.

"It's all right, Caroline," I said, trying unsuccessfully to comfort her. "It's all right. We knew this was going to happen."

"It isn't happening to you," she whispered.

"I know baby," I said. "I wish it was. I wish it was me instead of you."

I held her in the darkened room, listening alternately to the sounds of her sorrow and the wind whistling outside the window. After several minutes, she loosened her grip on my shoulders, took a deep breath, and lifted her head. "I have to use the bathroom," she said. "Would you take care of it for me and then come back and help me?"

"I'll be right there."

She rose and shuffled slowly out of the room like a ghost, still shrouded in the sheet. As soon as I heard the bathroom door close, I stood up, turned on the light, and walked back and stood over the bed. There, on her pillow, fanned out in the shape of a halo, was her beautiful auburn hair. It had apparently freed itself all at once while she slept.

I went into the kitchen and found a plastic bag, returned to the bedroom, and gathered the long strands. She and her mother had discussed what she should do with her hair if it fell out, and they'd decided to donate it to Locks of Love, a company that made wigs for children with cancer. My job was to preserve it, package it, and deliver it to her mother.

After picking the hair up and placing it in the bag, I changed the sheet and her pillowcase and walked back to the bathroom. She was sitting on a stool, looking at herself in the mirror. The sheet she'd been wearing had been replaced by a pink bathrobe. Small patches of hair remained on her scalp. She was tending to them with a pair of scissors. As I entered the room, she glanced up at me in the mirror, her eyes glistening.

"I'm hideous," she said.

"No. You're beautiful." Choking back my own tears, I walked up behind her and began to stroke her scalp with my fingers. The remaining hair on her head felt like soft down. "I've always thought you were the prettiest girl I've ever seen. I still do."

"Will you finish it for me like we talked about? I don't think I can bear to do it myself."

"Sure, baby."

I dipped a washcloth in warm water and ran it across her scalp. I took a bar of soap, lathered it in my palms, and rubbed it softly up the nape of her neck, back from her forehead, and around her temples and ears. I held her gaze in the mirror as tears streamed down her face.

"It's okay," I whispered. "Everything's going to be fine."

And then, still stroking her head, I reached into the medicine cabinet for my razor.

THURSDAY, NOV. 6

wo days later, I found myself standing with my hands against a gray block wall while a uniformed guard ran his hands up and down my arms, my back, stomach, chest, and legs. He clipped my driver's license and my bar card to a visitors log and took my photograph. When he'd met all his security requirements, he led me silently down a dim hallway, through a door made of steel bars, and into a poorly lit room with a round steel table in the center. There were four plastic chairs at the table, and I sat down. I'd been in hundreds of similar rooms, rooms painted in neutral colors and stained by nicotine and mildew. The musty air smelled of a mixture of floor wax and hot dogs. I could hear trusties rolling lunch carts down the hallway toward the cell block.

I sat nervously picking at my fingernails until I heard the unmistakable sound of shackles tinkling as the inmate shuffled toward the room. There was the sound of a muffled voice, then the metallic clang of the key turning in the lock. The door opened and a short-haired, fierce-looking female guard stepped through. She raised her nose as if to sniff me, then moved her head to the side, signaling her ward that it was okay to shuffle through the door. Without saying a word, the guard stepped back out and locked the door.

I looked at the forlorn figure before me and reached for her. Sarah, cuffed and shackled, fell into my arms and wept. I stroked her hair and listened to her desperate sobs. All I could say was, "I'm so sorry. I'm so sorry."

When the tears finally subsided, we sat across from each other at the table. The jail uniform was green and white striped. It looked like something out of a Charley Chaplain movie. Her face was badly bruised again, her nose swollen and purple. There was a bandage over her right eyebrow and deep scratches just beneath her throat. Her boyfriend, Robert Godsey, was lying in a hospital bed only a few blocks away with a fractured skull. His condition had been upgraded from critical to serious, and from what I'd been able to learn from the nurse on the hospital ward, it appeared that he would be okay.

"How did you get in here?" Sarah said quietly. I noticed she was clutching a wadded up piece of tissue in her hand. "They don't let the inmates have visitors for a week when they first come in."

"I told them I was your lawyer," I said, shrugging my shoulders. "They don't know me here."

"I didn't mean for this to happen, Joe. You have to believe that."

"I do. I believe you. But you're going to have to tell me exactly what happened so I can figure out the best way to handle it."

SCOTT PRATT

She took a deep breath, and I saw tears gathering in her eyes. She started to speak, then stopped and cleared her throat. She wiped her eyes and nose with the tissue.

"We both came home from work yesterday a little after five. I fixed him some supper, but he wouldn't eat. He was pacing around the house and kept disappearing into the bathroom. When he came out the last time, I saw a tiny white flake in his nose, and I knew. I knew he was using cocaine. I've used enough in my day to recognize it. No appetite, can't sit still, irritable—he had all the symptoms.

"So I tried to talk to him about it. I asked him if there was anything he needed to tell me, if he was having problems at work, if he felt like things weren't going to work out between us. He acted like he didn't know what I was talking about, so I mentioned the flake in his nose. He went berserk on me."

"That's obvious," I said. "Have you seen a doctor?"

"They took me to the emergency room before they brought me here," she said. "My nose is broken and they had to stitch the cut over my eye where he hit me with the fireplace poker."

The thought of my sister being beaten with a fireplace poker by an oversized brute enraged me, but I kept my mouth shut. The last thing Sarah needed was for me to start yelling or preaching or saying "I told you so."

"How many times did he hit you?" I said.

"I don't know. A lot. When he hit me with the poker, it knocked me backward and I fell across a coffee table onto the hearth. There was one of those little shovels that you use to clean out the ashes in the fireplace, and I picked it up and swung it at him. It hit him in the side of the head and he fell. His head hit the stone, and he just laid there. I tried to help him, but he wouldn't wake up, so I called 9-1-1."

She dropped her head into her hands and began to weep again. I stood up and rubbed her neck, but it was obvious that the kind of pain she was experiencing was beyond anything I could hope to comfort.

"Sarah, did you tell all of this to the police?" I said.

What she had described was clearly a case of self-defense. The force she'd used in defending herself was reasonable under the circumstances, especially considering the history of the relationship and the fact that she was being attacked with a fireplace poker. The facts wouldn't even support aggravated assault, let alone the attempted second-degree murder charge that had been filed against her.

She nodded. "I told them exactly what I told you."

I moved back around the table and sat down.

"Listen to me," I said. "It happened. You can't change it now. What you can do is fight with all your strength to make sure this doesn't ruin the rest of your life. They've charged you with attempted second-degree murder, which tells me that something isn't right. It's a Class B felony, maximum sentence is thirty years. Your bond is three hundred thousand, cash only, which is ridiculous under these circumstances. It's also more than I can raise right now, so you're going to be stuck here for a while. But I'm going to hire you a lawyer, a good one, and we'll make sure this turns out the way it should. In the meantime, I'm going to go talk to the district attorney and find out what's really going on."

"I know what's going on," Sarah said. "It's Robert's father. He has a lot of money and he has a lot of influence around here. He's a close friend of the district attorney. He brags about it all the time."

"Great. Small-time politics and criminal justice. My favorite combination."

Her face was battered and bruised, her green eyes glistening with tears, and my heart ached for her.

"I'm scared, Joe," she said. "I'm really scared."

I reached for her hands. "I know you're scared. But have faith. I'll make sure you get out of here. I promise."

Less than an hour later, I walked into the reception area of the district attorney's office in Crossville carrying the photos Fraley took the first night Godsey attacked Sarah. I also had more photos stored in my camera's memory, photos I'd taken just before I left the jail. I'd never met District Attorney General Hobart Denton and knew nothing about him. I'd called from the car and told his secretary I needed to see him and that I'd be there in just a few minutes. As I rounded a corner, I saw a plump woman wearing a high-necked green dress who looked to be in her mid-fifties. She eyed me warily as I stood in front of her desk.

"I'm Joe Dillard," I said. "I called earlier."

"Mr. Denton's busy."

"Then I'll wait."

"He's going to be busy all day."

"Then I guess you and I will get to know each other pretty well because I'm not leaving until I talk to him."

There was a door with Denton's name on it directly behind her desk, and I could hear someone talking. I walked around the secretary's desk, knocked twice on the door, and opened it. I could hear her babbling behind me, but I didn't care.

Hobart Denton was just hanging up the telephone when I walked through the door. His head was shaved and he had a bushy mustache. He reminded me of G. Gordon Liddy. He was wearing a gray suit with an American flag lapel pin just like the one Lee Mooney wore all the time. He stood as I approached.

"Who do you think you are, barging in here like this?" he said. He was short and wiry, and I could see a thick vein bulging in the middle of his forehead.

"My name is Joe Dillard." I didn't offer my hand. "I apologize for the intrusion, but I need to talk to you for a few minutes."

"I know who you are, and I know what you want to talk about. I don't have anything to say to you."

"Why are you holding my sister on a charge of attempted second-degree murder when any fool can see that she acted in self-defense?"

"Your sister nearly killed a resident of this district, a man who happens to be from a fine Christian family. Not to mention that she has a record longer than my leg."

"My sister defended herself against a man twice her size who was using her for a punching bag. He hit her with a fireplace poker before she finally hit him back. And this wasn't the first time he's done it."

"Ah yes," he said. "Are you referring to the other recent incident in which Mr. Godsey was badly beaten? He said you were the one that did it."

"I don't care what he said. He got what he deserved, both times."

I held the photos of Sarah up so he could see them. He glanced at them, but quickly looked away.

"These are from the first time," I said. "I just took some more. This one was even worse."

"You can tell it to a jury, Mr. Dillard. A Cumberland County jury who won't appreciate some drug-addled harlot coming into their county and attempting to kill one of their own."

"It doesn't matter where the jury's from. There's no way they'll convict her. Did he tell you he was hopped-up on cocaine?"

"The jury will convict her if I have anything to do with it," Denton said. "I intend to try her, convict her, and send her to the penitentiary where she belongs. Now I have work to do, Mr. Dillard. It's time for you to leave."

I stood there staring at him. "You have work to do? What kind of work? Is there someone else you need to railroad?"

"Get out of my office!" Denton roared.

I smiled at him. "You know something?" I said. "I'm going to enjoy this. I'm going to enjoy showing people that you're nothing more than a corrupt hick."

I spun on my heel and walked out the door, hoping I could get out of the district before he thought up a reason to have me arrested. My heart was pounding as I jogged through the courthouse lobby and out the front door to my truck.

Once I cleared the county line, I started thinking about Sarah. I'd been around the legal system long enough to know that if a prosecutor is bent on convicting someone and he has a judge in his pocket who will let him bend the rules, the chances of beating them at trial are slim.

Sarah was in real trouble this time. If I lost this fight, she was likely to lose the rest of her life.

FRIDAY, NOV. 7

The next morning, my cell phone rang at six. I'd been up for a half hour, sitting at the kitchen table drinking coffee and waiting for the sun to come up. The sky was just beginning to brighten, and as I looked out over the back deck, I could just begin to make out the silhouettes of the trees along the ridge line to the east. I walked over to the counter where the phone was charging and looked at the caller ID. It was Leon Bates.

"We need to have a sit-down," Bates said.

"When?"

"This morning. Right now if you can. It's pretty important."

"Where?"

"Someplace private. I don't want nobody seeing us or hearing what I have to say."

"How about here? There's nobody here but Caroline and me, and she won't be awake for a couple hours."

While I waited for Bates, I threw on some clothes, a jacket, and a pair of gloves. The temperature was in the low thirties, but the wind was calm. I thought it might be best if Bates and I took a walk around the property. That way Caroline wouldn't be disturbed when Rio inevitably started barking.

I called the dog, walked outside, and stood at the head of the driveway. Bates showed up in his black Crown Victoria a few minutes later.

"You up for a walk?" I said.

"Why not? Just let me grab my gloves. Is that dog going to tear my leg off?"

"Not unless I tell him to."

We walked down the driveway and behind the house, through the backyard, and onto a walking trail that I'd carved out of the woods several years earlier. Many of the trees had lost their foliage, and the leaves covered the ground like a vast green carpet. Dampness from recent rains gave rise to a slightly musty odor, an odor that always reminded me of playing in the woods behind my grandparents' home when I was a child. Rio ran ahead of us, lifting his leg next to tree trunks and chasing squirrels.

"Nice place," Bates said. He was wearing his dark brown cowboy hat, an image he often liked to portray to the media.

"Thanks. You should come out some time and bring the wife. We'll drink a few beers and swap a few lies."

"I might just do that. How's the missus?"

"Doing as well as can be expected under the circumstances."

"That cancer's a demon. Both my grannies died from it. My great-uncle too. The more they learn about it, the more it seems to spread."

I nodded my head in silence. Surely he didn't come all the way out here to talk about cancer.

"I heard about your sister," Bates said. "Sounds like a bum rap to me."

"It'll turn out okay. The DA down there is a jerk, but we'll figure out a way to beat him."

The woods were damp and cool, and I could see Bates's breath as we walked slowly along the path. The sun was just clearing the hills to the east, and streaks of pale yellow light were filtering through the branches and the few remaining leaves on the trees.

"So what brings you out here so early in the morning?" I said.

"Afraid I've got some bad news."

"How bad? The way things have been going lately, I'm not sure I can handle much more."

"There's a problem in your office. A serious problem. I need to be sure I can count on you before I make another move."

"Count on me for what?"

"To carry the prosecution through. To do what's right. It ain't gonna be easy."

"Why don't you just tell me what it is?"

"You give me your word you won't say anything to anybody?"

"Yes."

"That's good enough for me. I've got Alexander Dunn on tape and on video collecting two thousand dollars in extortion money from a man who runs a gambling operation out in the county."

I stopped in my tracks, stunned. Alexander? He was a jerk, but I didn't think he was a criminal. And I didn't think he needed money.

"Sorry to drop it on you like this," Bates said. "I need to move on Alexander while it's fresh, but I ain't gonna do nothing unless I know you're with me."

"Sorry," I said. "I'm having a little trouble wrapping my mind around this. You say you've got Alexander on tape? You set him up?"

"Yeah," Bates said with a slight chuckle. "He walked right into it. He's got no idea."

"How did this come about?"

"About a year ago I busted a bookie named Powers, big operation, especially for this part of the country. He was booking about fifty thousand a week. About a month after that I popped a casino that was set up in a big boat out on the lake. They'd run up and down the lake all night, gambling. Busted the operator and all the players."

"I remember both of them," I said. "It was all over the news. That's when I knew you were either crazy or serious about what you were doing. The cops and the prosecutors around here have always left the gamblers alone."

"What you didn't hear about was that three or four months after the arrests, after the cases went to criminal court, they wound up getting dismissed at the recommendation of the district attorney's office. The first case, the bookie, walked because Alexander Dunn told the judge that the sheriff's department had illegally wiretapped the bookie's phone."

"Did you?"

"Maybe, but we weren't gonna use any of it in court. We got enough information from the tap that we started putting pressure on some of the players and went at him that way. Then we set up a sting and popped him when he paid off a winner. I don't even know how Alexander found out about the tap.

"Then the second case got dismissed because Alexander told the judge we'd illegally obtained a search warrant for the boat and that the boat may have been in another county when we did the raid. I didn't know the county line ran right down the middle of the danged lake, but it seemed to me like Alexander was looking for ways to get the cases dismissed instead of helping us put these guys in jail. Even the customers walked."

"So you started looking at Alexander?" I said.

"Let's just say I was suspicious. A couple weeks ago, I arrested this ol' boy that lives on a farm out in the county and ran a little casino in what used to be the hayloft of his barn. Not real big time, but big enough. So I get him into interrogation and start threatening him. I threaten to bring the feds in, which I'd never do but he didn't know it. I threatened to arrest his wife. Told him I knew she was in on it too. Finally, after three or four hours, he told me he had some information that I might be interested in. Said it was big stuff. So I agreed to make a little trade with him if the information turned out to be useful. Turned out to be real useful."

We started walking again, slowly. I was having trouble believing what I was hearing, but Bates had no reason to lie to me.

"This boy said most of the people who run gambling operations around here—card games, bingo, video slots, tip boards, bookies, craps, roulette, you name it—used to make campaign contributions to the district attorney and the sheriff. Always in cash, even in years when there wasn't an election. They had sort of an unspoken understanding. I've never taken any of their money and never will, but a few months after Mooney got elected, Alexander started making the rounds. He told everybody there was a new deal. Monthly payments, cash, and he raised the stakes on them. My informant says they were all upset about it, but what were they gonna do? Call me?"

"So how'd you set him up?"

"I just waited for him to make his regular monthly pickup. Had cameras inside and outside the house and the informant wore a wire."

We turned a corner on the trail and started walking back toward the house. The quickly rising temperature had caused the air near the cool ground to condense, and a shroud of gray mist hung motionless among the trees. The thought of Alexander extorting money from gamblers blew my mind. He put forth such a polished public image, and he was so smug. Still, I took no pleasure in what Bates was telling me. It could lead only to a huge public scandal, with the district attorney's office at its center.

"Have you talked to Mooney about this?" I said.

"Not yet," Bates said, "but I'm going to. He's got a tough row to hoe ahead of him, being that Alexander's his nephew and Lee hired him and put him in charge of a bunch of big cases, at least until you came along."

"Maybe that's why he hired me," I said. "Maybe he suspected something."

"Maybe, but if he suspected something, he should have told somebody about it. This is gonna cause him some real problems."

"Any evidence that Mooney might be involved?"

"Nope. Not a bit."

"So why are you telling me all of this, Leon? Why don't you just turn it over to the feds and let them do their thing?"

"I don't trust the feds. Lee Mooney and his wife both have a lot of political connections. We turn this over to the U.S. Attorney and there's a good chance it goes away the same way my gambling cases did in state court. I want you to prosecute Alexander, and I want you to make sure the case is handled the way it should be handled."

"That won't be up to me, and you know it. That'll be Mooney's call."

"Trust me," Bates said, "you'll catch the case."

We made our way up the hill and back up the driveway to his Crown Vic. As he opened the door, he turned toward me and his eyes narrowed.

"Honest injun, Dillard," he said, "you up for this? All I'm asking you to do is what's right."

I nodded my head.

"That's all I need then. I'll have a little chat with the district attorney when the time is right."

Bates climbed into the car and started the engine.

"Hey Leon," I said, tapping on the window. He rolled it down. "You said you made a little trade for the information your informant gave you. What was it?"

He took off his cowboy hat and set it on the seat beside him.

"You didn't hear this from me," he said, "but I told him I'd make sure he didn't get no more than a year's probation, and I told him he could keep his equipment and keep right on doing what he's been doing for one more year. After that, I figure me and him will be even and all bets are off. You okay with that?"

I shrugged my shoulders and smiled. What could I say? It was just the high sheriff of Washington County doing business the same way it had been done for decades.

FRIDAY, NOV. 7

I looked around the room at the portraits of the generals and presidents hanging on the oak-paneled wall: Robert E. Lee, Stonewall Jackson, Ulysses S. Grant, William Tecumseh Sherman, Jefferson Davis, Abraham Lincoln. Sandwiched between them was a framed law degree from the University of Tennessee and certificates that said Jim Beaumont was licensed to practice law in Tennessee and in the federal courts.

Beaumont walked in a minute later carrying two cups of coffee, his graying brown hair still wet from his morning shower. I'd called him right after Bates left and told him about Sarah's case in Crossville, and he'd agreed to meet me at his office. He handed me a cup of coffee and sat down next to his antique mahogany roll-top desk. He was wearing a tweed vest over a white shirt and a string tie. He looked at me, and I could see compassion in his eyes.

"Never thought you and I would be talking under these circumstances," he said in his syrupy drawl. "I'm truly sorry about what happened to your sister."

"Thanks," I said. "Can you work it into your schedule? I know it'll be a pain driving back and forth to

Crossville, but you're the only guy around here I'd trust to handle it."

"Appreciate the confidence," Beaumont said, "but I've been thinking about this ever since you called, and there might be a better way to handle it than going into unfamiliar territory and trying a criminal case where the odds are likely to be stacked against us."

"I'm open to suggestions."

"This district attorney, Hobart Denton, I know a little about him. A friend of mine from law school's been practicing down there for more than thirty years. We've stayed in relatively close contact over the years. We talk on the phone every six months or so, take in a Tennessee football game once or twice a year, that sort of thing. He's told me quite a bit about Mr. Denton."

"Good or bad?"

"Let's just say he holds an extremely low opinion of the district attorney."

"We share the same opinion," I said. "I had the distinct displeasure of speaking to him face-to-face."

"Did you now?" Lines formed ridges across his forehead as he raised his eyebrows. "And how did that conversation go?"

"Not well. I'm afraid I made things even worse. I called him a corrupt hick."

Beaumont laughed richly. His laugh always reminded me of Santa Claus, a throaty "ho, ho, ho."

"You'll be pleased to know that from everything I've heard about Mr. Denton, you were right on both counts," he said.

"You said something about another way to handle it. What do you have in mind?"

"A little trick I learned a few years back dealing with another politician whose name I can't reveal. I know it's hard to believe, but politicians are human, and humans have secrets. I found that the key to getting a politician to do what you want him to do is to find his secrets and threaten to reveal them."

I'd always found Beaumont to be an intriguing character with his mixture of Western outfits, country charm, and genteel mannerisms. On the surface, he was the perfect Southern gentleman. But he'd been playing the game, and playing it well, for three decades, and I knew from experience that a person can't be effective for long in criminal defense without a willingness to act ruthlessly when the situation called for it. He apparently was of the opinion that this was the right situation. What he was suggesting was clearly blackmail.

"So how does one go about finding the secrets?" I said. "Hire a private investigator?"

"Exactly, but not just any private investigator. We need experience, we need professionalism, we need discretion, but more than anything we need results."

"From the look on your face, I'm assuming you have someone in mind."

He nodded slowly, the dimples in his cheeks barely showing as his lips curved into a shrewd smile.

"There are a couple gentlemen I met after doing some very thorough research. Both are retired FBI agents who spent most of their careers in Washington, DC, and both are very skilled in every phase of investigation. One lives in Atlanta. The other is in Boca Raton. I haven't spoken to them in a couple years, but I can tell you this—the work they did far exceeded my expectations."

"Expensive?" I said.

"Very, but compared to the cost of a trial two hundred miles away, it's a drop in the bucket."

"How much?"

"I'd say fifty thousand will cover everything, including my fee."

"How long will it take?"

"If they're able to get to it right away, probably less than a month. Would you like me to call them?"

"Absolutely."

He pushed himself up stiffly from the chair.

"Please don't take this personally, but they're extremely particular about the people they deal with. So with your permission, I'll make the call from the library."

"By all means."

Beaumont walked out of the room, leaving me there to ponder the portraits and think about the world in which I worked each day. Nothing was as it seemed. Nothing was real. Virtually everyone I dealt with, be it judge, victim, defendant, defense counsel, sheriff, boss, even coworker, had an agenda that had little to do with a quest for justice. When I went to work for the district attorney's office, I thought I'd be doing something right, something worthwhile, something I could feel good about. But I'd found the game was the same, and the side I was on was of no real consequence.

Beaumont returned twenty minutes later, a mischievous grin on his face.

"They're in," he said.

"When?"

"As soon as I wire them a twenty-five-thousand-dollar retainer."

"You'll have it tomorrow."

I stood and offered my hand to Beaumont.

"Do you think this will work?" I said.

"I have every confidence that these gentlemen will lift Mr. Denton's skirt up over his head, and by the time they're finished, we'll be intimately familiar with everything that's underneath."

I thanked him and turned to leave, but before I got to the door a question popped into my head.

"Hey Jim," I said, turning around. He'd already taken his seat behind the desk. "I've known you for a long time. Why haven't you ever told me about these guys? I probably would have used them a couple times."

He reached up and started stroking his goatee, rocking slowly back and forth in the chair. His eyes locked onto mine, and I knew, for once, I was about to get an honest answer from someone.

"Because you were my competitor," he said. "You still are."

FRIDAY, NOV. 7

She showed up out of nowhere, just like the first time. Fraley had been frantically searching for Alisha because without her we had very little chance of winning the motion hearing that was scheduled for Monday. Fraley said he believed Alisha's foster parents knew where she was, but they weren't telling him. He'd canvassed the downtown area, leaving his card at craft shops and the few art dealers in town. He'd gone to the university where he left notes for her on bulletin boards with instructions on how to contact him or me. He'd gone to the local arts center, asked around, and left another note on a bulletin board. For the last two days, he'd been cruising the mall, restaurants, the shopping centers—anyplace where there were a lot of people—approaching anyone he described as "earthy-looking," showing them her photograph and leaving his card.

I worked late Friday evening. I'd spent the last few days making sure everything was ready. Our witnesses were lined up—all but Alisha—and I'd read case after case, scrounging for anything that would help me with the arguments I'd have to make in front of Judge Glass. I was the last one out of the office, and by the time I stepped through the door into the crisp evening air, it was dark. A cold front had rolled in over the mountains, bringing with it the first snow of the year. Tiny flakes danced on the wind, brushing lightly against my cheeks as I walked through the empty parking lot.

I started my truck and was just reaching up to put it in gear when the passenger door opened. I turned my head and nearly jumped out. When she opened the door, the interior light hit her face and good eye, and I thought Natasha was climbing into my truck.

"You're looking for me," Alisha said. She was wearing a long, black overcoat and gloves, her head covered by a tan knit stocking cap. The long, flowing red hair I remembered from the park was tucked inside the coat. She turned her face toward me, and the same flesh-colored patch covered her right eye. Her left eye sparkled like a gemstone, and she smelled of pine-scented incense.

"Yes," I said, feeling a mixture of shock, relief, and fear. "Yes, I am. Do you want to go back in the office and talk?"

"I'd rather just ride if you don't mind."

She was the same size as Natasha, had the same face and hair. The only difference I could discern was the eye patch, but anyone could put on an eye patch. I needed to be sure. I had no intention of winding up dead by the roadside like the Becks.

"Do you have any identification?" I said.

"No, I don't."

"Please forgive me, but I'm going to have to ask you to prove to me that you're not your sister. You look just like her."

She smiled. She took her gloves off and reached up slowly with her right hand. Her long, slim fingers slid underneath the eye patch and lifted it, revealing a yellowed orb, covered by what appeared to be a milky cataract. I dropped my eyes immediately, feeling like a jackass.

"Thank you," I said. "I hope you understand."

I pulled out past the courthouse and turned left on Main Street, heading toward the rural community of Lamar and the Nolichuckey River. Now that she was there, I didn't quite know where to start. I found myself wondering whether she knew what I was thinking.

"You were right about Boyer and Barnett," I said as we made our way slowly down Main, "but we have to go into court on Monday and tell the judge how you knew."

"Do I have to testify?"

"I'm afraid so. If you don't, there's a chance that the judge will exclude all our evidence. If that happens, Boyer and Barnett will walk away."

She sat there in silence for a minute, the streetlights causing a strobe-like effect across her face.

"Why hasn't Natasha been arrested?" she said.

"We don't have any solid evidence against her. Not yet anyway."

"She was there."

"How do you know? I realize this must be difficult for you, but you have to explain *how* you knew about the murders."

"I'm afraid you'll find it hard to believe."

"Try me."

"It's been this way with Natasha ever since I can remember. When something extreme happens where she's involved, especially something violent that springs from rage, I can see it in my mind. It's like watching a movie on a screen, but the images appear in flashes, like black-and-white photographs."

I was struck again by the tone of her voice. It was a mellow soprano, almost melodic.

"And that's how you knew about Boyer and Barnett?" I said. "You saw them in a telepathic flash?"

My mind began to churn. I pictured myself questioning her during the hearing, her sitting on the witness stand in a shawl and hat with her eye patch and telling the court she was telepathic. Judge Glass would disallow her testimony, dismiss the case against Boyer and Barnett, and I'd be lynched by sundown. Unless, of course, I could find an expert witness who would agree to come to court and testify by Monday. But even if I could find one, Beaumont would stand up and object because if I was going to employ an expert, the rules required that I notify him and send him a report. Then again, I could argue that parapsychology was not recognized as a bona fide science, so the witness was not technically testifying as an expert, but merely as a witness who could illuminate the issues for the court. It might work. After all, everything Alisha had told us had turned out to be true. What other explanation could there be for her knowing what happened?

She was there, you idiot! She's wearing a contact lens over her "bad" eye and she's really Natasha playing some kind of sick game with you. Nah, there's no way. The juvenile records. Her mother. They confirmed that Alisha exists.

I glanced over at her, wondering whether I was sitting in the presence of yet another crazed murderer who intended to pull out a gun and blow my brains out as soon as we got out of town. But as we reached the city limits of Jonesborough, Alisha began to recount the night the Brockwells were murdered. She was awakened by what she thought was a nightmare sometime after midnight.

"I saw a woman's back," she said. "I didn't know who she was. It was dark, but I could see she was wearing a nightgown. I saw a hand on her shoulder, holding her. And the next image I saw was the ice pick in her back. I saw it over and over, and I knew. I knew it had to be Natasha."

"You're absolutely sure it was Natasha?"

"I see what she sees," she said softly. "At first, I kept telling myself it was just a nightmare. Mrs. Hamilton heard me screaming and came into my room. She held my hand and rubbed a cool washcloth on my face. I think I went back to sleep for a while, but then …."

She became silent. I didn't want to press her, but I had to know. She had to tell me everything.

"Then you saw the image of Mr. Brockwell?"

She nodded, sniffling.

"That was when I saw Sam and Levi. They shot Mr. Brockwell. I'm so sorry."

She began to sob, and I found myself thinking that she was either telling the truth, or she was one of the best liars I'd ever met. She seemed like such a gentle creature.

I leaned over and popped the glove compartment open, took out a napkin, and handed it to her.

"You don't have anything to be sorry for, Alisha. If it hadn't been for you, they'd still be out there killing people."

"I saw an image of Mr. Beck the day he was killed," she said through her tears. "He was standing next to a brick wall in the sunlight, holding his son in his arms. Then I saw his picture in the paper the next day. Natasha must not have been there when the Becks were killed because I would have seen something. But she at least saw Mr. Beck—I'm sure of it. And if I'd come to you sooner, maybe Mr. and Mrs. Brockwell would still be alive."

I reached over and squeezed her shoulder. "None of this is your fault."

As we drove south on Highway 81 toward the mountains, she sat quietly in the darkness. I asked her about Natasha, and she shook her head slowly and began to tell me about their lives. She said she and Natasha were born in Mountain City. Her father owned a Chevrolet dealership there, and the family was comfortable until she was eight years old. Then one day her father went out for a pack of cigarettes and never returned. The dealership was broke, she said, and her father had embezzled tens of thousands of dollars. There was an intense search, but he disappeared without a trace, taking his embezzled money with him.

Natasha was her identical twin, but she said she never felt the kinship, the closeness, that she'd read about among other twins. Alisha remembered Natasha as being surly and reclusive, almost paranoid, from the beginning.

"We both got kittens for our seventh birthday," she said. "Natasha's bit her on the finger. It bled and she cried. A little while later, I saw her take the kitten outside. It was the first time I saw the images. I was sitting on the couch with my kitten when this awful scene flashed in my mind. It was a kitten, tied down on its back, spread-eagled, and it was bleeding from the mouth. I went outside to find Natasha. She was behind the garage. She'd taken stakes from our tent and some string and tied the kitten down, just like I pictured it. She was pulling its teeth with a pair of pliers."

Natasha, she said, was unable to control her rage even in daycare. She attacked other children without hesitation, forcing her mother to remove her from the daycare and keep her at home. Not even her father, who was a strict disciplinarian, could control her. When their father left, the family moved back to Johnson City to be near Marie Davis's family. Marie took a series of menial jobs, leaving Natasha's care and schooling to Marie's mother. Natasha's behavior continued to worsen until one day, when the twins were thirteen, she set fire to her grandmother's home. Marie finally took her to a psychiatrist, who recommended that Natasha be committed to an institution.

"She was gone for two years," Alisha said. "They were the best two years of my life. When she came back, they said she'd be okay as long as she took her medication, but she stopped. By that time, my mother had suffered a nervous breakdown and she wasn't working anymore. She took lots of pills."

A little over a month after Natasha returned, Alisha awoke one night to find Natasha standing over her with an ice pick.

"I thought I was dreaming. I saw an image of myself lying in bed," she said. "As soon as I opened my eyes, she stabbed me."

"Why? Why would she do something like that?"

"Who can explain madness? Who can explain evil? Natasha is both, Mr. Dillard. She'll kill again if you don't stop her soon. Now that she's crossed that line, she'll never go back."

Doctors who treated Alisha at the hospital the night Natasha stabbed her called the police, who in turn called social services. Alisha was moved into a foster home for her own protection.

"Natasha told Mother that if she tried to send her back to the institution, she'd kill her," Alisha said. "Mother talked them into letting her stay. She promised she'd make sure Natasha took her medication. I think she did for a while after that, but Mother can barely take care of herself, let alone someone like Natasha."

"Isn't your mother afraid of her?"

"She's afraid of her, but she says Natasha needs her. They live off Mother's Social Security checks. And if something happened to Mother, Natasha knows she'd be right back in the mental institution."

She talked for a while longer as I wound through the back roads of the county. The snowfall had eased, and there were only occasional flakes rushing past the headlights like tiny shooting stars. Eventually, I brought the conversation back around to the hearing on Monday.

"Do you know Boyer and Barnett?" I said.

"They both grew up in our neighborhood. I went to school with Sam Boyer until Mr. Brockwell finally kicked him out for good. Levi's a few years younger than me, but I knew him."

"How would you describe them? What kind of people are they?"

"Poor, angry, neglected. Like a lot of kids in that neighborhood. Levi was especially mean. I saw him beat up Kerry Jameson one day. It was a long time ago. Natasha was in the mental institution. It was summertime, and a bunch of us were playing stickball in a field not far from my house. All Kerry did was call Levi a sissy. Kerry was older and bigger than Levi, but Levi picked up a stick and beat him so badly they had to take him to the hospital."

"Why would they kill for Natasha?"

"I don't know for sure, but Natasha started studying Satanism as soon as she got back from the institution. She liked the rituals and the philosophy. She tried to get me involved, but I didn't want any part of it."

"What's the philosophy?" I said.

"Do whatever you want. Please yourself. There are no consequences to your actions. If you feel like having sex, you have sex. If you feel like taking drugs, you take drugs. If you feel like killing someone, you kill them. They don't believe they're subject to the laws of man. If Natasha was controlling them, she was probably using a combination of sex, drugs, and satanic propaganda."

"Have you seen Boyer or Barnett lately?"

"I went over to my mother's on her birthday. I called first to see if Natasha was around, but she said Natasha had been out all night and was asleep. When I got there, Sam and Levi were just coming out the front door. They got in Sam's car and left. Mother said they spent the night in Natasha's room. She said they'd been hanging around a lot."

"When was that?"

"August ninth."

"Doesn't Natasha have the same kind of telepathic connection with you that you have with her?"

"No, but she can do something that I can't. She can interfere with electricity somehow. She does something with her mind, something that somehow overloads electrical circuits. I've seen her do it. It's very frightening."

I thought about what Fraley had told me the morning after Natasha was arrested. He said he was in the middle of interrogating Sam Boyer when the power seemed to surge and some of the lights in the building exploded.

"Alisha, can I trust you to show up on Monday morning?"

All I had to do was hand her a subpoena, and then if she failed to appear, I could get a brief continuance and have her arrested and held as a material witness. But I couldn't do it. Part of me hoped she would stay away and let me take my chances with the judge. After listening to her and observing her for an hour, I no longer suspected that she might be involved in the murders in any way. She was so beautiful, so serene, so seemingly pure. I was genuinely concerned for her safety, and I knew I'd never forgive myself if something happened to her.

"Do you know what Alisha means, Mr. Dillard?" she said.

I shook my head.

"It means truth. I'll be there."

"Aren't you afraid of what Natasha might do?"

"I have something much more powerful than Natasha."

"Really? What is it?"

"I have faith."

I thought about the photographs of the six murder victims, the wild look in Natasha's eyes in the courtroom, the message on my bathroom mirror.

"I'm afraid you'll need more than faith if Natasha decides to come after you."

She turned and looked out the window for a few minutes. When she turned back, she was smiling warmly.

"I'm not worried," she said. "I have faith in God, and I have faith in you."

SATURDAY, NOV. 8

got a hold of Tom Short, my forensic psychiatrist friend, early on Saturday morning. I thought he'd be skeptical of Alisha's claim that she received telepathic signals from Natasha and was fully prepared to deal with a barrage of wry sarcasm. But instead, after listening to what Alisha had told me, Tom surprised me by saying there had been some interesting progress made in parapsychology in recent years and gave me the telephone number of a woman who lived in Sea Island, Georgia.

"Her name's Martha King," Tom said, "marvelous-looking woman. Probably forty or so, tall, shiny black hair, jasmine eyes, terrific body."

"Is that how you describe her to your wife?"

"I don't think I mentioned her to my wife, now that you mention it. She has a doctorate in parapsychology, and she's also what they call a seer."

"A seer? What's that?"

"A person who can see things others can't see. A person who knows things he or she couldn't—or shouldn't—know. A psychic. I met her at a conference in Hilton Head five or six years ago. She convinced me."

"So you think it's really possible?" I said. "I guess the better question is do you think I can convince a judge that it's possible?"

"Give her a call," Tom said. "I promise it'll be an experience you won't forget."

I dialed the number. After a couple rings, a woman's voice answered. Once I was sure I was talking to the right person, I told her who I was, that Tom had suggested I call, and gave her a brief outline of my situation with Alisha, Natasha, and the hearing on Monday morning.

"My biggest concern is that I'll get kicked out of court because the traditional scientific community doesn't recognize telepathy," I said.

"They don't recognize it officially," Ms. King said. Her voice was pleasant, with an accent that told me she'd either been raised or educated in England. "But there are a great number of psychologists, physicists, and mathematicians who absolutely believe that telepathy is real. They simply haven't proven it yet in a controlled, scientific setting, or if they have, they haven't reported it."

"That doesn't do me much good," I said. "I have to convince a judge that my witness is reliable."

"Perhaps your judge will have an open mind about it," she said. "It really isn't that hard to accept. Thoughts are a type of electromagnetic energy, although we don't yet understand precisely how the energy originates or is dispersed. Is the idea that a person can generate a wave of energy that can be received and interpreted by another person so ludicrous? Especially in the case of identical twins? You might want to gather some of the research that the British have done on identical twins and mental telepathy and present it to the court. I'm sure you'd find it fascinating."

"What about telekinesis?" I said. "My witness says her twin sister doesn't have the same telepathic connection, but she can interfere with electricity. Have you seen evidence of that?"

"I've seen things far beyond the ability to manipulate electrical fields. The human mind is a powerful, powerful tool when one knows how to use it."

"What are the chances that you could catch a plane here tomorrow and testify for me on Monday morning?" I said. "The state of Tennessee will take care of all the expenses, and I'll make the travel arrangements myself."

There was a long silence.

"Oh my," she said. "Could you excuse me for a moment?" She sounded like something had upset her. I waited for at least three minutes, the line dead silent. Finally, she came back on.

"I apologize. I've just had a bit of a fright," she said. "I'm trembling all over."

"Is everything all right?"

"I'm afraid not," she said, "and I'm afraid I'll have to turn down your offer to testify on Monday."

"I'm sorry to hear that," I said. "May I ask why?"

"I'm afraid I can't tell you precisely, but I sense that something very evil is going on around you. I don't believe there will be a hearing on Monday."

SUNDAY, NOV. 9

The house where Lee Mooney and his wife lived was tucked into a small grove of white oak trees just off the thirteenth hole at a country club halfway between Boones Creek and Jonesborough. As Leon Bates pulled his car into the driveway, he marveled at the sheer size of the place. The house was three stories, finished with brick and stone, and looked to be at least five thousand square feet. How could one man, one woman, and one child possibly use all that space?

It had been a warm day, a welcome break from the unseasonably cold weather of the past couple weeks. The sun was shining brightly, and Bates felt its warmth on his face as he walked to the front door and rang the bell. He was greeted by a pink-faced Lee Mooney, fresh from the links, still wearing a blue sweater vest and matching blue pants. Bates had called Mooney early in the morning to tell him he had something of grave importance he needed to talk about, but Mooney had put him off until after his Sunday golf game.

Mooney led Bates through an opulent foyer dominated by a crystal chandelier, across marble tile and cherry floors into a beautifully furnished study that looked out over the golf course.

"Drink?" Mooney said as Bates sat down in a plush, high-backed leather chair.

"No thanks."

"Don't mind if I have one, do you?"

"Knock yourself out. It's probably a good idea."

"I see you wear your uniform even on Sunday," Mooney said.

"I wear it when I'm working."

"So you're working today?"

"Sure am. That's why I'm here."

Bates watched as Mooney finished fixing a vodka martini. He dropped three olives from a jar into his glass and carried the glass to his desk. Rather than sit down in the seat next to Bates, Mooney slid in behind the desk.

"To what do I owe the pleasure?" Mooney said.

Bates leaned forward, rested his elbows on his knees, and watched Mooney carefully.

"Ain't no point in beating around the bush, Lee. I arrested Alexander Dunn this morning."

Mooney's complexion immediately changed from pink to purple and his mouth tightened. He began to slowly spin the martini glass with his right hand.

"I assume that was a joke," Mooney said.

"Afraid not. I arrested him for extortion and soliciting a bribe for now. I'm going to have Dillard look at the case and see what else he can come up with."

Mooney took a long drink from the martini and set it gently back down on the desk. Bates had to give him credit. Besides the change in color, Mooney had exhibited barely any reaction to the news. He shook his head.

"Extortion? Alexander? I don't believe it."

"Maybe you'll believe it when you see the video, but for now, I'll just play the audio."

Bates reached into his back pocket and produced a small CD player that contained a recording of the night Alexander collected two thousand dollars from Bates's informant. He pushed the button and allowed the recording to play from start to finish. When it ended, Bates picked the recorder up and put it back in his pocket. Mooney drained the rest of the martini and began to finger his handlebar mustache.

"Alexander's been begging me to make a deal," Bates said. "He says it was all your idea. He wants to give you up. He's even willing to wear a wire on you."

"Doesn't surprise me," Mooney said calmly.

"Any truth to it?"

"What do you think?"

Bates leaned back in his chair and stretched his arms above his head, savoring the moment. Bates was a sheriff, a good one, but he was first and foremost a politician. Opportunities like this were rare, and Bates planned to make the most of it.

"I think it's time for you and me to make a deal," Bates said. "The way I see it is this little situation could go real bad for you unless I was to see my way clear to put a certain spin on it. The way I see it is I can either tell folks around here that I suspect the district attorney has been involved in illegal activity but I can't prove it, or, later on down the road if the word leaks out, I can tell them that we investigated Alexander's accusations thoroughly and there is absolutely no evidence that the district attorney was involved in any way. I can tell them that Alexander is desperate and is trying to save his own skin by smearing his boss. And coming from me, people will believe it."

"What about your recording? It alludes to me." Bates noticed beads of sweat forming at Mooney's temples.

"Digital recordings can be altered pretty easy," Bates said. "Computers are fine tools."

Mooney rose from the chair and walked back over to the bar. Bates watched Mooney's hands closely as he poured another drink. They weren't even trembling.

"You said something about a deal," Mooney said. "What is it you want?"

"Not much. You've got ambitions. I've got ambitions. Me? I think I'd make a fine state senator when my term as sheriff is up. But in order for me to be a senator, I'm gonna need a lot of political and financial support. I believe you could help me with both of those things. But in the meantime, I want you to stay out of Dillard's way and let him make sure Alexander gets what he deserves. I also want your word that you'll support me in everything I do from this day forward. If I bust a gambler, I want him prosecuted. Same with drug dealers, pimps, prostitutes, whatever. You make me look good, and I'll make sure you don't go to jail."

"Sheriff, take a look around you," Mooney said as he walked back to the desk. "Expensive furniture, expensive antiques, expensive art, cherry molding, imported tile, vodka that costs a hundred dollars a bottle. I have plenty of money. What makes you think that I would ever get involved in something like this, despite what my nephew claims?"

"Your wife went to see a divorce lawyer when she caught you sleeping with Rita Jones last year," Bates said. "Can't say as I blame you. Rita's a looker. But stuff like that gets around pretty quick in a small place like this. The way I figure it is that you thought you might be out on your ear, and since you'd gotten used to living the way you do, well, I reckon you just needed another source of income and those gamblers were easy pickin's. But it appears as though your wife has forgiven you. Either that or it'd cost her too much money to divorce you. Am I right?"

A smile crossed Mooney's face as he stood over Bates, drink in hand.

"You know a lot, don't you, sheriff?"

"It pays to know a lot."

Bates rose and stuck out his hand. "So do we have a deal? In exchange for me keeping this ugly matter under my cowboy hat, you support me a hundred and ten percent from now on. And when the time comes for me to move on up in the world of politics, you'll make a substantial campaign contribution, publicly endorse me, and get your friends to do the same. Plus, you stop shaking down the gamblers, give Alexander's case to Dillard, and stay out of his way."

Mooney took Bates's hand and squeezed.

"Have you spoken to Dillard about this?" Mooney said.

"I talked to him, but I said nary a word about you."

"Anyone else know about it?"

"The jailers know Alexander's in jail. My informant heard what Alexander had to say, but I took care of him. That's it."

"Good. Then I guess we have a deal."

Mooney set his drink down on the desk and led Bates back through the house to the front door. As Bates stepped back out into the sunshine, he heard Mooney clear his throat behind him.

"Sheriff, do you mind telling me how you caught Alexander?"

Bates turned and grinned. "It was good old-fashioned police work is all."

"Hmm, good for you. Bad break for me, huh?"

"Brother, let me tell you what my granddaddy used to say when I told him I thought I'd caught a bad break. 'Leon,' he'd say, 'the sun don't shine up the same dog's butt every day. If it did, it'd warp his ribs.'"

Bates tipped his hat to the district attorney, got in his car, and drove away.

MONDAY, NOV. 10

I took the money Jim Beaumont needed to him Saturday morning after I talked to Martha King, and then spent the rest of the weekend trying to distract myself. I ran six miles both Saturday and Sunday, cleaned out the garage, fixed a leak in an upstairs faucet, mopped all the floors in the house, did a couple loads of laundry—anything to keep busy. I slept fitfully Sunday night. Images of Natasha kept haunting my dreams. At four fifteen on Monday morning, I had a vision of Natasha standing over me while I slept, ice pick in hand, and I bolted upright. Sweat was pouring out of me, so I went into the bathroom and took a shower. I didn't even bother trying to go back to sleep.

Caroline's mother, Melinda, walked through the door at seven, right on time. She was a tall and elegant woman, sixty-eight years old. She'd agreed to stay with Caroline during the day until the worst of the sickness passed.

"Why is there a sheriff's car out there?" Melinda said as I gathered my things.

"We had a little problem with someone. Nothing to worry about."

She looked at me suspiciously. "It doesn't have anything to do with the girl who went after you in the courtroom, does it?"

"It might, but I think we've got it under control. If everything goes well today, she'll be in jail by Wednesday."

"For what?"

"For committing crimes against the peace and dignity of the great state of Tennessee."

"How's Caroline?" Melinda said.

"She still has a fever, and I don't think she slept very well. I'm worried about her."

"Well, her mother will take good care of her. You can run along and save the world."

The truth was that I didn't care much for Melinda, although I refrained from saying anything to Caroline. She was a cold and manipulative woman who reminded me very much of my own mother. But I was relieved to have her around. I knew I could count on her to look after my wife.

I was glad to see Alisha standing at the corner of the convenience store when I pulled in. She was wearing the same dark coat and tan cap she'd been wearing Friday. She got into the truck and smiled weakly. She had very little to say on the way to the courthouse. We arrived a little before eight, and I escorted her up the steps to my office. The hearing was scheduled to start at nine. I hadn't heard anyone say anything about it being postponed or canceled, so I made some coffee and brought a cup to Alisha.

Fraley walked in just a couple minutes later in his usual jovial mood. He was wearing a brown jacket that had a small tear in the right shoulder seam and I noticed a stain on his white shirt.

"Well, if it isn't the phantom," Fraley said when he saw Alisha.

"Alisha Davis, meet Hank Fraley," I said.

She smiled and nodded at Fraley. "We met at the park, but we haven't been properly introduced."

"Speaking of the park, where did you disappear to?" Fraley said. "I talked to Dillard for a couple minutes and when I started back down to talk to you, you were gone."

"When you live with someone like Natasha, you learn to disappear," she said. "As soon as Mr. Dillard turned his back, I started walking down the hill toward the lake. Then I walked along the bank. There wasn't anything magical about it."

"I talked to a woman on Saturday who explained some things about telepathy to me," I said to Alisha while Fraley poured himself a cup of coffee. "I tried to get her to come and testify, but she said there wasn't going to be a hearing."

"No hearing?" Fraley said. "Why not?"

"She didn't say. She just said she sensed something about evil being around me."

"I know how she feels," Alisha said. "I have a bad feeling about this."

"Don't worry, you'll do fine. Just answer the questions the best you can."

"That's not what I mean. I just have this nagging feeling that something very bad is happening."

"Happening? You mean now?"

"Yes. Something isn't right."

Lester McKamey sat on the cold concrete bench and sulked. The guards had rousted him early and taken him to a holding cell near the sally port. They'd refused to bring him any breakfast, telling him food wasn't allowed in the holding cell. He'd been there for two hours, and his stomach was churning and growling. To make things worse, if they didn't hold his hearing in the morning, he'd be stuck at the courthouse and would miss lunch too. Being locked up was bad enough. Did they have to starve him to boot?

A fat transport deputy in a khaki uniform unlocked the cell door. The clock in the drab, gray hallway said it was seven forty-five, far too early to go the courthouse.

"Why are y'all takin' me over there already?" Lester whined. "Court don't start 'til nine."

"What difference does it make to you, boy? You can sit on your butt over there as good as you can sit on your butt here."

"I ain't gonna get fed 'til suppertime," Lester said.

"Tell it to somebody who cares."

The guard led Lester down a short hallway. The steel door buzzed and clanged as the bolt released. The door slid back into the wall, and Lester walked through to yet another steel door twenty feet down the hall. It slid open, and Lester could feel the cool morning air. A white van sat idling in the open sally port. Lester climbed into the back, conscious that another inmate was already there. Lester didn't look at the other inmate as the guard chained his shackles to a steel ring on the floor. He wasn't in the mood for idle conversation.

As the van bounced along toward the highway, Lester thought about his prospects. He'd been arrested for his third DUI in eighteen months after being stopped at a sobriety checkpoint a month ago. The cops also tacked on driving while suspended—second offense, violation of the seat belt law, violation of the implied consent law, and misdemeanor possession of marijuana for half a joint they found in the ashtray. His momma and daddy had refused to post his bail, and he'd been stuck in jail ever since. His lawyer, a fresh-faced punk who probably didn't know jack, had filed a motion claiming the roadblock violated Lester's constitutional rights. If the lawyer was right, Lester would be home by suppertime. But if he was wrong, Lester was looking at six more months of eating cheap peanut butter and bologna.

The courthouse was less than two miles from the jail, so the ride lasted only a few minutes. Lester continued to sulk and stare at the floor as the guard unchained the other inmate. Once his own chain was unlocked and pulled through the ring, Lester climbed out. He thought he recognized the other guy as they shuffled toward the steps that led to the courthouse holding cell, but he wasn't sure. He'd get a better look when they got upstairs.

The guard led them through the door, up the steps, and into the holding area. Lester leaned on one foot, then the other, as he waited for the fat guard to unlock the cell. The other dude shuffled into the cell ahead of Lester and plunked himself down on the concrete bench. Lester took a seat on the floor across from him. The guard slammed the cell door and walked out, leaving the two of them alone. The courthouse bailiffs were in charge of

SCOTT PRATT

holding-cell security, but they didn't pay much attention. The last time Lester had been in the cell, a fifty-something lesbian with big teeth had talked on the phone on the other side of the counter for almost an hour. When she hung up, she disappeared until it was time for Lester to go in front of the judge.

The guy across from him was leaning over on his elbows with his face in his hands. He was wearing the standard-issue orange jail jumpsuit. He was lanky and had long, black hair that Lester figured had been dyed since the roots were a different color. Why would anybody dye their hair black like that? It made the guy look like a zombie.

Wait a minute. Wait just a minute. Could it be? Lester cleared his throat.

"S'up, dude?" Lester said.

The zombie lifted his chin. It was him. The baby killer. Lester had seen him on television a bunch of times. *What's his name? Zombie baby killer, that's what. Why would they leave me alone in a cell with a baby killer? I'm just a drunk.*

Lester decided to play dumb, act like he didn't recognize the dude. Maybe he'd even get the zombie to say something Lester could use later on to cut a deal and get out of jail.

"I'm fixin' to get out of here," Lester said.

"That right?" said the zombie.

"My lawyer says they violated my rights by settin' up a road block out in the middle of nowhere."

The zombie responded by dropping his face back into his hands.

"What's your name, dude?" Lester said.

"What do you care?" the zombie said through his fingers.

"Easy, man, ain't no need to get your panties all in a wad. I was just tryin' to be friendly. Whatcha doin' over here today?"

"Beating the hell out of a bald-headed little redneck if he doesn't shut his mouth."

"Wow, you are one hostile dude," Lester said. He stood up and walked to the barred window at the back of the cell that looked out over the parking lot behind the courthouse, still stinging from the remark about his bald head. He'd thought about getting one of those rugs like his uncle Keith, but they were too expensive. Besides, he didn't want to put up with all the mess he'd hear from his drinking buddies if he suddenly showed up with a full head of hair.

Lester watched another van pull up and saw a stocky, black-haired boy get out of the back, wearing the same orange jumpsuit that he and the zombie were wearing. It was the other baby killer. He remembered this one's name because he had a younger brother named Levi. His brother was pretty much worthless, but at least he wasn't no baby killer.

"Looks like we're gonna have company," Lester said.

A couple minutes later, Lester heard the sound of shackles rattling in the hall. The door opened, and Levi came shuffling through, followed by a different transport deputy. The deputy stuck his key in the barred door and opened it. Lester had heard the news about the first baby killer wanting to cut some kind of deal with the

DA's office, and he knew there wasn't but one way to cut a deal. You had to rat somebody out. This could get interesting.

The kid walked into the cell without looking at either Lester or the zombie. He sat down on the concrete bench next to the zombie and stared at the wall while the deputy locked the cell door.

"I'll be back to pick you up at noon, Levi," the deputy said.

What was that? He called the boy by his name. Lester had never heard a guard or a deputy call an inmate by name. Sometimes they'd call them "inmate" or "prisoner," but usually it was "maggot" or some profane insult. They never called anybody by name. He shook his head. If the deputy was coming back to pick up Levi at noon, that meant Lester's hearing wouldn't be held until at least one thirty. He'd have to sit in the cell and twiddle his thumbs all morning. *Why won't they feed the inmates in the courthouse holding cells? I'm gonna have Daddy call the congressman when I get out of here.*

The clock behind the counter outside the bars said ten after eight. Lester could smell coffee brewing and could hear a couple bailiffs laughing beyond the door that opened onto a hallway that led to the courtroom. He put his back against the wall and slid down to sit on the floor.

"I hear you're planning to make a deal," a voice said. Lester looked at the baby killers. The young one, Levi, was staring at the zombie, who still had his face in his hands. Levi's voice was calm, his empty eyes locked onto the zombie's head.

"You shouldn't believe everything you hear," the zombie said without moving.

Levi leaned toward him and hissed, "You gonna snitch on me?"

"I'm not snitching on anybody."

"You're a liar. And a coward."

"You don't know anything, man," the zombie said, and he stood up and started to move toward the window. Before he could get out of range, Lester saw Levi rock back and lift his knees to his chest. His shackled feet flew forward, and the zombie's knees buckled. Lester slid into the corner and pulled his ankles beneath him as Levi leaped onto the zombie's back and drove him face-first into the concrete floor.

A sickening *crack* as the zombie's teeth shattered. Levi straddling him, grabbing two handfuls of hair, pulling his head backward and smashing it into the concrete, over and over. Blood flying, the zombie groaning.

Lester in the corner, frozen with fear as droplets of blood landed on his face and arms. Levi grunting and mumbling, the awful thud of the zombie's head hitting the floor again and again and again and again. Lester watching Levi drive his knees into the zombie's shoulder blades, wrapping the chain that connected his bloodied handcuffs around the zombie's neck. The veins in Levi's forearms bulging. The veins in his temples bulging. Levi squeezing. The zombie dying. Lester closing his eyes.

Voices, loud and excited, coming from the other side of the bars. The sound of metal against metal as they scrambled to unlock the cell door. Cursing. More grunting. The sound of boots scraping. Lester opening his eyes. Levi being dragged from the zombie's prone body. A pool of dark blood spreading out, coming nearer, chasing Lester deeper into the corner. A deputy kneeling over the zombie's body.

Lester screaming.

A bailiff came into the office at eight twenty and said there was a problem in the holding area. I asked Alisha to stay where she was and hurried down the steps with Fraley right behind me. Another bailiff buzzed me through the barred steel door. Levi Barnett was sitting on a metal chair to my right with his head hanging and a bailiff looming over him. I noticed blood on his hands as I passed by. A short, bald-headed inmate was being led out the door. He was crying. When I got to the holding cell, I froze. Lying face down in a huge pool of dark blood was Sam Boyer. He wasn't moving, didn't seem to be breathing.

A bailiff was standing next to Barnett. Everyone else had disappeared, like rats scurrying from a sinking ship.

"Is he dead?" I said to the bailiff.

"'Fraid so."

"You put them in the same cell?"

"We ain't got but one holding cell," the bailiff said. "But it wasn't me that done it. The transport officers was the ones what brought them in and put them in the cell."

"This is unbelievable," I said. "Wasn't anyone in here watching them? Aren't you supposed to keep an eye on them?"

"They was alone for just a few minutes."

I walked over and stood in front of Barnett. Anger pulsed through me like a radio signal. I wanted to strangle him. My chances of getting enough evidence to convict Natasha were dead, along with Boyer.

"Doesn't matter what happens in the other cases now," I said. "You're going to prison for the rest of your miserable life."

Barnett lifted his head and looked at me with dull, colorless eyes.

"I ain't going to no prison," he said. "I'm going to hell with you."

Judge Glass sent word that the hearing would be postponed for two weeks, so I gave Alisha a ride back to Johnson City. The brilliant light in her blue eye seemed to have dulled. She remained quiet for the first ten minutes of the trip.

"Does this mean you won't be able to arrest Natasha?" she said as we rounded a curve near the old Burlington Industries plant.

"I'm afraid so. I think Boyer was going to testify against her. Without him, all we have is circumstantial evidence. It isn't enough to arrest her, let alone convict her."

"You need to be careful," she said. "You know what she's capable of."

Images of Natasha plunging an ice pick into Mrs. Brockwell's back and into Alisha's eye ran through my mind.

"Alisha, would you have any idea where the ice pick might be?"

"No," she said, shaking her head. "I'm sorry. I don't know where it is."

I gave her my home and cell phone numbers when I dropped her off at the convenience store and told her to call me anytime, day or night.

"Stay safe," I said as she stepped out of the truck.

She turned and gave me a mournful look.

"What's wrong?" I asked. "Do you want me to see if I can arrange police protection for you?"

"No. It's not me I'm worried about. You're a good man, Mr. Dillard. I hope I see you again."

MONDAY, NOV. 10

L evi Barnett pondered his bloody hands as he rode silently in the back of the transport van back toward the juvenile detention center. He was looking at the blood of a traitor, the blood of a coward. Sam Boyer wouldn't be making the trip to the other side. He'd sold himself out to the laws of man, and Levi had made him pay the price.

The pathetic cops had made him sit there for almost three hours while they took their photographs and their blood samples. The big cop who'd arrested Levi at the motel and then tried to interrogate him had showed up and scraped some of the blood off Levi's hands. He'd tried again to interrogate Levi, but Levi had refused to say a word. Levi spit on the floor as he thought of the scrawny little bald-headed dude sitting in the corner of the cell. Didn't offer to help Sam, didn't say a word, didn't make a move. All he did was watch and scream like a little girl.

He knew Natasha would be pleased. She'd come to visit him at the juvenile detention center three days earlier. The guards there were so stupid. All Levi had to do was put her on his visitors list. When she arrived,

SCOTT PRATT

they led Levi to a visiting room and left the two of them alone for an hour. Levi knew the guards were watching on video, but they couldn't hear a thing. Natasha had laid out her plan, and Levi had executed the first step to perfection. All that was left was for him to complete the second step, and Natasha would take care of the third.

Levi lifted his hands over his head and stretched. Even though he'd just committed a murder, the transport deputy hadn't cuffed him in back or put a waist chain on him. The policy at the juvenile detention center was that all prisoners going to court were to be cuffed in front. Another deputy was along for the ride as extra security, but as long as Levi's hands were in front of him, he could do what he needed to do.

The van pulled up in front of the detention center, and Levi looked out at the dull, yellow concrete block building. It was a single story with four-inch openings for windows and an exercise area that was surrounded by chain link and concertina wire and was just a little bigger than his cell. What little food Levi had eaten tasted like plastic, and the guards, like the other inmates, were all morons. None of them were armed, and Levi mused briefly about what it would be like to walk in with a weapon and slaughter every last one of them.

But old man Finney was armed, as was the extra deputy. Both carried stainless steel .357 magnum revolvers in holsters on their hips. Old man Finney was the transport deputy the sheriff's department assigned to the juvenile detention center. Every time someone from the detention center needed a ride to court or got hauled off to a juvy home downstate, Finney came and picked them up. Levi couldn't stand the old hypocrite. He wore bifocal glasses with black rims and always had his stupid sheriff's hat on. He called people by their first name and tried to make them think he was their friend. Some friend. Take you to court where you have to sit and listen to some blueblood judge run his mouth and then take you straight back to jail.

Levi waited for the door to open. Finney reached in and started fumbling with the lock that secured the chain through the steel ring on the floor while the other deputy, a young, pasty-looking dude with a buzz cut and acne scars who Levi had never seen before, stood back and chewed on a toothpick. As soon as Levi saw Finney get the lock released and start pulling the chain, he raised both arms over his head and came down hard on the back of Finney's neck. The old man grunted. His bifocals flew off his face, and his hat went rolling toward the front of the van. Levi wrenched Finney's revolver from its holster and pointed it at the pasty guard, who was fumbling with his holster. The guard's mouth was open, and Levi saw the familiar look of fear in his eyes. Before the guard could get a firm grip on the revolver, Levi blew a hole through his chest.

Levi turned back toward the van and stood there watching as old man Finney fumbled around trying to find his glasses. When his fingers finally clutched them, he pushed them onto his nose and rolled slowly over onto his back.

"Levi, what are you going to do?" Finney said.

"What do you think I'm going to do?" Levi said as he raised the revolver and pointed it at Finney's forehead.

"Levi, please. I've never mistreated you."

"You don't want to stay in this world. It's full of bad people. Think of it as a favor."

"No, Levi, please. I have a family. They need me." Finney raised his hands in front of his face. "Levi! *I've tried to be your friend!*"

Levi pulled the trigger and watched curiously as a chunk of Finney's forehead separated from his face and splattered against the interior wall of the van. Finney's body jerked once, and then he was still.

"Yeah, I was thinking about that a little earlier," Levi said. "Some friend."

Levi closed the door. He saw his reflection in the mirrored-glass window. As he looked at himself, he thought about how far he'd come. Not long ago, he'd been a nobody, a poor boy with no education and no future. But all that had changed with Natasha. She'd taught him the ways of Satan, and now he was a celebrity. Everyone knew his name. Everyone feared him. He even received fan mail in jail.

Levi looked down at the fallen guard. A soft, gurgling sound was coming from the wound in his chest. Levi thought about putting a bullet in his head to finish him off, but instead he looked at the building. He could see people looking out the windows. A guard ran up and locked the front door while talking on a cell phone. They'd be coming soon.

Levi raised his middle finger defiantly toward those who were peering out at him. There would be no prison for Levi—not now, not ever. Soon he and Natasha would walk together with Satan.

He fired one shot at the building, then slowly pushed the barrel up tight beneath his chin.

And pulled the trigger.

MONDAY, NOV. 10

After I took Alisha back to Johnson City, I drove home to check on Caroline. She was sleeping, but Melinda said she still had a fever. I drove back to Jonesborough, finished up some work on my other cases, and went to lunch alone. When I returned, Fraley was sitting in a chair in front of my desk with his feet up. He was smoking a cigarette and putting the ashes in a coffee cup.

"You're not supposed to smoke in this building, big boy," I said. "If Alexander smells it, he'll call the police and have you arrested."

"If he calls the police, I'll crush his skull like a peanut shell," Fraley said, taking another long drag.

"Some morning, huh?" I said.

Fraley blew a smoke ring. "You haven't heard, have you?"

"Heard what?"

"About Barnett. He overpowered Deputy Finney in the back of the transport van, got a hold of his weapon, and shot himself in the head."

I felt my knees weaken and sat down behind the desk.

"He's dead?"

"Dead as Elvis. It was a .357 magnum. In under the chin and out the top of his skull. The bullet took a bunch of his brain with it, what little he had."

I ran my fingers through my hair, still unable to completely digest what I'd just heard.

"Is Finney …?"

"Didn't make it. Levi shot him in the head. They sent another deputy along for extra security, a kid named Huff. Killed him too."

My stomach started churning, and I suddenly wished I'd skipped lunch. Both of our murder suspects were dead. Two deputies were dead. We had a third suspect in the murders, but we didn't have enough evidence to arrest her, and now the only two people who could have provided us with that evidence were dead. I wondered how much Alexander Dunn's little leak to the media had to do with what happened.

"So where does this leave us?" I said.

"If you want to look on the bright side, it leaves us with two dead scumbag murderers. I say good riddance. Now we don't have to prosecute them, don't have to feed and clothe and shelter them, and we don't have to waste electricity killing them."

"Your compassion never ceases to amaze me."

"My compassion is with the innocent people they terrorized and murdered. But if you're anxious to look at the bleak side of things, we're pretty much left with nothing as far as Natasha goes."

"What are we going to do about her?"

"Let me drop this little tidbit on you. I drove up to the detention center when I heard the chatter about the shooting. While I was there, I went in and asked the guards about Levi's visitors. He's only had one besides his aunt. Guess who?"

"You're kidding me."

"Three days ago. Signed in under her own name and everything."

My phone rang and I picked it up.

"Is Special Agent Fraley back there with you?" It was Rita Jones.

"He is."

"Mr. Mooney would like to see both of you right now."

Fraley and I made the short walk down the hall to Mooney's office. We found him pacing back and forth between his flags with his hands folded behind his back. Instead of sitting, Fraley and I both stood behind the chairs in front of his desk. He paced for more than a minute, occasionally fingering his handlebar mustache. Finally, he spoke.

"This is a disaster," Mooney said, "a *disaster* of magnanimous proportion. Do the two of you have any idea what happened today?"

It sounded like a rhetorical question to me. Of course we knew what happened, but I'd learned long ago that the best answer to a rhetorical question was no answer at all, so I kept my mouth shut. Fraley did the same.

"Do you know that the reputation of law enforcement in this community was ruined today? *Ruined!* I've spent the last two years of my life trying to make the people here feel safe, make them feel confident about the men and women who are responsible for providing them with safe streets and an efficient court system. I've tried to hire people who are fair and compassionate to victims and defendants alike. And now, in a three-hour span, every bit of credibility we've been able to establish is gone."

I stood there staring down at his desk, focusing on nothing. I told myself that the man had given me a job, and since Caroline had come down with cancer, he'd also probably saved me from bankruptcy. The least I could do was stand quietly while he ranted. Suddenly, he stopped pacing and faced us.

"I want you to know that I hold the two of you at least partially responsible for this," he said.

Fraley and I exchanged an incredulous glance. Since Mooney was my boss, I thought it best that I do the talking.

"Lee, I know you're upset," I said. "Everyone is. But pointing fingers won't do anyone any good."

"Don't patronize me!" he snapped. "When bad things happen in an organization people get blamed. It's called accountability in case you've never heard of it. Those held accountable for whatever has happened usually resign or get fired. At the very least, they change the way they do business. So pointing fingers is exactly what I need to be doing. I have to show the people of this district that we're accountable when something goes this monumentally wrong."

"Explain to me how any of this was our fault in any way," I said.

"*You're* the one who ordered arrests on the basis of information you received from a confidential informant," he said, pointing at me. He turned to Fraley. "And *you*, a veteran TBI agent, went along with it. And as I understand it, your confidential informant had absolutely no personal knowledge of what happened. She didn't see a thing. Because of that, you gave an opening to the defense. Because of that, they filed motions to suppress and a hearing was scheduled. And because of that, Boyer and Barnett wound up in the same cell and now both of them, along with two police officers, are dead! Do you see what I'm getting at?"

I'd read plenty of appellate opinions in which judges convoluted logic to the point of sophistry, but this was beyond even them.

"Our informant was exactly right about everything, and without her, we would've had more victims," I said.

"We do have more victims! And we all look like idiots!"

He was shouting now. His face looked like a candy apple with eyes.

"What do you want from us, Lee?"

"What do I want from you? I want you to make this right! I want you to redeem yourselves and this office! I want that girl arrested. I want her kept alive long enough for you to convict her of first-degree murder in a very public trial. And then I want her executed. *That's* what I want from you!"

"We don't have enough evidence to arrest her, Lee. We needed Boyer."

"Then find some! Plant some! Manufacture some! Do whatever you have to! I want her locked up by the end of the week."

"We'll do what we can, Lee," I said.

"Get out."

Fraley and I spun and walked out as quickly as dignity would allow. Instead of going back to my office, I turned toward the stairs and started down. Neither of us said a word until we were outside. I stopped by a bench near a Civil War-era cannon.

"Can you believe that? He actually tried to blame us for Boyer and Barnett."

"He seemed a little out of sorts," Fraley said.

"And do you know what's even worse? He thinks the only way to redeem himself and the office is with an execution. Redemption through bloodshed."

"Redemption through bloodshed. Sort of like salvation through bloodshed, isn't it?"

"If we don't come through for him, it sounded to me like the axe is going to fall on somebody's neck, and I'll bet you a dollar to a doughnut that somebody will be me."

Fraley reached out and patted me on the shoulder, and I saw the glint in his eye.

"Don't worry about that," he said. "Ol' Fraley's got you covered."

"What do you mean?"

"Back when I first got out of the academy, an old buddy of mine told me that if I was going to last in this business, I'd need to learn to deal with bosses and politicians who were looking for fall guys. He taught me to learn to cover my butt. So when we were walking back to Mooney's office, I turned on my cover-my-butt gadget."

Fraley reached into his inside jacket pocket and pulled out a device that was thin and shiny.

"Was it that? An iPod?" I said.

"No, no, no. This, my friend, is a digital, voice-activated recording device. Top of the line. I never leave home without it."

"And it was on while Mooney was ranting?"

Fraley pushed a button, and I could hear Mooney's voice.

"Wait, let me find my favorite part." He searched through the diatribe for a few seconds.

"Here it is," he said, and Mooney's voice came through loud and clear: *"Then find some! Plant some! Manufacture some! Do whatever you have to! I want her locked up by the end of the week."* Fraley looked at me and grinned.

"I love you, man," I said, and I grabbed his neck and planted a kiss on his cheek.

MONDAY, NOV. 10

"Y'all better be careful," a deep voice said from behind me. "People will say you're in love."

I turned around to see the face of Wild Bill Hickok, back from the dead in the form of Jim Beaumont. Beaumont bowed stiffly and tipped his hat. Today's string tie was made of rawhide with a round piece of polished turquoise mounted on a platinum clasp at his neck.

"I hate to interrupt your affair, Mr. Dillard, but I have a very important matter I'd like to discuss with you."

I told Fraley I'd catch up with him later to form a strategy for dealing with Natasha and turned back to Beaumont.

"Let's walk," he said.

We started walking leisurely up the brick sidewalk, past the International Storytelling Center and the Eureka Hotel toward the west end of Main Street. The unpredictable November weather had changed yet again, and the past few days had been warm and pleasant.

"News from the investigators already?" I said.

"No, not yet. There are some things I need to tell you. I wish I could have done it sooner, but I was bound by the rules of ethical conduct and client privilege. I hope you'll understand."

"Of course."

"Now that Mr. Boyer has expired, the rules say I'm no longer bound by privilege," Beaumont said. "I'll start by telling you that you were right about Miss Natasha Davis. She was deeply involved in all six murders."

"Then why can't we find any evidence?" I said.

"Being insane doesn't make her stupid. She wasn't at the first crime scene, but she ordered Boyer and Barnett to commit the murders because Mr. Beck attempted to share his faith in God with her."

"What were they doing down on Marbleton Road?"

"It started at a rest stop on the interstate. They'd been to Knoxville for some kind of goth festival. On the way back, their car started overheating so they pulled into the rest stop to let it cool down. Mr. Beck approached Natasha. She became angry and gave the other two the order to kill the family. She drove the car back to town, and the boys took the Becks down to Marbleton, shot them, and drove their van back to Johnson City."

"You said she ordered them. Why did she have so much control?"

"Boyer said she controlled them in a variety of ways, but I think it was primarily with two things. She was generous with sex, and she was generous with drugs. She's also an attractive young lady, or at least Boyer believed she was. Beyond that, she put the two of them in a position where they were competing for her attention and affection. She played them against each other. She introduced them to satanic rituals and philosophy and used that as a means to gain further control. Boyer believed the first murders, the Becks, were a test. She was testing their loyalty. He said shooting everyone in the right eye was Barnett's idea. Apparently there's some kind of painting or print of the Eye of Providence in Natasha's home. She hated it, so Barnett shot everyone in the right eye as a symbolic gesture to Natasha."

"And the inverted crosses and running over their legs?"

"Boyer's way of keeping up in the competition."

"What about the Brockwells?" I said. "Why did they kill them?"

"Natasha allowed Boyer to pick their next victim. Boyer said he hated Mr. Brockwell because Brockwell humiliated him when he expelled him from school. They did surveillance on the house for a couple days and then went in and did the deed."

"Was Natasha there?"

"She killed Mrs. Brockwell with an ice pick."

"Boyer saw her do it?"

"Yes. She also accompanied them to the woods where Mr. Brockwell was shot. She gave the order."

"Any chance Boyer told you where Natasha hid the ice pick?"

"I asked him. He said he didn't know. Don't you have any other physical evidence?"

"Nothing solid," I said, "but with what you've told me, if you'll sign a sworn affidavit, I might be able to get a warrant to get a DNA sample from her. We've got some hairs from the Brockwells' place that we haven't been able to match up with anyone."

"I'll have to make an inquiry with the Board of Professional Responsibility first, but I'll do it no matter what they say," Beaumont said.

"Forget the BPR. Those people are nothing but a waste of oxygen."

"I agree, but I'll give them the courtesy of a call anyway. It wouldn't surprise me if they tell me I have to remain silent, even if it allows a murderer to remain free."

"All right, just let me make sure I've got this straight," I said. "Natasha manipulates Boyer and Barnett into forming a sort of mini-satanic cult. She shoves the dogma and ritual down their throats in what appears to be a successful effort to gain control of them. They run into the Becks randomly at a rest stop where Mr. Beck approaches Natasha and wants to talk to her about God. She gets angry and orders her boys to kill them. A couple weeks later, they decide they liked it and they kill the Brockwells. Is that pretty much it in a nutshell?"

"Almost," Beaumont said.

"What did I miss?"

"There are two other things I need to tell you. First, Boyer said Natasha took a necklace from Mrs. Brockwell after she killed her. It was a twenty-four-karat gold cross on a gold chain."

"We searched her house. Didn't find it," I said.

"Maybe she's wearing it."

I tried to picture Natasha in my mind the day I confronted her in the courtroom, but I couldn't remember whether she was wearing a cross. Mrs. Brockwell's family hadn't said anything about a missing necklace, which meant it was either new or she didn't wear it often. If it was relatively new, and if she purchased it with a credit card, we might be able to identify it. *If* Natasha was wearing it, which I doubted.

"Thanks, we'll check it out," I said. "And what's the last thing?"

"Do you remember the article in the paper after the Brockwells were killed in which you referred to the killers as cowards?"

"I didn't read it," I said, "but I remember saying it."

"Apparently the comment didn't sit well with Mr. Barnett. Boyer said the night they were arrested at the motel, Natasha told Barnett it was his turn to pick the victim. They were about to head for your house."

MONDAY, NOV. 10

As I was walking back up the steps to the office, my cell phone rang. I looked down and recognized my mother-in-law's cell phone number.

"Her fever's getting worse," Melinda said. "And she's talking like she doesn't know where she is. I'm taking her to the emergency room."

"I'll be right there."

I turned and ran back down the stairs and out to my truck. I called Rita Jones on the way to the hospital and told her where I'd be, and I called Fraley and told him everything Jim Beaumont had shared with me. Fraley said he'd get a hold of Beaumont, draft an affidavit, and take care of the warrant himself. I was glad to be free of it for a while because suddenly I didn't care about Boyer or Barnett or Natasha. All I cared about was Caroline.

I raced to the hospital, breaking nearly every traffic law ever written along the way. I saw Melinda's car in the emergency room parking lot, got out, and rushed inside. I found Melinda pacing in the waiting room.

"Where is she?"

"They took her back as soon as we got here," Melinda said. Her face was drained of color, her eyes darting nervously around the room.

"Can't we go with her?"

"They told me to wait out here. I think it's serious. They mentioned something about an infection."

Over the next ninety minutes, I paced constantly around the waiting room, to the parking lot, back to the waiting room, to the nurses' station where I was told at least five times that a doctor would be out to talk to me as soon as Caroline was stabilized. They wouldn't give me any information about what was wrong with her or how she was doing. The only thing the nurse would tell me was that they were "treating" her. I didn't want to call Jack or Lilly until I knew more, and Melinda had turned stone-faced and silent. All I could do was pace and think.

As I paced, thoughts kept flashing through my mind: Sarah being beaten, Lilly being attacked by a dog, Boyer dead on the floor. Barnett sitting in the chair: *"I'm going to hell, with you."* I walked back in from the parking lot and glanced across the emergency room lobby. An elderly man in a long sweater was making his way to a chair with the aid of a wooden cane. He reminded me of the old man who warned me of the curse.

Oh, Caroline ... this is my fault. I'm so sorry.

I remembered the old man's voice as I was walking out of the coffee shop: *"One of you has to die."* Had I been wrong to ignore the warning? Had I been too cavalier? Too full of hubris to recognize the threat to my family? And if the old man was right and the curse was real, what was I going to do? I couldn't just go to Natasha's and kill her. What would I tell the police? That I was defending myself from a satanic curse? Good luck selling that to a jury.

Finally, a doctor I recognized came into the waiting room. Collins Reid was the oncologist who was overseeing Caroline's chemotherapy program. He wore a white medical coat and had thick, longish black hair and a beard that covered a pale, round face.

"How is she?"

"Let's go back into the private area," he said, and he led Melinda and me down a short hallway into a large room that was furnished with three brown overstuffed chairs and a matching couch. As I looked around the room, I realized that it must be a place for families to grieve. There were prints of Jesus with the Lord's Prayer and the twenty-third psalm beneath them. My throat tightened.

"I really don't understand this," Dr. Reid said when we all sat down. "Her white cell count was fine when we drew blood before her last chemo treatment. Her count has dropped, which is normal with chemotherapy, but the problem is that it dropped so low that she became what we call neutropenic, which in turn made her vulnerable to a variety of infections. She's now developed a condition known as sepsis, which basically means her bloodstream has become filled with bacteria. I'm afraid it's quite serious."

"What does 'quite serious' mean?" I said. "Is this life-threatening?"

He ran his fingers through his hair and sighed. I could tell from his demeanor, and from the way he was avoiding eye contact with me, that he was extremely concerned about Caroline.

"I'm afraid it is. She's going to be in isolation for a while. We'll treat her with antibiotics. Her survival depends on how she reacts to the antibiotics. And I'll tell you this up front, patients often develop further complications from the antibiotics."

"Isolation?" I said. "Does that mean I can't see her?"

"I'm sorry. She has to be in a sterile environment. We can't risk having anything, or anyone, around her until we get the infection under control."

"How long?"

"It's hard to say."

"How long before I can see her?"

"Please, Mr. Dillard, take it easy. This type of thing happens rarely, but unfortunately, it happens. I've seen patients recover in a short amount of time, and I've seen them require months of hospitalization. But Caroline is relatively young and up until the cancer diagnosis, she'd been healthy. All we can do is follow the treatment plan and hope her youth and strength get her through this."

"Is she in pain?"

"She's sedated now. She shouldn't be feeling any pain …."

As the doctor continued to talk, I felt myself slipping into a deep psychological void. I could hear him, but his words sounded distant and muffled. Time suddenly seemed to slow, and I found myself contemplating particles of dust that were illuminated by sunlight pouring in through a window. By the time the doctor left, I'd entered into what must have been emotional shock.

I couldn't talk, I couldn't move, I couldn't even think. Melinda said something to me before she left, but I had no idea what it was.

I don't know how long I sat on the couch, but I eventually forced myself to get up and walk over to admissions. My legs felt as though they were dragging a ball and chain as I made my way through the bustle of people coming and going through the main lobby. I sat down in front of the clerk and somehow managed to give her my insurance card and the information she needed. Caroline, she said, had been moved to an isolated room near the intensive care ward.

I got up and wandered back through the lobby, not knowing what to do or where to go. I'd never felt so helpless. The thought of Caroline lying alone in a hospital bed, hooked to tubes and monitors and fighting for her life, caused my throat to constrict so tightly that I had to stop, lean against the wall, and gather myself. As I walked down the hallway, I caught a glimpse of a small cross on a sign just to my right. It was the hospital chapel, and I felt myself being pulled toward it as though by force of gravity. I opened the door and looked inside. The chapel was empty. There were eight pews, four on my right and four on my left, and a simple altar at the front of the room.

I took a deep breath and walked in. It was quiet, the air perfectly still. As I moved slowly to the altar, tears began to stream down my face. I tried to control it, but there were so many emotions running through me—sorrow, pain, fear, sympathy, anxiety—by the time I reached the altar, I was sobbing.

And then I did something I hadn't done since my mother told me there was no God.

I got down on my knees, bowed my head, and prayed.

PART III

TUESDAY, NOV. 11

Hank Fraley drove with a feeling of excitement mixed with anxiety. It had taken him only half a day to secure a search warrant for Natasha's DNA sample and the necklace, and now, after a night of tossing and turning, he, Norcross, and two other agents were heading to Natasha's to execute the warrants at 7:00 a.m. A cold, overcast dawn was breaking, and Fraley flipped on the windshield wipers as a light rain began to fall.

Norcross sat in the passenger seat. He was wearing a brown suit covered by a black overcoat and a tan, button-down shirt that was too tight for his muscular neck.

"Hey Thor," Fraley said, "I've been thinking about this psycho, and I'm betting she's got something special planned."

"What makes you say that?"

"Think about it. She goes down to the juvenile detention center and meets with Barnett three days before the hearing. She knows that Boyer is about to rat her out. She knows their little train has come to the end of the tracks. So she talks Barnett into killing Boyer and then himself. He goes out in a blaze of glory, gets a whole bunch of press. But I don't think she's the type to let Barnett steal the spotlight for long."

"What do you think she's planning?" Norcross said.

"I don't know for sure, but I'm thinking it'll be some kind of mass-murder-suicide thing. Maybe a shopping mall, maybe a school. That seems to be a popular way of going out these days."

"Let's hope we can arrest her and lock her up before she does it."

"I doubt it. Once we show up and get the DNA sample, she's going to think the bomb's about to drop. She'll do something."

Fraley was tired, still haunted by nightmares of the two children on Marbleton Road. He wanted this case to be finished. He wanted to get back to working stolen-car rings and chop shops, maybe a nice white-collar embezzling case.

"I hate dealing with people like her," Fraley said, "because the chances are we won't be able to get rid of her."

"What do you mean?" Norcross said.

"I mean she's probably crazy enough to stay out of prison. They'll send her to a mental institution, put her back on her meds, keep her five or ten or twenty years, and turn her loose. And as soon as they let her out, she'll go back off her meds and start killing people again. People like her are the same as cancer. The only way to really get rid of them is to kill them."

They rounded a bend and the white frame house came into view. Sitting outside was Marie's powder-blue Chevy sedan that was at least twenty years old. Fraley had seen the car and run the tag back when he was doing surveillance on Natasha. As Fraley pulled up behind the car, he took a closer look. The paint was faded and cracking, and the vinyl top was peeling. The tires looked like they wouldn't make it around the block.

Fraley led the way up the steps to the front door, flipping off the safety on his pistol as he climbed. When he reached the top, he moved to the right and unholstered the gun. Norcross banged on the door with his fist and stepped to the side while the two other agents moved around to cover the back. A dog started to bark immediately.

"Police! Search warrant!" Norcross yelled.

A long minute passed and Norcross banged on the door again. "Open the door! Search warrant!"

Fraley saw a shadow pass across the window and heard the sound of feet shuffling inside. The door cracked open, and Marie Davis stuck her pale head outside.

"What do y'all want?" she said.

Fraley stepped forward slowly, wary of what, or who, might be behind Marie.

"We have a search warrant that allows us to take a sample of Natasha's hair for DNA testing. The warrant also allows us to search for a gold necklace."

"I don't want y'all in here again," Marie said.

"Open the door and step back," Fraley said. "If you don't, we'll kick the door in and arrest you for obstruction."

The door creaked as it opened, and Fraley and Norcross entered the house. It was dark and quiet. All the shades had been drawn, and the television was off. It smelled of stale smoke and mildew. Marie went immediately to the kitchen table and lit a cigarette. She was wearing the same flowered robe that she wore the first time Fraley came to her house.

"Where's Natasha?" Fraley said.

"Asleep," Marie said, motioning with her head toward the hallway.

"She won't be for long with that dog barking."

"She probably took something. She could sleep through Armageddon," Marie said.

"Don't you have any lights in this place?" Fraley said as he looked around the trailer.

Marie walked across the kitchen into the small den, turned on a lamp beside her recliner, and went back to the kitchen.

"Have you seen an ice pick since the last time we were here?" Fraley said.

Marie shook her head and blew out a long stream of gray smoke.

"How about a necklace? A gold cross on a gold chain."

Marie stared down at the table in front of her, saying nothing.

"Lying to a police officer is a felony, Ms. Davis."

"I didn't lie to you. I didn't say nothing."

"Have you seen a gold cross on a gold chain or not?"

"I ain't telling you nothing."

Fraley looked at her. She was obviously in poor health, hiding behind tinted glasses, her skin as pale as a full moon, liver spots covering her bony hands. He imagined her sitting alone in a dark, silent house, her perception clouded by drugs, waiting for Natasha to return, wishing that death would take her. He might have felt sorry for her, but how could he feel sorry for someone who had brought a cancer like Natasha into the world? And now, it appeared Marie was protecting her.

Norcross, who had gone to the back to retrieve the other two agents, walked into the kitchen.

"Ms. Davis here says Natasha's sleeping," Fraley said. "I'll go first. Thor, you're right behind me, Danny behind you. Jimbo, you stay here and keep an eye on Ms. Davis. If she moves, shoot her."

"What happened to the other dog?" Jimbo said to Marie. "There were two last time I was here."

Marie shrugged her shoulders, staring down at her cigarette.

Fraley moved cautiously down the darkened hallway, gun raised. The door to Natasha's room was closed, so he reached out and carefully turned the knob. The door opened silently; the room was as dark as black ink. Fraley stepped soundlessly inside. He could hear steady breathing in the corner. He looked over his shoulder to see Norcross's frame filling the doorway and slid his hand along the wall to find the light switch. He flipped it on.

Natasha was lying on top of the bedspread on her stomach, sound asleep. A black T-shirt covered her to mid-thigh. Her arms were beneath the pillow under her head. Fraley turned to Norcross and gave him a hand signal. Norcross took the handcuffs from their pouch on his belt and crept toward the bed. Fraley stepped to the foot, ready to grab Natasha's ankles as soon as Norcross made his move. Danny provided cover. Fraley holstered his weapon and nodded, and Norcross dropped his knees into the small of Natasha's back and grabbed both of her forearms.

"Police!" Norcross yelled. "Stay facedown!"

Natasha screamed as Norcross wrenched her arms behind her back and snapped the handcuffs on her wrists. She tried to squirm and kick, but Fraley had a solid hold on her ankles and the sheer weight and strength of Norcross rendered her helpless.

Natasha started screaming profanities. Fraley watched as Norcross lifted her off the bed and dragged her down the hallway. Once he got her to the den, he laid her on her stomach in the middle of the floor and straddled her.

"Don't move," Fraley said. "We have a warrant to take a hair sample from you and to search the house."

"I hate you!" Natasha screamed. She continued to struggle. "I hate cops! I hope your children burn to death!"

"Danny, hold her legs," Fraley said. "Norcross, turn her head to the side and hold her still."

Natasha continued to scream profane insults as Fraley pulled a small evidence bag and a pair of tweezers out of his jacket pocket.

"Hold still, sweetie pie," Fraley said. "This won't hurt a bit."

Fraley knew that the best DNA sample would come from the roots of Natasha's hair, so he maneuvered the tweezers close to Natasha's scalp as she struggled and spat and cursed. He plucked five hairs, put them in the bag, and sealed it. He was just starting to get off his knees when he noticed the chain around Natasha's neck. It was gold.

"Hold her right there," Fraley said. He got up and went back to Natasha's bedroom, rifled through a couple drawers until he found a T-shirt, and went back into the den.

"Put this over her head and turn her over," he said to Norcross. "I don't want her spitting all over me."

Norcross did as Fraley said. When he turned Natasha over, Fraley saw that a gold cross was indeed hanging on the chain.

"Look guys," Fraley said. "Isn't that nice? She's put a personal touch on it. The cross is hanging upside-down from the chain. We're going to take this, Miss Davis. I hope you don't mind."

Fraley fumbled with clasp while Natasha let loose a steady stream of expletives. It took almost a minute to get it unhooked. He pulled the chain from beneath Natasha's neck. When Fraley had bagged the necklace, he looked at Norcross's face. The big man was flushed and beginning to sweat.

"Turn her back over and get the cuffs off her," Fraley said. "I think we have everything we came for."

Natasha went silent as Norcross rolled her over. Fraley held his gun on her while Norcross unlocked the cuffs, pulled the T-shirt off her head, and stepped carefully away.

"Don't leave town," Fraley said as the agents began to back toward the kitchen. Jimbo opened the door, and light seeped into the dim interior of the room. "As soon as we get the results back from the lab and figure out where this necklace came from, we'll be back to get you."

Suddenly, the light bulb in the lamp that Marie had turned on exploded with a loud *pop!* Fraley heard the bits of glass fly against the inside of the lamp shade and when he looked toward the lamp, he could see smoke rising.

Natasha slowly pulled herself to her knees and glared at Fraley. She began to speak her gibberish, and Fraley felt the hair on the back of his neck stand up.

Then, with her freakish eyes boring in on Fraley, she said, "Don't worry. I'm not going anywhere. I'll be waiting for you."

TUESDAY, NOV. 11

F raley looked up at the clock as he walked through the door of the small house he rented on Cranston Street. Almost midnight. It had been an exhausting day, beginning with the raid at Natasha's. As he opened the closet door to hang up his coat, Fraley heard the familiar meow of his golden-eyed tabby. He felt the cat rubbing against his leg and reached down to pick it up.

"How's Clementine tonight?" Fraley said, scratching lightly around her ears and down her back. "I'll bet you're hungry. Sorry Pops was so late getting home."

Fraley walked into the kitchen, set the cat down gently, and opened a can of food.

"How about tuna and bacon tonight?" he said. "Good for your ticker."

Fraley scraped the food into a plastic bowl and stood watching as Clementine enthusiastically went about devouring it.

"Pops is gonna get out of these smelly clothes. You let me know when you're ready to go out."

Immediately after the raid, Fraley had made the hundred-mile drive to Knoxville to hand deliver Natasha's hair samples to the lab. While he was there, he convinced the lab supervisor the DNA comparison should be given top priority, which meant he should hear something by tomorrow afternoon.

After driving back, Fraley set about trying to identify the necklace he'd taken from Natasha. The cross was somewhat unique in that it had been manufactured in the form of a ribbon with a small diamond at its center. He began by driving to Gladys Brockwell's daughter's home. He showed her the gold cross, but she said she'd never seen it. She also said her mother had become an avid Internet shopper. If she'd purchased the necklace over the Internet, Fraley knew the forensic computer analysts could find the transaction. The problem was it could take days, even weeks.

So Fraley hit the streets. He showed the necklace to eight different jewelers before he found someone who recognized it and could identify the manufacturer and the regional distributor. Once he had the distributor's name, Fraley tried to contact them by phone, but by that time it was nearly seven o'clock and no one was manning the company's switchboard. It would have to wait until morning.

After grabbing a bite to eat, Fraley had gone to the hospital to see Dillard. He found him in the intensive care waiting room looking haggard and worried. He hadn't shaved, the lines in his forehead look drawn and rigid, and there were dark circles beneath both eyes. Though Dillard barely spoke, Fraley had stayed until eleven forty-five. He remembered the agony of his first wife's death, the feelings of emptiness and loneliness, and he knew it was better for Dillard to have someone around. Besides, he lived only a couple blocks away.

Dillard had managed to say that he'd finally called his children, but he'd instructed both of them to stay at school until the weekend. He said he hoped Caroline would be out of intensive care by then, but the way he said it made Fraley think it would probably be much longer. Dillard had also pointed out Caroline's mother in the waiting room. He said he thought she somehow blamed him for Caroline's illness because she was all the way across the room reading a book. She left around nine without speaking to Dillard.

Fraley tried to tell Dillard about the raid at Natasha's and the progress he'd made with the necklace, but nothing he said seemed to have any effect. It was like talking to a mannequin. Sheriff Bates showed up around nine, so for a little while, Fraley at least had someone to talk to.

Fraley donned his favorite flannel pajamas and went to the refrigerator. He picked up a can of Budweiser and went into the den. Just as he was about to sit down, Clementine meowed again, signaling that she was ready. Fraley opened the front door and let her outside. He sat down in the recliner, sipping his beer and watching a rerun of his favorite show, *Law and Order.* Just as he finished his beer, he heard the cat scratching, got up, and let her back inside.

"Pops is bushed," he said, "and he's going to bed."

An hour later, a noise awakened him. He lay in bed listening for a few seconds, heard it again. It was a soft thump, as though someone was knocking on the side of the house. It sounded like it was coming from just outside the back door. Fraley sat up and reached into the drawer of his bedside table and retrieved his pistol. Leaving the lights off, he crept through the house in his pajamas, stopping briefly at the closet to pick up a flashlight. He moved silently to the front door, let himself out slowly, tiptoed down the front steps, and moved along the wall on the side of the house, his heart pounding. The wind was whipping, and the ground beneath his bare feet was cold and hard. When he reached the corner of the house, Fraley flipped on the flashlight. The small backyard was quiet and still except for the wind. He walked slowly all the way around the house, finding nothing. As he doubled back, he heard a scraping sound. He looked toward the sound and realized a maple that needed trimming was rubbing against the house in the wind.

Fraley's feet were beginning to go numb because of the cold, so he moved quickly back around the side and up the steps. Clementine regarded him curiously as he locked the door behind him.

"Sorry honey," he said. "I guess Pops is getting a little jumpy in his old age."

Fraley bent over, picked up his pet, and carried her off to the bedroom. Ten minutes later, he was sound asleep, his left hand resting on his beloved cat, his right hand resting on his revolver.

WEDNESDAY, NOV. 12

'd been at the hospital for thirty-six hours, unable to sleep or eat, barely able to communicate. The sparse news I received about Caroline was dire, and I kept experiencing feelings of desperation and hopelessness. My head was pounding, my throat dry, and it seemed that every joint in my body ached whenever I attempted to move.

The intensive care waiting room was recently constructed, a large open space with a skylight above, comfortable chairs, and tapestries on the walls. Jack and Lilly were calling every hour or so for updates, but I didn't have the heart to tell them how serious Caroline's condition really was. Fraley and Leon Bates both stopped by sometime during the evening, but I had very little recollection of anything they said.

I was sitting in the chair with my eyes closed and my feet propped up on a table in front of me when my cell phone rang. I opened my eyes to find that I was the only person left in the waiting room. I picked the cell up off the table next to me and didn't recognize the number that was calling. I looked at my watch, twelve minutes after two in the morning. I pushed the button and lifted the phone to my ear.

"She's killing the policeman! She's killing the police-man!" a female voice screamed.

"What? Who is this?"

"Natasha! She's killing him!"

I suddenly recognized the frantic voice. It was Alisha.

"Who?" I said. "Which policeman?"

"Mr. Fraley! You have to help him!"

I stood up, unsure what to do.

"Where are they?"

"I don't know! He's in bed!"

I pushed the button on the phone and started running down the hall toward the stairs. Along the way, I dialed 9-1-1.

"9-1-1 dispatch, what's your emergency?" a female voice said.

"This is Joe Dillard. I'm an assistant district attorney, and I'm calling to report a murder in progress," I said breathlessly as I started down the steps.

"A murder in progress?" she said in a skeptical voice. "Where are you, sir?"

"I'm on my way there. You need to send someone to Hank Fraley's house. He's a TBI agent and he lives on Cranston Street."

"Do you have the address?"

"No! Hank Fraley! TBI agent! Cranston Street! He's being attacked right now! Get the police and an ambulance over there!"

I pushed my way through the door that led to the parking lot and entered the cold night air. The wind was blowing so hard that it almost knocked me off balance as I ran to my truck.

"Did you say your name is Joe Dillard?" I heard the dispatcher say.

"Yes! I'm an assistant district attorney. Have you sent a patrol car?"

"How do you know that a murder might be in progress, Mr. Dillard?"

"What difference does that make?" I yelled. "It's happening!"

I jumped into the truck and tossed the cell phone down on the seat next to me. Fraley's house was a short distance from the hospital. If I got there in time, maybe I could get my hands on Natasha, or at the very least, keep Fraley alive until the paramedics arrived.

It took me only a couple minutes to get to Fraley's. I parked the truck near the curb right in front of the house and turned on the emergency flashers, hoping the police would see them and know exactly where to come. As I sprinted toward the front door, I realized I wasn't armed. I stopped, turned around, and raced back to the truck. I opened the passenger side door and reached beneath the seat where I kept a tire tool and a jack. I felt the cold steel of the tire tool, pulled it out, and ran back to the house and up the front steps. The house was completely dark. I opened the storm door and grabbed the doorknob, hollering Fraley's name at the same time. The door was locked. I broke out a window with the tire tool, reached inside, and unlocked the deadbolt and the knob.

I kept telling myself that Alisha was wrong, that she'd probably just experienced a nightmare, that there was no way Fraley would let Natasha get the best of him.

"Fraley!" I called as I stepped into the den. I'd only been in the house once, the night Fraley rode with me to Crossville to get Sarah, but he'd given me a little tour. He showed me the pictures of his family that he'd hung on the wall and his medals from serving in the 101st Airborne Division in Vietnam.

The house was dead silent. As I crept down the short hallway toward Fraley's bedroom, gripping the tire iron tightly in my right hand, I felt the temperature drop, and I knew Natasha had been there. I heard sirens in the distance just as I reached the bedroom. The door was open slightly, so I gently pushed it with the tire iron. I reached around the doorway with my left hand and slid it against the wall until I felt a light switch.

The scene I encountered caused my knees to buckle and I staggered toward the bed, trying to keep my balance. Fraley was face up, his eyes and mouth wide open. I stood over him and reached down to feel his carotid for a pulse, but he was perfectly still. Fresh blood was everywhere. It covered his face, arms and pajamas. I forced myself to look more closely and could make out several puncture wounds, including one in Fraley's right eye. There was blood on the walls, even on the ceiling. The bedroom window was open. Natasha must have made her exit through the window. As I backed awkwardly away from the bed, I noticed something on the floor. It was Fraley's pistol, and it, too, was covered in blood.

I reached down and picked up the pistol, the sirens outside growing louder with each passing second. As I tried to decide what to do next, several images again began flashing through my head: the Becks' bullet-riddled bodies; Norman Brockwell and his wife, brutally murdered; Sarah's battered face; Lilly on the ground, fighting for her life; Boyer's body on the holding cell floor; Fraley's death stare; and Caroline lying alone, dying from a blood infection. Again, I heard the old man's warning: *"If the curse is real, and I believe it is, there's only one way to break it. One of you has to die. … One of you has to die. … One of you has to die."*

Fraley's car keys were on the bedside table. I knew a shotgun would be in it. I grabbed the keys and hurried out the door, intending to find the shotgun and take off in my truck. The sirens were louder. The place would soon be filled with uniformed officers and paramedics. If I stuck around, I'd be stuck there for the rest of the night.

Instead of opening the trunk, I jumped in and started Fraley's car.

WEDNESDAY, NOV. 12

The heavy winds were pushing a thunderstorm, and as I drove the cruiser across town, a blinding bolt of lightning tore through the blackened sky followed by a clap of thunder that reminded me of an artillery burst. I was conscious on some level that what I was doing was wrong, but after seeing Fraley's body and the horrific way in which he died, I wasn't thinking rationally. About halfway to Natasha's house, I punched Leon Bates's number into my cell.

"Natasha killed Fraley," I said when Bates answered in a sleepy voice. "I'm going after her."

"What? Killed Fraley? When?"

"A few minutes ago. I just left his house. She stabbed him to death. She stabbed him in the eye."

"What do you mean you're going after her?" Bates said.

"It's time somebody put a stop to this."

"Now you wait just one tick there ol' buddy. You can't go tearing after a suspect with murder in your heart."

"She's responsible for all of these deaths," I said. "She's terrorized me and my family. She's threatened me. She even left a threatening message in my house. I'm going, Leon. You can't stop me."

"And what are those beautiful children of yours going to do if she kills you? Especially if Caroline doesn't make it?"

I hung up on him as soon as he mentioned Caroline's name. It was the thought of saving her life that was driving me. If I could kill Natasha, maybe it would break the curse, and maybe Caroline would be okay. I tried not to think about what Bates said about my children. I willed myself to think only about what Natasha had done to Caroline and Lilly and Fraley and the Becks and the Brockwells. By the time I got to Natasha's neighborhood, I was in a blind rage.

I parked Fraley's car a couple blocks from Natasha's and rifled through the trunk. It turned out to be a bonanza—a twelve-gauge pump shotgun, fully loaded with seven shells of double-ought buckshot, and a flashlight. I stuck Fraley's bloody pistol in my belt and walked quickly up the road in a driving rain. When I got to the driveway, I jogged toward an old Chevy that was parked in the driveway and felt the hood. It was warm.

I crouched beside the car for a few moments, watching the house and listening. Nothing was moving, the house and yard were dark except for the occasional flashes of lightning. I became aware of my clothing. I was still wearing the same clothes I'd worn to work the preceding morning. I'd left my jacket at the hospital, and my shirt was soaked and sticking to me. A cold chill ran through me. I decided to move.

I walked slowly up on the front porch and turned the doorknob. It was unlocked, but it squeaked slightly as I opened it. I crouched again and moved just inside the door. Another flash of lightning exploded above me, briefly illuminating an image of Marie Davis sitting in her recliner. I pushed the button on the flashlight and panned the kitchen and den. Marie, wearing her flowered robe, was staring straight at me, her face like white paper behind the tinted glasses. I moved toward her slowly, still in a crouch.

"Where is she?" I whispered.

She looked away for a brief second, and I heard air rushing through her nostrils. When she turned back, she raised her right hand, her index finger pointing toward the back of the house. She mouthed the word "outside."

I moved back out through the front door, went down the steps, and put my back against the front of the house. From there, I started sliding along the wall until I got to the corner. I peeked around the side, looking for any sign of Natasha or a dog, seeing nothing. I slid along the side wall until I got to the corner. I raised the flashlight and scanned the backyard. Still nothing. Just as I started to move around the corner, I thought I sensed movement behind me. I was conscious of another lightning strike and searing pain, and then … darkness.

I don't know how long I was unconscious, but when I woke up, I was flat on my back with rain pelting down on me, stinging my face. I opened my eyes and first tried to lift my head, but the pain in my temples was so intense that I nearly threw up. I closed my eyes and lay still, thoroughly confused until I suddenly remembered where I was. Hunting for Natasha. Trying to save my wife. But something had happened. Either I'd been struck by lightning, or someone had hit me.

I tried to sit up, but my arms and legs were restrained. I turned my head from side to side and could see that my wrists were tied to something that had been driven into the ground. Stakes? I pulled against them with what little strength I had, but neither of them moved. I lifted my head and could see that my legs were both restrained in the same fashion. As I lay my head back down on the cold, soaked earth, I could feel something warm running down the back of my neck, and I knew it must be blood.

The kitten. Natasha's kitten.

I started tugging at the stakes again, ignoring the pain that was surging down my spine and radiating through my entire body.

C'mon, Joe! C'mon!

I tried desperately to push the stakes away from me and pull them toward me. I thought if I could loosen them enough in the ground, I'd be able to pull them up. As I strained against the ropes, I heard a snarl just a few feet away. I turned my head just as a bolt of lightning flashed and could make out a hooded figure standing beneath a small tree. In the figure's hand was a thick leash, and attached to the leash was a snarling Doberman. A sickening chill overtook me. It was Natasha. My heart began to pound even harder in my chest. She wrapped the leash around the trunk of the tree a couple of times, secured it, took a few steps, and stood directly above me. I knew if I didn't find a way to free myself soon, I'd be dead.

"I like seeing you this way," she said in a calm voice. "If I had more time, I'd build a cross and do it right."

She knelt, her knees almost straddling my head. I watched as she reached with her right hand to retrieve something. She picked up a hammer, the one she must have used to drive the stakes into the ground. Slowly, she reached into a coat pocket and pulled out an ice pick. She began waving the pick back and forth in front of my eyes.

"Have you come to arrest me?" she said. "Or have you come to kill me? I think you're here to kill me. And what does that say about you, Mr. Dillard? It says you're no different from me. You came to punish me for violating your Christian laws, just like I punish those who deserve it. Or did you come to sacrifice yourself so others might live? Do you have a Christ complex, Mr. Dillard? Do you?"

She bent close to the ground and put her lips next to my ear.

"I wish I could crucify you," she whispered, "but since I can't nail you to the ground, I'll have to settle for this."

She moved quickly to her right, still on her knees. I saw her hold the ice pick against my right forearm, felt the stab of the steel point. She raised the hammer and brought it down hard. I moaned as the pick drove through my flesh. The pain was unspeakable, but I refused to scream or beg for mercy. The rage I'd felt before I was knocked out had returned. I hated her. I hated her passionately, completely. I wanted to kill her. I put an image of blowing a hole through her with the shotgun in my mind and kept straining against the ropes.

She pulled the ice pick out, sending another shock of pain through me, then straddled me and began whispering in my ear again.

"The smell of your blood will drive Zeus wild," she said. "As soon as I finish, I'm going to let him taste you. He hates you anyway. I told him you killed his sister. How's your daughter?"

She scooted to the left and drove the pick through my other forearm. A wave of nausea came over me, and I turned my head to the side and vomited. I didn't want to drown in my own vomit, but the thought crossed my mind that it might be better than what Natasha had in store for me. She crawled around to my right foot, and I braced again for the pain. But as she lifted the hammer, I heard another voice. A female voice.

"Stop hurting him, Natasha."

Was I hallucinating? Maybe, but when I looked at Natasha, there was a look of surprise, maybe bewilderment, on her face.

"You!" Natasha hissed as she slowly stood.

I heard a squishing sound, footsteps, and looked back and to my left. It was Alisha, and in her hands she held Fraley's shotgun. The dog continued to snarl and bark furiously. It was straining against the leash.

"Leave him alone, Natasha," Alisha said. "Let him go."

"Or what? Are you going to shoot me?" Natasha started walking slowly toward her sister as she spoke. "You're the good daughter, the gentle soul, the Wiccan princess. You've never hurt anything in your life. You don't have the strength."

"Stop or I'll kill you."

SCOTT PRATT

"Go ahead!" Natasha yelled. "You can't hurt me! Don't you know who I am? I'm the daughter of Satan!"

She began to speak in the same language I'd heard at the courthouse, continuing to move toward Alisha. As she spoke, she quickened her step. Suddenly, she raised the ice pick and threw herself at Alisha.

The shotgun belched thunder and fire and smoke, and Natasha was lifted off the ground. I heard a heavy thud as she landed, and I strained to see if she was moving. Alisha dropped the shotgun and knelt next to me. She began working on the ropes holding my arms. As soon as they were free, I tried to help her loosen the ropes on my ankles, but my fingers wouldn't work. Blood was pouring out of the wounds in my forearms, and when I tried to stand, pain and dizziness forced me back to my knees. I looked over at Natasha—she was face up a few feet away. Her shirt was stained with dark blood.

She bleeds. I guess she's mortal after all.

I crawled over to the shotgun and picked it up. The dog had suddenly gone silent. I didn't want to kill it, but if it broke free and came after us, I knew I wouldn't have a choice. Alisha hooked her hand beneath my arm and helped me get to my feet. I noticed headlights coming down the road toward the driveway. I turned back and stood looking down at Natasha. My forearms felt like they were on fire, and my head felt like it was about to explode with every beat of my heart. With Alisha still holding my arm for support and using the shotgun as a crutch, I knelt next to Natasha and felt for a pulse.

Nothing.

Ding dong, I thought. *The wicked witch is dead.*

WEDNESDAY, NOV. 12

"**H**elp me get to the side of the house," I said to Alisha as she pulled me up from my knees. "Someone's coming."

The storm had lost some of its ferocity, but rain continued to fall. We got to the corner of the house just as the car pulled into the driveway. As it moved closer, I recognized the Crown Victoria. It was Leon Bates.

I turned to Alisha and gently touched her cheek. Her long hair was plastered to the sides of her face, rainwater dripping from her chin.

"You have to go now," I said. "You have to get out of here. I don't want him to see you."

"What? What do you mean?" she said. She was in a state of semi-shock.

"Go in the back door, get those wet clothes off, and stay inside until they come to question you. Tell them you don't know what happened. Tell them you were too scared to look outside."

"But why?" she said. "I … I …."

I was thinking about Lee Mooney and Hobart Denton and their desire to see someone suffer publicly for crimes that had been committed in their district. I was thinking about political agendas and scapegoats. I was thinking about how corrupt the system could be.

"Please, Alisha, I know how things work. I'm afraid of what they might do to you. They might arrest you. They might charge you with murder. I'm not going let it happen."

The interior light in Bates's car came on, and I heard the door slam.

"Go," I said. "Please, just go inside and don't ever say a word to anyone."

She looked at me, her face a mosaic of fear, confusion, and sadness. I saw her make the decision, and she disappeared around the corner of the house. I heard the door to the back porch creak, and I knew she was safe.

Without Alisha, I was unable to stand for more than a few seconds, and I dropped once again to my knees. The beam of a flashlight was slowly making its way toward me.

"Here!" I yelled, immediately regretting it because of the pain. The beam was on me instantly, and then Leon Bates was over me, water pouring off the plastic covering his cowboy hat.

"Brother Dillard! Are you all right?"

"No."

"What happened? Where is she?"

I pointed over my shoulder with my thumb. "Over there. She's dead. Watch out for the dog."

Bates walked to the spot where Natasha lay. I watched as he surveyed the scene: the body, the stakes and the ropes, the shotgun, the ice pick. The Doberman didn't make a sound. I saw Bates pick up a shovel and examine it closely with the flashlight. He looked toward the back of the house and disappeared from sight for a minute. When he returned, he stood over me again.

"You're bleeding like a stuck hog, Dillard," he said. "We best get an ambulance out here pronto."

He hoisted me to my feet, and we made our way to his car. As he opened the back door on the passenger side, he told me to hold still.

"I've got some plastic in the trunk," he said. "Let me cover the seat. I don't want you bleeding all over my vehicle."

Once I was in the backseat, Bates got on the radio. I felt myself sliding into unconsciousness. Time passed, I don't know how much, and then Bates was leaning over me again, checking my wounds.

"You gotta stay awake now," he said. "Don't go slipping into a coma on me."

I was conscious of him kneeling next to me, dabbing the wounds on my arms with something. I opened my eyes and saw a first-aid kit sitting on the ground.

"Talk to me, Dillard," he said.

I opened my eyes and tried to focus, but I felt the energy ebbing out of me like an ocean tide.

"Who killed her?" Bates said.

"I did," I whispered.

"I don't reckon that's true, brother. Don't take no genius to figure out what happened over there. Somebody got staked out on the ground, and judging by the blood on the ice pick and the shovel and the wounds to your head and your arms, I'm guessing it was you. I don't reckon you was in much shape to defend yourself after she whacked you in the head with that shovel and tied you up, so somebody had to help you, and I reckon that somebody is the person who left those wet footprints on the back porch when she went in the house."

"No," I said, shaking my head as much as I could without passing out from the pain. "No, Leon, don't. Please."

"Why?" Bates said. "Why are you doing this?"

"She saved my life. She had to kill her own sister. She's already paid enough. Please don't throw her to the wolves. Just let her be."

He stared at me for a long moment, his mouth slightly agape. Even in the state I was in, I could almost see the wheels turning in his mind as he pondered his next move. His eyes suddenly flew open wide, and I knew he'd experienced some kind of revelation.

"You with me? You with me, Dillard?" he said as he shook my shoulder. "You understand what I'm saying?"

I nodded as best I could.

"All right, here's the deal. You found Fraley's body, you knew it had to be Natasha that killed him, so you came over here to check it out and you called me on your way. Once you got here, she ambushed you in the backyard. She staked you out and drove that ice pick through your arms. Just when she was about to finish you off, I showed up. I tried to get her to back off, but she came at me and I killed her. That makes a whole lot more sense, and it makes me a hero."

"It was Fraley's shotgun," I whispered.

"I got a shotgun, son. I always carry a shotgun in my car. I'll just run up there and get Fraley's, wipe it down real good and put it back in his car. Where was it?"

"Trunk."

"Okay. Do we have the story straight? They'll be here any minute."

"Thanks," I whispered.

"No need to thank me. You helped me out with the judge, but we're even now. You understand? Me and you are even."

SIX MONTHS LATER ...
FRIDAY, MAY 15

I'm sitting in the vacant jury room just down the hallway from the courtroom in Jonesborough. Jim Beaumont, his blue eyes gleaming like a South Pacific island lagoon, is brushing a tear from his cheek as he recounts the story.

"You should have seen the look on his face when I plopped those pictures down on his desk," Beaumont says. "He thought I was there to beg for mercy or to try to make some kind of deal. I made a deal all right. The deal of the century!"

He's laughing, and it's infectious. My diaphragm begins to cramp slightly as I pound the table. I've heard the story at least a half dozen times, but each time he tells it, he enhances it a little.

"The one with that girl sitting on his thumb was my favorite. I nearly peed on myself when I saw it! Ho, ho, ho, ho, ho!"

Prostitutes, and the younger the better.

That was the secret his retired FBI guys unearthed in Cumberland County. It took them just over two weeks to find out what was beneath Hobart Denton's skirt, another three days to set him up and get their video and photographs. The girl cost me five thousand dollars, but I considered it money well spent.

"He wilted like an orchid in a blizzard!" Beaumont said. "I thought he was gonna run over to the jail and let Sarah out himself!"

"Stop," I said, holding up my hands and trying to catch my breath. "You're killing me."

His mood changed suddenly as something caught his eye. It took only a second before I realized what it was. I'd taken my jacket off when we entered the room and hung it on the back of my chair. I was wearing a short-sleeved shirt, and Beaumont was looking at the pink scars in my forearms.

"They're fading," he said.

I put my arms on the table, embarrassed. "Yeah. They don't hurt anymore."

"You've been through a lot, you and your wife."

"We're still standing."

I passed out in the ambulance on the way to the hospital the night Natasha met her demise, and when I woke up almost twenty-four hours later, Caroline, Lilly, and Jack were all standing over me. Caroline's white cell count had risen during the early morning hours as quickly as it had fallen a couple days before, and although the doctors attributed her miraculous recovery to their regimen of antibiotics, I wondered whether the explanation was something far beyond their—or my—understanding.

Caroline had since endured a breast reconstruction and another round of chemotherapy. She still had six weeks of radiation to face, but her hair was starting to come back in and during the entire ordeal, she's missed less than two weeks of work. I'd loved and respected Caroline since I was a teenager, but as I watched her deal so bravely with the calamity of cancer, my respect for her grew exponentially with each passing day.

Hank Fraley's daughter took him to Nashville to be buried less than a week after he was killed. I was still a little woozy from the concussion caused by the blow to my head, but my family and I made it to the funeral. I was amazed at how much Fraley's daughter, whose name was Jessica, resembled the photograph of Fraley's wife that he'd shown me in his office. Jessica was a beautiful young woman, very gracious. I cried when they put him in the ground. He'd become a good friend, and I missed him.

Sarah was released the same day Jim Beaumont had his meeting with Hobart Denton. She stopped going to church. I dropped by to see her at least three times a week, but she was withdrawn and sullen. She said she hadn't heard from Robert Godsey. I suspected she might be drinking again.

Leon Bates convinced every law enforcement agency in the region—and the media—that he killed Natasha in self-defense. A Johnson City detective came and questioned me in the hospital, but the questions were cursory and he didn't stay long. I didn't tell him the truth, but I didn't regret it. Bates had since become a folk hero. He appeared on a half dozen national talk shows and let the news leak that he was thinking about running for state senator when his term as sheriff expired. He told me a couple weeks ago he might even consider a run for the United States Senate.

I agreed to a plea deal with Alexander Dunn's attorney. Alexander pleaded guilty to one count of accepting a bribe as a public official and agreed to serve six months in jail and another two years on probation. Despite the fact that Leon Bates told me Lee Mooney wasn't involved in the extortion scheme, Alexander's attorney convinced me otherwise. After that, I couldn't bring myself to drop the hammer on Alexander. I was still working as an assistant district attorney, but I found it difficult to look Mooney in the eye every day.

I hadn't seen or heard from Alisha Davis, but my experience with her and Natasha changed me in a fundamental way. I still didn't believe I knew the answers to questions of eternity, but I'd become much more reverent, and instead of just gazing at the rising sun each morning and shallowly pondering how everything came about, which had long been my habit, I took a little time to pray.

A bailiff stuck his head through the door to the jury room where Beaumont and I were talking.

"The judge is ready for you," he said.

I stood and put on my jacket. Beaumont did the same.

"This is unusual, isn't it?" he said.

"I guess it is."

We walked out to the courtroom, and I took my seat at the prosecution table. Beaumont went straight to the podium as his client stepped through the bar and walked up to be arraigned.

The elderly woman Billy Dockery attacked and robbed was in a coma, but this time Dockery cut his hand breaking into her house and left his blood at the scene. Dockery was charged with attempted first-degree murder, burglary, and theft over five thousand dollars. His momma posted his bond, but he was looking at forty years in prison.

This time, I intended to make sure he got what he deserved.

Thank you for reading, and I sincerely hope you enjoyed *In Good Faith*. As an independently published author, I rely on you, the reader, to spread the word. So if you enjoyed the book, please tell your friends and family, and if it isn't too much trouble, I would appreciate a brief review on Amazon. Thanks again. My best to you and yours.

Scott

ABOUT THE AUTHOR

Scott Pratt was born in South Haven, Michigan, and moved to Tennessee when he was thirteen years old. He is a veteran of the United States Air Force and holds a Bachelor of Arts degree in English from East Tennessee State University and a Doctor of Jurisprudence from the University of Tennessee College of Law. He lives in Northeast Tennessee with his wife, their dogs, and a parrot named JoJo.

www.scottprattfiction.com

ALSO BY SCOTT PRATT

INJUSTICE FOR ALL

By

SCOTT PRATT

This book, along with every book I've written and every book I'll write, is dedicated to my darling Kristy, to her unconquerable spirit and to her inspirational courage. I loved her before I was born and I'll love her after I'm long gone.

Justice – the quality of being just, impartial, or fair.
Webster's New Collegiate Dictionary

PROLOGUE

Three years ago …

My name is Joe Dillard, and I'm leaning against a chain-link fence watching a baseball game at Daniel Boone High School in Gray, Tennessee, on a spectacular, sun-drenched evening in early May. The sky is a cloudless azure, a mild breeze is blowing out toward left field, and the pleasant smell of freshly cut grass hangs in the air.

There are five of us watching the game from our spot near the right-field foul pole: me, my wife Caroline, her best friend Toni Miller, my buddy Ray Miller (Toni's husband), and Rio, our German shepherd. The Dillards and the Millers have been watching our sons play baseball together for ten years, alternately rejoicing in their success and agonizing over their failure. Rio is a relative newcomer—he's been around for only three years—but he seems to enjoy the games as much as we do.

Ray Miller and I have much in common. We're both lawyers. After many years of practicing criminal defense, I switched to prosecuting a few years back while Ray remains on what I now call the "dark side." I rib him on a regular basis about defending scumbags, but I know he does it for the right reasons and I respect him. He doesn't cheat, doesn't lie, doesn't try to pull tricks. He tends to see things in black and white, much like me. We both despise the misuse of power, especially on the part of judges, although Ray is a bit more venomous than I in that regard. We're close to the same age, and we're devoted to our families.

We watch the game from our position in the outfield, away from the players and the other parents, because none of us wishes to distract our sons. We don't yell at them during games like other parents. We don't criticize the umpires or the coaches. We just watch and worry. If something good happens, we cheer. If something bad happens, we cringe.

My son, Jack, is the star hitter on the Boone team. Ray's son, Tommy, is the star pitcher. Back in November, both of them signed national letters of intent to continue their baseball careers at the Division I collegiate level. Jack signed with Vanderbilt, and Tommy signed with Duke. It was one of the proudest moments of my life.

This evening's game has been intense. It's the finals of the district tournament, and if Boone beats Jefferson High, they move on to the regional. If they lose, their season is over. Jack doubled off the left-center field fence in the first inning with runners on second and third to put Boone up 2-0. Jefferson's cleanup hitter hit a solo home run off Tommy Miller in the second. Jack came up again in the fourth and hit a home run, a long moon shot over the center-field fence, to put Boone up 3-1. In the top of the fifth, Tommy walked the lead-off hitter, and the next guy laid down a bunt that Boone's third baseman misplayed, leaving Jefferson with runners on second and third with nobody out and their cleanup hitter coming to the plate. Tommy threw two great pitches to get him down 0-2, but the next pitch got away from Tommy just a bit and hit the batter in the thigh. Jefferson's coaches, players, and parents all started screaming, accusing Tommy of hitting the kid on purpose. It looked as though a fight might break out, but the umpires managed to calm things down. Jefferson scored two runs when the next batter hit a bloop single to right field, but then Tommy struck out three in a row. The game is tied with Jack leading off for Boone in the bottom of seventh, which is the final inning in a high school game.

"They'll walk him," Ray says. I turn and look at him incredulously. He's wearing sunglasses that shield his dark eyes. He's an inch shorter than me at six feet two, but he's thicker through the chest and back. His long, brown hair is beginning to gray and is pulled back into a pony tail, and his forearms, which are leaning against the fence, look as thick as telephone poles.

"You're nuts," I say. "They don't want to walk the lead-off man in a tie game in the last inning. They'll pitch to him."

Jack digs into the batter's box and takes his familiar, wide, slightly open stance. He's a big kid, six feet two inches and a rock-hard two hundred and ten pounds. He has a strong jaw and a prominent, dimpled chin—a "good baseball face"—as the old-time scouts would say. He's crowding the plate like he always does, daring the pitcher to throw him something inside.

The first pitch is a fastball, and it hits Jack between the eyes before he can get out of the way. I hear the awful thud of the baseball striking his head all the way from the outfield. Jack's helmet flies off. He takes a step backward but doesn't go down, and then he starts staggering slowly toward first base. The umpire, who is as stunned as everyone else, jogs along beside him, trying to get him to stop. I sprint down the fence line toward the gate, watching Jack as his coaches scramble out of the dugout to his side. By the time he gets to first base, I can see blood pouring from his nose.

I make my way through the silent crowd and onto the field. Jack's coaches have taken him into the dugout and sat him on the bench. One of them is holding a white towel over Jack's face. I see immediately that the towel is already stained a deep red. The coaches step back as I approach.

"They did it on purpose," the head coach, a thirty-year-old named Bill Dickson, says. "They haven't come close to hitting anyone else."

I bend over Jack and gently remove the towel. His head is leaned back, his mouth open, and he's staring at the dugout roof. The area around both of his eyes is already swelling, and there's a deep, nasty gash just above the bridge of his nose. He's bleeding from the cut and from both nostrils.

I put the towel back over the wound.

"Jack, can you hear me?"

"Yes."

"Who am I?"

"Dad."

"Do you know where you are?"

"Boone High School. Dugout."

"What's the score in the game?"

"Three three, bottom of the seventh."

"Has anyone called an ambulance?" I say to Coach Dickson.

"They're on the way, but it always takes them fifteen or twenty minutes to get here."

I can sense someone beside me, and I turn my head. It's Ray, Caroline, and Toni.

"He all right?" Ray asks.

"He's coherent."

"Let me see."

I pull the towel back again. Caroline gasps, and a flash of anger runs through me like electric current. How could they do this? *Why* would they do this? It's just a baseball game. Jack has been hit dozens of times in the past but never in the face. And Coach Dickson is right; their pitcher displayed excellent control until Jack came to the plate in the seventh. They hit him intentionally.

I gently replace the towel and look at Ray. I'm thinking seriously about grabbing a bat from the rack and going after Jefferson's coach.

"You don't want to wait for an ambulance," Ray says. "We need to take him now."

"Why?"

"His pupils are different sizes. There's already a lot of swelling. I've seen this before, Joe. He might be bleeding internally." Ray was a medic in the Navy for eight years, so he knows what he's talking about. At that moment, Jack leans forward and vomits on the dugout floor.

"We have to go," Ray says. "Right now."

Caroline and Toni rush off to get the cars while Ray and I each drape one of Jack's arms over our backs and lift. Coach Dickson holds the towel in place to try and slow the bleeding as we walk Jack out through the gate. Just before we reach the parking lot, he loses consciousness, and I feel a sense of dread so deep that I nearly pass out myself.

He regains consciousness after we put him in the backseat, but during the ride to the hospital, he's in and out. He keeps saying his head feels like it's going to explode. I call the emergency room on my cell phone along the way, and they're waiting when we arrive. They take Jack immediately into a trauma room, and in less than ten minutes they've taken him to surgery. A doctor comes out to talk to us briefly. He says that Jack is suffering from an acute epidural hematoma. In layman's terms, he says, Jack's brain is bleeding. A neurosurgeon is going to perform an emergency craniotomy to drain the blood, relieve the pressure, and repair the damage.

We wait for three agonizing hours before the neurosurgeon comes out. The waiting room is filled with Jack's coaches and their wives, his teammates and their parents, plus dozens of his friends from school who were either at the game or heard about what happened. Everyone falls silent when the surgeon, a dark-haired, serious-looking, middle-aged man wearing scrubs, asks Caroline and me to step into a private room. My daughter, Lilly, who is a year younger than Jack and was sitting in the bleachers behind home plate when Jack was hit, grabs my hand and comes into the room with us.

"I'm told you didn't wait for the ambulance," the doctor says gravely as soon as the door closes behind us. "Whose idea was that?"

"Why?" I ask. "Was it a mistake?"

"Under some circumstances, it could have been. But this time, it was the right decision. If your son had bled for another ten or fifteen minutes, I don't think he would have made it."

"So he's all right?"

"He's in recovery. It's a serious injury, but thankfully, we got to it in time. We'll keep him in intensive care for a day or two. He's going to have a heckuva headache, but we can control the pain with medication. He'll have to take it easy for a couple months, but after that, he should be as good as new."

"When can we see him?"

"He'll wake up in about a half hour. He'll be groggy, but you can talk to him for a few minutes."

We thank the doctor, and Caroline, Lilly, and I embrace silently. Caroline and Lilly are crying, but I'm so relieved I feel like I could float on air. We walk back out to the crowded waiting room. Ray and Toni Miller, along with their son Tommy, are standing just outside the door. When the group sees Caroline's tears, I can sense that they think the news is bad. Ray looks at me anxiously and I smile.

Caroline walks straight to Ray, reaches up, wraps her arms around his thick neck, and squeezes him tightly.

"You saved his life," I hear her say through muffled sobs. "You saved our son's life."

PART I

CHAPTER ONE

The moment Katie Dean began to believe she'd been abandoned by God was on a Sunday afternoon in August.

It was late in the summertime in Michigan. Katie, along with her mother and brothers and sisters, had returned home earlier from the First Methodist Church in Casco Township. At seventeen, Kirk was her oldest sibling; then Kiri, sixteen; then Katie, who was just two months shy of her thirteenth birthday. Kody was the baby of the family at ten. They were gathered around the dining room table, waiting for their mother to bring the platter of fried chicken in from the kitchen.

The fresh smell of Lake Michigan floated through the open dining room windows, mingling with the sweet odors of chicken and garlic mashed potatoes. After lunch, Katie and Kiri were planning to pack a small basket with a thermos of ice water, suntan lotion, and magazines and hike to the sand dunes above the lake where they would spend the afternoon lying in the sun and giggling about the Nelson boys who lived just up the road. It would be their last visit to the dunes this summer. School was starting back the next morning.

Richard Dean, Katie's father, sat on the other side of the table, staring into a glass of whiskey. He was thin and pale with a thatch of dark hair above his furrowed brow. He was upset, but that wasn't unusual. It seemed he was always upset.

Richard Dean was distant, as though he wasn't part of the world everyone else lived in. He never kissed Katie, never hugged her, never told her that he loved her. He was like a ticking bomb, always on the verge of another explosion. Katie's mother had told the children that Father was sick from the war in Vietnam. She said he'd been wounded and captured by Viet Cong soldiers near the Cambodian border in 1970 and had spent four years in a prison in Hanoi.

Katie's father didn't have a job, but Katie knew the family lived off money he collected from the government every month. Her mother couldn't work because she had to stay home and take care of Father all the time. He drank lots of whiskey, smoked cigarettes one after the other, and Katie had seen him lock himself in his room and not come out for a week at a time. Sometimes she'd hear him screaming in the middle of the night.

Father had picked them all up from the church parking lot just after noon. He didn't attend church, but he drove the family there and picked them up every Sunday at precisely twelve fifteen. When Father pulled into the church parking lot earlier, Katie's mother had been talking to a man named Jacob Olson near the front steps. Katie didn't think there was anything unusual about it— Mr. Olson was a nice man—but as soon as Mother got into the car, Father lit into her. He called her a slut. White trash. He was yelling and spitting. The veins on his neck were sticking out so far Katie thought they might burst through his skin. When the family arrived home, the first thing Father did was open a bottle of whiskey. He filled a tall glass and sat at the dining room table while Mother, Kiri, and Katie cooked in the kitchen and the boys went about setting the table. They all stepped lightly around Father. They never knew when he might strike, like a rattlesnake coiled in the grass.

Katie was still wearing the flowered-print dress Mother had made for her out of material she bought from the thrift store in South Haven. It was Katie's favorite summer dress, light and airy and full of color. She was looking down at the hemline that crossed her thighs, trying to imagine the pink carnations coming to life, when Mother walked in carrying the chicken.

"Here we are," Mother said. She had a forced smile on her face. She put the platter down in the middle of the table. Steam rose from the chicken, and through it Katie caught a glimpse of Father's face. He was already halfway through his third glass of whiskey. His eyes had reddened, and the lids were beginning to droop.

"Chicken," Father muttered into his whiskey glass. "Damned fried chicken's all we ever get around here."

Mother attempted to remain pleasant. "I thought you liked fried chicken," she said, "and I'd appreciate it if you wouldn't use that kind of language around the children."

"The chiddren," he slurred. "Probly ain't mine anyways."

"Richard!" Mother yelled. She rarely raised her voice, and Katie shuddered. "How dare you!"

Father lifted his chin and turned slowly toward Mother.

"How dare me?" he said. "How dare *me*? How dare *you*, you whore! How long you been giving it up to Olson anyways?"

"Stop it, Father," Kirk pleaded from Katie's left. Kirk was blond-haired and blue-eyed like Katie and Mother. He was tall and paper thin, wiry strong but teenage awkward. Father whipped his head around to face Kirk.

"Watch your mouth, boy," he said, "and don't call me Father no more. Go look in the mirror. You don't look nothing like me."

He turned back to Mother.

"Does he, darling? None of 'em look like me. They look like ... they look like ... Olson!"

"Please leave the table if you're going to talk like that," Mother said.

Katie felt the familiar twinge of fear in her stomach. She watched as Father's face gradually turned darker, from pink to purple.

"Leave the table?" Father bellowed. "You think you can order me around like a slave?"

"Please, Richard." There was a look of desperation in Mother's eyes.

"*Please, Richard,*" Father mocked her hatefully. "I'll show you please, by God, and thank you very much too!"

Father stood on wobbly legs, knocking his drink over in the process. Whiskey spilled out and stained the tablecloth as he stumbled off toward his bedroom. The aroma filled Katie's nostrils, sickening her. She hated whiskey. She hated everything about it.

Katie, along with the others, sat at the table in stunned silence, waiting for Mother to say something. She'd seen Father's outbursts before—all of them had—but this one was as vicious as any they'd ever experienced.

"It's all right," Mother said after what seemed to Katie like an hour. "He's just not feeling well today."

"He shouldn't talk to you that way," Kirk said.

"He doesn't mean it."

"Doesn't matter. He shouldn't do it."

Katie heard heavy footsteps coming from the direction of Father's bedroom and looked around. He was moving quickly toward them. He raised a shotgun, pointed it in Mother's direction, and pulled the trigger. Katie thought her eardrums had burst. Mother went straight over on her back. A spray of pink mist seemed to hang in the air above the table. Katie's joints froze. She urinated on herself.

She watched in terror as Father pumped the shotgun and swung it around toward Kirk. A second horrific explosion.

Then Kiri.

Then her …

CHAPTER TWO

A s the bailiff calls criminal court into session, I look around the room at the anxious faces and feel the familiar sense of dread that hangs in the air like thick fog. Nearly everyone in the gallery has committed some transgression, some violation of the laws of man. It's an odd conglomeration of check-kiters, drunk drivers, burglars, drug dealers, rapists, and killers, all irretrievably bound together by one simple fact—they've been caught and will soon be punished. Less than 5 percent of them will actually continue to protest their innocence and go to trial. The rest will beg their lawyers to make the best deal possible. They'll plead guilty and either be placed on probation or face confinement in a county jail or a state penitentiary.

The courtroom itself looks as though it was constructed by a humorless carpenter. The colors are dull and lifeless, the angles harsh and demanding. Portraits of dead judges adorn the walls behind the bench. There's an awkward sense of formality among the lawyers, bailiffs, clerks, and the judge. Everyone is disgustingly polite. The behavior is required by the institution, but beneath the veneer of civility runs a deep current of hostility borne of petty jealousy, resentment, and famil-iarity. I'm never comfortable in a courtroom. There are enemies everywhere.

Sitting next to me is Tanner Jarrett, a twenty-five-year-old rookie prosecutor fresh out of law school. He's a political hire, the son of a billionaire state sena-tor who will no doubt soon be a United States senator. Tanner looks out of place with his fresh face and boy-ish demeanor. He's handsome, with strong jawbones that angle sharply to a dimpled chin beneath inquisitive brown eyes and a thick stand of black hair. He's bright, capable, and extremely likable. It seems he's always smil-ing. Tanner will handle forty-seven of the forty-eight cases on today's docket. He'll resolve a few of them by plea agreement and agree to continue the rest. I'm here only to receive a date for an aggravated rape case that's going to trial.

Judge Leonard Green takes his seat at the bench. Green is mid-sixties, tall and lean, with a hawkish face and perfect silver hair. He moves with the effeminate gait of a drag queen on stage. He's a miserable example of a human being, and he hovers over us from his perch on the bench, scanning the crowd like a vulture searching for carrion. Green could just as easily give my trial date to Tanner and let him pass it along to me, but because I'm handling the case for the district attorney's office, the judge insists that I appear in court. He knows that I have no other reason to be here, but he won't call the case early so that I can go on about my business. He'll make me sit here for hours, just because he can. If I leave the courtroom, he'll call the case and then hold me in contempt of court because of my absence. Such are the games we play.

Green leans to his left and whispers in the clerk's ear. She shakes her head and whispers back. I notice a look of concern on her face, a look I've seen hundreds of times. It means that Green has spotted a potential victim and is about to indulge his ever-present, masochistic need to inflict pain or punishment on an unsuspecting victim.

"Case number thirty-two thousand, four fifty-five, *State of Tennessee versus Alfred Milligan*," the clerk announces.

I turn to see Alfred Milligan, who appears to be in his late fifties but is probably at least ten years younger, rise from his seat in the gallery. Milligan looks like so many others that inhabit the seemingly bottomless pit of criminal defendants. He's decimated by a lack of nutrition, probably caused by a combination of poverty and alcohol or drug abuse. He uses a cane to walk. What's left of his black hair is greasy and plastered to his forehead. He's wearing what is most likely his best clothing, a black T-shirt with "Dale Earnhardt" written in red across the front and "The Legend" written in red across the back, and a pair of baggy blue jeans. He saunters to the front of the courtroom and looks around nervously.

"Mr. Milligan, you're charged with driving under the influence, seventh offense. Where's your lawyer?" Judge Green demands.

"He told me he'd be here later in the morning," Milligan says.

"Mr. Miller represents you, correct?" The judge is talking about my friend, Ray Miller, and there's a gleam in his eye that tells me he's about to exact a little revenge. Judge Green hates Ray, primarily because Ray isn't the least bit afraid of him and lets him know it on a regular basis. They've been feuding bitterly for years, but lately it has seemed to escalate. Two weeks earlier, my wife and I were dining with Ray and his wife at a restaurant in Johnson City when Ray spotted Judge Green eating by himself at a table in the corner. Ray walked over and started an argument about the judge's practice of locking the courtroom doors at precisely nine o'clock each morning and jailing anyone who arrives late. The conversation grew heated, and with everyone in the place listening, Ray called Judge Green a "sissy in a black robe." He voiced the opinion that the judge had probably been beaten up by bullies as a boy and now used his robe to seek symbolic vengeance whenever the urge struck him. I told Ray later that his indiscretion could cost him dearly. His response was, "Screw him. I hope his legs grow together."

Green turns back to the clerk. "Has Mr. Miller notified the clerk's office that he would be late this morning?"

The clerk shakes her head sadly.

"Then he's in contempt of court. Let the record show that Mr. Miller has failed to appear in court at the appointed time and has failed to notify the clerk's office that he would either be absent or late. He is guilty of contempt of court in the presence of the court and will be taken to jail immediately upon his arrival."

Just as I'm about to say something in Ray's defense, Tanner Jarrett stands suddenly and clears his throat.

"Excuse me, Your Honor," Tanner says. "Mr. Miller called me early this morning. He's filed a motion on Mr.

Milligan's behalf, and we're supposed to have a hearing today. But since the court doesn't typically hear motions until after 11:00 a.m., Mr. Miller told me he was going to take care of a matter in chancery court before he came down here. I'm sure that's where he is."

"He's supposed to be *here*, Mr. Jarrett," the judge snarls. "Right here. Right now."

"With all due respect, Your Honor, the state isn't ready for the hearing now. I told my witness to be here at eleven o'clock."

"Sit down, Mr. Jarrett," Green says coldly. He turns his attention to Alfred Milligan, who has been standing silently at the lectern. "Mr. Milligan, your case is continued. The clerk will notify you of the new date. You're free to go."

I sit there seething impotently as Milligan walks out of the courtroom. Nothing would please me more than to jerk Green off the bench and beat him to a bloody pulp. All it would cost me would be my job, my law license, and a few months in jail. I stare up at Green, hoping to catch his eye and at least give him a silent look of contempt, but he ignores me and begins calling cases as though nothing out of the ordinary has happened. I'm afraid for Ray. I wish I could go out into the hallway and at least call him, but I know if I do, Green will call my case and do the same thing to me that he's just done to Ray.

Ray walks through the side door a little before ten. As soon as Green sees him, he stops what he's doing and orders Ray to the front of the courtroom.

"You're in contempt of court, Mr. Miller," the judge says triumphantly. "I called your case at nine o'clock. You weren't here, and you hadn't notified the clerk's office of your absence as is required under the local rules. Bailiff, take Mr. Miller into custody. His bond is set at five thousand dollars."

Ray is wearing a brown suit. His hair is pulled back tightly into his signature ponytail. He looks up at the judge with hatred and defiance in his eyes. I can see the muscles in his jaw twitching, and his complexion is darkening noticeably. I immediately begin to hope he has enough sense to keep his mouth shut. He's helpless right now. There's nothing he can do. But if he stays calm and doesn't do or say anything stupid, he can take up this fight later. If he does it right, he'll be exonerated, and the judge will be the one who has to answer for his actions. But if he says something he shouldn't—

At that moment, Ray speaks. "I've been right about you all along, you gutless wonder. I hope you enjoy this because from this day forward, I'm going take a special interest in you. You'd better grow eyes in the back of your head."

"Cuff him!" Green yells at one of the bailiffs, who has sheepishly walked up behind Ray and is reaching for his arm.

"Keep your hands off me," Ray growls, and the bailiff takes a step back.

I stand and walk to my friend. I take him gently by the arm and begin to lead him toward the hallway that leads to the holding cells. "C'mon, Ray," I say calmly. "This only gets worse if you stay." He comes out of his rage and his eyes settle on mine. The rage has been replaced by desperation and confusion.

"I'm going to jail?" he asks in a tone that is almost dreamy.

"I'll go to the clerk's office and post your bond as soon as I can break away from the courtroom," I say. "You'll be out in an hour."

"I'm signing an order suspending you based on your threat, Mr. Miller," Judge Green says as we walk out the door. "And I'm reporting you to the Board of Professional Responsibility. You'll be lucky if you ever practice law again."

CHAPTER THREE

ix months later, I'm sitting on a metal stool in
the death row visitor's section of Riverbend
Correctional Facility in Nashville. Riverbend is
what they call a modern, state-of-the-art facility. It's
sprawling and modern, but my experience tells me the
place is misnamed. Men who spend time in a maximum-
security prison do not come out "corrected." They come
out more cunning.

On the other side of a thick pane of Plexiglas
is thirty-eight-year-old Brian Thomas Gant. I was
appointed to represent Gant nearly fifteen years ago. He
was my first death-penalty client, accused of murdering
his mother-in-law and raping his five-year-old niece.
There was no forensic evidence against him—DNA testing hadn't yet become the gold standard—and seemingly no motive for the crime. But the niece, a youngster
named Natalie Booze, told the police that the man who
raped her "looked like Uncle Brian." The police immediately focused their investigation on Gant, and the girl's
story quickly changed from "looked like Uncle Brian"
to "it *was* Uncle Brian." He was arrested a week after
the crime was committed. I did the best I could at trial,

but I couldn't overcome the young girl's testimony. He was convicted of first-degree murder and two counts of aggravated rape a year after his arrest. He's been on death row ever since.

After her uncle was shipped off to the penitentiary, Natalie Booze had a change of heart. She told Gant's wife that she wasn't sure that it was Uncle Brian. It happened so fast. She was asleep when the rapist came into her room. It was dark. The account was completely different than what she'd testified to at trial. It didn't matter though. Gant's appellate attorneys asked Natalie to sign an affidavit swearing that she now believed she'd been mistaken when she identified Brian Gant at trial. She signed the affidavit and the attorneys filed it. Both the prosecution and the appellate courts ignored it.

Several years after Gant was convicted, after DNA testing had been developed, his wife paid a private laboratory nearly forty thousand dollars to test three pieces of evidence from the crime scene: a pair of panties his niece was wearing, a nylon stocking his mother-in-law was wearing, and a pubic hair that was found on the niece's sheet. The lab was able to extract DNA samples from all three pieces of evidence, and none of them matched Gant. Armed with this new evidence, his appellate attorneys were able to get a hearing in front of a judge, who summarily denied their request for a new trial. The Tennessee Court of Appeals upheld the judge's ruling, and Gant remains here in this terrible place. I'm convinced he's innocent, but once a jury finds a man guilty in a death-penalty case, the odds against overturning the verdict are overwhelming.

"What are you doing down here?" Gant asks pleasantly. He's put on some weight since I last saw him, and the hair at his temples has turned gray, but he seems to be in good spirits.

"I'm here to witness an execution, believe it or not."

"Johnson?"

"Right. The murder he was convicted of happened in our district. My boss dumped this on me at the last minute. How's your appeal going?"

"It isn't. Unless Donna can somehow hand them the guy who did it on a silver platter, I'm the next one on the gurney."

Donna is Gant's wife. I see her at the grocery store once or twice a month, but I avoid talking to her whenever possible. Despite the fact that her mother was murdered, Donna has steadfastly maintained her husband's innocence and has become obsessed with getting him exonerated. Back when I was representing Brian, she swore to me that Brian was at home in bed with her the night the crime took place, and she testified to that at trial, but the prosecutor successfully argued to the jury that she was just protecting her husband.

"When are you scheduled?" I ask.

"Three weeks from today."

"I had no idea, Brian. Have you run the DNA profile Donna got from the lab through the Department of Corrections database? They might get a hit."

"We've tried, but they refuse to do it."

"Your lawyers can't force them?"

"How could they force them?"

"Get an order from a judge."

"What judge? Every judge I've run across has upheld my conviction. I'm just a convict now. I'm on death row. No one is interested in helping."

"Anything I can do?"

"I appreciate the offer."

"I'm sorry about everything, Brian. I'm sorry I didn't do a better job."

His eyes soften and he smiles, and I immediately feel even more guilt.

"The Lord works in mysterious ways, my friend," he says. "Don't blame yourself. You did what you could, and I have no hard feelings toward you. The Lord will take care of this, and if He sees fit not to, then I won't question His judgment. If He calls me to Heaven, then he must have a purpose for me there. I'm at peace."

"You have to keep fighting."

"Like I said, I'm at peace. I've placed myself in God's hands and washed myself in the blood of the lamb. I'll accept my fate with a song on my lips and love in my heart."

We sit there for a few minutes in awkward silence. I can't think of anything else to say. Finally, Brian stands up.

"I think I'll head on back to my cell now, Mr. Dillard, but I appreciate you coming. I really do. It makes me feel good to know that you care. God bless."

Eight hours later, just before midnight, I'm back at the prison, only now I'm sitting on a folding chair on a polished concrete floor just outside the execution chamber. Dull, gray paint covers the concrete block walls, and pale light emanates from fluorescent bulbs hidden behind sheets of opaque plastic in the drop ceiling. The room is colorless, the air so still it's stifling. I'm feeling queasy and claustrophobic and want nothing more than to get out of here.

The condemned is a white man named Phillip Johnson. Twelve years ago, Johnson brutally raped and murdered eight-year-old Tanya Reid no more than ten miles from my house. He did unspeakable things to the child, then dumped her body in a culvert near the South Central community and covered it with brush. A couple boys looking for frogs in the creek bed discovered Tanya two days later.

I was an outsider looking in during Johnson's trial—he was represented by the public defender's office—but from everything I heard and read, there was no doubt about his guilt. He was a sex offender who'd already served seven years for fondling a young girl and was on parole, living in nearby Unicoi County, the day he snatched Tanya Reid from her driveway. His semen was found on the little girl's body, her blood and hair were all over the backseat of his car, and he confessed.

I've been sent here to witness the execution on behalf of the people of the First Judicial District and my boss, the man they elected as their attorney general. His name is Lee Mooney, and he was supposed to do this himself, but he called me into his office yesterday and said he'd decided to attend a conference in Charleston and would be gone until Friday evening. He then assigned this unpleasant task to me. I wasn't offered the option of refusing.

Tanya Reid's family is here—her mother, father, and three grandparents—and they smile at me tentatively. I'd introduced myself to them earlier, just as my boss had instructed. They're simply dressed and quiet, grossly out of place so near this chamber of death. I remember the parents' pleas on television the day after their child was abducted. They appear to have aged more than double the ten years it's taken to bring their daughter's killer to what they believe is his rightful end. Their hair is gray, their shoulders slumped. They're languid nearly to the point of being lifeless.

I must admit I'm conflicted about the death penalty. Philosophically, or intellectually, I just can't cuddle up to the notion that a modern, civilized government that forbids its people from killing should be allowed to kill its people. But when I imagine putting the proverbial shoe on my own foot … well, let's just say I know in my heart that if someone had kidnapped, raped, tortured, and murdered either of my children, I'd want them dead. I'd want them to suffer. I also know that I'd be perfectly capable of doing the killing myself. Maybe the state legislature should consider passing a law that allows the victim's family the option of killing the condemned. They could also give them the option of killing the condemned in the same manner in which the victim was killed. Perhaps that particular form of revenge would provide the closure they seem to crave so deeply.

Sitting in the front row are two representatives from the media back home, both young female newspaper reporters, dressed in their dark business suits. So much time has passed since the crime occurred that the state and national media have moved on to more pressing matters. Tanya Reid is old news, perversely obsolete in our fast-moving society. As I look at them, I can't help but wonder what kind of effect this is going to have. They're young journalists, at once inexperienced and arrogant, even condescending as they prepare their "concerned" look for the live shot outside the prison later on. I wonder how they'll feel about their love affair with professional voyeurism after they've watched a man die fifteen feet from their notepads.

At precisely the appointed time, they bring Johnson out into the death chamber in a white hospital gown, cuffs, and shackles. A steel wall separates the witnesses from the condemned. There's a window, much like the one through which newborn babies are viewed in a maternity ward. I muse over the irony for a moment, then put it out of my mind.

Johnson is short and doughy with neatly cut black hair, a double chin, and a clean-shaven face. The monster is forty-one years old, but he looks no more than thirty. He's spent nearly half his life in prison, but if you replaced the hospital gown with a jacket, slacks, and a tie, he'd look like the neighbor who passes the collection plate in church on Sunday mornings.

The prison's representatives are here too. Warden Tommy Joe Tester is leading Johnson into the chamber, followed by two massive prison guards in black uniforms. The chaplain, a physician, and two stone-faced medical technicians wearing white coats follow only a pace behind.

Johnson stops his shuffle and looks out over the audience mournfully. No one from his own family has come to watch him die. Until this point, he has at least attempted to remain stoic, but his lips begin to tremble and his shoulders slump. As the guards help him onto the gurney, he begins to weep. The guards remove his cuffs and shackles and replace them with leather straps that are attached to the gurney. Then they step back against the wall.

"That's it, cry," I hear Tanya's father mutter from his front-row seat. "Go out like the coward you are."

The warden, dressed in a navy blue suit, steps forward holding a piece of paper.

"Phillip Todd Johnson," the warden says in a nasally Southern twang, "by the power vested in me by the State of Tennessee, I hereby order that the sentence of death handed down by the Criminal Court of Washington County in the matter of *State of Tennessee versus Phillip Todd Johnson* be carried out immediately. Do you have any last words?"

There's a brief pause, and then a pitiful wail.

"I'm sorry," Johnson cries. "I'm so very sorry. I couldn't help myself. May God forgive me."

I don't know what God's attitude toward him will be, but the State of Tennessee doesn't seem to be in a forgiving mood.

"May God have mercy on your soul," the warden says as the executioners efficiently hook an IV into Johnson's left forearm.

There are three different drugs waiting to be injected into his body: five grams of sodium thiopental, which will render him unconscious; followed by one hundred milligrams of pancuronium bromide, which will block the neuromuscular system and cause his breathing to cease; and one hundred milliliters of potassium chloride, which will stop his heart. All three doses would be lethal on their own, but the state wants to make absolutely sure he's dead and that he doesn't feel a thing. Those who are enlightened about such things consider this to be the most humane method of killing a human being.

Johnson continues to cry as the chaplain prays. Suddenly, the microphone inside the death chamber is turned off. All we can do now is watch. The prison physician steps forward while one of the EMTs walks behind a wall, presumably to release the first dose of fatal drugs. I want to close my eyes, but I can't. Even though I find the entire matter hypocritical and disgusting, I'm riveted. Thirty seconds after the EMT disappears, Johnson's chest rises, his eyes flutter, and he is still. The thought crosses my mind that the death he's just been given was so much more serene than the one he doled out to little Tanya. Even so, I wonder how what I've just witnessed could possibly be called justice.

I sit in the seat for a moment, feeling awkward, not quite knowing what to do. Then the family rises, and I do the same. The show's over—figuratively for the audience and literally for Johnson—and I hurry out into the night.

If yo enjoyed the beginning of *Injustice for All*, you can purchase here via Amazon:

<u>Injustice for All</u>
Again, thank you for reading!

Scott

MAY 0 2 2023

Made in the USA
Middletown, DE
05 June 2019